we
are
the
ants

we
are
the
ants

shaun david hutchinson

Simon Pulse

NEW YORK   LONDON   TORONTO   SYDNEY   NEW DELHI

SIMON PULSE

An imprint of Simon & Schuster Children's Publishing Division

1230 Avenue of the Americas, New York, New York 10020

First Simon Pulse hardcover edition January 2016

Text copyright © 2016 by Shaun David Hutchinson

Jacket photograph copyright © 2016 by Cubird/Getty Images

All rights reserved, including the right of reproduction in whole or in part in any form.

SIMON PULSE and colophon are registered trademarks of Simon & Schuster, Inc.

For information about special discounts for bulk purchases, please contact Simon & Schuster Special Sales at 1-866-506-1949 or business@simonandschuster.com.

The Simon & Schuster Speakers Bureau can bring authors to your live event. For more information or to book an event, contact the Simon & Schuster Speakers Bureau at 1-866-248-3049 or visit our website at www.simonspeakers.com.

Jacket designed by Regina Flath

Interior designed by Hilary Zarycky

The text of this book was set in Adobe Garamond Pro.

Manufactured in the United States of America

2 4 6 8 10 9 7 5 3 1

This book has been cataloged with the Library of Congress.

ISBN 978-1-4814-4963-2 (hc)

ISBN 978-1-4814-4965-6 (eBook)

For Matt, my favorite alien

TWO POSSIBILITIES EXIST: EITHER WE ARE
ALONE IN THE UNIVERSE OR WE ARE NOT.
BOTH ARE EQUALLY TERRIFYING.

—*Arthur C. Clarke*

Chemistry: Extra Credit Project

Life is bullshit.

Consider your life for a moment. Think about all those little rituals that sustain you throughout your day—from the moment you wake up until that last, lonely midnight hour when you guzzle a gallon of NyQuil to drown out the persistent voice in your head. The one that whispers you should give up, give in, that tomorrow won't be better than today. Think about the absurdity of brushing your teeth, of arguing with your mother over the appropriateness of what you're wearing to school, of homework, of grade-point averages and boyfriends and hot school lunches.

And life.

Think about the absurdity of life.

When you break down the things we do every day to

their component pieces, you begin to understand how ridiculous they are. Like kissing, for instance. You wouldn't let a stranger off the street spit into your mouth, but you'll swap saliva with the boy or girl who makes your heart race and your pits sweat and gives you boners at the worst fucking times. You'll stick you tongue in his mouth or her mouth or their mouth, and let them reciprocate without stopping to consider where else their tongue has been, or whether they're giving you mouth herpes or mono or leftover morsels of their tuna-salad sandwich.

We shave our legs and pluck our eyebrows and slather our bodies with creams and lotions. We starve ourselves so we can fit into the perfect pair of jeans, we pollute our bodies with drugs to increase our muscles so we'll look ripped without a shirt. We drive fast and party hard and study for exams that don't mean dick in the grand scheme of the cosmos.

Physicists have theorized that we live in an infinite and infinitely expanding universe, and that everything in it will eventually repeat. There are infinite copies of your mom and your dad and your clothes-stealing little sister. There are infinite copies of you. Despite what you've spent your entire life believing, you are not a special snowflake. Somewhere out there, another you is living *your* life. Chances are, they're living it better. They're learning to speak French or screwing their brains out instead of loafing on the couch in their boxers, stuffing their face with bowl after bowl of Fruity Oatholes while wondering why they're all alone on a Friday night. But that's not even the worst part. What's really going to send you running over the side of the nearest bridge is that none of it matters. I'll die, you'll die, we'll all die, and the things we've done, the choices we've made, will amount to nothing.

Out in the world, crawling in a field at the edge of some bullshit town with a name like Shoshoni or Medicine Bow, is an ant. You weren't aware of it. Didn't know whether it was a soldier, a drone, or the queen. Didn't care if it was scouting for food to drag back to the nest or building new tunnels for wriggly ant larvae. Until now that ant simply didn't exist for you. If I hadn't mentioned it, you would have continued on with your life, pinballing from one tedious task to the next— shoving your tongue into the bacterial minefield of your girl-friend's mouth, doodling the variations of your combined names on the cover of your notebook—waiting for electronic bits to zoom through the air and tell you that someone was thinking about you. That for one fleeting moment you were the most significant person in someone else's insignificant life. But whether you knew about it or not, that ant is still out there doing ant things while you wait for the next text message to prove that out of the seven billion self-centered people on this planet, *you* are important. Your entire sense of self-worth is predicated upon your belief that you matter, that you matter to the universe.

But you don't.

Because we are the ants.

I didn't waste time thinking about the future until the night the sluggers abducted me and told me the world was going to end.

I'm not insane. When I tell you the human race is toast, I'm not speaking hyperbolically the way people do when they say we're all dying from the moment our mothers evict us from their bodies into a world where everything feels heavier and brighter and far too loud. I'm telling you that tomorrow—January 29, 2016—you can kiss your Chipotle-eating, Frappuccino-drinking, fat ass good-bye.

You probably don't believe me—I wouldn't in your place—but I've had 143 days to come to terms with our inevitable destruction, and I've spent most of those days thinking about the future. Wondering whether I have or want one, trying to decide if the end of existence is a tragedy, a comedy, or as inconsequential as that chem lab I forgot to turn in last week.

But the real joke isn't that the sluggers revealed to me the date of Earth's demise; it's that they offered me the choice to prevent it.

You asked for a story, so here it is. I'll begin with the night the sluggers told me the world was toast, and when I'm finished, we can wait for the end together.

7 September 2015

The biggest letdown about being abducted by aliens is the abundance of gravity on the spaceship. We spend our first nine months of life floating, weightless and blind, in an amniotic sac before we become gravity's bitch, and the seductive lure of space travel is the promise of returning to that perfect state of grace. But it's a sham. Gravity is jealous, sadistic, and infinite.

Sometimes I think gravity may be death in disguise. Other times I think gravity is love, which is why love's only demand is that we fall.

Sluggers aren't gray. They don't have saucer-wide eyes or thin lipless mouths. As far as I know, they don't have mouths at all. Their skin is rough like wet leather and is all the colors

WE ARE THE ANTS · 7

of an algae bloom. Their black spherical eyes are mounted atop their heads on wobbly stalks. Instead of arms, they have appendages that grow from their bodies when required. If their UFO keys fall off the console—*boom!*—instant arm. If they need to restrain me or silence my terrified howls, they can sprout a dozen tentacles to accomplish the task. It's very efficient.

Oddly enough, sluggers do have nipples. Small brown buttons that appear to be as useless to them as most men's. It's comforting to know that regardless of our vast differences and the light-years that separate our worlds, we'll always have nipples in common.

I should slap that on a bumper sticker, © HENRY JEROME DENTON.

Before you ask: no, the sluggers have never probed my anus. I'm fairly certain they reserve that special treat for people who talk on their phones during movies, or text while driving.

Here's how it happens: abductions always begin with shadows. Even in a dark room, with the windows closed and the curtains drawn, the shadows descend, circling like buzzards over a reeking lunch.

Then a heaviness in my crotch like I have to pee, growing

painfully insistent regardless of how much I beg my brain to ignore it.

After that, helplessness. Paralysis. The inability to struggle. Fight. Breathe.

The inability to scream.

At some point the sluggers move me to the examination room. I've been abducted at least a dozen times, and I still don't know how they transport me from my bedroom to their spaceship. It happens in the dark space between blinks, in the void between breaths.

Once aboard, they begin the experiments.

That's what I assume they're doing. Trying to fathom the motives of an advanced alien race who possess the technological capacity to travel through the universe is like the frog I dissected in ninth grade trying to understand why I cut it open and pinned its guts to the table. The sluggers could be blasting me with deadly radiation or stuffing me full of slugger eggs just to see what happens. Hell, I could be some slugger kid's science fair project.

I doubt I'll ever know for certain.

Sluggers don't speak. During those long stretches where my body is beyond my control, I often wonder how they communicate with one another. Maybe they secrete chemicals the way insects do, or perhaps the movements of their eyestalks is a form of language similar to the dance of a bee. They could also be like my mother and father, who communicated exclusively by slamming doors.

I was thirteen the first time the sluggers abducted me. My older brother, Charlie, was snoring his face off in the next room while I lay in bed, translating my parents' fight. You might believe all doors sound the same when slammed, but you'd be wrong.

My father was a classic slammer, maintaining contact with the door until it was totally and completely shut. This gave him control over the volume and pitch, and produced a deep, solid bang capable of shaking the door, the frame, and the wall.

Mom preferred variety. Sometimes she went for the dramatic fling; other times she favored the heel-kick slam. That night, she relied on the multismash, which was loud and effective but lacked subtlety.

The sluggers abducted me before I learned what my parents were arguing about. Police found me two days later, wandering the dirt roads west of Calypso, wearing a grocery bag for underwear and covered in hickies I couldn't explain. My father left three weeks after that, slamming the door behind him one final time. No translation necessary.

· · ·

I've never grown comfortable being naked around the aliens. Jesse Franklin frequently saw me naked and claimed to enjoy it, but he was my boyfriend, so it doesn't count. I'm self-conscious about being too skinny, and I imagine the sluggers judge me for my flaws—the mole in the center of my chest shaped like Abraham Lincoln or the way my collarbone protrudes or my tragically flat ass. Once, while standing in the lunch line waiting for shepherd's pie, Elle Smith told me I had the flattest ass she'd ever seen. I wasn't sure how many asses a twelve-year-old girl from Calypso realistically could have been exposed to, but the comment infected me like a cold sore, bursting to the surface from time to time, ensuring I never forgot my place.

Part of me wonders if the sluggers send pervy pics back to their home planet for their alien buddies to mock. *Check out this mutant we caught. They call it a teenager. It's got five arms, but one is tiny and deformed.*

It's not really deformed, I swear.

When the sluggers had finished experimenting on me that night, the slab I was resting on transformed into a chair while I was still on it. During previous abductions, the aliens had locked me in a totally dark room, attempted to drown me, and once pumped a gas into the air that made me laugh until

I vomited, but they'd never given me a chair. I was immediately suspicious.

One of the sluggers remained behind after the others disappeared into the shadows. The exam room was the only section of the ship I'd ever seen, and its true shape and size were obscured by the darkness at the edges. The room itself was plain—a gray floor with swirls that gave it the impression of movement and that was illuminated by four or five lights beaming from the shadows. The slab, which had become a chair, was obsidian black.

My limbs tingled, and that was how I realized I could move again. I shook them to work out the pins and needles, but I couldn't shake the impotence that rattled in my skull, reminding me that the aliens could flay me alive and peel back my muscles to see how I functioned, and there wasn't a goddamn thing I could do to stop them. As human beings, we're born believing that we are the apex of creation, that we are invincible, that no problem exists that we cannot solve. But we inevitably die with all our beliefs broken.

My throat was scratchy. Even caged rats are given water bottles and food pellets.

"If you're testing my patience, I should warn you that I once spent three weeks in a roach-infested RV with my family on the antiquing trip from hell. Twenty-one days of Dad getting lost, Mom losing her temper, and my brother finding any excuse to punch me, all set to the glorious song of Nana's deviated septum."

Nothing. No reaction. The slugger beside me waggled its eyestalks, the glassy marbles taking in a 360-degree view. They were like one of those security cameras hidden under a shaded dome; it was impossible to know where they were tracking at any given moment.

"Seriously, it was the worst trip of my life. Every night we all had to lie still and pretend we couldn't hear Charlie polishing his rifle in the overhead bunk. I'm pretty confident he broke the world record for the most number of times a kid's masturbated while sharing breathing space with his parents, brother, and grandmother."

A beam of light shot over my shoulder, projecting a three-dimensional image of Earth in the air a few feet in front of me. I turned to find the source, but the slugger sprouted an appendage and slapped me in the neck.

"I really hope that was an arm," I said, rubbing the fresh welt.

The picture of the planet was meticulously detailed. Feathery clouds drifted across the surface as the image rotated leisurely. Tight clusters of defiant lights sparkled from every city, as bright as any star. A few moments later, a smooth pillar approximately one meter tall rose from the floor beside the image of the earth. Atop it was a bright red button.

"Do you want me to press it?" The aliens had never given me the impression that they understood anything I said or did, but I figured they wouldn't have presented me with a big shiny button if they hadn't intended for me to press it.

The moment I stood, electricity surged up my feet and into my body. I collapsed to the floor, twitching. A strangled squeal escaped my throat. The slugger didn't offer to help me, despite its ability to grow arms at will, and I waited for the spasms to recede before climbing back into the chair. "Fine, I won't touch the button."

The projection of the earth exploded, showering me with sparks and light. I threw up my arm to protect my face, but I felt no pain. When I opened my eyes, the image was restored.

"So, you definitely *don't* want me to press the button?"

Under the watchful eyes of my alien overlord, I witnessed the planet explode seven more times, but I refused to budge from my seat. On the eighth explosion, the sluggers shocked me again. I lost control of my bladder and flopped onto the floor in a puddle of my own urine. My jaw was sore from clenching, and I wasn't sure how much more I could take.

"You know, if you just told me what you wanted me to do, we could skip the excruciating pain portion of this experiment."

They restored the planet again; only when I tried to sit, they shocked me and blew it up. The next time the image was whole, I scrambled to the button and slammed it with my hand. I was rewarded with an intense burst of euphoria that began in my feet and surged up my legs, spreading to my fingers and the tips of my ears. It was pure bliss, like I'd ejaculated a chorus of baby angels from every pore of my body.

"That didn't suck."

I lost track of how many times I pressed the button. Sometimes they shocked me, sometimes they dosed me with pure rapture, but I never knew which to expect. Not until I saw the pattern. It was so simple, I felt like an imbecile for not seeing it sooner. Being shocked until I pissed myself probably hadn't helped my problem-solving abilities.

Those shocks and bursts of euphoria weren't punishments and rewards, nor were they random. They were simply meant to force me to see that there was a causal relationship between whether I pressed the button and whether the planet exploded. The sluggers were trying to communicate with me. It would have been a much more exciting moment in human history if I hadn't been wearing soggy underwear.

I decided to test my theory.

"Are you going to blow up the planet?"

SHOCK.

"Am I going to blow it up?"

SHOCK.

I finally gave up and stayed on the floor. "Is *something* going to destroy the earth?"

EUPHORIA.

"Can you stop it?"

HALLELUJAH!

My eyes rolled back as a shiver of bliss rippled through me. "How do we stop it?" I looked to the slugger for a clue, but it hadn't moved since slapping me. What I knew was this: when I pressed the button, Earth didn't explode. When I didn't, it did. It couldn't be that simple, though. "Pressing the button will prevent the destruction of the planet?"

UNADULTERATED RAPTURE.

"So, what? All those other times I pressed it were just practice?"

BABY ANGELS EVERYWHERE

"Great. So, when is this apocalypse set to occur?" I wasn't sure how the aliens were going to answer an open-ended question, especially since they'd never answered me before, but they were capable of interstellar travel; providing me with a date should have been cake. A moment later the projection of the earth morphed into a reality TV show called *Bunker*, and a hammy announcer's voice boomed at me from every-where at once.

"This group of fifteen strangers has been locked in a bun-ker for six months. With only one hundred and forty-four days remaining, you won't want to miss a single minute as they com-pete for food, water, toilet paper, and each other's hearts."

"You guys get the worst stations up here." The commercial faded and Earth returned. "So, one hundred and forty-four days?" It took me longer than I'll admit to do the math in my head. "That means the world is going to end January twenty-ninth, 2016?"

SWEET EUPHORIA.

I never got tired of being right.

When my head cleared, I came to the conclusion that the sluggers were screwing with me. It was the only logical explanation. I refused to believe that they had the power to prevent the world's end but had chosen to leave the decision up to a sixteen-year-old nobody.

But if it wasn't a joke, if the choice was mine, then I held the fate of the world in my sweaty hand. The aliens probably didn't care one way or another.

"Just to be clear: I have until January twenty-ninth to press the button?"

EUPHORIA.

"And if I do, I'll prevent the planet's destruction?"

EUPHORIA.

"And if I choose not to press it?"

The earth exploded, the projection disappeared, and the lights died.

8 September 2015

I darted across the dawn-drenched lawn in front of my duplex, gushing sweat in the muggy Florida heat and shielding my privates with a trash can lid I'd stolen from a house a couple of streets over, hoping Mr. Nabu—who sat on his patio, reading the newspaper every morning—was too busy scouring the obits for names of friends and enemies to notice my pasty white ass scramble past.

After my second abduction, I began hiding a duffel bag with spare clothes behind the AC unit under my bedroom window. The sluggers don't always return me totally naked, but when they do, I assume it's because it amuses them to watch me attempt to sneak from one end of Calypso to the other without being arrested for indecent exposure.

As I dressed, I tried to wrap my brain around the possibility that the world was going to end, and the absurd notion that aliens had chosen me to determine whether the apocalypse would happen as scheduled or be delayed. I simply wasn't important enough to make such a crucial decision. They should have abducted the president or the pope or Neil deGrasse Tyson.

I don't know why I didn't press the button for real when I had the chance other than that I don't think the aliens would have given me such a long lead time if they hadn't wanted me to consider my choice carefully. Most people probably believe they would have pressed the button in my situation— nobody *wants* the world to end, right?—but the truth is that nothing is as simple as it seems. Turn on the news; read some blogs. The world is a shit hole, and I have to consider whether it might be better to wipe the slate clean and give the civilization that evolves from the ashes of our bones a chance to get it right.

I used the spare key under the dead begonia by the front door to sneak into my house. The smell of cigarette smoke and fried eggs greeted me, and I sauntered into the kitchen like I'd come from my bedroom, still bleary-eyed and sleepy. Mom glanced up from reading her phone. A cigarette hung from the tips of her fingers, and her curly bleached hair was pulled back into a messy ponytail. "About time. I was calling you, Henry. Didn't you hear me calling you?" My mom is shaped like an eggplant and often sports bags under her eyes of the same color.

I leaned against the door, not planning to stay. Alien abductions always make me feel like I need a boiling bleach shower. "Sorry."

Nana smiled at me from the stove. She slid a plate of pepper-flecked fried eggs onto the table and set the mayo beside it. "Eat. You're too skinny." Nana is gritty and hard; she wears her wrinkles and liver spots like battle scars from a war she'll never stop fighting. She's the gristle stuck between Time's teeth, and I love her for it.

Mom took a drag from her cigarette and jabbed it in my direction. "I called you a hundred times."

Before I could reply, Charlie stomped into the kitchen and swiped my plate. He ate one egg with his hands as he flopped into a chair, and then set to work on the rest of my breakfast. Sometimes it's difficult to believe Charlie and I come from the same parents. I'm tall, he's short; I'm skinny, he used to be muscular, though most of it turned to fat after high school; I can count to five without using my fingers. . . . Charlie has fingers.

"Henry didn't hear you because Henry wasn't home." Charlie smirked at me as he grabbed a fistful of bacon from the plate in the middle of the table. He grimaced at Mom. "Do you have to smoke while I'm eating?"

Mom ignored him. "Where were you, Henry?"

"Here."

"Liar," Charlie said. "Your bed was empty when I got home from Zooey's last night."

"What the hell were you doing in my room?"

Mom took a drag off her cigarette and stubbed it out in the ashtray. Her mouth was pursed and tight like a bright pink sphincter, and her silence spoke louder than any slammed door. The only sounds in the kitchen belonged to the eggs frying on the stove and Nana whistling the *Bunker* theme song.

"I couldn't sleep so I went for a walk. What's the big deal?"

Charlie coughed "bullshit" under his breath; I replied with one finger.

"You're not . . . sleepwalking . . . again, are you?"

"I was walking, Mom, but I was definitely awake."

Charlie whipped a toast wedge that struck me below my eye. "Two points!"

"Did you just try to blind me with toast? What the hell is wrong with you?" I grabbed the toast off the floor to throw it away, but Charlie held out his hand and said, "Don't waste it, bro."

Mom lit another cigarette. "No one would blame me if I smothered you both in your sleep." I think my mom might have been pretty once, but the years devoured her youth, beauty, and enthusiasm for anything with an alcohol content of less than 12 percent.

Nana handed me a paper bag stained with grease. "Don't forget your lunch, Charlie."

I peeked inside the bag. Nana had dumped two fried eggs, three strips of bacon, and hash browns at the bottom. Broken yolk oozed over everything like sunny pus. "I'm Henry, Nana." As soon as she turned her back, I tossed the sack lunch into the garbage can.

"Do you need a ride to school, Henry?" Mom asked.

I glanced at the clock on the microwave. If I hurried, I'd have enough time to shower and walk to school. "Tempting. I've read that beginning your day by doing something absolutely terrifying is good for you, but I'm going to pass."

"Smartass."

"Could you drop me off at Zooey's?" Charlie mopped up the last of *my* eggs with the projectile floor toast and stuffed it into his fat mouth.

"Don't you have class this morning?" I asked, knowing full well Charlie had withdrawn from all his classes but still hadn't told Mom.

WE ARE THE ANTS · 23

"I can swing you by the community college on my way to work," Mom said.

"Thanks. Great." Charlie faked a smile with gritted teeth, but I knew he was dreaming up a hundred ways to cause me excruciating pain, most of which likely involved his fists and my face—my brother isn't terribly creative, but he is consistent.

For the record: if the sluggers ever abduct Charlie, I'm certain he'll earn the anal probe.

"Henry, I need you home right after school today."

"Why?" I stopped my excruciatingly slow exit from the kitchen even though I needed to get out of there and take a shower if I didn't want to be late.

"I'm working a double at the restaurant, so you'll have to look after Mother tonight."

Charlie jeered at me behind Mom's back, and I wanted to punch that smug look off his face. "What if I have plans?" I didn't have plans, but the dismal state of my social life was none of her business.

Mom sucked on her cigarette; the cherry flared. "Just be home after school, all right? Can you do one fucking thing I ask without arguing?"

"Watch your mouth, young lady," Nana said from the stove, "or you can go straight to your room without supper."

"Sure," I said. "Whatever."

. . .

On the day I was born, photons from the star Gliese 832 began their journey toward Earth. I was little more than a squalling, wrinkled, shit-spewing monster when that light began its sixteen-year journey through the empty void of space to reach the empty void of Calypso, Florida, where I've spent my entire, empty void of a life. From Gliese 832's point of view, I am still a wrinkled, shit-spewing monster, only recently born. The farther we are from one another, the further we live in each other's pasts.

Five years in my past, my father used to take me and Charlie deep-sea fishing on the weekends. He'd wake us up hours before sunrise and treat us to breakfast at a greasy diner called Spooners. I'd stuff myself full of grits and cheesy eggs. Sometimes I'd really indulge and order a stack of chocolate-chip pancakes. After breakfast we'd head to the docks, where Dad's friend Dwight kept his boat, and we'd aim for carefree waters.

I always sat at the bow, dangling my feet over the side, letting the water tickle my toes as we sped through the intra-coastal toward the deep sea. I loved how the sun and salt spray perfused my skin, filling me with the memory of light. God surely meant for humans to live like that. He hadn't intended for us to wither into desiccated husks in front of brightly lit screens that leeched away our summer days one meme at a time.

The fishing trips began well enough. We'd swap dirty jokes that Mom would have killed us for hearing or telling; Dwight would find us a suitable place to drift; Dad would bait my hook, patiently explaining what he was doing as he worked the squid or bait fish onto the barbed end; and we'd cast our lines and wait for the fish to bite. Not even Charlie's unending nut punches and nipple twists ruined the mood. Those times were as perfect as any I ever had, but the good times never lasted.

My doctor once explained that it was an inner-ear problem. Something to do with balance and equilibrium affecting my spatial orientation. Honestly, I don't understand how my ears affected my stomach, but I took his word for it. There I was, laughing and smiling and enjoying the day—fishing pole gripped in my hands, bare feet propped on the railing—when the nausea would strike. The boat tilted, the deck melted under my feet and sloped toward the water. My skin burned, and my mouth watered. I'd try to breathe normally, but I could never get enough oxygen.

I was on a sinking ship in the middle of the expanding ocean, terrified, sick, and unable to do a goddamn thing about it. The boat would rock, dipping and swaying with the waves, and I'd fight the queasiness. I'd barter with God.

I'd pray for anyone, angel or demon, to keep me from being sick, but no one was listening or they didn't care. My puke splattered into the water—chunks of my breakfast still recognizable—someone, usually Charlie, would make a joke about chum, and I'd crawl into the cabin and curl up on the padded bench for the remainder of the fishing expedition.

Eventually, Dad gave up trying to include me and left me behind. One Saturday morning I woke up and discovered his car gone, Charlie's bed empty. Then Charlie started high school and was too cool to go fishing anymore. He was too cool for everything. He divided his time between watching porn, masturbating, and trying to figure out ways to score liquor to impress his mouth-breather friends. I was convinced that high school transformed boys into porn-addicted, chronic-masturbating alcoholics.

I was wrong. It turns them into something much worse.

Most of Calypso is paradise, and is home to some of the wealthiest families in South Florida. Rich teenage boys are also porn-addicted, chronic-masturbating alcoholics, but they have access to better porn and booze. They also have cars and money. I have neither, which means I started CHS with two strikes against me.

High school is like those fishing trips with my dad: I want to be there, I want to enjoy myself like everyone else,

WE ARE THE ANTS · 27

but I always end up huddled on the floor, praying for the end.

Jesse once told me that if I focused on a fixed point on the horizon, I would be okay, but Jesse hanged himself in his bedroom last year, so the value of his advice is dubious at best.

Ms. Faraci stood at the Smart Board trying to explain covalent bonds, which we were supposed to have reviewed the previous night. Judging by the downcast eyes and bored expressions worn by most of the class, I was the only one who'd actually done it.

Ms. Faraci doesn't care about societal conventions. She rarely wears makeup, frequently shows up to class in mismatched shoes, and is obscenely passionate about science. Everything excites her: magnetism, Newtonian dynamics, strange particles. She's a pretty strange particle herself. And she never lets our apathy discourage her. She'd teach chemistry with jazz hands and finger puppets if she thought that would inspire us. Sometimes her enthusiasm makes me cringe, but she's still my favorite teacher. There are days when her chemistry class is the only reason I can stomach school at all.

"Hey, Space Boy." Marcus McCoy whispered at me from the back of the classroom. He has money and a car. I ignored him. "Yo, Space Boy. You do the chem worksheet?" Muffled laughter trailed the question. I ignored that, too.

I stared at the illustrations of molecules in my book, admiring the way they fit together. They had a purpose, a destiny to fulfill. I had a button. My mind wandered, and I fantasized about the end of everything. About watching all the Marcus McCoys of the world die horrible, bloody deaths. I'm not going to lie: it made me want to masturbate.

"Space Boy . . . Space Boy." Their sadistic giggling irritated me almost as much as the nickname.

On my left, Audrey Dorn sat at her desk, scrutinizing me. She has an easy Southern smile, calculating eyes, and usually dresses like she's on her way to a business meeting. She's the kind of girl who doesn't believe in "good enough." We were friends once. When she noticed I'd seen her staring, she shrugged and returned her attention to Faraci.

"Come on, Space Boy. I only need a couple of answers."

I glanced over my shoulder. Marcus McCoy was leaning forward on his elbows so that his biceps bulged in his tight polo for everyone to appreciate. He wore his thick brown hair parted neatly to the left, and he flashed me his entitled grin. No doesn't mean to Marcus what it means to those without money and a car.

"Do your own homework, Marcus."

Adrian Morse and Jay Oh, two of Marcus's buddies, snickered, but it was aimed at me, not him.

"I don't have little green men to do it for me," Marcus said, drawing even more attention.

"What's so funny?" Ms. Faraci scowled at me and Marcus. She took the sharing of electron pairs seriously.

"Nothing," I mumbled.

Marcus said, "Nothing, Ms. Faraci," barely able to finish the sentence before cracking up.

I have Charlie to thank for outing me to the entire school. He was a senior when I was a freshman, and he considered telling everyone I'd been abducted by aliens and turning me into a social pariah his greatest achievement. I don't know who thought up the nickname Space Boy, but it stuck. Most of the kids in my class don't even know my real name, but they know Space Boy for sure.

When the bell finally rang for lunch, Ms. Faraci caught me at the door and pulled me aside. I stared at my shoes when Marcus passed. Adrian whispered, "Space Boy sucks alien dick," on his way out. To the best of my knowledge, sluggers don't have dicks, which probably makes it difficult to masturbate. People have a lot of theories about why boys fall behind in school when they become teenagers, but all I'm saying is that I'd probably get a lot more schoolwork done if I didn't have a dick.

Ms. Faraci sat on the edge of her desk. "Rough day?"

Page 30 — SHAUN DAVID HUTCHINSON

"Not the roughest."

Her concern made me uncomfortable. It was one thing to be ridiculed by my classmates, another to be pitied by a teacher. "You're a smart kid, Henry, with a real knack for science. You're going to show those boys one day."

Maybe that's true, but cliché platitudes rarely help. "Is it possible for the world to end suddenly?"

Ms. Faraci cocked her head to the side. "Well, sure. There are any number of scenarios that could lead to the extinction of all life on Earth."

"Like what?"

"Asteroid impact, gamma radiation from a nearby supernova, nuclear holocaust." She ticked the list off on her fingers before she stopped and narrowed her eyes. "I know high school is rough, Henry, but blowing up the planet is never the answer."

"You've clearly forgotten what high school is like from my side of the desk."

Marcus slammed me against the inside of the bathroom stall. The rickety partitions shook, their bolts rattled, and he invaded my personal space. The edge of the toilet-paper dispenser dug through my jeans and into the backs of my thighs, and he thrust his palm against my chest and leaned all his weight onto me. His cologne filled my nostrils with the scent of freshly mown grass. Marcus McCoy always smelled like summer.

I thought I heard the door and tried to check it out, but Marcus grabbed my jaw, silencing me. He dug his thumb into my cheek and eliminated the remaining space between our bodies, his kiss impatient and rough. His scruff scraped my lips, he ran his hands up my back and across my cheeks and down the front of my pants so quickly, I could hardly react.

"Cold hands!" I ducked out of Marcus's crushing hug to peek over the top of the stall door and make certain we were still alone. I buttoned my pants and adjusted myself.

Marcus was pissing into the toilet when I turned back around. He grinned at me over his shoulder as if I should be honored to watch him pee. "My parents are in Tokyo this weekend."

"Again?"

"Awesome, right?" He zipped up and pulled me by the back of the neck into another kiss, but it felt like he was trying to excavate my face with his tongue. Anyway, I was paranoid someone was going to catch us, so I disengaged from his lips and stumbled out of the stall. "Where you going, Space Boy?"

"We agreed you weren't going to call me that anymore."

"It's cute. You're cute, Space Boy." We stood at the sinks and both admired Marcus's reflection in the mirror— his smooth olive skin and aquiline nose combine with his dimples and muscles to make him unbearably handsome. Worse still, he knows it. Then there's me. Round cheeks, big lips, and an angry zit on the side of my nose that resisted all attempts at eradication. I couldn't fathom why Marcus wanted to hook up with me, even if it was only in secret.

Marcus fished an oblong pill from his pocket and dry-swallowed it. "What do you say?"

"About what?"

"Staying at my house this weekend?"

"I don't know. My mom expects me to look after my grandma and—"

"Your loss, Space Boy." He smacked my ass so hard, I could already feel the welt rising.

I brushed my wavy hair out of my eyes and off my forehead. I hate my hair, but I let it grow long because I hate my ears more. "You could swing by my house. Nana will be there, but we'll tell her you're the pool boy."

Marcus wrinkled his nose like he'd accidentally wandered into a Walmart and found himself surrounded by poor people. "You don't have a pool."

I wonder how he'd react to the end of the world. To

finding out his charmed life is nearing its end. He'd been mauling me at every opportunity since we'd returned from summer break, but we only hung out at his house when his parents were gone. I wager his reluctance to been seen with me in public has less do with his concern about his friends finding out he's hooking up with a boy and more to do with them finding out he's hooking up with Space Boy.

I was deluding myself. We would never be more than this—whatever *this* was.

"If you knew the world was going to end but you could prevent it, would you?"

Marcus was busy gazing at his reflection. "What?" He'd probably clone and fuck himself if the technology existed.

"Would you—" The bathroom door swung inward to admit a beefy kid sporting a buzz cut. He nodded at us and stepped up to a urinal.

Marcus shoved me into the hand dryer. I yelped as the sharp metal jabbed into my shoulder, and he just waltzed out the door. "Catch you around, Space Boy."

The kid at the urinal laughed. "Fucking pansy."

The Meteor

It begins with excitement. The date is 24 January 2016. Frieda Eichman of Grünstadt is the first to identify the asteroid, using the telescope her father gave her for her thirteenth birthday. He's been dead these last twenty years, but he would have been proud. Though the asteroid is given the provisional designation 2016BA11 until its orbit can be confirmed, Frieda knows she will name it the Jürgen Eichman in honor of him.

Space agencies around the globe—NASA, UKSA, CSA, CNSA, ISRO, CRTS, ROSCOSMOS—release statements assuring citizens that though asteroid 2016BA11's trajectory will bring it near Earth, it does not pose a threat. At the top levels of every government, they know this is a lie.

On the night of the Jürgen Eichman event, families gather

outside to watch it streak across the night sky. They hold each other tightly and remark at its beauty, at how lucky they are to witness this once-in-a-lifetime cosmic marvel. Marshmallows are roasted, wine is consumed in heroic quantities, stories are shared. Some who know the truth dine on bullets.

As the Jürgen Eichman looms ever larger in the night sky, as big as the moon and then bigger, people around the world realize something is wrong. The asteroid isn't going to pass harmlessly by. It is going to become a meteor. Most are paralyzed with fear. What can they do? Where can they go? You cannot run from the hand of God.

Frieda Eichman stands alone in an empty field and watches the heavens burn. She whispers, *"Ich habe dich so sehr, Papa verpasst."*

On 29 January 2016, at 1:39 UT, the Jürgen Eichman impacts the Mediterranean Sea. It is approximately the diameter of London. Those within three thousand kilometers of the impact witness a fireball larger than the sunrise over the horizon. Within a minute their clothes combust, grass is set ablaze. Everything is burning, including people. Seismic shocks follow. They radiate from the epicenter, shaking the ground like buried thunder, traveling the globe in less than twenty minutes. The earthquakes are shadowed by the air blast, which vaporizes nearly everything in its path. Houses are demolished, people killed, ancient trees ripped from the ground. Hours later a tidal wave hundreds of kilometers tall washes the earth clean.

Ash and dust bedim the sky, blocking the sun's light. Those few who survive the initial impact die slowly, frozen and alone.

Of the four fundamental forces, gravity is considered the weakest, despite its theoretically endless range. Gravitational forces attract physical bodies to one another. The greater their masses, the greater their attraction. We are pulled toward the ground by gravity, gravity keeps the moon in orbit around the earth, and our planet is held captive by the sun because of gravity. But gravity isn't limited to celestial bodies, it applies to people, too. Though rather than being determined by mass, its force is determined by popularity.

Popularity is teenage heroin. Kids who have tasted it crave more; those who have it in abundance are revered as gods; and even those who have never basked in the light of its glory secretly desire it, regardless of what they may say to the contrary. Popularity can transform an otherwise normal kid into a narcissistic, ego-obsessed, materialistic asshole.

Not that I would know. I have never been, nor wanted to be, popular. Popularity is the reason Marcus ridicules me in public and makes out with me when we're alone. He texted me a couple of times, still trying to convince me to spend the weekend at his house, but I didn't respond.

He was pretending not to watch me from his locker as I dodged other students who were too busy staring at their phones to notice they were in my way. I wondered how Marcus would have reacted if I'd marched up to him and kissed him for the whole school to see. Not that I ever would.

Chemistry is my oasis, and I'm usually the first person to arrive, but today Audrey Dorn beat me and was at her desk, alternating between staring at her phone and watching the door.

I waved at Ms. Faraci when I entered, but she was busy drawing chemical structures on the board and didn't notice.

"You've got to watch this." Audrey faced her phone to me when I reached my desk. "It's one of those Japanese prank shows. They put this guy in a coffin with a bunch of dead squid and leave him there."

I slid into my seat. "Claustrophobia *is* hilarious."

"Maybe another time." Two girls walked in, and Audrey shrank reflexively, but they didn't even look at us. "Listen,

Henry . . ." She leaned across the aisle and spoke in a whisper. "I saw you coming out of the restroom yesterday."

"Was my fly down? Did I forget to wear underwear again? I hate when I do that."

"I know what you were doing in there." Audrey's eyes darted all over the room. "And I know *who* you were doing it with."

More students trickled in as the two-minute bell rang. "Nice try, Veronica Mars, but I have no clue what you're talking about."

"You bite your lip when you're lying, Henry."

"And yours move when you're being a nosy fuckmuppet."

"Did you just call me a fuckmuppet?"

"If the hand fits . . ."

Audrey stiffened. "Whatever. I was only trying to help."

"Your concern for me is touching. Too bad it's not sincere."

The stragglers rushed in as the final bell rang, filling the empty seats. Ms. Faraci dove into a review for our upcoming exam, but I couldn't concentrate on anything except Marcus. Unless Audrey had a secret spy camera in the boys' toilets, all she could know was that we'd both been in the restroom at the same time. Anyway, she was the only person at CHS snoopy enough to monitor when and where I took a whiz.

My phone buzzed in my pocket, and I jumped in my

seat, which distracted Ms. Faraci, causing her to lose her train of thought and launch into a tangent about the importance of understanding atomic structure. As soon as she turned her back, I checked my phone. It was from Marcus, though he came up as All-Star Plumbers. His idea.

ALL -STAR PLUMBERS: bleachers. lunch. i'll bring the footlong.

It was risky meeting him while Audrey was playing detective, but I wanted to see him, especially since I'd turned down his offer for the weekend. Even when I hate Marcus, I miss him when we aren't together. He doesn't fill the yawning hole left by Jesse, but sometimes he makes it hurt slightly less.

I texted a quick reply and then stowed my phone.

Faraci was reviewing the different types of chemical reactions when the door at the front of the class swung open to admit a guy I didn't recognize. He was tall and dangerous with spiky black hair and a fuck-you grin. Lean muscles danced under his crisp shirt. He stood in the doorway, his thumbs hooked through the belt loops of his gray shorts until the entire class was staring at him.

"Someone called for a nude model?"

Ms. Faraci sputtered as she tried to reply. Those students not gaping at the strange kid whispered to one another about him. Marcus wore a wolfish smirk, which caused something savage to rumble in my chest.

"I'm sorry," Ms. Faraci said, "who are you?"

"Diego, obviously." He spoke with an ease that was probably rehearsed; no one could be so composed under the withering scrutiny of twenty sets of eyes. "I'm not really a nude model. Yet."

I wondered if Ms. Faraci was having trouble speaking because the interruption had thrown her off her game and she was trying to figure out where in her lecture she'd left off or because she was imagining what Diego would look like naked too. Finally she rushed out from behind her desk and ushered Diego into the hall. I strained to listen but couldn't hear anything over the din of excited conversations.

After a few moments Ms. Faraci leaned into the room and said, "Henry, can you come out here? Bring your things." I gathered my books, wishing, not for the first time, that I could turn invisible. Ms. Faraci patted my arm when I reached the door. "Henry's one of my best students. He'll show you to your class."

"I will?"

"Diego's new." Ms. Faraci handed me a crumpled printout. "He got a little turned around."

Behind us, the class was descending into chaos without supervision.

"I'll do him . . . it. . . . I'll take Diego to his class." At that moment I wished I were a dickless alien, but my verbal diarrhea only made Diego smile. It was a cute smile, lopsided and charming.

Ms. Faraci mouthed *thank you* and rushed inside as Dustin Collier fell out of his desk and crashed into the supply locker where Ms. Faraci stored the volatile chemicals.

I slung my backpack over my shoulder and led Diego toward the exit. "You're supposed to be in history with Mrs. Parker this period. It's across campus in the social studies building."

Diego took his schedule, folded it neatly, and slipped it into his back pocket. "Lead the way, Sacagawea."

"What?"

"Because you're my guide? And we're going to history? Forget it." Diego's voice was deep and hummed like the constant vibration of the sluggers' ship.

The humid air pummeled us as soon as we left the air-conditioned science building, but I was still grateful for the excuse to escape the classroom. I took the long way to the social studies building.

"So," Diego said, "your science teacher's a little out there."

"Yeah."

"But she seems cool."

The confidence Diego exuded when he'd burst into my class

appeared to be waning, and he fidgeted, shoving his hands into his pockets, then crossing his arms, then putting his hands back into his pockets. I was never good at small talk, preferring not to talk at all. Talking is how bad things happen. But Diego seemed uncomfortable with the silence, so I gave it a try. "Science is my favorite. It's precise, and everything has an explanation. Plus, sometimes we get to blow shit up."

"I can see the appeal."

"It's so weird." Once I began babbling, I couldn't stop. "Like, the smaller things get, the crazier science becomes. When you start talking about p-branes and quantum immortality and entanglement . . . Well, it's just cool is all."

Diego stared at me with X-ray eyes. It was like he could see through my clothes and skin, straight to the meat of me. I quickly changed the subject. "You just move here or something?"

"Or something." Diego quickened his pace. The way he avoided looking at me reminded me of Jesse at the end— the odd hesitation before each smile, the sudden silences that rose between us. At the time I hadn't thought much of them, but that's what makes hindsight such a bitch.

"I didn't mean to pry."

"It's not you," Diego said. "It's just a reflex. I moved from Colorado."

The first thing that popped into my mind was, "Jack Swigert was from Colorado."

"Who?"

"Jack Swigert? Apollo 13 astronaut? Nearly died in space trying to reach the moon?" I stuffed my hands into my pockets when Diego shook his head. "I read a lot."

"Books are for ugly people."

"And old women. My nana reads a book a day. Of course, she's got Alzheimer's, so she could read the same book over and over and it wouldn't make a difference to her. She used to write in her journal every day. I kind of picked up the habit from her."

"So you're a writer?"

"I write sometimes—mostly about stuff that happens to me, and occasionally different ways the world might end—but I'm not a writer."

Diego laughed, and the rich, sincere sound of it made me smile. "That sounds . . . odd. I paint."

"Landscapes?"

"Lots of 'scapes."

"I can't even draw stick figures. I sat next to a kid in middle school who specialized in turning the illustrations in his textbooks into dicks and vaginas. I doubt there's any real-world application." I couldn't stop rambling, so I bit the inside of my lip to shut myself up.

We reached the social studies building. It was a squat, two-story structure that was begging to be torn down. The paint was peeling, and the classrooms smelled moldy and damp. "Here we are. Two nineteen is on the second floor."

"Thanks for being my guide."

"Sure. Oh, and you should avoid sitting in the front row; Mrs. Parker's a spitter."

Diego tapped his temple. "Noted. See you later, Henry . . ."

"Denton."

"Diego Vega." He climbed the stairs, and I walked in the direction of the football field. "Hey, Henry!" I stopped and turned around. Diego was leaning over the railing of the second floor, and I had to crane my neck to see him. "You think *you'll* ever go into space?"

"I'd say it's pretty likely."

Twenty minutes later Marcus was pawing me under the bleachers while I kept a lookout for spiders and tried not to feel like a dirty cliché. He didn't even say hello when he saw me because he was too busy slipping his tongue into my mouth and putting his hands down my pants. It would have been sweet if I thought he were actually happy to see me rather than just plain horny.

My stomach churned, and I pushed Marcus away to avoid burping in his mouth. "Sorry, I skipped breakfast."

Marcus grabbed his crotch. "I've got something you could—"

"I changed my mind about this weekend," I said, cutting him off before he ruined the moment.

"Really?"

"Yeah. My mom's preoccupied with work, and Charlie can look after Nana."

Marcus uncapped his bottled water and took a swig. "Too late, Space Boy."

"Why?" My voice was crumbling, and I struggled to shore up its supports.

"After you blew me off, I decided to throw a little party."

"Oh." Marcus twisted my nipple. I slapped his hand away. "Dick!"

"It's not even a party, really. More like an intimate gathering of friends."

"Next time." I pinched my leg through my jeans and focused on the pain. I had no right to be upset; I'd bailed on him first. It's not like I expected him to sit home all weekend, pining for me, but would it have killed him to act a little disappointed?

"Definitely." Marcus checked the time on his phone. "Come on, Space Boy. Bell's gonna ring soon, and I didn't invite you out here to talk."

11 September 2015

On Friday, Marcus hardly acknowledged I existed. I loath admitting I wanted him to pull me into the restroom to make out or send me a text, begging me to come to his party. Anything to prove he gives a shit. To occupy my mind and keep me from spiraling out of control, I tried to come up with an explanation for why the sluggers chose me to save the planet.

I think most people would have pressed the button the moment they realized the stakes. Most people are motivated by their own self-interest, and pushing the button would ensure their survival. But I am not most people. Maybe that's why the sluggers chose me: they weren't sure what I'd do.

On the surface, it seems like there are a million reasons to press the button—great movies, books, sex, pizza with everything, bacon, kissing—but those things mean nothing. The universe is more than thirteen billion years old. What is the value of a single kiss compared to that? What is the value of an entire world?

It's too much to wrap my brain around, which only leads me back to wondering why I've been chosen. There are smarter people who could make a more informed decision, and dumber people who'd make a quicker one.

The sluggers didn't abduct them, though, they abducted me, and all I can do is be honest.

I trudged through the front door when I got home from school, and all I wanted to do was make a sandwich, take a nap, and sleep through the weekend. But Mom and Nana were huddled around the kitchen table, staring at a shoe box stuffed with papers and envelopes like they were water moccasins. Mom's cheeks were flushed, and she was sucking on her cigarette—puff-puff-ash, puff-puff-ash. I considered skipping my snack and retreating to my room, but I couldn't sleep on an empty stomach.

I regretted my decision immediately.

"Henry, tell your mother she's not putting me in a nursing home."

Mom rolled her eyes, which she knew Nana hated, and

blew a cloud of smoke into the air. "Mother, you need someone to look after you."

"I can look after myself."

"Before I moved you in with us, you were eating rancid meats and hadn't paid your water bill in three months."

Nana crossed her arms over her sagging breasts—fucking gravity. "I had water."

"Because you ran a hose from Mr. Flannigan's house through your kitchen window!"

"I am not an invalid, Eleanor." She spoke with a quiet fury, her anger reducing to a hard crust you'd need a hammer to chip away.

Mom laughed in her face. "When was the last time you showered? Or brushed your teeth?"

"That's irrelevant."

"I've got two children, Mother, I don't need a third."

"I would rather die than live in one of those places."

They glared at each other across the table. The air between them a toxic cloud of cigarette smoke and resentment. I was certain they'd forgotten I was there, and the intelligent decision would have been to sneak away, but I was thinking with my rumbling stomach rather than my brain.

"Nana doesn't belong in a nursing home, Mom."

"Mind your own business, Henry."

Nana stood and shuffled to the fridge. "Go to your room and wait for your father to get home." She lingered before the open doors, staring at the shelves of food.

"Daddy's gone," Mom said, her fight evaporating. "He's been dead a long time."

"That's a terrible thing to say," Nana mumbled. "I think he'd like pot roast for supper."

Nana's forgetfulness was cute at first—she'd call us by the wrong names, mix up our birthdays, send us Christmas cards in the middle of summer—but it isn't cute anymore. Sometimes she looks at me, and I see nothing but a deepening abyss where my grandmother used to be. She's becoming a stranger to me, and I'm often nobody to her. Then she'll turn around ten minutes later and tell me I'm her favorite grandson. Nana's doctors believe her memory will continue to deteriorate. Good days outnumber the bad now, but eventually only bad days will remain.

"I'll come home right after school," I said. "Don't put her in a home."

Nana unloaded butter, tomatoes, and a package of chicken thighs onto the table. Whatever she was cooking, it wasn't pot roast.

Mom fumbled with her cigarettes and lit another. "Whatever. It's not like we can afford it anyway, especially with the way you and your brother eat." She glanced at the shoe box of unpaid bills. "Waiting tables isn't exactly the path to riches."

"Get a new job then," I said. "You studied cooking in France. You should be running a restaurant."

"Henry—"

"Come on, Mom. You know I'm right. I bet there are tons of restaurants that would hire you. If you'd just try to—"

"Henry," she said. "Shut up."

Charlie and his girlfriend, Zooey Hawthorne, barged into the kitchen, carrying grocery bags, oblivious to the tension that clung to the walls like splattered grease. I never thought I'd be glad to see Charlie.

"Who's hungry?" he asked, dropping his bags onto the table, which pushed Nana's growing collection of odd ingredients aside. "Zooey's making pasta carbonara, and I thought Nana could bake an apple pie."

Zooey kissed Nana's cheek and led her away from the fridge. "You have to give me your recipe. It's so yum." Zooey is taller than Charlie, slender, with skin like a buckeye, and spacey brown eyes. Way too good for my dipshit brother.

I was still waiting for Mom to pick up our argument from where we left off, while Charlie and Zooey unpacked groceries like we were some kind of happy family. Like this was normal.

"I'll skip the food poisoning tonight," I said.

Charlie grabbed my arm, squeezing hard, and pulled me into an awkward hug. It threw me off-balance. Charlie doesn't hug me—we don't hug each other—it isn't our thing. Wedgies, wet willies, dead legs, and broken noses—those are our things. "Family dinner, bro."

Mom shook her head. Her shoulders were slumped and her back bowed, giving her the impression of having a hump. "Charlie, I don't think tonight—"

"We're pregnant."

Zooey and Charlie snapped together, linking hands and sharing a goofy grin. She rubbed her still-flat belly and said, "Ten weeks. I wasn't sure at first, even after I took a dozen home tests, but I went to my gyno and she confirmed it and . . . we're pregnant!"

"I told Mom to have you neutered," I said, and Charlie boxed my ear.

"Show some respect, kid."

"Kid?" My brother is a kid. Sure, he can drink, smoke, and kill during wartimes, but he's still a dumb kid. He pees on the toilet seat and doesn't know how to operate the washing machine, and it was only a couple of months ago that he shoved a peanut M&M so far up his nose that we had to take him to the emergency room to have it extracted. Charlie has no business having a baby when he's just a baby himself.

But Charlie and Zooey stood in the middle of the kitchen, smiling and smiling, waiting for someone to congratulate them or tell them they were ruining their lives. The longer they waited, the more strained their smiles became, cracking around the edges. They might have waited forever if Nana hadn't broken the silence.

"Young man, do your parents know you're having a colored girl's baby?"

"Nana!" I said, mortified by what she'd said but laughing at her the way you'd laugh at a toddler screaming "fuck!" in the middle of a crowded department store.

Charlie and Zooey latched on to Nana's anachronistic racism and wrung out a chuckle that turned into a torrent of laughter. We were so busy being mortified by what Nana had said and uncomfortable at our own response that we didn't notice Mom crying until she said, "Oh, Charlie."

The pasta carbonara smelled delicious, but I didn't expect I'd get to eat any because of the yelling and fighting and Charlie's occasional hysterical outbursts. Once the shock wore off, Mom got around to listing the various ways Zooey and Charlie were ruining their lives, and Charlie's only defense consisted of shouting loud enough to drown her out.

I could have settled the argument by informing them that I wasn't going to press the button. If the world needed someone as pathetic as me to save it, we were better off dead. Nana wouldn't be shipped off to a home, and Charlie and Zooey wouldn't be saddled with a little parasite neither of them was ready to care for. I'd be doing them a favor. Only, I'm still not sure what I'm going to do.

I found a bag of stale potato chips under my bed and munched on the crumbs. I was too worked up to sleep, but not bored enough to do homework, so I killed an hour on the Internet, which is how I ended up stalking Marcus's SnowFlake page. It was flooded with comments about the party, and it looked like he was going to be hosting more than just a few friends. Based on what I read, I guessed he'd invited every kid at CHS. Well, almost every kid.

Marcus probably hadn't even waited an hour after I'd turned him down before organizing the party.

Fuck it.

I shut off my computer and flopped across my bed, letting my head fall backward so that the blood rushed to my brain. The pressure increased, and I counted the quickening *thud-thud-thud* of my heartbeat. I wondered how long I'd have to stay upside down before I passed out. How long after that before I'd die. I wondered what Jesse had thought about after he'd stepped off the edge of his desk and dangled on the end of the rope. Charlie has a buddy who works for Calypso Fire Rescue, and he said Jesse's knots were the best he'd ever seen. A perfect noose on one end, and a textbook clove hitch on the other. Once Jesse took the plunge, he couldn't have changed his mind even if he'd wanted to.

I wonder if he thought of me in his final seconds. Or about his mom and dad, or his dog, Captain Jack, that he had put to sleep only a few months earlier. Maybe random thoughts invaded his brain the way they often do right before you fall asleep. Thoughts like how he'd never taste chocolate again or about the homework he'd neglected to finish. I doubt he thought of me at all.

If I die before deciding whether to press the button, will the sluggers abduct someone else and force them to choose, or will they let the world end? I should ask.

No . . . fuck it.

I'm being stupid. If Marcus doesn't want to be seen with me, why kiss me at all? I remember the first time it happened. I'd hung around after Faraci's class to ask her a question about our lab. I went to the restroom after, and knocked into Marcus on his way out. I thought he was going to rearrange my face, but he kissed me. It was the first time since Jesse had died that I'd felt anything. I knew, even then, Marcus was never going to be my boyfriend or write me sappy love letters. I'll never have with him what I had with Jesse—I doubt I'll have that again with anyone—but I want to be more than Marcus's stand-in. To him, I am the cheap pair of sunglasses you buy on vacation because you know you won't care if you break or lose them.

Fuck it.

Nothing matters. If I don't press the button, the world will end in 140 days. Marcus's party, Charlie's baby, Mom's job, Nana's memory. None of it matters. The sluggers didn't give me a choice, they gave me freedom.

So what if Marcus hadn't invited me? He hadn't *not* invited me. No matter what happened, I could always let the world end and the universe forget. It would forget the party and Calypso and Earth. It would forget Charlie and Zooey and Marcus and Mom and Nana. It had already forgotten Jesse, and if I let it, it would forget me, too.

I could write my name across the sky, and it would be in invisible ink.

I showered and dressed, settling on jeans and a short-sleeve plaid shirt I'd borrowed from Jesse once and never returned. It had looked better on him, but that was true of everything. My hair was hopeless, so I did my best to make it appear purposely messy.

My stomach roiled as uncertainty gnawed at my apathy-fueled courage. I doubted Marcus would be thrilled I was crashing his party, and I wasn't sure whether I was going because I didn't care or because I was hoping to prove that Marcus did.

Mom, Charlie, and Zooey were still talking in the kitchen; at least they seemed to have agreed upon a temporary cease-fire, probably thanks to Zooey, who's far more level-headed than either my mom or brother. Nana was reading a book on the couch and watching *Bunker*. I waved when I left, but she didn't notice.

Audrey Dorn was waiting in the driveway in her cobalt blue BMW, a present from her parents on her sixteenth birthday. She smiled when I climbed into the car, and leaned toward me like she was going to hug me, but hesitated and reversed course when she saw the look on my face.

"Thanks for the ride."

"I was surprised you called." Even wearing Jesse's shirt I felt underdressed compared to Audrey. She was wearing jeans too, but hers probably cost more than my mom made in a month, and her silver halter top sparkled like the noon sun on a calm ocean. "You used to hate parties."

"I still do."

"Did Marcus invite you?"

"No."

Audrey *mmmhhhmmmed* at that, which made me regret calling her. I wouldn't have, but Marcus lives on the other side of Calypso, and it was too warm outside to walk. She put the car in gear and sped off. At least she hadn't pestered me about why I was going.

"You ready for the chem exam?" Audrey asked. I'd never driven with her, and it was a strange experience. She drove with both hands on the wheel, checked her mirrors religiously, and always used her turn signals. She even kept the music so low I could barely hear it.

"No."

"I'd heard Faraci was supposed to be an easy A."

"Joke's on you. Maybe she'll zone out and accidentally mix sodium phosphide with water and kill us all with phosphine gas."

Audrey giggled, but it sounded forced and more like a hiccup. "I've missed you, Henry."

I didn't know how to respond. Audrey was doing me a favor driving me to Marcus's party, but I'd only called her out of desperation. Sometimes I wondered if I was being too hard on her. We'd both lost Jesse, and most of the time I thought we were both to blame for his suicide. But it was easier to stay mad at her, and it wasn't like she didn't deserve it. I pulled a ten-dollar bill from my pocket and stuffed it in the cup holder. "For gas."

We drove the rest of the way in silence.

Marcus lives in a mansion. Not one of those faux McMansions that everyone seems to live in these days, but an actual mansion with two garages, twelve bedrooms, a formal dining room, and a kitchen the size of a tennis court, which is ludicrous to me since, as far as I know, Mr. and Mrs. McCoy never cook.

Audrey drove past the security gate and parked on the side of the winding driveway. Sloppy rows of expensive cars sparkled under the decorative lights strung from the palm trees that kept vigil over the yard.

I was a fraud; I didn't belong. No one had invited me, and no one would miss me if I fled.

"If you're having second thoughts, we can grab a bite at Sweeney's instead." Audrey was in my head, and I wanted her out. "I haven't eaten there in ages."

"Me neither." In fact, I hadn't been to Sweeney's since the last time Audrey, Jesse, and I had gone together. We'd shared a tower of onion rings and celebrated Jesse being cast as Seymour in the CHS production of *Little Shop of Horrors*. Jesse sang all the time. He was singing the night I realized I loved him. It wouldn't surprise me to learn he'd been singing when he died.

"Henry?"

I shook Jesse from my thoughts. "If you knew the world was going to end, and you alone had the power to prevent it, would you?"

"Of course."

"Why?"

"What do you mean?"

A shiny black pickup truck parked beside Audrey's car, and four girls from our class spilled out, chatting and smiling, probably sharing the delusion that they were going to have the best night of their lives. "Give me one reason why you think humanity deserves to live."

I recognized the look she was giving me. The poor-pathetic-Henry look that made me want to gouge out her eyes with a plastic knife. "If this is about Jesse—"

"Forget it."

"What?"

"Do you honestly believe any of this is important? That in a hundred years, one of your great-great-great-whatevers is going to write about how you went to a party, got hammered, and tried to avoid being groped by every boy with hands? None of this matters, Audrey. We're all fucked." I opened the car door but didn't get out.

Audrey's bottom lip trembled, and tears welled in her

eyes. It was a dirty trick, and she knew it. "I miss Jesse too, but you deserve better than Marcus McCoy. Please tell me you get that."

"If I really deserve better, then maybe Jesse shouldn't have killed himself."

I was out and walking toward the house before Audrey could kill the engine and follow. Calling her was a mistake, and I vowed to walk home before asking her for another ride.

The two-story tall front doors of Marcus's house were wide open and welcoming. Couples and crowds flowed in and out—their cheeks flushed, pleasantly drunk—stumbling and stoned or just laughing at some joke I'd never hear. I was worried as I entered that they'd see me and cringe, wonder who let Space Boy in, but no one noticed me. I snagged a beer from the kitchen and wandered through the house. I knew the rooms; the rooms knew me. Marcus and I had made out on that leather couch, I'd gone down on him under that baby grand piano, he'd chased me through the library and caught me on the stairs. We'd fucked on that counter and that floor and in that bathtub. After all we've done, I'm still his dirty secret.

Marcus fucks Henry. In the grammar of our relationship, I am the object.

I chugged my beer and grabbed another.

"Henry Denton?"

Diego Vega was standing with his back against a wall, holding a bottled water. He said something to the girl standing near him and met me at the keg. He was wearing faded jeans and a thin orange hoodie that made him stick out like that one dead bulb in a string of lit Christmas lights. When he reached me, he gave me a stiff one-armed bro-hug.

"Only in school a week and already at the coolest party in Calypso. I'm impressed."

Diego buzzed with energy, like the physical confines of his body couldn't contain him. "I've never been in a house this big."

I sipped my beer and tried to think of something witty to say. I hadn't expected to see Diego, but I was glad he was there. "They've got two pools."

"What?" Diego cupped his hand to his ear. Someone was blasting shitty power-pop in the other room, and it was drowning out our voices.

"Come on!" I pulled Diego away from the kitchen, toward the family room. I was hoping it would be empty, but there was a group playing pool. It looked like girls against guys, and the girls were kicking ass. The music wasn't as loud, though. "That's better."

Diego took in the room. Shelves stuffed with books were built into three walls, and a TV dominated the fourth. "How rich is this guy?"

"Marcus?" I shrugged. "The McCoys are super rich. His dad's an investment banker or something."

"Who?"

"Marcus McCoy? The guy who lives here?"

Diego smacked my chest. "That's his name! He's in my econ class. It's been driving me crazy." He had dimples like quicksand, and his hazel eyes reminded me of the sluggers' skin. "Anyway, I was hoping I'd run into you."

"Bullshit."

"Seriously."

"Why?"

Diego shrugged. "You're the only person I've met who hasn't asked me what kind of car I drive."

"Well, then you're the only person at this party who actually wants me here."

"I doubt it."

"That's because you're new." Diego had an honest face, but I found it difficult to believe he'd come to the party to see me when I was practically invisible to everyone else. "How're you liking Calypso?"

"Honestly? It's weird. Sometimes there are too many

people and I just want to find a quiet closet to read in. Other times I want to surround myself with as many people as possible. But I love the beach. I'm there so often, my sister jokes about buying me a tent so I can sleep there."

"Keep the zipper locked or you'll wake up being spooned by a bum."

"So long as I get to be the little spoon."

Diego's laugh made me smile in spite of myself. Maybe I'd been wrong to fear the party. I'd been there an hour, and not only had it not turned into a disaster, I was actually having fun.

"You'll have to work that out on your own." I finished off my beer and set the cup down on a bookshelf ledge.

We lingered in that awkward stage of a conversation where there was no logical next topic but the silence hadn't yet grown uncomfortable.

"If you knew the world was going to end, and you could press a button to prevent it, would you?"

Diego raised his eyebrow. "Is there something I should know?"

"It's a hypothetical question."

"Then hypothetically, yes."

"Why?"

"Because I'm not keen on dying."

WE ARE THE ANTS • 65

The girls at the pool table squealed with delight, razzing the losers. I tried to block them out. "But you're going to die anyway."

"Sure, when I'm old."

"You could die at any time. A freak lightning strike could fry your heart, or you could drown in a molasses tsunami."

Diego's face was difficult to read. He seemed to take my question seriously, but I hoped he wasn't going along with it while he devised a way to escape. "If I don't press the button, I'm definitely dead. At least if I press it, I've got a chance at a long life. I like having choices."

Having choices is the problem. Everything would be easier if someone told me what to do: push the button, stop seeing Marcus, get over Jesse. The problem with choices is that I usually make the wrong ones.

Diego reached out and brushed a stray lock of hair off my forehead. "Sorry, that was driving me crazy."

"Great, now everyone's going to figure out my secret identity."

"Space Boy?" Diego said, smiling. "They already know."

My smile disappeared, and my defenses snapped up. I shoved my way past Diego without a word. His apologies bounced off my back because I was fucking bulletproof. I needed to leave, to escape the house and party and all those artificial people, but the front was crowded, so I stumbled onto the patio, where it was quieter and I could breathe.

"Space Boy!"

Marcus and a mixed group, some of whom looked familiar, were sitting around a patio table by the hot tub. Natalie Carter lounged across his lap. The moment he said my name, I became visible. People who hadn't noticed me before were suddenly glaring at me like I was covered with festering sores. They parroted "Space Boy" and invented semicreative variations of their own. None stung as badly as when Diego had said it.

"Who the fuck let you in?" Marcus's voice was cough syrup, but his words were acid.

"Front door was open." A burning pang began in the center of my chest and spread to my limbs. Marcus was treating me like I was nobody—less than. I wondered how his friends in the hot tub would react if they found out what we'd done where they were lounging.

Marcus elbowed Adrian Morse. "We need to start charging at the door. Keep out the trash."

I'm sure when Adrian's mom looks at him in the mornings or brushes his sweaty hair off his forehead while he sleeps through a fever, she thinks he's a nice boy, but when I look at him, all I see is a demented thug with an inferiority complex and hardly a thought of his own bouncing around in his empty head. "I can get rid of him."

"If only getting rid of your herpes was as easy," I said.

Adrian stood, but Marcus pulled him back. There was a dangerous gleam in Marcus's eyes, a flicker that scared me. "Fuck it. I'm feeling charitable. Space Boy can stay. Maybe he can phone home and convince the aliens to join the party. If you do, ask them to bring ice. We're running low."

I had no intention of remaining at the party. All I could think about was how I'd been so wrong. I never should have come. Once Marcus was done torturing me, I planned to leave and never speak to him or anyone else again.

"But first," Marcus said, "you have to take a shot."

From where Marcus's friends sat and stood on the patio, drinking and smoking and judging, I felt their contempt. It burned through my skin, melted the fat from my body, chewed through my muscles until I was nothing but a skeleton—bleached bones held together by duct tape and the tattered remnants of my pride.

Jay Oh flicked a bottle cap at me that bounced off my chest and skittered across the table. "What would aliens want with a jizz stain like him? Aren't there better people to abduct?"

"Better looking, certainly," Marcus said, which earned

him a kiss from Natalie. He kept his eyes on me while she sucked his lips.

And I stood there and took it because I was an object. We were all objects to Marcus McCoy.

Marcus began chanting, "Shot, shot, shot!" and it was taken up by the drunken horde surrounding me. Adrian set up a round of shots, sloshing a dark brown liquid into the glasses, spilling some over the sides. Marcus watched me with a manic, sweaty grin.

Adrian finished pouring and rolled his eyes. "Space Boy's a little bitch. He won't—"

I grabbed the nearest shot glass and threw it back. The liquor tasted like pureed licorice and blood. I shivered as it hit my empty stomach. When I finished, I downed a second shot. "Thanks for the drink." I tossed the glass onto the table and left.

Their laughter hounded me, but I refused to look back. The world was going to end, and none of this mattered. I tried to convince myself I was all right.

But I was so far from all right.

I was too drunk to walk home, and I couldn't find an empty room to hide in, so I ended up sitting by the edge of the lap pool, obscured by fake rocks and palm trees. The pool was far enough from the house that I wasn't worried about being found, but still near enough that I could hear their laughter. I couldn't escape it. I couldn't escape being Space Boy.

The moon was hardly a scratch in the sky, but underwater lights illuminated the tiled bottom of the pool. All the way down to the deep, deep end. It had to be eight or nine feet. I bet I'd sink. It would have been easy to roll over the side, fully clothed, and let the weight of denim and cotton drag me to the bottom while my last breaths escaped my lungs. The world was spinning around me, so maybe the alcohol in my blood would prevent my survival instinct from kicking in, and I could drown peacefully without all that unnecessary flailing and screaming.

It didn't matter why the sluggers had chosen me, only that they had. Hell, why wait for the world to end at all?

Diego was wrong. Pressing the button wouldn't give me choices. Only this. Only humiliation. Loneliness. Death was easier. I could lean forward and let my weight carry me into the water. Gravity would do the rest. Everything would end, and all I had to do was let it happen.

The moon grew brighter and multiplied the shadows. They encircled me, blotting out the light. I shook my head to clear the vertigo. I needed to piss, but I didn't want to go back inside. I could always piss in the pool.

My breath caught in my throat, and the hairs on my ears rose. I tried to look around but couldn't. I tried to call out, but no words escaped my lips. I was paralyzed.

Oh, I thought as the moon's light blinded me, and the shadows grasped at me with green-brown fingers, *I didn't expect to see you here.*

World War III

North Korea fires the first missile. After years of threats and insane posturing, it's Fox's early cancellation of *Bunker* that provokes North Korea's supreme leader to action. He demands to view the finale, but is ignored. If Fox won't resurrect *Firefly*, they're certainly not going to bring back *Bunker*.

The North Korean missile detonates prematurely, but the aggressive act puts the world's nations on high alert. The leaders of the European Union recommend diplomacy. China and Russia deploy their military forces to strategic positions throughout the world while suggesting that the US capitulate to North Korea's demands.

Dennis Rodman travels to North Korea as an unofficial ambassador on a mission of peace but is taken into custody the moment he disembarks from the plane. A video of him being torn apart by a pack of starving house cats is the most popular video on YouTube for seven hours, before it is displaced by an elderly woman who inhales helium and sings Michael Jackson's "Thriller."

Despite stern warnings from the United Nations Security Council, North Korea fires a second missile, striking Osaka, Japan. Thousands die. Japan and the United States declare war on North Korea. The joined forces of Russia and China advise that retaliatory attacks against North Korea will not be tolerated.

The United States Armed Forces invade North Korea on 29 January 2016 at 20:03 GMT. Russia responds by launching a nuclear missile at Universal Studios Florida, proclaiming that if they can't visit the Wizarding World of Harry Potter, no one can. The United States obliterates Moscow and urges all patriotic Americans to boycott vodka.

China, taking advantage of the chaos, launches its full arsenal of nuclear weapons at key US targets, initiating a full-blown thermonuclear war that ultimately renders the planet a desolate wasteland incapable of supporting life.

The only survivors are the contestants of *Bunker*, forgotten by Fox producers after the show's cancellation. Unaware of what has occurred on the surface, they eventually run out of food and draw lots to decide who they're going to eat first.

14 September 2015

I woke up laughing. For a few disorienting seconds, I thought I was still on the spaceship. The sluggers had shown me a projection of the earth exploding again, along with the big, red button, but they hadn't shocked or blissed me. They simply offered me the choice and waited to see what I would do. Maybe that's why I was laughing. Averting the apocalypse shouldn't be so easy. It should require elaborate schemes hidden from the public to keep them from panicking. It should demand sacrifice and tearful good-byes and Bruce Willis.

Obviously, I didn't press it.

When I regained my senses and realized I wasn't on the sluggers' ship anymore, the laughter died in my throat. My back was damp, and something sharp dug into my hip. My hair, my boxers, and my chest were wet. I stank like stagnant canal water. When I sat up, I spit, in case some of the water had gotten into my mouth.

The moon was dark, and clouds obscured the stars. I had no idea where I was. I remembered being at Marcus's party, sitting by the pool—then I was on the ship—but I had no idea how I'd ended up floating on a sea of sandspurs and goose grass. The sluggers had stolen my jeans and Jesse's shirt, but at least they'd left me my boxers. A teenage boy running around Calypso in his underwear is odd, but a teenage boy running around Calypso naked is a felony.

My legs trembled as I stood, and I listed dangerously. I focused on the horizon like Jesse had said to, but without the moon, the sky and ground bled into one another. Eventually, my eyes adjusted, and I was able to pick out a few distant shadows. I set sail for those.

I walked for ten minutes, carefully picking my way through the weedy field, forced to stop occasionally to pluck a spiny sandspur from the tender skin between my toes, cursing the sluggers for never dropping me off anywhere interesting. I hope before the world ends, they drop me off somewhere I've never been—Paris or Thailand or Brazil. Anywhere has to be better than Calypso.

The shadows turned out to be jungle gym equipment. Towers and monkey bars, the various structures connected by wooden bridges. I didn't recognize the playground, but I did recognize the Randy Raccoon mascot painted on the wall of the nearest building. This was my old elementary school. It had changed since I was a boy. There used to be a metal geodesic dome that I'd climb to the top of and leap from, trying to break my ankle so I'd be sent home. I wasn't Space Boy back then, I was Hillbilly Henry because of a cowboy hat I'd worn every day for weeks. I don't even remember where I got it, but I hardly took it off. Not until Matt Walsh stole it during recess and pissed on it. No one but me had seen him do it, and Mr. Polk—my third-grade teacher—accused me of peeing on it myself and trying to blame Matt. When my father picked me up from school and asked me where my hat was, I told him I lost it. He spanked me so hard with a wooden spoon, the handle broke.

Ben Franklin Elementary was too far from home to walk, so I trudged to the front of the school. I was exhausted, my legs ached, and my head felt like the sluggers had unspooled my brain through my ears and then stuffed it back in wrong so that it resembled a bowl of gray linguini. Needless to say, I was overjoyed when I saw a pay phone next to a wooden bench near the student drop-off area. The phone booth was decorated with faded stickers for bands I'd never heard of and brands that sounded only vaguely familiar—relics of rebel kids long since assimilated into adulthood. I picked up the receiver, trying not to imagine the hundreds of snot-nosed brats that had probably groped it, and prayed it still worked. The dial tone was the most beautiful sound I'd heard in ages.

My finger hovered over the numbers. It was late, but I didn't know how late. It had been eleven or twelve when I was sitting by the pool—those shots had skewed my perception of the passage of time—but the sluggers could have kept me for an hour or five. Waking up my mother was out of the question, and Charlie would sleep through the end of the world, so I knew he wouldn't answer his phone. I didn't know my father's number or if he even still lived in Florida, and Audrey was the last person I wanted to see. I only knew one other number.

The first indignity was having to call collect. Pay phones should be free. If you're desperate enough to need one, it's probably an emergency and you don't have change. It's not like boxer shorts come with pockets. I hadn't even known that you *could* make collect calls until Jesse explained it to me one morning after the sluggers had dropped me off near his house. The information had seemed about as useful as Latin, until the first time I actually needed to use it.

I pressed zero and followed the prompts, first dialing Marcus's number, then speaking my name into the receiver, and, finally, waiting.

The second indignity was hearing Marcus ask who it was three times and then pause, as if he were actually considering whether to accept the charges, before muttering a weary yes. His voice was drowsy and annoyed. "Henry?"

"Were you sleeping?"

"Obviously. It's, like, three in the morning."

I forced a laugh. "I figured you'd be drinking until dawn."

Marcus paused. "Drinking? What the fuck, Henry? I've got school tomorrow. So do you."

School? Seriously? The sluggers had kept me on their ship for at least two whole days. I hate when they do that.

The third indignity was listening to Marcus speak to me in that condescending tone, knowing I couldn't tell him to eat a dick because I needed him to pick me up, and having to pretend it was Sunday when my brain was telling me it was still Friday.

"I wouldn't have called if it weren't important."

"Couldn't you have called someone else?"

"No."

The silence on Marcus's end of the line worried me that he'd hung up, but he coughed, and the phlegmy noise was a relief. "What's the big emergency?"

"I'm at Ben Franklin Elementary, and I need you to pick me up."

"Funny."

"I'm not joking."

"Dude, that's way out by Beeline. What're you doing there?"

The fourth indignity was that Marcus already knew the answer but wanted to hear me say it. "Can you get me or not?"

Part of me wanted him to refuse. To hang up the phone and fall back to sleep, wake up the next morning believing my call had been some crazy, late-night, Chinese-food-fueled dream. But he said, "Give me a few minutes to get dressed."

No one memorizes phone numbers anymore. They call "Mom" or "Dad" or "Assface." The entries in their phones are completely divorced from the ten-digit numbers that make calling people possible.

I tried to bring my cell phone onto the ship with me a couple of times. I'd slept with it clutched in my hands, stuffed in my underwear; I'd even duct-taped it to my thigh once. The sluggers had ditched the phone but left the tape. I'm not ashamed to admit that I screamed when I pulled it off the next day. I thought if I could sneak my phone aboard, I could snap some grainy photos, record some video, maybe grab GPS coordinates to prove I wasn't lying. As an added bonus, I'd be able to call for help if the sluggers dropped me off far from home.

I finally gave up and memorized the numbers of everyone I knew worth calling. The list was short.

Marcus zipped into the parking lot in a sleek black Tesla. His poor taste in music reached me before he did; the car vibrated from the bass, and Marcus sang loud and proud.

When he pulled to a stop in the loading zone, I caught my reflection in the car's tinted windows before Marcus pushed open the door. My hair was tangled and stiff from the dried water, my chest was streaked with mud, and I was wearing the boxers with the kissing whales Jesse had given me for our first Valentine's Day. I'm pretty sure whales don't actually kiss.

"Looking hot, Space Boy." Marcus, of course, looked perfect. His hair had just the right amount of wave in the front, and he was dressed in khaki shorts and a V-neck T-shirt. He didn't look at all like someone who'd recently rolled out of bed.

"Can you not call me that?" I started to climb into the car when Marcus shouted, "Whoa, whoa! Hold on." He dug around in the backseat and retrieved a towel for me to sit on, and one of his track jerseys to wear. It was crusty and reeked of salty sweat, but it still smelled better than I did. "Thanks."

We barely made it out of the parking lot before Marcus

started in on me. "Is this some sort of Space Boy thing?"

I leaned my head against the window and watched Ben Franklin Elementary disappear, trying to ignore Marcus. For him, the party was two days ago—old news—but the things he'd said, the way he'd treated me, were still fresh wounds for me. Being desperate for a ride didn't mean I was willing to forgive him.

Marcus smacked my arm. "Those aliens lobotomize you or something?"

"I don't want to talk about it."

"You were totally abducted, weren't you?" Marcus fired off a high-pitched cackle that made me fantasize about punching him so hard in the balls that the trauma traveled back through time and rendered his ancestors sterile, thus wiping Marcus McCoy from history. "What'd they do to you? Anal probe? That's it, isn't it?"

"Totally," I mumbled. "Why do you even want to know?"

"I'm curious."

"Bullshit. You just want the gory details so you can tell your asshole friends how Space Boy got bummed by aliens."

Marcus's eyes widened. "Did you really?"

"No!"

Despite being the only car on the road, we caught every red light. When Marcus pulled to a stop, he slid his hand across the center console and rested it on my thigh, slowly inching toward my crotch like he thought I wouldn't notice. "I was dreaming about you when you called."

"Funny, I was dreaming about you, too."

"Yeah?"

"It was great. I showed up at your party, and you didn't publicly humiliate me. Of course, that's how I knew it was a dream." I peeled his hand off my leg.

"Lighten up, Henry."

I despised his bully logic. If I did nothing when taunted or teased, I was a pussy. If I fought back, I was accused of taking things too seriously. He hides behind the excuse that he's only fooling around, that everyone else needs to learn how to take a joke. Normally, I would have let it pass, but I was too exhausted, too sore, and too upset. It was one indignity too far.

"Do you think this is funny for me? Having to call the guy who humiliates me one second and gives me boners the next to rescue me from the middle of nowhere at three in the morning? Do you think this is my idea of a good fucking time?"

The light turned green, but the car didn't move. Marcus looked at me curiously, but I had no idea what he was thinking. "I'm glad you came to my party."

"What?"

Marcus shrugged. "I should have invited you, but I didn't figure you'd come. I'm glad you did."

That wasn't even remotely close to what I'd expected Marcus to say, and I didn't know how to respond. Moments of sincerity from him are rare, but he can be sweet when he thinks no one is watching. That's the only thing that kept me coming back, but it wasn't enough anymore. Marcus finally drove on and, when we'd gone a bit farther, I said, "You called me trash. You made me *feel* like trash."

"Chill, Henry. You need thicker skin." Marcus glanced at me, but I refused to look him in the eyes. "Anyway, I tried to find you to apologize, but you'd left."

"Whatever."

Marcus cut the wheel and pulled into a Taco Bell. The pink-and-purple lights cast a garish glow on the empty parking lot. He parked the car, unbuckled his seat belt, and turned toward me. His smile was gone, replaced by an earnestness that unnerved me. "It's more than sex to me, you know."

"What is?"

"Us."

"Are we an us?" With Jesse I'd never needed to define our relationship. From the beginning, we'd felt like a unit. Jesse was my parallel subject—I always knew he was on the other side of the ampersand—but I didn't know where I stood with Marcus. Was I his object or something more?

Marcus ground his teeth. His jaw muscles twitched. He was looking at me like having to answer a simple question was beneath him. Like I was beneath him. "Henry . . ."

I got out of the car. We were only halfway home, but it was closer than I'd been. "I'll walk from here."

"Get in the car, Space Boy."

I slammed the door as hard as I could, relishing the hollow thud, but Marcus ruined it by rolling down the window, so I gave him the finger in case he hadn't understood me the first time.

"Come on, Henry. I got up in the middle of the night for you. Doesn't that prove something?" His voice betrayed no sarcasm, no condescension. It was almost enough to make me believe he cared.

"It proves you thought you could trade a ride home for a hand job."

Marcus gripped the steering wheel so tightly that his knuckles turned white. He wasn't used to people telling him no. He grew up surrounded by people who convinced him he deserves everything he wants and that no one should refuse him anything.

A red pickup truck barreled into the drive-thru, the

modified exhaust announcing to the world that the driver had a micro-penis. I noticed the Calypso High bumper sticker at the same time Marcus did. "Get in the car, and we'll talk about it, Henry."

"It doesn't matter anymore."

Once the truck reached the pickup window, the driver would be able to see Marcus. They'd see me standing next to Marcus's car. After a moment's hesitation, he peeled out of the parking lot, leaving me stranded again.

I walked the rest of the way home, sticking to the shadows to avoid catching the attention of cops on patrol. Calypso is a quiet town, and the police often have nothing better to do than pester anyone who looks like they don't belong, and that includes teenage boys walking home in the middle of the night wearing kissing-whale boxers and a running singlet.

This is my life. A parade of humiliation and suffering. Before Jesse, I could deal with being Space Boy. He knew about the abductions but never made me feel like a freak. Before Jesse, I knew that no matter what happened to me, I could soldier on so long as we were together. But I'm living in an After Jesse world where I ache from missing him and nothing makes sense. My boyfriend and best friend both abandoned me. Marcus was using me for sex. I am a punch line at school, a ghost at home.

I hate Jesse for leaving me behind. If he asked, I would have walked into the air with him.

I was wrong to believe that the sluggers had given me freedom. Going to the party changed nothing. If anything, it made my life worse. I no longer cared why they'd chosen me to decide the fate of the earth. It didn't matter.

By the time I reached my house, my feet cut and sore, I decided I would never press the button.

Fuck it. Let the world burn.

22 September 2015

After the party, I kept to myself and counted down the days until the end of the world—129 for the math-impaired. Almost two weeks had passed since Marcus ditched me at Taco Bell, and he hadn't tried to apologize. No texts, no notes, no gropes in the restroom during lunch. The only thing that changed is that he calls me Space Boy twice as often, which only toughens my resolve not to press the button.

If the sluggers were looking for someone to save the world, they chose the wrong guy. Marcus would press the button to save his own ass, Audrey would do it because she honestly believes every person on the planet deserves to live, and I'm sure even Charlie would do it, but only because the button is red and he likes bright things.

I'm not sure what Jesse would have done. He had this

way of seeing the truth about a person. He understood people in a way I never could. Maybe he would have saved the world because it deserved to be saved, or maybe he wouldn't have pressed it because he figured we'd only wind up finding some other way to annihilate ourselves. Whatever choice he might have made, it would have been the right one. Jesse was the best of us. Definitely the best of me.

Not that it makes a difference. The sluggers chose me and, as far as I'm concerned, life is like a game of *Whose Line Is It Anyway?* Everything's made up, and the points don't matter.

I was pretending to pay attention to Ms. Faraci while she taught us about buffers and pH by leaning on my fist and covering one eye, keeping the other open to look like I was awake. Mom and Charlie were still fighting whenever they were in the same room, so I wasn't getting much sleep at home. I must have dozed off because the bell rang, startling me. Marcus slapped the back of my head as he passed, and threw a nickel on my desk. It bounced off my book and rolled on its edge to the floor. "Keep the change, Space Boy." Adrian dropped a handful of them at my feet, laughing so hard, he looked like he was going to give himself a hernia.

I watched them go and, when I turned around, caught Audrey eyeing me. "What?"

"Someone started a rumor that you trade blow jobs for nickels behind the gym."

"That's stupid," I said, looking at the change on the floor.

"They seem to think it's hilarious."

"If I'm supposedly some kind of nickel whore, and they're giving me spare change, doesn't that mean—"

Audrey flapped her hands in exasperation. "Just ignore them."

"Whatever."

She was huffing like she was dying to give me more unsolicited advice, but she said, "Forget it," instead, gathered her books, and left.

Audrey hadn't tried to talk to me since the party, and I was grateful for the silence. The last thing I want is for Audrey to tell me how sorry she is or make some lame attempt to fix our friendship. I'm content to let the world end with our friendship as dead as Jesse.

"Henry, may I speak to you for a moment?" Ms. Faraci sat behind her desk and caught me as I tried to sneak out.

"I'm kind of on my way to lunch and—"

Ms. Faraci picked up a Scantron sheet and set it on the edge of her desk. Even from a distance, the red lines were visible and plenty. "You failed your exam, Henry. This isn't like you."

I shuffled forward to look at the grade. I hadn't failed the exam, I'd bombed it hard. We'd taken the test the Monday after Marcus's party, and I knew I'd tanked it when I turned it in. "It's just one test."

"If someone is giving you a hard time, I can speak to them."

"Please don't."

Ms. Faraci bit back whatever she was planning to say. "I know high school can be difficult."

"Is this the part where you tell me it gets better, and that if I toughen up and make it through the next two years, my life will be awesome?" I hoisted my backpack higher on my shoulder. "Can I go?"

"I'd like to give you the opportunity to do some extra credit."

"Pass."

"An essay on a science-related topic of your choosing."

"I don't have time."

"Maybe you could ask Audrey Dorn to help you; I've seen you talking, and she's got the highest average in the class."

"Definitely not, but thanks anyway."

"You've got a real talent for science, and I don't want to see your grade suffer. Think about it, okay?" Ms. Faraci's voice was sincere, and I didn't want it to be. I wanted her to be like the rest of my teachers: bored, jaded, and counting down the seconds until retirement.

"Sure, whatever." I took off before she could detain me any longer. Even though I didn't have anywhere to go, I didn't want to spend my lunch period with a teacher.

My locker was in the art building, which was quiet and centrally located. When I reached it, I dialed in the combination and grabbed my lunch. I heard the door open at the end of the hall, and turned to see Diego Vega enter. I hoped he hadn't seen me.

"Henry Denton!"

Damn. He was waving like we were best friends. It was hot as balls outside, but he was wearing a green sweater over an oxford shirt and tie that made him look like he'd gotten lost on his way to a polo match, only his tie was askew and his collar flaps out. It was probably as contrived as everything else about him.

Diego sidled up to me as I slammed my locker door shut, and said, "You've been avoiding me."

"Guilty."

"If it's about what I said at the party—"

"Forget it. I'm used to it." I wanted to leave out the west exit, but the north doors were closer, so I headed for them.

"Cafeteria's the other way."

I kept walking. "I don't eat in the cafeteria."

Diego trotted along beside me. This kid wasn't going to give up. "Please tell me you don't eat in the restrooms. That would be too tragic."

"There are benches near the library."

Diego crinkled his nose. "Even worse." He tried to drag me by the arm, but I pulled away. "Come on. I don't have anyone to sit with. You'd be doing me a favor."

"Trust me, I wouldn't be doing you any favors." We'd both stopped walking, and for some reason, my feet wouldn't start again. Diego's sincerity, which I'd been fooled by at the party, was back in full effect. The thing was, I wanted to believe him. I considered for a moment that maybe he hadn't known what he was doing when he'd called me Space Boy. Maybe he was exactly what he seemed.

"Just, whatever. My rep's no better."

"I doubt that."

"For real. I'm sure they'll come up with a nickname for me any day now."

I shrugged because it was easier to go with him than to continue arguing. "Fine, but if you call me Space Boy again, I'm gone."

Diego slung his arm around my shoulders. "Deal."

. . .

I hadn't eaten in the cafeteria since the middle of sophomore year. Jesse, Audrey, and I always sat together. We were a unit. After Jesse, I stopped eating inside.

Not much about the cafeteria had changed. It was loud and jagged, and I made myself small. Most people were sitting in the same groups with the same people they'd known all through high school. We aren't just defined by who *we* are, but by who our friends are. It's funny that we put so much importance on something that won't mean shit once we graduate.

"You hungry?" Diego asked. "I'm starving. My sister is hardly home to cook, so I've been living on delivery pizza and microwave popcorn." He slid into the lunch line, grabbed a tray, and tossed on a bag of chips, mac and cheese, a pudding cup, and something the serving guy claimed was chicken potpie. "Food here is so much better than at my last school. We were happy if all we got was E. coli."

I cringed looking at Diego's lunch. "I'm not sure that qualifies as food."

Diego shuffled to the cashier and fished money from his pocket. "Sometimes you have to learn to adjust your expectations to survive."

"How bad *was* your last school?"

"Pretty much a prison." Diego grabbed his tray and

waded into the sea of tables and chairs. I followed him to a table with a couple of free seats, and watched him tear into his lunch while I dumped mine out of its paper bag.

"Is that meatloaf?" Diego grabbed my sandwich without asking and peeled back the plastic wrap. He sniffed it before I could snatch it back.

"Yeah." A thick slice of meatloaf rested between the bread, one side slathered with mayo, the other with ketchup. A mixture of sunflower seeds and raisins rolled around freely at the bottom of the bag.

Diego talked with his mouth full of mac and cheese. "My mom made great meatloaf. It was my favorite."

I tossed the sandwich aside. "We had meatloaf last week, and it was terrible then." Diego frowned, so I said, "Sometimes my grandma packs my lunch. She's a little senile. I should be grateful we didn't have any gravy left."

"It could be worse." Diego tossed me his potato chips; I was too hungry to refuse the gift. "You do anything fun this weekend?"

"Mostly hid in my room to avoid my mother and brother. He knocked up his girlfriend and dropped out of college, and my mom's not taking it so well." Diego probably didn't want to hear about my fucked-up family, but I couldn't think of anything else to talk about.

"What about your dad?"

"Not around." I was content to let it drop there, but Diego had this way of looking at me that made me keep talking, like I was afraid to let the silence creep up between us. "My parents divorced when I was younger, and my father disappeared. I haven't heard from him in years."

"Oh."

"Yeah."

Diego had eaten most of what he'd bought, but there was still some potpie he was eyeing like he couldn't decide whether to finish it. "Did you stay at the party after I decided to see how much of my foot I could shove in my mouth? I tried to find you, but that house is huge. I got lost in a closet for an hour. It was fun."

"About as much fun as a throbbing hemorrhoid."

"Tell me how you really feel."

The last thing I wanted to be reminded of was Marcus's party. "I don't really do parties."

"They're not my thing either."

"What *is* your thing?"

"Painting."

"That's right. You're an artist."

"When you say it, it sounds like an insult."

"Artists always seem so self-involved. Everything is about

their art." I chuckled to let him know I was teasing. "I mean, come on. What's up with all the self-portraits?"

Diego was quiet for a moment, but the empty space was filled by the chaotic noise from other tables. I hoped I hadn't offended him. "Artists have to learn how to paint what's in the mirror, even if what they see is a total shit show." He gave in and scooped up the last bite of potpie. "If you can't paint yourself honestly, everything else you paint will be a lie too."

"I didn't realize artists were so self-aware."

"Yeah, well, being self-aware only means that we *know* we're assholes." Diego shrugged and pushed his empty tray to the side. "Anyway, that's what my ex-girlfriend used to tell me."

"Ex-g-girlfriend?" I tried not to stutter, but I couldn't help it, and ended up drooling. "Shit." I forced a laugh and wiped my lip with a napkin.

Diego pretended not to notice, but I caught him grinning. "Her name was Leigh. She'd tell you I was the biggest prick in North America. Probably the world."

Having recovered from my sudden inability to keep saliva in my mouth, I said, "Did you break up because you moved here?"

"Nah, we were done way before that."

"Sorry."

"I'm not. She was only using me for my big prick. Didn't I mention that?"

I snorted and laughed. The students at the other end of the table glared at me, which only made it harder to stop. "I know the feeling."

"You got a . . . ?"

"Not really," I said. "Maybe. I don't know. He's a big prick too." I considered telling Diego about Marcus, but I hardly knew him, and it wasn't my secret to tell. It would destroy Marcus if word got out he was hooking up with Space Boy. "Why'd you move to Calypso?"

Rather than answer, Diego looked at the table and the walls and over my shoulder—everywhere but at me.

"I get the feeling you don't want to talk about it. I was only trying to make conversation," I said.

"It's complicated." I thought Diego was going to explain, but instead he said, "What do you do for fun around here?"

Diego's unwillingness to discuss why he moved from Colorado to a shit hole town in the limp dick of the nation only made me more curious. Maybe he was shipped off by his parents as punishment for robbing liquor stores or cheating on history exams. Or maybe he was a secret government operative whose mission was to befriend me and discover what I knew about the sluggers. That actually made more sense than anything else. Still, I hated secrets. Jesse had kept secrets. Maybe if he hadn't, he'd still be alive. Only, Diego wasn't Jesse. Diego was nobody to me, and I didn't want to piss him off by prying.

"You already went to the biggest party of the year. What more do you want?"

Diego leaned back in his chair. "Something exciting."

"What'd you do in Colorado?"

"Stuff."

"Stuff?"

"Yeah," Diego said. "Hung out with friends, avoided my parents. Stuff. All of it very exciting. I miss it." He looked far away, like he'd traveled there in the silence between our words. That's the problem with memories: you can visit them, but you can't live in them.

"Then why don't you go back?" I regretted asking the moment the question left my mouth. Shadows crowded Diego's face, and every muscle tensed up. Shoulders, fists, cheeks. I cleared my throat and said, "All we've got here are beaches, but you already know about those."

"Let's go."

"Where?"

Diego grabbed his tray, already half standing. "The beach. We'll bail on class, and you can show me around Calypso.

I've got a car. We'll get some sandwiches and hang out."

Jesse and I skipped once in tenth grade. It was the first week he got his driver's license. Vice Principal Marten nearly caught us trying to sneak off campus, but Jesse's car was faster than Marten's golf cart. We drank beer on the beach and lay in each other's arms until the sun was only a memory burned into our brains. He'd said, "You know, I think I love you, Henry Denton," and I believed him. I believed all of Jesse's lies.

"I can't."

Diego slumped back into his seat. "It's cool."

"Maybe some other time."

Rather than giving me a guilt trip, Diego said, "Any time," and I knew he meant it. "So, tell me about these aliens of yours."

I twisted a bit of sandwich wrap around the end of my index finger, watching it turn grape red. Diego snapped his fingers in front of my face. "I'm not making fun of you."

"I didn't—"

"You can't bullshit a bullshitter."

"It's not something I talk about."

"Then you should write about it."

"Drop it."

Diego was either oblivious or determined or simply a giant prick like his ex-girlfriend had said. "Writing's like painting. You have to write about yourself before you can write about anything else."

I was done talking, but I couldn't figure out how to shut Diego up. It was like something inside of him had malfunctioned, and he was going to keep rambling until his batteries died.

"There's an amazing world out there for you to discover, Henry Denton, but you have to be willing to discover yourself first."

The bell rang, saving me, and we all rose like Pavlovian dogs, eager to run to our next classes. Except Diego. He was still sitting, like he was waiting for me to say something, but I didn't know what. Finally I said, "What if I don't give a shit about the world?"

Diego gathered our trash and frowned. "I'd say that's pretty fucking sad."

"Why?"

"Because the world is so beautiful."

4 October 2015

Nana leaned on the shopping cart as we strolled through Publix, ignoring the other customers who shot us pissed-off glares every time she blocked the aisle to scan the shelves for some item from the crumpled list in her hand.

"What about pork chops?" she asked. "I could stuff them. Maybe fry some okra."

"Sounds good." I grabbed a jar of spaghetti sauce and tossed it in the cart, which was filling up rapidly because Nana couldn't decide what she wanted for dinner. So far she'd suggested tacos, salmon with spinach, shepherd's pie, and lasagna, and we'd gathered the ingredients for each. "Did you teach Mom how to cook?"

Nana kept shuffling down the aisle as if she hadn't heard me. I started to repeat the question when she said, "Eleanor

WE ARE THE ANTS · 101

loved to watch me in the kitchen when she was a little girl, but I was never much of a cook. My grandmother passed her recipes to my mother, and she passed them to me, but your mother doesn't need recipes. She's quite gifted."

I grimaced. "So the Lewis women have been inflicting that meatloaf on their families for four generations?"

Nana smacked my arm. "For your information, your mother loves my meatloaf."

"Get real. She spits it out in her napkin and flushes it down the toilet. Haven't you ever noticed how often she visits the can on meatloaf nights?"

Nana hit me again, harder. "That's for lying to your grandmother."

I smiled and hugged her. She felt small and fragile, the way ice over a lake thins as the weather turns warm. Cracks were beginning to appear on the surface, but she'd always been a stubborn constant in my life, and I refused to count her out.

"It was your father," Nana said as we moved from one aisle to the next. "He encouraged your mother to become a chef when they were still in high school."

"If she loves it so much, she should quit waiting tables and get a job cooking."

"Cooking reminds her of him." Nana stopped the cart

and seized a box of couscous, ignoring the frustrated grunt of a red-faced man as he squeezed past us. "Sometimes, Henry, remembering hurts too much." She patted my arm, her wrinkled fingers like dry carrots.

"Then they shouldn't have gotten divorced."

"Life rarely works out the way we plan it."

"He left because of me, didn't he?"

Nana stopped pushing the cart. She leaned on it heavily like it was the only thing holding her up. "Why would you think that?"

"It was my fault. I know it."

"You know that's not true, Henry." Her words were sharp, and they stung more than her slap. She continued walking. "Now, enough of this. Tell me one good thing that happened to you today."

At first I thought she was joking, but she was lucid and totally serious. "Nothing happened."

"One thing, Henry."

"It was a boring day."

Nana motioned for me to grab a gallon of milk as we passed the dairy case. "When I was sick—so sick, I thought I would die—sometimes the highlight of my day was that I hadn't soiled myself."

"Gross!"

"When the days are darkest, dear, you latch on to happiness wherever you find it."

Mom hadn't let me or Charlie see Nana when she was going through chemotherapy, and we didn't talk about it after, either, but the specter of death had haunted us for months. Even when her doctors said her cancer was in remission, I still felt the weight of death in Nana's house. I figured if she could find joy during those terrible times, I could give her one good thing. "I had lunch with this guy. It was pretty okay."

"Does this young man have a name?"

"Diego Vega." I liked the way it rolled off my tongue. "He's new. We've been eating together the past few days."

Nana tossed creamed corn and green beans and artichoke hearts into our cart. "I like new. New is mysterious. Tell me about him."

Lunch with Diego had become a thing, against my better judgment, but with each day that passed, I learned more about him. He lives with his sister, Viviana, who is a neat freak; his favorite cereal is Fruity Oatholes; he loves superhero movies, even that train wreck *Green Lantern*; he drives a twelve-year-old Jetta named Please Start that frequently doesn't; and his greatest fear is being murdered by his time-traveling self from the future. We both had things we refused to discuss—I steered away from asking him why he moved, and he didn't bring up the sluggers—but Diego had become part of my life by default, and I didn't hate it. In fact, I began looking forward to lunch, to discussing our favorite bands and which teachers were probably doing it in the break room.

"There's not much to tell."

"Don't lie to your grandma."

I knew she was trying, but there was nothing going on, and nothing likely to happen. "He's just a friend, Nana."

"Why?"

"He had a girlfriend, which means he's probably not looking for a boyfriend. Honestly, neither am I."

"Well, a regular old friend is still a good thing to have. Since Jesse passed, I've been worried about you. And what happened to the young woman who used to come around? She always brushed my hair."

"It's complicated. Everything's complicated." Only, sometimes I wonder if it has to be. I could call Audrey anytime, and we could pick up our friendship like nothing happened. But something *did* happen. Jesse is dead, and it's my fault or her fault or both our faults. There's no room in my life for Audrey in this After Jesse world.

"Still, Charlie—"

"Henry."

Nana frowned. "Henry's dead."

"No, I'm Henry. Your grandson."

"That's not funny, Charlie." Nana shook her head and kept on like I hadn't interrupted her. "It's nice that you've made a new friend. You should invite him over for dinner."

It seemed pointless to even consider it. Pointless to put in the effort to get to know him when the world was going to end. Except, I could imagine him sitting between Mom and Nana, kicking me under the table as my brother unleashed his most embarrassing stories about me. I could picture Diego sitting where Jesse once had, and that stirred up emotions—both pleasant and painful—I wasn't equipped to deal with in the cereal aisle of the grocery store.

"Maybe," I said. "Just so long as you promise not to cook meatloaf."

16 October 2015

Charlie banged on the bathroom door while I brushed my teeth. Every time the mirror fogged over, I had to clear it with the palm of my hand, which didn't really help. I hadn't seen much of my brother since the big baby announcement, which meant my life had been quieter and more bruise-free than usual. He'd spent most of the last month with Zooey or couch surfing at various friends' houses, but now that he was back home, he seemed hell-bent on making up for lost time.

"Open the door! I'm gonna be late for work."

I spit a mouthful of toothpaste into the sink. "I'll be out in a second." I'd been brushing my teeth for the last five minutes, and didn't have anything else I needed to do in the bathroom, but I still took my time, rinsing my mouth and shaving and making sure no stray boogers were hanging out of my nose.

The banging finally stopped, but that's how I knew something was up. Charlie was nothing if not relentless. He once went four days without food when he was little because Mom had refused to buy him a stuffed giraffe he wanted.

Still damp from the steam, and wearing only a towel, I hurried to my bedroom. The door was open, and I was greeted by the sight of Charlie standing beside my desk, pissing into my trash can. When he saw me, he didn't stop—not Charlie—instead he flashed me a toothy, sadistic grin. The kind that makes me wonder if my brother is a sociopath. I didn't know what to do other than stand there in total disbelief while he finished, shook off the last drops, and zipped up his fly.

"Oh," Charlie said, "was that your homework? If Mom finds out you didn't turn it in, you're in a lot of trouble." I didn't think it possible for me to hate my brother more than I did, but I should have known better. "Get it? *You're in* a lot of trouble?"

I glanced at the black plastic trash can and then at my brother. Trash can, brother, trash can, brother. "What kind of fucking psycho pisses on someone's homework?"

"You don't need to be a little bitch about it. Anyway, I told you to get out of the bathroom."

"Charlie! You pissed on my homework! In my bedroom!"

Drops of urine had splattered out of the wastebasket and clung to the side of my desk. "I can't believe Zooey didn't have an abortion the moment she realized she was pregnant with your demon spawn!"

Before I could stop him—before I even knew what was happening—Charlie charged across the room and clamped his hand around my throat. He slammed me into the door, grinding my shoulder blades against the wood. "Don't you ever fucking talk about my kid like that." He didn't even yell. That was the scariest part. His voice was this calm, steady thrum. But he didn't need to yell for me to hear how deadly serious he was.

I slapped Charlie's wrists, not that I was strong enough to break free. I may have been afraid, but I refused to back down. Die right then at Charlie's hands or die in 105 days from an unknown disaster. It made no difference to me. "Please, you're such a fuckup, you'll probably scar that little parasite for life and then abandon it like Dad abandoned us." My voice croaked from my throat as air fought to escape.

Charlie released me. His chest heaved and sweat rolled down his temples. He loomed over me despite being shorter. For a moment I thought our fight was done, that Charlie was finished with me, but I was mistaken. I didn't even have time to block before he sucker-punched me in the gut. I cried out and clutched my stomach.

"Dad didn't abandon us," he said. "He abandoned you."

I struggled to breathe, to look Charlie in the eyes and call him a liar. Tell him he was the worst fucking brother in the universe. That I would have been better off an only child. But I didn't say any of those things. I didn't say anything at all.

"He was so ashamed of what a pathetic loser you were that he couldn't stand being around you. Everyone you care about either runs away or kills themselves, and you think *I'm* a fuckup."

I shoved Charlie out of my room and slammed the door. I leaned against it, slid to the floor, and put my head in my hands. I wasn't crying because of what Charlie said; I was crying because, deep down, I knew he was right.

All day at school, I couldn't stop thinking about my fight with Charlie. About what he'd said. When my parents divorced, they didn't sit me and Charlie down to explain what was happening. One day Dad was just gone, and we stopped talking about him like he'd never existed in the first place. All traces that he'd ever lived at our house disappeared. In my heart I'd always known he'd taken off because of me. It wasn't a coincidence that he left only a few weeks after my first abduction.

I was so caught up in my own thoughts that I hardly knew what was going on around me at school. I ignored

Audrey when she asked me if I wanted help studying for our next chemistry exam, I blew past Ms. Faraci before she could keep me after class again, and I planned on ditching Diego at lunch too. I was on my way to my locker when Marcus pulled me into an empty art room. Sketches done in charcoal and pencil plastered the walls, and I wondered which ones, if any, belonged to Diego.

"What the hell, Marcus?" He'd nearly yanked my arm out of the socket, and I'd already been abused enough for one day.

Marcus was fidgety. His eyes were wide and manic, his shirt was untucked, and a cluster of pimples that reminded me of the constellation Andromeda dotted his forehead, but he still smelled like summer. "How's it going, Space Boy?"

"Don't call me Space Boy." A growl crouched in my throat.

"I haven't seen you in a while."

The classroom was empty, but Mr. Creedy often let students work on projects during lunch, so I expected we wouldn't be alone for long. "Aren't you afraid of being seen talking to Space Boy, or are you going to throw more nickels at me?"

Marcus shook his head. His bangs fell over his forehead, and he flicked them back. "No . . . I missed you, Henry."

I tapped my lips with the tip of my finger. "Wouldn't it

be great if we had a magical device that allowed two people to talk over long distances any time they wanted? They could call it a talky-box."

Marcus closed the gap between us and placed his hand flat against my chest. I felt the familiar tingle, and I hated that I missed it. "I know you don't believe me, but I like you. I don't want us to be over."

We were so close, I could feel the heat radiating off his skin. I wanted to tell him that I missed him too. It would have been easy to give in and go to some storage closet, to kiss him and forget about all the yesterdays and tomorrows. But I couldn't forget wanting to die by his pool the night of the party, or walking home because he thought I was a joke. "I can't be one thing to you behind the bleachers and another in front of your friends."

Marcus sneered. "I get it. You've got a new boyfriend, and you don't need me anymore."

"Boyfriend? What are you talking about?"

"I've seen you together at lunch."

"Diego?" Marcus flinched when I said the name. "He's a friend, nothing more."

"Was I just someone you banged to get over your dead boyfriend?"

Marcus had never spoken to me like that before. I

honestly didn't think he cared enough about me to be jealous. "No! Jesus, Marcus."

"Then come to my house tonight. My parents are attending a fund raiser and won't be home until late." Gone was the swagger he used like a glamour to hide this needy boy who was begging me to come home with him.

"If I say yes, how long before the next time you humiliate me to amuse your friends?"

"It won't be like that."

"I want to believe you. . . ."

"Space Boy, you were my first." His voice trembled. I hadn't known, which made it worse.

I wanted to stay angry, but this Marcus would have invited me to his party. He would have introduced me to his friends. This was the most real he'd ever been, but it wouldn't last. The moment we walked out of the classroom, his cocksure veneer, the spit and polish, would return. I wasn't going to spend my last days on Earth as the butt of his jokes. I may not be sure I want to live, but I'm sure I don't want to live like that.

"Marcus, I can't."

His armor snapped into place. The vulnerable boy I might have said yes to disappeared, and I'm not sure I'll ever see him again. "I'm not surprised Jesse hanged himself. I'm just surprised he didn't do it sooner." Marcus shoved me against the wall as he stormed out.

I spent my lunch sitting outside the library, trying to comprehend how my life had gotten so fucked up. First my father left, then Jesse. Neither Charlie nor Marcus told me anything I hadn't already considered.

It has been 268 days since I got the phone call from Mrs. Franklin telling me Jesse committed suicide. He left no note, gave no explanation, but I still know it was my fault. He killed himself because of me. Because I loved him too much or not enough. I don't know why; all I know is that it was my fault.

Charlie's and Marcus's words festered in me, and by the time I got to PE, I wanted to hurt someone, anyone. To make them feel how I felt. Narrow rows of lockers separated by benches, fellow students changing into their gym clothes, and the pungent odor of sweat and body spray made my skin itch. I wanted to get dressed for class and get out as quickly as possible.

I shouldered past a couple of kids, and opened my gym locker. Nickels poured out. There had to be hundreds of dollars worth of them spilling to the floor, and I just stared as they fell.

Adrian Morse stood a few feet away by the water fountain

with Gary Neuman, Chris Weller, and Dean Gold, laughing his ass off. It must have taken them at least an hour to get all those nickels into my locker, all for a moment's cheap laugh.

The sound in my ears narrowed until all I could hear was that psychotic cackle. I felt something inside me break in that moment. It wasn't just what had happened that day; it was as if all the preceding days, all the hate I'd been hoarding and the guilt I'd buried, erupted, breaking my ability to contain them any longer. I ran toward Adrian and launched myself at him, not caring if he beat the crap out of me. I swung wildly, a berserker bloodlust overriding my rational mind. I screamed at him, but can't remember what I said.

Adrian tried to protect his face, but my fist connected with something solid, and that only made me fight harder. It seemed like hours but was probably only seconds before he kneed me in the crotch, knocking the breath out of me. I fell to the ground, and he kicked me, but I roared back and tackled him, slamming his back against the lockers, pounding him with my fists. I was beyond pain, beyond all reason. I didn't care about anything. Not me, not Jesse, not Marcus. The world was ending, and there were no more consequences. I think I was going to kill him.

Coach Raskin wedged himself between us, yelling at us to break it up, and wrestled me away from Adrian. I struggled to free myself from his powerful grip, but Coach was too strong for me. I shook myself loose and glared at Adrian, sprawled on the locker room floor. Blood ran from his nose, and I smiled. I spit at his feet and left.

Mom didn't talk to me until we were in the car. She'd come straight from work, still in her uniform, her apron stained with ketchup and potato soup. After I buckled my seat belt, I examined my bloody, bruised knuckles. My hand hurt when I flexed it, but it was a good hurt. An anchor.

Because Adrian had started it with the nickels, Principal DeShields opted for a month of Saturday detentions rather than suspension. I would have preferred the suspension.

"Do you want to tell me what's gotten into you, Henry Jerome Denton?"

"That asshole had it coming."

Mom slapped me across the face. My cheek stung, and I touched my jaw while she glowered at me. "You sound like your father." She cranked up the radio and peeled out of the parking lot, headed for home. My mom had never hit me before, but I think I deserved it.

"It's true, you know."

"What is?"

I turned down the music. "That Adrian deserved it."

"That doesn't excuse fighting."

"I know."

Mom sighed, shook her head. "It's been rough for you, Henry, I know, but you can't do this. You're flunking three classes, getting into fights. I hardly see you because you're always locked in your room."

I wanted to tell her she'd know what was going on with me if she ever bothered to ask, but she was so concerned with Charlie and Nana, or too tired from working to bother with me. Aliens abduct me, and she pretends I'm sleepwalking. My boyfriend killed himself, and we don't even talk about it. Like my father, Jesse's name just disappeared from her vocabulary. I would have told her anything, everything, if she had asked, but I knew she wouldn't.

"If the world were going to end, but you could stop it, would you?"

Mom drove for a while without answering. I thought she hadn't heard me, and I leaned my head against the window. Finally she said, "Some days I think I would. Other days, probably not."

"What about today?"

Mom's shoulders bowed downward. "What do you think, Henry?"

Nanobots

They're hailed as a marvelous breakthrough in modern medicine. Their inventors, two scientists from South Africa, are awarded the Nobel Prize for Medicine for their work. The tiny robots are too small to see with the naked eye, but are capable of cooperating to eradicate any disease and to repair any damage done to the human body. The Fixers, as they're called, usher in what many refer to as the Golden Age of Humanity.

Despite warnings from paranoid extremist groups, governments around the world approve Fixers for widespread use. Billionaire philanthropists donate their entire fortunes to fund efforts that bring Fixers to impoverished nations, making certain that every human on the planet in need is able to receive treatment.

Within one year, cancer becomes little more than a nuisance—curable with one treatment and no side effects.

Within two years, HIV, cerebral palsy, Huntington's disease, blindness, polio, and male pattern baldness are eradicated. They become footnotes in history.

Genetic defects are repaired in utero.

Two years, nine months, seven days, and two hours after Fixers are approved for public use, the world experiences its first full day without a single death. It is the day humanity becomes God.

It begins on 26 January 2016 at 7:35 a.m. EST at a Starbucks in Augusta, Georgia. Donald Catt, already irritated over having to wait in line, completely loses his cool when the barista doesn't know how to make *his* drink the way *he* likes it. Despite the barista's attempts to calm him, Donald refuses to leave until he gets what he wants, prepared exactly the way he wants it.

The store manager eventually calls the police. Donald Catt resists, and the officers have no choice but to Taser him. The electrical shock causes a Fixer, deployed to repair Donald's erectile dysfunction, to malfunction. It scrambles the Fixer's software and initiates self-replication.

Fixers were designed to replicate under strictly regulated conditions, but the damaged Fixer replicates uncontrollably, at an exponential rate, using whatever materials are at hand. That includes still-twitching, undercaffeinated Donald Catt.

Attempts to quarantine Georgia are unsuccessful, and the new Fixers, whose sole function is to replicate, consume the entire planet in three days, leaving behind nothing but an ocean of gray goo.

20 October 2015

My situation at school deteriorated. Marcus and Adrian glued my locker shut and wrote *Space Boy gargles alien balls* on the door in permanent marker, and I couldn't walk the halls without being stalked by whispers and cruel laughter. I tried to ignore them, but that only made them meaner. In PE, Adrian's been keeping his distance, but I've noticed the murderous glares he shoots me across the gym. I started something I'm certain he's determined to finish.

Diego is still a mystery, but I enjoy spending time with him. He listens when I need to vent, talks when I don't want to, and knows more about literature than anyone I've ever met. The only thing about him that unnerves me is the dark look that falls over him when I tell him about something that Marcus said or that Jay Oh and Adrian have done. It's like a completely different person replaces the smiling Diego I've come to know. And then, quicker than a summer storm, it disappears, leaving me to wonder if I imagined his reaction.

Nothing will make me change my mind about the button, but I'm trying my best to maintain the status quo for the days that remain. I figure if I keep my head down, maybe I can serve out the balance of my life sentence in relative peace. Wake up, go to school, go home. Repeat until the world ends.

The house was quiet when I got home from school—Mom wasn't screaming at anyone, and Charlie wasn't being Charlie. It was nice. Living in a house with my mother, brother, and Nana means that someone is usually shouting or dashing from one room to the next as if everything is of monumental importance. I wish they understood how little their actions matter. With the end of the world looming, I can finally see the pointlessness of everything. How the whole of human civilization is nothing more than a mosquito's annoying buzz to the universe.

My stomach rumbled, so I figured I'd make a snack and watch TV while there was no one around to bother me. The fridge was pretty barren, so I settled for peanut butter and jelly. The bread had some mold on it, but I cut it off, too hungry to care.

A sonogram with HAWTHORNE, ZOOEY printed across the bottom clung to the refrigerator door—held in place by a magnet from our favorite Chinese takeout joint. The picture looked like a miniature monochrome galaxy, teeming with stars and worlds and boundless potential. I took the sonogram to the kitchen table and tried to determine which part of the amorphous blob was my future niece or nephew. It was a game: find the fetus. Was it too early to know the sex? Probably. Not that it mattered. It wasn't even a baby yet. It was just a little parasite, and it would never be anything else.

A shadow fell across the table, startling me. Nana hovered to my left, staring at the picture over my shoulder. "Jesus, Nana, you scared the crap out of me."

Nana's flaccid, wrinkled cheeks pulled back into an impish grin. "Mission accomplished." She eased into the seat next to mine and snatched the sonogram, turning it this way and that, examining it from every angle. "What the devil am I looking at?"

"Charlie and Zooey's kid. I think."

"Are you certain? It looks like an ink blot test." Nana covered her right eye. "I see Jonah and the whale."

"I won't tell Zooey you called her a whale."

Nana snorted. "I wonder if they've thought about names."

"Probably not. I call it the little parasite."

"I like that," Nana said. "That little parasite is lucky. Its life is just beginning, while mine is nearly over."

"Don't say that."

"You'll understand when you're my age, Henry. You spend your life hoarding memories against the day when you'll lack the energy to go out and make new ones, because that's the comfort of old age. The ability to look back on your life and know that you left your mark on the world. But I'm losing my memories. It's like someone's broken into my piggy bank and is robbing me one penny at a time. It's happening so slowly, I can hardly tell what's missing."

I tried to think of the right thing to say, but sometimes the right thing to say is nothing.

"I look at people and I don't know them. Yesterday, I spent twenty minutes trying to figure out who the grumpy woman sitting beside me was before I realized it was your mother." I laughed, and Nana offered me a feeble smile in return. "I've led a rich life, Henry, but I'm terrified of dying a pauper."

While there are some memories I wish I could dispose of, sometimes my memories are the only things that keep me sane. There are times when I walk along the beach and smell the hot tar and sand, and I think of all the summer days Jesse and I spent lying in the sun, making our plans to rule the world. Then there are times when I see something funny on TV or hear a great song, and I pick up my phone to text Jesse before I remember he's dead, and the wound tears open, bloody and raw all over again. A person can become a part of you as real as your arm or leg, and even though Jesse is dead, I still feel the weight of that phantom limb. I have a thousand amazing memories of Jesse, but his suicide is leaking into those recollections, poisoning our past. I can hardly remember him without hating him for taking his life and leaving me alone in mine.

I honestly don't know whether it would be better to forget or be able to remember, but it physically hurts being forced to watch Nana diminish. Charlie and Zooey's baby will never know the terror of creating memories only to lose them, but Nana knows all too well.

"I love you, Nana."

I was sitting in the living room, flipping through the channels, unable to find anything worth watching, when Charlie and Zooey came home. I didn't want to be in the same room with Charlie, but I wasn't about to leave and let him think he'd beaten me. He mumbled about needing to take a shower before stomping toward the bathroom.

Zooey looked cute in a pair of little jean shorts and blousy white top. I've never been able to figure out what magic my brother cast to make someone like her stay with him. To want to have a kid with him. When they first began dating, I assumed she must have been blind, but she wasn't. She actually and improbably seemed to like Charlie. Love him, even.

"Whatcha watching?" Zooey asked. She flopped down onto the couch with a thick book and a legal pad.

I'd stopped on the *Bunker* live feeds, but no one was doing anything interesting. You could watch for hours and never see any good action. It was a miracle the producers were able to cobble together enough entertaining footage for three weekly shows. "Nothing."

I tossed the remote to Zooey and started to stand, but she said, "Don't leave on my account. I have so much studying to do."

"What class?"

She rolled her eyes and glanced at her book. "Just a stupid history survey."

"Sounds like a blast."

"I hate it. Not history—history's pretty cool—just the way they cram two thousand years of human civilization into a five-month class." Zooey shook her head. "Seriously, it's like history for dummies. No, strike that. It's like white male history for dummies. The professor totally ignores every major contribution by anyone who wasn't a white dude."

She talked about history the way I felt about science. Science is all around us. We *are* science. It governs our bodies, how we interact with the world and universe. But most people are too stupid to realize it. They think science is optional. Like if they refuse to believe in gravity, they can simply ignore it.

"Is that what you want to do?" I asked. "Be a historian, I mean."

"No," she said. "I think I want to be a psychologist." Zooey flashed me a wry smile. "To be honest, I'm not even a hundred percent certain about that."

"You've definitely got the patience for it. You'd have to, dating my brother and all."

"Who knows? Maybe I'll major in history, too, and become a historical psychologist."

"Is that even a thing?"

Zooey shrugged. "Got me."

Talking to her was easy. Even when she was watching the TV with one eye, I felt like she was really listening to me. Like she actually cared. "If you knew the world was ending, and you had the chance to stop it, would you?"

"Of course." Zooey rubbed her belly. She wasn't even showing yet, not that I could see. "Why do you ask?"

"Oh," I said. "It's for a school project."

"That's interesting."

I shook my head. "Not really. Like I said: it's just a school thing."

Zooey turned toward me, giving me her undivided attention. "Not the question—the fact that you'd even need to ask."

"You don't think there are some pretty compelling reasons for wiping the earth clean and starting over?"

"No," she said, "but clearly, you do."

I didn't get the opportunity to respond because Charlie returned, his shirt sticking to his still damp body. He flopped down between me and Zooey and grabbed the remote, which was my cue to leave. Though she didn't say anything, I felt Zooey's eyes on my back as I left the room.

I was surprised when Diego texted me later that evening to meet him outside in twenty minutes. He refused to tell me where we were going, but Charlie and Zooey had ordered pizza and traded her history homework for baby name books, so I was especially grateful for the opportunity to escape.

Diego grinned when I hopped into the car, and didn't even wait for me to buckle my seat belt before throwing Please Start into drive and lurching toward our destination, which didn't take long to deduce.

"We could have walked here," I said when Diego parked on the side of the beach road. It was empty, save for a couple of packs of cyclists that whizzed past, wearing those obscenely tight spandex shorts.

"I didn't want to carry *that*." He pointed at a long black duffel bag in the backseat.

"Are those the tools you're going to use to kill and dismember me?"

Diego rolled his eyes. "If they were, do you think I'd tell you?"

"I'd tell *you*."

"As if. I'm pretty sure the only thing you could dismember is a sandwich." Diego hoisted the bag over his shoulder. "Speaking of, there's a sack with subs on the floor. Grab the pop, too." He started down the dunes, and I had to hustle to catch up. By the time he stopped, my shoes were full of sand, so I kicked them aside and peeled off my socks.

"If I'd known we were going to the beach, I would have worn flip-flops."

"You usually do. I hadn't expected you to be in fancy dress."

"Fancy?" I tried to ignore my burning ears, but I'd be lying if I said I hadn't put some thought into my outfit. Still, it was only jeans and a V-neck tee. Compared to Diego, though, I suppose I was a little dressy. He was wearing khaki shorts and a green tank that showed off his lack of tan lines and his impressive shoulders. I tried not to stare at the way his muscles rippled when he moved, but I rationalized that it would be insulting not to admire them a little. "Anyway, at least I can pick a style and stick with it."

"What's that supposed to mean?"

"Preppy one day, surfer the next. It's like you can't decide who to be."

Diego shrugged. "I like to try new things. You don't go to a buffet and only eat spaghetti all night."

"Still, it's weird." I walked to the edge of the water and breathed in the salt air. The sun had set, but the western sky was the color of peach skin, while the sky over the ocean was a clear lapis blue. The moon was a bright smile, hovering high to the south. "Is this the surprise?"

Diego knelt beside the bag and lifted out a navy tube and black tripod. It slipped, and I rushed to help. "It's my sister's telescope. I thought you'd enjoy looking at the stars."

"I guess." I'd never looked through a telescope before, and I'd always wanted to, but I kept waiting for Diego to crack an alien joke or ask me about the abductions, even though he hadn't mentioned either in weeks.

After twenty minutes of trying to set up the telescope, Diego threw his hands in the air and admitted defeat. I had no idea what I was doing, but I tried to aim it at something interesting anyway. "You know," I said, as I fiddled with the knobs, "I kind of like that you suck at something."

"Me? You're crazy. I suck at lots of things. Stargazing, for instance. And Ping-Pong. I'm the world's worst Ping-Pong player." Diego busied himself with spreading out a ratty blanket that had been wadded up in the bag with the telescope. "Anything?"

I peered through the eyepiece and tweaked it until I managed to bring Neptune more or less into focus. "Check it out."

Diego sprang to his feet and peeked through the lens. "Is it supposed to be that small?"

"It's almost three billion miles away. Even traveling at the speed of light, it would still take about four hours to reach." I tried to imagine standing on that cold, distant planet, breathing hydrogen and helium, viewing Earth from the other side of the solar system. I wondered if it was lonely out there on the edge of space, so far from the light and warmth of the sun. "I bet I can find Saturn. We can probably see its rings."

"It's not a very good telescope, is it?"

"Better than nothing."

Diego patted the tube. "Viv got it cheap, I think. She's not a telescope expert."

"And you are?"

"No." Diego swiveled the telescope to another part of the sky and looked through the eyepiece. He kept adjusting the knobs, but I don't think he knew what he was doing. "I just thought I could show you something beautiful." He glared at the telescope. "Or try to, anyway."

I trudged back to the blanket, flopping down and staring at my toes. It was one of the most considerate things anyone had done for me, and that twisted my stomach into knots. "Why are you so nice to me?"

"I've got a soft spot for lost causes."

"I'm not your charity case."

Diego abandoned the telescope and sat across from me. The way he looked at me—with curiosity or pity, I couldn't tell which—made me wish I'd ignored his text. "It was a joke, Henry."

"That's what Marcus always says."

"That's because he's a douche."

"He's not. I mean, yeah, he is, but sometimes he's okay."

"Wait." Diego's eyes widened. "Please tell me Marcus isn't the guy you've been fooling around with."

"No," I said, but it was obvious I was lying when my voice broke. "Damn it." I stood and walked to the water, let the waves run over my toes. If I dove in, maybe I could swim off the edge of the world. When I heard Diego behind me, I said, "Don't you dare tell anyone."

"I won't."

"I'm serious."

"I know how to keep a secret."

"That's obvious."

I waited for Diego to decide I was too much trouble, to leave or fight with me. Something. He simply stood beside me while the moments passed and my anger drained into the ocean. Then he said, "Do you actually like him?"

"I thought I did."

"He's not the kind of guy I figured you'd go for."

"He isn't."

"Then why?"

"Because he's not Jesse." It was the first time I'd admitted it to myself. Marcus and Jesse were so different. Jesse had never called me Space Boy, he never would have hit me, hadn't cared what his friends thought, and I'd never felt ashamed of who I was with him. Jesse had loved me.

But that's a lie, isn't it? If Jesse had loved me, he wouldn't have left me. "Marcus isn't a bad guy. He can be sweet."

A wave splashed across my feet and sloshed up my legs, soaking the cuffs of my jeans. In the dark it was difficult to see where the ocean ended and the sky began; I could pretend the sky curved down and around, and that it was possible to walk on the clouds. But even though I wasn't looking at Diego, I felt the pull of him, the way he distorted everything around him so I didn't know what was right or real anymore.

"What about all the names he calls you? The shit he and his friends put you through? A guy who does that . . . Well, he's not really boyfriend material. I mean, is that honestly who you want to be with?" Diego's voice contained a dangerous undertow. He hardly sounded like the boy who'd flung himself into my chemistry class, pretending to be a nude model. "Well, is it?"

I knew the answer. Jesse Franklin was who I wanted to be with. Jesse, who'd wrapped his arms around my waist and kissed my neck and told me it was going to be okay after I fought with my mom, and who stayed up all night on the phone with me when he went to Rhode Island to visit his family for Christmas, and we watched the sunrise together even though we were separated by 1,377 miles. That was who I wanted to be with. But he was dead. "Maybe that's what I deserve," I said under my breath.

"What?"

"It doesn't matter."

"Of course it does."

"We're all going to die."

"Which is why it matters." Diego stood beside me quietly for a few seconds before he returned to the blanket. "Hungry?"

He tossed me a sub—roast beef with all the veggies. I didn't have the heart to tell him I hated onions.

"Thanks." I unwrapped it and ate it even though I wasn't hungry. Diego didn't know what he was talking about. He didn't know Marcus, he didn't know Jesse, and he didn't know me. If he did, he'd understand.

"I met Jesse freshman year. I knew who he was; everyone knew Jesse Franklin. It wasn't that he was popular, but he had this way of dominating a room. No matter how many other people were there, you couldn't help noticing Jesse.

"Of course, he talked to me first. I never would have had the courage to approach him. It was during lunch. I always sat alone, reading, and he walked up to my table, all smiles and perfect hair, and asked me if my name was Daniel. I told him it wasn't, but he insisted I looked like this guy Daniel he'd known from summer camp. Finally he asked me my name. But it wasn't just Jesse standing there. It felt like every kid in the cafeteria was at my table asking. I've never done well under pressure, so when I opened my mouth to answer, I said, 'I don't know,' instead."

Diego snorted and laughed.

"Jesse gave me this crazy look and was like, 'You don't know your own name?' and all I could do was nod, even though in my brain I was screaming, 'Henry Denton! My name is Henry!' Jesse eventually returned to his own table. I was sure I'd blown my only chance to get to know him."

"But you hadn't," Diego said.

"No." I felt a tear burning in the corner of my eye, but I refused to acknowledge it. I wasn't going to cry in front of Diego. "I ran into him at the mall a few weeks later. Actually, he'd found out my name from one of his friends, and when he saw me with my mom shopping for shoes, he chased after me, yelling my name. My mom thought he was a lunatic, but all he wanted to do was give me his number."

Diego finished his sub and tossed the crumpled wax paper into his duffel bag. "Your Jesse sounds like a cool guy."

My Jesse. He wasn't anyone's Jesse anymore. "He was the best. We spent almost every second together, and when we were apart, it hurt—it physically hurt. My entire life revolved around Jesse, but in the end, it didn't matter. He slipped a noose around his neck and hanged himself without saying good-bye. No note, no text, no last voice mail. The last thing he said to me was that I needed a haircut, like it was just another day. Only, it wasn't any other day. It was the day before he committed suicide. If everything matters, wouldn't Jesse have said something more meaningful? Wouldn't he have wanted to do more than hang out and watch TV like we always did? Wouldn't he have at least left me a note to explain why he felt he had to die, instead of leaving me here alone, wondering why. Why is Jesse dead? Why am I not?"

I waited for Diego to answer. I wasn't sure how he had expected this night to go, but I doubted it was this. There was nothing he could say that would change my mind, but I waited for him to try. Instead he said, "Do you think we could see *them* with the telescope?"

"Them?"

"The aliens."

"I don't want to talk about it."

"Okay, sure." A moment later he said, "I believe you, you know."

"I don't need you to believe me."

"I know. It's one of the things I like most about you." It caught me off guard, and I didn't know how to reply. Diego stood up, brushing the sand off his shorts. He peered through the telescope again. Maybe he was looking for the sluggers, maybe he just wanted to see the stars and dream of a world beyond this one while I sat on the blanket and remembered Jesse. Dreams are hopeful because they exist as pure possibility. Unlike memories, which are fossils, long dead and buried deep.

We stayed at the beach for a while longer but, no matter how much we fiddled with the telescope, the stars never seemed so far away.

Sometimes I wonder if the sluggers sent Diego Vega to Calypso to test my resolve. It makes more sense than his persistent attempts to be my friend when everyone else at school barely notices me. His reluctance to talk about his past coupled with the fact that I haven't been abducted since Marcus's party makes me seriously consider that this is simply an elaborate experiment and Diego is nothing more than a variable in a slugger equation. For all I know, it might not even matter whether I press the button. Not that I've changed my mind about that.

The Friday before Halloween, Principal DeShields allowed students to wear costumes to school, though the list of prohibited items was extensive and included:

Masks

Weapons (real or fake)

Excessive cleavage

Wearing underwear on the outside of clothes

Fake blood (or bodily fluids of any kind)

Glitter

Vampire teeth (which may or may not have fallen

into the weapon's category)

Clown costumes of any kind

I didn't wear a costume, but Marcus showed up as Captain America, and I overheard Audrey claim to be Joan of Arc, which was fitting. Ms. Faraci was supposed to be an oxygen molecule, but her outfit—pieced together with coat hangers, duct tape, and cardboard—carried the unfortunate whiff of homemade desperation. It's both cool and mortifying to have a teacher so passionate.

Marcus, Jay, and Adrian spent the entire period whispering to one another, cutting up like they didn't think anyone could hear them. I did my best to ignore the name-calling and laughter, and between the impending end of the world and Diego, I hadn't spent much time worrying about what fiendish plans Marcus and his boys were cooking up.

Before the bell rang, I noticed Diego waiting outside the

door. He grinned at me and waved. We *were* only friends, but I hoped Marcus saw him. It was tough to tell whether Diego had dressed up like a surfer for Halloween—wearing board shorts and a tank top—or if he was just trying on another style. Anyway, it never seemed to matter what Diego wore; he always looked like he belonged. I envied that about him, since I never belonged anywhere.

The classroom became bedlam when Ms. Faraci dismissed us for lunch. I'd started hanging back, waiting for Marcus and the others to leave first. Adrian especially enjoyed shoving me into the edge of my desk, leaving me with bruises across my thighs, so I'd learned it was best to remain seated until they were gone. Diego stood at the threshold of the door, leaning from one foot to the other.

"Ah, my nude model has returned." Ms. Faraci waddled around her desk and lifted the oxygen molecule over her head, setting it on the floor. She looked strange and lumpy in her faded unitard.

Diego blushed. "Yeah. Sorry about that. First-day jitters."

I shouldered my bag and hurried for the door. "Have a good weekend, Ms. Faraci."

"Henry, wait." I flinched, knowing what she wanted. "About your extra credit."

My chemistry grade was the last thing I wanted to discuss

in front of Diego. And I had a perfectly horrible BLT waiting in my locker. Of course, the *B* was actually butter and the *T* was probably tuna—I really needed to stop letting Nana pack my lunches. "Can we talk about it later?"

"Your last quiz was an improvement, but you still need to do the extra credit project to pull your grade up. You need at least a B to get into physics next year."

"I'll think about it." I inched closer to the door with every word.

"It can be anything, Henry. Essay, experiment, song and dance. Just give me something I can slap a grade on." She was practically begging.

The last time a teacher cared so much about my academic welfare was in first grade. All the standardized tests said I was a below-average reader, but Mrs. Stancil kept me after school every day to tutor me. I don't remember when the blocks of words began to make sense, but by the end of that school year I'd gone from book hater to bookworm. But this was different, and I wanted to tell Ms. Faraci not to waste her time. None of this would matter in ninety-one days.

"You should write a story, Henry," Diego said, stepping into the classroom. "Henry likes to write, you know."

Ms. Faraci's eyes widened with delight. "I did *not* know that."

I prayed for the sluggers to take me away, but they didn't answer. They were probably using their alien technology to spy on me, laughing their eyestalks off. "Don't listen to Diego. He lies. Pathologically. He can't help himself."

"Did I ever tell you that I was almost an English teacher? I spent a year studying medieval literature." Ms. Faraci's molecules were jittery with excitement. "I would love it if you wrote a story."

With Diego and Faraci both gaping at me, hope and optimism relentlessly beaming from them, my resolve began to fizzle. "What would I write about?"

"Write what you know," Diego said.

"But I don't know anything."

Ms. Faraci shook her head. "Oh, Henry, don't you understand? You know everything."

It was a stupid idea to schedule PE immediately after lunch.

Coach Raskin informed us after we'd dressed that we were going to be running four miles—mandatory participation—with him jogging behind us screaming inspiration in the form of personal insults, as if that were actually going to work. Yes, I did want to go home and cry to my mommy. No, I did not care that a one-legged octogenarian could outrun me.

I managed to jog the first mile, but the air was thicker than tree sap, and the pizza I'd eaten for lunch instead of the "BLT" squirmed in my stomach like a bottled-up squid. I tried to keep up my pace for the second mile, but I developed a stitch in my side, right under my ribs, and I was panting so hard, I thought I would faint. When everyone else had finished and gone to the locker room to change, I still had two laps to go, and Coach Raskin made sure I completed them.

The first bell had already rung, so the showers were empty, which I was grateful for. Showers after gym had been mandatory in middle school, and I'd spent years perfecting how to be naked for the least amount of time. The other boys seemed comfortable in their own skin; I felt like an alien. If I hadn't been soaked with sweat and smelled like the inside of one of Charlie's sneakers, I would have doubled up on deodorant and skipped the shower. But since I was already going to be late for last period, I decided it didn't matter. Besides, I didn't want to reek when Diego took me home.

Even though he'd clearly mentioned his ex-girlfriend—possibly to make sure I knew he wasn't into me—I am more confused by him than ever. But I know what it means that I get excited when I see him and bummed when I don't. I'm starting to like him, and that's a losing scenario for everyone. Even if the world wasn't coming to an end, Diego and

I are an impossibility. Beyond all reason, he wants to be my friend but would never be interested in more.

Even if things were different—if the world weren't ending and Diego were into me—I can't take the chance that it was my fault Jesse hanged himself and that I might cause Diego to do the same. It might seem ludicrous to believe I caused Jesse's suicide, but in the dearth of answers he left behind, it makes as much sense as anything else.

The warning bell rang, and I rushed to rinse the last of the shampoo from my hair and shut off the water. I retrieved my towel from the hook on the wall and tried to dry off in the humid air. The best I could hope to do was mitigate the disaster.

I was drying my hair, the towel draped over my head, and didn't hear their footsteps.

They were on me before I knew what was happening. One on each arm, dressed in black, wearing alien masks. They weren't *my* aliens. The oval eyes gave them away. There were no shadows, either, and sluggers wouldn't have grabbed me and slapped a sweaty hand over my mouth to prevent me from screaming.

The three aliens wrestled me to the floor. They were stronger, but I kicked and bucked and tried to run, dignity be damned. My knee slammed into the tile floor, and my leg went numb. An alien stuffed a pair of boxers into my mouth, while another bound my wrists together with tape. My shoulders ached from struggling like they were going to pop out of their sockets. When they finished with my hands, they pulled my legs out from under me and secured my ankles, leaving me prone on the wet, mildewed floor. I sobbed and tried to breathe, but I snorted water up my nose instead.

This is how I die. In the midst of the chaos in my mind, that's the thought that calmed me. This didn't matter. Nothing they did to me was important. I'd been ready to let the world end, prepared to sit back and wait for the apocalypse. What did it matter if I died a few weeks early? What did I matter at all?

"Hurry up!"

"Where's Coach?"

"Taking a dump."

"Bring it, bring it!"

The tile was slippery, and I swung my legs around, trying to squirm away. The tallest alien kicked me in the testicles with his grass-stained sneaker. The pain was excruciating, and it clawed through my stomach and up my spine. I gagged, trying not to puke with the underwear in my mouth. My vision blurred around the edges, and I thought for a moment the sluggers *had* come to save me. But no one was coming to save me.

Everything hurt. It hurt to move and breathe. I wished they'd kill me and be done with it. I looked up; one of them stood over me with a five-gallon bucket. I swore I saw him grinning through his garish alien mask. "Now you can be an alien too, Space Boy." He tilted the bucket and poured green paint on my chest and legs and arms. It was cold and spread across my stomach like pancake batter.

"Close your eyes, Space Boy." I clenched my eyes shut and held my breath as he emptied the bucket over my head.

"Shit, guys, come on. Time's up."

I heard the empty thud when the bucket hit the floor.

"Hold on. One more thing." I was too afraid to move when one of them pulled something down over my head. I blew paint out my nostrils and, when I breathed, it smelled like latex and cut grass.

I lay sprawled on the shower floor, waiting for the next kick, but it didn't come.

Look at you. Look at what you've become without me. Jesse's voice was muffled through the paint and whatever else covered my head. But it wasn't him. Jesse was dead. I'd seen his body. His parents had insisted on an open-casket funeral, and I'd looked. Despite my brother's warning not to, I'd looked. He was so dead, and that last image of Jesse was the one that remained with me. Dead was the way I saw him from that point forward. *You're a punch line, Henry. The butt of a cruel joke.*

It wasn't Jesse.

I'm beginning to think you should have hanged yourself rather than me. I probably would have cried over you, but I wouldn't have come to this. Jesus Christ, you're fucking pathetic. I don't know what I ever saw in you.

It wasn't Jesse. I repeated that over and over. Jesse was dead, Jesse had loved me, Jesse never would have said those things.

I only killed myself because of you. To escape you. You smothered me, Henry Denton. You loved me to death. You should be dead, not me.

It wasn't Jesse, couldn't have been Jesse, but he was right. I should be dead. I wish I were dead. Because you can only die once, but you can suffer forever.

Coach Raskin discovered me at the end of last period when he came to shut off the lights. Finding me victimized and covered in green paint on the shower floor probably confirmed his opinion of my weakness. I'm willing to bet there was some small part of him that thought I deserved it. He cut the tape around my wrists and ankles, moved me into his office, and gave me a towel, but he refused to let me go home.

Principal DeShields arrived shortly after and hammered me with questions: Who had attacked me? Had I provoked them? What were their names? Why was I in the showers? I did my best to provide answers, but my head throbbed, and the fluorescent overhead lights buzzed, bright and sickly. I wanted to go home, clean the paint off, and never return to CHS again. I didn't mention smelling Marcus's cologne because it would have pitted his word against mine, and he had the benefit of both a car and money.

The paramedics' arrival saved me from further interrogation, but aside from scraped knees and elbows, and slightly swollen testicles, I was unhurt. They took my vitals anyway and tried to clean some of the paint from my face and around my eyes. The police arrived next.

"Are you Henry Denton?"

The officer stood in the doorway of Coach Raskin's office. Her name tag identified her as Sandoval. She was stiff-backed with serious eyes and a crooked nose. I should have been grateful to see her, but this made it real. She'd file an official report, and everyone would know I'd been assaulted. Now I had no chance that this would quietly disappear.

Principal DeShields straightened her cream-colored jacket and shook Sandoval's hand. Her dour frown met Sandoval's humorless eyes, and it looked like a competition to see who could take my situation more seriously. "I'm Margaret DeShields, principal of Calypso High School." Then she fell silent, like she'd planned a whole speech but had forgotten it.

"I need to speak to the victim," Sandoval said. I wasn't Space Boy or Henry Denton; I was The Victim. Coach Raskin's office was cramped, and I had to gulp for breath to get enough air into my lungs. Sandoval must have read my mind because she said, "Alone."

Everyone cleared out, but Principal DeShields hovered outside the doorway, probably mentally strategizing damage control.

Officer Sandoval produced a reporter's notepad and pen from her pocket and turned the full weight of her somber gaze upon me. It was the kind of look I knew could extract the truth the way a dentist tears free a rotten molar. Only, Sandoval wouldn't use Novocain. "Walk me through what happened."

I recounted the attack, sticking to the facts and avoiding conjecture. Even though I was sure I knew the identities of the three aliens who attacked me, I couldn't prove it. Officer Sandoval listened closely but didn't write anything down. I didn't tell her about Jesse speaking to me.

"They were wearing masks?"

"Yeah."

"Did you hear their voices? Could you identify them if you heard them again?"

Marcus McCoy had called me Space Boy so many times that I knew by heart the way his faint Southern accent stretched out the *a* and clipped the *y*, but doubt lingered. Maybe I'd imagined it—his voice, the smell of summer. I didn't want to believe Marcus was capable of attacking me. "No. Nothing."

Sandoval frowned and scribbled in her notebook. "Do you know why anyone would have targeted you?"

I could have given her a hundred reasons:

> I was Space Boy.
> Marcus was still pissed I'd refused to hook up with
> him again.
> Adrian wanted revenge for our fight in the locker
> room.
> I was Space Boy.
> I was weak.
> Fuck it, fuck this place, fuck them all.

"It's Halloween," I said. "And I was an easy target."

Officer Sandoval pursed her lips—she definitely wasn't buying that line of bullshit. However, I'd endured enough shame for one day. I was sure Principal DeShields, Coach Rankin, or anyone else she asked could tell her what she wanted to know. I was done talking.

The sharp rattle of a slamming door outside the office caused Officer Sandoval to glance over her shoulder, but I knew who it was before the shouting began.

My mom had come to take me home.

The sluggers abducted me from the bath. I'd spent two hours under running water, scrubbing with washcloths and loofas until my skin was red and raw. My mom kept trying to invade the bathroom under the guise of offering me different methods of removing the paint—the oddest of which was a stick of butter—and I had to lock the door to get any privacy.

Diego sent me a handful of text messages, at first asking where I was, then begging me to let him know I was all right. I felt terrible about not returning his texts, but I couldn't bear any more pity. Especially not from him.

I also figured out what the One More Thing was while Mom drove me home from school. A photo of me sprawled on the shower floor—bound and green, wearing only a gray alien mask—had spread virally through SnowFlake, each new person who shared it heaping on derision. I tried to trace it back to the original poster but eventually gave up—Space

Boy had become an international phenomenon. I was *Raumjunge* in Germany, *Garçon Cosmique* in France, 宇宙 の少年 in Japan, *Chico Cósmico* in Spain, and *Ruimtejongen* in the Netherlands. At least Marcus had blurred out my junk before exposing me to the world.

"I'm not pressing the goddamn button!" I shouted. My voice didn't echo in the exam room. The darkness devoured it in a way that reminded me of the auditorium where I'd watched Jesse rehearse *The Snow Queen* freshman year. He only had a small part, but he spoke his lines as if he were the lead. His strong tenor reached even the back row where Audrey and I sat, she doing her homework, and I unable to take my eyes off the boy flapping his wings, willing us to believe he was a crow.

The rotating projection of the earth disappeared, but the button remained, as either a taunt or a promise. I didn't know which, and I didn't care. Fuck it.

"Why me?" Though the sluggers had left me alone in the room, I knew they were watching. They were always watching. "If you can save Earth, then do it! Why do you need me?"

Even if they had answered, I doubt I would have comprehended them any more than a rat would understand the reasons a scientist dropped him in a maze and forced him to navigate it for the cheese at the end.

I was startled by a slugger who appeared from the darkness and approached me at a crawl. I'd never noticed before, but it had tiny legs that grew from it like a centipede's. They were absorbed back into its body when it halted.

"What?"

From my supine position on the metal slab, the sluggers had all looked the same, but this one was close enough that I could distinguish fractal patterns on its skin in a million shades of green and brown. The deeper I followed, the farther they led. And they weren't static, either. The intricate designs changed in subtle ways. I sat up, swung my legs around, and slid off the edge of the slab.

"Is that how you communicate with one another?" I wondered aloud as I observed the body markings swirl and transform in an endless dance. They were beautiful. I shed my anger standing there, sloughed off the dead weight of it.

"Do you want me to press the button?" The slugger didn't respond. It simply lingered, motionless except for the designs on its skin and its round eyes floating on their stalks. "If you want me to press it, I will, but you've got to promise never to send me back."

Without my anger to support me, I faltered. My legs trembled, and I collapsed to the floor. I searched for the horizon but saw nothing. Without my anger, I was adrift and drowning. Marcus had attacked me and Nana had Alzheimer's and Jesse had killed himself and Charlie was having a baby. I was helpless to stop any of it; I'd been robbed of hope as surely as Nana was being robbed of her memories.

"Please don't send me back."

The alien turned and crawled toward the darkness. I thought it was abandoning me, but it stopped at the edge of the shadows and waited. This behavior was new, and I watched it curiously. After a moment, a floppy appendage grew out of the upper half of its body and waggled in the air, almost like it was waving at me.

"Do you want me to follow you?" My voice was thick with mucus, and I scrubbed away my tears with the back of my hand. The slugger waved until I stood up, and then its arm melted back into its body.

The slugger led me into the shadows. I'd always imagined there were walls behind the dark, and I was surprised when there weren't. The shadows enveloped me, and I stopped and held my hand an inch in front of my face. It wasn't simply dark; it was the complete absence of light. My heart began to race, but I walked on. I was prepared to spend my life in a cage as the centerpiece of their intergalactic zoo if it meant never returning to Calypso.

The farther I walked, the more confident I grew. I kept

my hand extended in front of me to avoid stumbling into anything. I didn't even know if the slugger was still there; I just kept walking. I wondered how it could see without light, and it dawned on me that the darkness was probably natural to the aliens. The lights in the exam room were for my benefit. The possibilities were endless and exciting. Did their eyes perceive heat? Radiation? Maybe they could see my atoms, and I was merely bits of organic code for them to manipulate. The sluggers were so fundamentally different from humans that it was a wonder they understood me at all. How ugly we must look to them, spilling light into every dark corner to push back the shadows, blinding ourselves to the true beauty of emptiness.

Thank God for nipples.

My hands brushed against something smooth, and I halted. I searched for a door or handle but found nothing. "What now?" As if to answer, a hole appeared in the wall, and a narrow beam of light struck my face. I threw up my arm to cover my eyes. I'd been in the dark so long, the light hurt. When I lowered my arm, I screamed, thinking the sluggers had jettisoned me into space. I stood surrounded by stars. I dropped to my knees, comforted by the solidity of the floor even though I couldn't see it, expecting at any moment to be sucked into the gelid void, frozen and dead. It took a moment for my brain to process that I wasn't floating in space. I perceived no walls, no ceiling, no floor, yet that I was alive proved that some kind of barriers protected me. The slugger who'd led me into the darkness was gone, as was the hallway from which I'd come. It shouldn't have been possible. I was surrounded by heaven. The sun, the moon, the earth, and all those living stars. They weren't static like in pictures taken from impossibly far away—they breathed, they glowed. They were future and past, possibility and memory. They were beautiful.

"I never knew there were so many," I whispered. We are merely pieces of a grander design, even more insignificant than I imagined. When the earth ceases to be, all those stars will shine on. Our deaths will mean nothing to them.

"I feel so small." No one replied. I wondered as I watched the stars, really seeing them for the first time, whether they could see me, too.

Time Travel

It begins a thousand years from now. Dr. Jiao Hatori discovers time travel.

A new and exciting industry emerges from the breakthrough. Those willing to pay the exorbitant fees are shifted backward in time to view history firsthand. Time tourists can finally discover the truth of who shot JFK, they can watch the first majestic performance of *Hamlet*, they can dine with Cleopatra or Queen Elizabeth I or Amelia Earhart the evening before her ill-fated flight. Future humans infest history like cockroaches.

The problems begin when the North American Alliance's prime minister sends soldiers to the year 2213 to prevent the Texas uprising that turned much of what was once known as the United States into an atomic wasteland. The plan succeeds, which is the problem.

History becomes fluid. Factions with varying agendas fight to rewrite the events of the past to their advantage. The government that controls the past controls the future.

The Guilde Immuable, an anti-time travel organization, forms in response to the deconstruction of the past. Citizens applaud its goals while condemning its methods. Its members destroy art and literature, kill famous figures throughout history, demanding time travel cease or they will dismantle the whole of time. They sow chaos to bring attention to the plundering of humanity's history.

World leaders declare war on the Guilde Immuable, vowing never to bow to the will of terrorists.

Emmanuel Roth arrives in Geneva on 29 January 2016 to destroy the Large Hadron Collider, the site of the groundbreaking discovery of gravitons, without which time travel would be impossible. Emmanuel knows that scientific progress cannot be stopped, and that someone else will eventually discover gravitons, but he admires the symbolism of the act.

At 10:19 UTC, Emmanuel detonates a fission bomb, atomizing the Large Hadron Collider, CERN, and most of Switzerland. Emmanuel is unaware that the Large Hadron Collider is active. An infinitesimal fraction of a second prior to the bomb's detonation, two particles collide with such fierce velocity that they form a micro singularity—a black hole too small to see with the naked eye. It would have lacked the energy to sustain itself under normal conditions, however, the fission bomb provides it with all the energy it requires to grow and become self-sustaining. As the earth's core is devoured by the black hole, the resulting radiation vaporizes the outer layers of the planet and expels them, and all life, into space.

The future destroys the past destroys the future.

3 November 2015

Mom let me stay home from school on Monday but refused to allow me to skip Tuesday. She believed that the sooner I returned to my normal routine, the sooner I, and everyone else, would forget about The Incident. That's what we're calling it. It's certainly better than referring to it as the Everyone Saw Henry Denton's Blurry Balls in That One Picture escapade. Anyway, it's impossible to forget about something that haunts me every time I close my eyes. I have to shower with the curtain drawn back and the door locked. And forget about sleep. Dawn and I have become fast friends, and I don't expect that will change any time soon.

Tuesday morning I was sitting at the kitchen table nursing my second cup of coffee and wondering if I knew anyone I could score something stronger off of when Charlie strolled in wearing a dress shirt and tie. He grabbed a Mountain Dew from the fridge and chugged it.

"Come on," he said, hardly looking at me. "I'll take you to school on my way to work."

I was the only person in the kitchen, so Charlie had to have been speaking to me, but he'd never offered me a ride to school before. "You don't even have a car."

"Hurry up, Henry, I don't want to be late." Charlie grabbed my backpack and headed out the front door, leaving me to toss my dishes in the sink and follow.

Charlie's Jeep was running when I got outside. The engine rumbled and coughed and smelled like burning oil, but it actually worked. I swung into the passenger seat. "Holy shit, dude. You fixed it."

"It was nothing," Charlie said, but the giant smile plastered on his face said otherwise. It was the first time I remembered seeing my brother proud of anything other than a particularly putrid fart. The guy beside me, I didn't know him. The aliens must have replaced him with a robot.

Charlie stalled the Wrangler when he put it in reverse, and swore like it was his primary language. I figured I still might have to walk, but he threw it into neutral, got it started again, and we took off. I hadn't expected the Jeep to make it out of the driveway under its own power. Charlie had taken something that was broken and made it whole again.

"What's up with the fancy tie?" I asked. Charlie hadn't even worn a tie to Jesse's funeral, but today he was decked out in a dress shirt, gray pants, and a black-and-silver-plaid tie.

He tugged at the neck. "Zooey's dad gave me a job."

"Doing what?"

"Computer stuff." Charlie shrugged like it was nothing. "Fixing laptops and helping stupid people figure out their e-mail."

As a kid, Charlie had disassembled everything he could get his hands on—CD players, watches, our clothes dryer—but he'd never shown much interest in putting them back together. Somewhere along the way he changed, and I missed it.

"What about college?"

Charlie sighed. "I've got responsibilities, Henry. Anyway, I'm not cut out for more school."

"Is this what you want?"

"I love Zooey. We'll figure the rest out as we go." We hadn't spoken much since he pissed on my homework, but my attack and humiliation at the hands of Marcus made my fight with Charlie seem petty and unimportant. Brothers fight, and then they move on.

"What do you even know about babies? You can barely look after yourself."

Charlie punched me in the arm, but Nana could've hit me harder. "Look who's talking, *Space Boy*."

"You're a dick."

The brakes squealed and the body shuddered when Charlie stopped at a red light. "Listen, you can't let people intimidate you, bro."

"I wasn't intimidated, Charlie; I was attacked." I could still feel the tape around my wrists, see the smooth patches where it had torn the hair from my arms, and my groin ached when I took a deep breath. Every movement was a reminder that I was a joke, every pain a reminder that I was better off not pressing the button.

Charlie gripped the cracked leather steering wheel so hard, his knuckles turned white. "Guys like that . . . They're pussies."

"Thanks for the brilliant insight."

"I'm serious." The light turned green. Charlie gunned it, trying to shift quickly through the gears, but it stuck in third, and the transmission chewed metal like it was grinding bones. "If I'm going to beat someone up, they'll see me coming. Only cowards attack a kid in the showers."

I knew, in his own way, my brother was trying to make me feel better, but Charlie doesn't know the meaning of subtle. He probably can't spell it either. I looked out the window to discourage him from talking; it didn't work.

"You need to cut it out with the alien crap." Charlie nodded to himself. He was conveniently forgetting the fact that he was the big mouth who told the whole school about the "alien crap" in the first place. "You make yourself a target."

"So you're saying I asked for it? That I got what I deserved?"

Charlie backhanded my shoulder. "Jesus, Henry, you know what I mean."

"You're not a father yet, so stop trying to act like one."

Charlie was quiet until we pulled up to the front of CHS. He stopped me when I tried to hop out of the Jeep. "If you want people to treat you normal, you have to act normal."

A few of the other students being dropped off cast stealthy glances in my direction. Space Boy was back for their amusement. "I never asked to be treated normal, Charlie. I just want to be left alone."

Someone left an alien mask on my chair in Ms. Faraci's class that I discovered when I slipped in right before the final bell. I wasn't kidding about what I said to Charlie—I really did want to be left alone. I made certain I was the first person out of class and the last person in.

I froze when I saw the mask. I recognized it immediately, and the memories of the attack rushed at me in a torrent I couldn't stop. I felt the paint oozing down my skin. Felt them kick me in the balls. But I refused to let them see me upset. I made my bones steel and my skin chain mail. I was diamond on the outside, and I would not break.

Inside, though, I was already broken.

"What's the matter, Space Boy?" came the hideous whisper. I didn't look at them. I just stood by my desk, willing the mask to disappear.

"Henry? Is there a problem?" Ms. Faraci's voice sounded scratchy and distant, like a faded recording. "Henry?"

I yelped when she touched my shoulder. She saw the mask and reached past me to grab it. "Who put this here?" The rest of the class stared at me, at their desks, and no one spoke up. The attention made everything worse. I should have brushed the stupid alien mask to the floor. But I hadn't, and now Ms. Faraci was going to wave that thing in the air until someone copped to leaving it on my desk.

"Tell me immediately, or I will simply fail you all for the semester." Ms. Faraci was trembling. I should have been flattered that she cared, but I hated the feeling of every student in the classroom looking at me, despising me. I doubted she'd actually flunk everyone, but there was a chance, and they would blame me.

"Adrian did it." Audrey Dorn spoke loudly and clearly. She turned to look Adrian in the eyes. "I saw him put it on Henry's desk."

"Bitch!" snarled Adrian, but Ms. Faraci rounded on him.

"Get your bag and report to Principal DeShields's office at once." She towered over Adrian as he gathered his belongings, glaring at me and Audrey and Ms. Faraci.

"I need a pass," Adrian said in a voice resembling a growl.

Ms. Faraci shoved the alien mask at him. "Here's your pass."

Adrian elbowed me on his way out, likely already plotting his revenge.

Even though he had gotten into trouble, and Audrey had handed Faraci his head on a platter, I was the one people would talk about. The one they'd laugh at between classes. My skin began to itch like I'd been sunburned and blistered, and my stomach filled with bile. Ignoring Ms. Faraci's concerned shouts, I fled the classroom for the restroom. I clamped my hand over my mouth to keep from puking until I reached the toilet. It wasn't food that made me sick; it was knowing that I was Space Boy, that I would always be Space Boy. That poison infected every cell, and I vomited so hard that I felt my muscles tear from my ribs. It wasn't enough.

"Henry?"

I recognized Marcus's voice and threw my shoulder against the stall door. My nostrils burned with snot and bile, and I wiped my mouth with the back of my hand.

"I told Faraci I forgot my book in my locker, but I wanted to make sure you're all right."

"Get the fuck out!" I was shaking, scared of what he might do. "I know it was you."

Marcus's shadow floated back and forth across the tile floor, but he didn't try to open the stall. "It was only a joke."

I wasn't sure whether Marcus was talking about the mask on the chair or The Incident. Not that it mattered. "That wasn't a joke, Marcus; it was felony assault! What's next, acid in my face? I hear hot tar and feathers is a real crowd pleaser." I was trembling so badly, the door rattled, but my rage was the only thing keeping the terror at bay.

I imagined Marcus standing in front of the sinks, trying to figure out the right thing to say to make me see he wasn't to blame. Telling himself he was a good guy, and it was my fault if I couldn't take a joke. I wished it were Audrey on the other side of that door. I wished I'd forgiven her and that we were friends again, because without Jesse, I was alone. I got my phone out of my pocket and began typing a text to send her, begging her to rescue me from Marcus, but I deleted it and put my phone away.

"For what it's worth, I'm sorry," Marcus said after a few moments of silence. I'd begun to think he'd left. "Are you going to tell anyone?"

"Don't worry, Marcus, I'll keep your secrets. All of them. I don't want people to find out about what we did any more than you do."

• • •

Diego found me during lunch, sitting on a bench beside the library. The weather was too warm to eat outside, but I couldn't endure the cafeteria with all those people looking at and talking about me. I didn't have an appetite anyway. "I texted you a couple of times." There was coldness in his voice, a distant calm. I was sure he knew about the attack, had probably seen the pictures, but he was being maddeningly blasé.

"More like thirty."

"I was worried."

"I wasn't in the mood to talk."

Diego nodded and sat beside me. He was wearing flip-flops that exposed his flat feet and hairy toes. "Who attacked you, Henry?"

"I already went through this with the cops."

"I'm not the cops."

"Just drop it, all right?"

"I've told you about my sister, right?" Diego didn't wait for me to answer. "Viv was wild when we were growing up. She's got her shit together now, but when we were kids, I didn't think she'd make it out of high school without a felony record." He coughed and cleared his throat. "She was great, though. When I was seven, I think, we had this storm come through that knocked out the power for hours. Our parents had gone into town, and I was so scared. Viv found a bottle of champagne in the back of the fridge and made us champagne ice cream. We played penny poker until our parents got home. My pop whipped us both pretty good, but it was worth it.

"Another time, when I was nine, Viv was climbing this huge cottonwood in our backyard. Dad had told her a million times not to, but that was probably exactly why she did it. She slipped and fell, smacked her face on a branch coming down. Came screaming to me, all bloody and purple. Thing was, she wasn't worried about her nose being broken; she was scared of being grounded for climbing that stupid tree. Mom lost it when I took Viv inside. I told her I was playing ninja and had tackled Viv and accidentally broken her nose.

"When my pop got home that night, he beat me so hard, he ruptured my spleen." Diego chuckled like a ruptured spleen was hilarious.

I looked for self-pity in Diego's eyes, tried to figure out why he'd told me. "Did your dad really do that?" Diego lifted his T-shirt. A faded scar ran down his stomach to his navel, marring the smooth tan skin. Another scar, jagged and more fresh, cut across his left side above his hip. He dropped his shirt back down before I could examine it further. "I'm sorry that happened to you, but what's your point?"

Diego clenched his fists, took deep, even breaths. He said, "I protect the people I care about, Henry."

"It doesn't matter who attacked me."

"It matters to me." For a moment I considered telling him it was Marcus, and probably Adrian and Jay, who'd attacked me. Maybe he would have turned them in; maybe he would have beaten them bloody. All I know is that he wouldn't have done nothing. Which is why I didn't tell him.

"The sluggers—"

"Who?"

"The aliens," I said. "I call them that because they look like slugs. Well, they told me the world is going to end soon."

"How soon?"

"January twenty-ninth."

Diego arched his eyebrow. "That's pretty specific."

"It's the end of life on Earth. Specificity matters."

"Did the . . . sluggers tell you how?"

I shook my head. "But they told me I could prevent it. All I have to do is press a red button on their ship."

"Strange. And sort of anticlimactic."

"I thought so too."

Most people would have written me off as a delusional lunatic, but Diego treated me like he believed what I was saying, or at least believed that I believed it. "So at Marcus's party, when you asked me about saving the world, you weren't speaking hypothetically?"

"Not so much."

"Did you press it?"

"Not yet." Admitting that to Diego, telling him about the button and the end of the world, made the burden slightly more manageable. It was still my decision, no one could make it for me, but I didn't have to carry the weight of it alone.

"It'd be easier not to," Diego said. "Wouldn't it?"

"Yes," I whispered.

"Because you miss Jesse." The muscle along Diego's jaw pulsed, and it was a while before he spoke again. "You've already made up your mind, haven't you? That's why you won't tell anyone who attacked you. The world's going to end; why rock the boat, right?"

"No. I don't know." I'd admitted more to Diego than I'd meant to. "Do you want me to press it?"

"I think I want you to want to press it."

"Oh." It wasn't the answer I'd hoped for. I didn't want to be responsible for the fate of humankind. I could barely be responsible for myself. We sat in silence, each roaming our own thoughts until the bell rang and the walkways flooded with chatty students on their way to classes. The one good thing to come from being attacked was that Principal DeShields transferred me from gym to study hall. Diego escorted me to my new class without asking, and I didn't tell him how grateful I was.

Before I went inside, Diego tugged my sleeve and said, "So, I know it's still a couple of weeks away, but my sister's having a Thanksgiving barbecue. It's absolutely going to be lame, but it'd be cool if you dropped by."

The suddenness of Diego's invitation confounded my ability to speak. After what I'd told him, I was sure he'd want to distance himself from me. "We usually do family dinner."

"I figured, but you could come before . . . or after."

"Why me?"

Diego cocked his head, looked at me with his green-brown eyes before he said, "Because I can be myself around you, even if I don't know who I am yet."

"Oh."

Diego broke into a welcome grin. "Anyway, you've got to try Viv's potato salad before we all die."

"It's that good?"

"No," he said, "it's terrible. But you can't believe how bad it is until you taste it."

I laughed in spite of myself. "I'll think about it."

"Good enough for me."

4 November 2015

I leapt out of bed at 5:16 a.m., awakened by Chopin's Sonata no. 2. I knew what time it was because I stubbed my toe on my desk, knocking over my alarm clock, which fell onto the cord of my lamp and dragged it to the floor, breaking the bulb into a hundred invisible pieces that I was sure I would step on later. By the time I steadied myself and made certain my toe wasn't broken, I had so much adrenaline pumping through my veins that it was like I'd snorted a cup of coffee grounds.

Bleary-eyed and ready for war, I stumbled into the living room, but I wasn't the first to arrive.

Nana sat at the piano, which she hadn't played since her memory began to fade. Her bony back straight, her fingers swept the keys delicately, then hard, alternately caressing and torturing music from them. Mom stood behind her, arms rigid at her sides. I was about to ask what the hell was going on, but Mom held her finger to her lips before I could interrupt. A moment later Charlie and Zooey joined us. The little parasite bulged in Zooey's belly, and she rested her hands on it. Mom didn't need to tell them to remain quiet.

As my anger faded, Nana's song consumed me. I'd grown up listening to Nana play the piano—she had even tried to teach me when I was little, but gave up because I had clumsy fingers—and I'd heard stories of the concerts she'd played in her youth before she married and had my mother. This was different. These notes were raw. They rose and fell, soared as the chords were layered atop one another. They ached and bled, and we bled with them. This was every fear and horror her mind could conjure. The music showed us what she couldn't say. All her emptiness and despair. The hollowness of her mind without her memories. The way she saw the world as a cold, dead place. She'd tried to tell me, to tell us all, but I hadn't really heard her until that moment.

Abruptly, Nana stopped. Her fingers paralyzed, arched over the keys. She tried to continue, searching desperately for the right chords, but the notes were discordant. She banged the piano, her frustration mounting. "I can't remember how it goes!"

Mom rested her hand on Nana's shoulder. "Mother, it's the middle of the night—"

"What're you doing in my house? Get out of my house!" Nana didn't see us. She saw people, but not us. She fixated on the song, her arthritic fingers hunting recklessly for the next note.

"Nana—" I tried, but she screamed, "Leave me the hell alone, all of you!" and slammed the keys. Mom's shoulders shook. I stood helplessly, unsure what to do. I was worried Nana was going to hurt herself.

Charlie brushed past me and sat on the bench beside Nana. Without speaking, he began to play. Haltingly at first but, as his confidence grew, each note flowed from the one that preceded it. Charlie's song, though different from Nana's, stoked her memory, and she began again. He played a joyful counterpoint to her plaintive dirge—his notes light and hopeful to drive back the desolation of the future. I've never heard anything like it and doubt I ever will again.

Nana sighed as the song ended—the final note lingering in our ears—stood, and shuffled back to her room.

I'm not sure whether we were more stunned by Nana's behavior or Charlie's. Zooey kissed his cheek as he wrapped his arm around her shoulders. "We're going back to bed. I have to work early."

I can't help thinking that if we live long enough, we'll all eventually forget the lives we've lived. The faces of people closest to us, the memories we swore we'd hold on to for the rest of our lives. First kisses and last kisses and all the passion between the years. We have to watch Nana's life slipping away from her like a forgotten word. I thought I understood what's happening to her, but this isn't like being robbed a penny at a time. Memories aren't currency to spend; they're us. Age isn't stealing from my grandmother; it's slowly unwinding her.

"I can't do this anymore," Mom said.

I held her hand. "You won't have to."

10 November 2015

Mathematics rules the universe. The earth orbits the sun, traveling at an average speed of 107,200 kilometers per hour. The actual speed can be determined at any point in the earth's orbit by using the distance to the sun and the specific orbital energy. The earth also completes one full rotation every 23 hours, 56 minutes, and 4.09 seconds, and has an axial tilt of 23.4 degrees. Because of the constancy of the math that governs these events, I can tell you with absolute certainty that on May 1, 2091, the sun will rise over Calypso at exactly 6:45 a.m. and will set at 7:57 p.m.

Scientists even theorize that if you could take the position, speed, trajectory, and mass of every object in the universe and feed it into a supercomputer, you could predict the future of everything.

Predicting my routine over the days after the attack was far easier. I lost myself in the minutiae of life. Charlie drove me to school each morning, and I watched him grow more comfortable in his shirt and tie, and more confident in his role as a father-to-be, though he still found time to torture me—his new favorite game was to stick his finger in my mouth every time I yawned. Diego and I continued to eat lunch together. Sometimes we skipped the cafeteria, but most days we found the quiet end of a table and pretended the other seats were empty. I still haven't figured out why he's wasting his time on me when he could easily fit in with any clique he wanted. He's a chameleon that way. He seems to change personalities the way he changes styles, and that makes it difficult to figure out who he is. The only times I catch a glimpse of the real Diego Vega are when he's talking about books or art.

Sometimes I think about pushing him to talk about his family, about why he moved to Calypso from Colorado, but my goal is to simply survive until the world's end, and that does not include antagonizing Diego.

Nana officially resigned from lunch-making duty, and on Tuesday, Mom packed leftover fried chicken, which I shared with Diego. I offered him the thigh and kept the leg for myself. He peeled off the skin and ate it first, savoring each bite. "This is killer."

"My mom uses ground unicorn horn and the blood of virgins for the coating." In truth, I don't know what's in her chicken, but I love it. Laughter drew my attention away from Diego, toward the lunch line where Audrey Dorn stood with her arms extended like she was frozen mid-pirouette. I didn't understand what was happening at first because her scoop-neck shirt was brown, and I couldn't see the spilled soda until the rivulets reached her white pants. All the kids at the nearby tables were cracking up, but Adrian Morse was doubled over. I hoped he pissed himself.

"Don't you know that girl?" Diego asked.

"Audrey?"

"Looks like she's having a rough day."

Audrey shook the soda from her hands, not caring who she flung the drops on, and stormed out of the cafeteria, leaving her lunch tray on the floor. Adrian stood up and did a fairly accurate impression of her stance and walk. Possession of the mask hadn't been sufficient proof for Principal DeShields to link Adrian to my attack, but harassing me with it had earned him a three-day suspension. He'd returned more vicious than before.

"I don't want to sit through study hall," I said, trying to change the subject.

"It's better than PE."

"True, but Mr. Weiss spends the entire period posting on Brony forums—"

"That should surprise me, but doesn't."

"And Chloe Speedman smacks her lips when she chews gum, which she does constantly. If I have to spend another hour there, I might consider self-immolation as a form of protest."

Diego leaned over his tray, his arms resting on either side, and poked around his lunch for any crumbs he might have missed—he was the only person I knew who ate faster than Charlie—but there was nothing left. "Let's ditch."

"And do what?"

"Whatever."

"I hear whatever's fun this time of year."

Diego rolled his eyes. "Come on, man. Don't you want to get out of here?"

"Yeah, but—"

"How can you make an informed decision about whether to save the world if you never leave your tiny part of it?"

The bell rang, but we didn't move. Diego was staring at me so hard, it was like he was trying to force his thoughts into my brain. I know it was only my imagination, but I felt like I could hear a chorus of Diegos encouraging me to say no to class and yes to anarchy. Diego was one variable no equation could predict. Being in survival mode for the next seventy-five days didn't have to mean I couldn't have fun.

"Fine, but we're not going to the beach."

Diego and I loitered on the side of the math building while we waited for the final bell to ring. Vice Principal Marten patrols the parking lot between classes, making sure only students with passes escape. He locks the gate the rest of the time, but it's hardly a deterrent, since all you have to do is hop the curb and drive around it.

VP Marten cruised the lot for a couple of minutes after the last bell before heading back toward the administration building. Diego grabbed my arm and motioned for me to follow.

"Who gives their kid an eighty-thousand-dollar car?" Diego asked. He was eyeing Marcus's Tesla, though he could have been talking about any of the cars. The parking lot was full of Lexuses, BMWs, and Mercedes.

"The McCoys."

Diego raised an eyebrow and glanced again at Marcus's sleek ride. Even though I hated him, I couldn't deny it was a beautiful machine.

We reached Diego's car, and he breathed a sigh. He stuck the key in the ignition and turned; nothing happened. Not even the car's characteristic wheeze that I'd come to know well. "Come on. Please Start, please start, please start." Diego cranked the ignition again, but Please Start refused to. "Maybe the battery's dead."

While Diego tinkered under the hood, doubt gnawed at my resolve. Mr. Weiss wouldn't care if I snuck into study hall a few minutes late. I could've lied and told him the cafeteria burritos gave me stomach cramps, even though I'm smart enough never to eat those cheesy laxative bombs. This was a stupid idea. Skipping class wasn't going to change my mind about pressing the button. It wasn't going to bring back Jesse or make Marcus and Adrian disappear. Even if we found something to do, my shitty life would still be waiting for me when the fun ended. I was about to say so when Diego slammed the hood and said, "She's toast."

"I guess we should go to class." I tried to sound crestfallen as I grabbed my bag and got out of the car. That's when I saw Audrey speed-walking toward us. It was really more of a trot.

"Problems?" she asked.

"We *were* planning to ditch," I said.

Audrey glanced nervously over her shoulder. "Were?"

"Car trouble," I said.

"I hate to break it to you, but Marten's headed this way."

Diego sighed. "We're not going anywhere in this thing."

I swore I could hear the predatory whirr of Marten's golf cart approaching.

Audrey fidgeted with her keys. She kept looking behind her, her eyes wide and dodgy. "Listen, I'll give you a ride off campus if you want, but we should hurry."

"It might be safer to go back to class." I'd agreed to skip school with Diego; catching a ride with Audrey hadn't been part of the plan.

Diego snorted. "No way. Marks will give me detention. I don't do detention."

"Now or never." Audrey took a couple of steps toward her car and disarmed the alarm.

I wasn't paranoid. I could definitely hear the golf cart's motor. I'd earned some sympathy because of the attack, but I doubt I'd be able to weasel out of a detention if Marten caught me trying to skip. "Fine. Let's go."

Nobody said much as we left campus. Vice Principal Marten chased us out of the parking lot, but he couldn't catch Audrey's V8. I wasn't sure what Diego and I were going to do without a car after Audrey dropped us off. Ratting out Adrian for the mask didn't make us even. She pulled into a CVS and parked.

Diego hopped out and stretched his legs. "Thanks for the save."

WE ARE THE ANTS · 183

"Yeah," I mumbled.

Audrey looked at me in the rearview mirror. "I never pegged you for a skipper."

"You're one to talk."

I noticed she'd changed out of her soda-stained clothes, and into jeans and a tank top. "I . . . yeah . . . I needed to get out of there."

"I know the feeling." Diego wandered to her side and offered her his hand through the open window. "I'm Diego Vega, by the way."

"Audrey Dorn."

"Henry's told me nothing about you."

Audrey flashed him a wry smile. "I bet."

"Seriously," Diego said. "All I know is that you used to be friends."

"It's . . . whatever," I said. We'd managed to escape school, but we didn't have a car, and I didn't want to spend the rest of the day in a drugstore parking lot. "Where were you headed?"

"Home, probably," Audrey said. "Me and Leah and a couple of other girls had plans to go to the fair tonight, but they've been avoiding me lately."

Diego perked up. "Fair?"

"It comes around every year," I said.

"Is it far? I haven't been to a real fair ever."

"I don't know. Maybe we could go this weekend."

"What else are you going to do today?" Audrey asked. "It's not like you've got a car."

Diego was so excited, he was practically bouncing up and down, and I didn't want to disappoint him. Hanging out at the fair with Audrey wasn't how I'd planned to spend my afternoon, but she had a point.

"Come on, Henry," Diego said. "It'll be fun, I promise."

"Do you think you can stand hanging out with me for a few hours?" Audrey's lips hinted at a smirk I knew well.

I sighed dramatically. "You did sort of save my ass—"

"Twice."

"So I suppose I can make an exception."

Audrey shrugged. "Then I guess we're going to the fair."

The last time I attended the fair, Audrey and I were still friends, and Jesse was alive. I thought Jesse was happy, though in retrospect, the signs were there that he was going to fall apart. It wasn't any one big thing; it was the way all the little things added up and compounded. He didn't kill himself because of a single overwhelming problem; he died from a thousand tiny wounds.

Audrey walked ahead of me and Diego, moving with the line, which was longer than we'd anticipated. Clearly, we weren't the only ones skipping the last two classes of the day, but it still wasn't as busy as it would have been on a Friday night or Saturday afternoon.

"There's no way you survived living in a house without Internet." Audrey's head was cocked to the side, and she jutted out her hip. "Please tell me you're joking."

Diego shoved his hands into his pockets and shrugged. "Wish I could."

Diego had been telling us about life in Colorado to kill time while we waited to buy the bracelets that would let us on every ride at the fair. He'd casually mentioned having to go to the library to check SnowFlake, which led to the conversation we were having. "Next you're going to tell us you didn't have cable, either," I said.

"No TV at all," Diego said, a shy smile on his face that made me wonder if he was messing with us.

Audrey inched forward with the line. "Were your parents Amish?"

"Nope. Just poor." He said it with a simplicity that expressed no regret and asked for no pity. It was just a statement of fact.

Audrey began to stammer. "I didn't . . . I didn't mean . . ."

Diego patted her arm. "Don't worry about it."

"Seriously . . . I . . . I . . ."

"Her family wasn't always rich," I said. "Her mom invented this recyclable paper coffee cup that holds in heat but keeps the outside from burning your hand."

"Seriously?"

Audrey blushed and glanced at the trampled grass under her feet like she was considering digging a deep hole and crawling into it. "My . . . my mom's a genius."

"My mom knits sweaters for cats." Diego's deadpan delivery was so good that I didn't know whether he was telling the truth, and I busted up laughing at the image of grumpy cats in ugly sweaters. Audrey relaxed; I was in awe of Diego's ability to always know the right thing to say.

At the front of the line, Audrey and I got into a fight when she tried to pay for all of our tickets. Diego stealthily paid the admission while we were arguing, causing me and Audrey to join together in righteous indignation. But all was forgotten and forgiven by the end of our first ride on the Pirate Ship.

We stared at our twisted reflections in the mirror maze, ate powdered-sugar-dusted elephant ears, banged out our aggression on the bumper cars, and got sticky fingers from cotton candy. I was sweat-soaked and flushed, and I couldn't remember the last time I'd laughed so loudly or smiled so often without having to fake it.

Diego grabbed my and Audrey's hands and pulled us toward the flying saucer with the garish blinking lights. "Whatever that is, I want to ride it!" His curiosity was insatiable, his joy infectious. He approached everything he did like it was both the first and last time he was ever going to get to do it.

Audrey glanced at me knowingly, and not because of the obvious UFO reference. The last time I'd ridden the Gravitron was with Jesse. He killed himself sixty-eight days later. I said, "I'm okay," and we crowded onto the ride, shoving past some preppy parents who dragged their whining, disinterested brats alongside them. The dark, muggy interior was a nineties fossil, a dream frozen in amber. The ride whirled around and tilted up and down, but it never moved forward. We shuffled to our narrow slats along the wall and leaned against the cracked and taped vinyl panels. I tried not to think about the parade of filthy people who had previously stood in my place, sweat matting their hair, soaking into the headrest.

"All right, partners!" shouted the lanky-haired, metal-band reject at the center of the Gravitron. "Let's get this thing a-movin' and a-shakin'. Yee-haw!"

"I bet he drinks heavily to smother the shame of what his life has become, and dies of liver failure by forty-three," I said. Diego laughed, and I wanted to preserve the sound in a jar for the days when laughter was scarce.

"Yeah, right," Audrey shot back. "Two funnel cakes says that's you in ten years!"

"In ten years, we'll all be gone."

Audrey gave me a perplexed look, but Diego shouted, "Fuck that! I'm gonna live forever!" as the ride fired up and the room lurched into motion. Diego howled—earning us glares from the preppy parents who probably presumed we were drunk—and the wave of bad music continued to assault our ears as Creed blurred into Nickelback.

The trucker-hat-wearing scarecrow at the controls continued yee-hawing like anyone cared. We were swept up in the spin and in the smell of metal and vomit and bleach. I was swept up in Diego Vega. In the way he sounded like he honestly believed he'd never die despite my telling him the whole world was on borrowed time; in the way he looked at me like I was someone other than Space Boy, a way that was impossible and endless. Diego looked at me and saw *me*. No one had seen me since Jesse.

The ride spun faster, so fast that gravity squatted on my chest and pushed the air from my lungs, and then faster still. Jesse fought the centrifugal force and flipped onto my panel, straddling me, his curly blond hair hanging in my face, his body pressed against mine. Audrey glared at us, disgusted, and the conductor yelled for Jesse to return to his slab. Jesse ignored him. Rules didn't apply to Jesse Franklin, and I loved him for it.

We were whirling around so fast that Jesse couldn't hold his head up any longer and buried his face in my neck, his chapped lips grazing my skin. He was insane, and I told him so as I wrapped my arms around him so tightly that nothing would ever tear us apart.

I nipped at Jesse's ear and ran my hands up the back of his shirt. His skin was sticky with sweat. He smelled like the ocean.

"Never stop," whispered Jesse.

"I don't plan to," I promised, and meant it.

The ride slowed, and our bodies began to separate, but that only made me hold Jesse closer. He kissed me so hard that I cut my lip on his teeth.

Jesse and I disappeared into a world where we two alone existed.

"Honestly," said Audrey as the ride slowed to a stop, "can you stop dry humping my best friend?"

But we pretended we didn't hear her, and I wrapped my arms around Jesse's neck, and he kissed me like the world had fallen out from under our feet. We were two bodies floating in space, brighter than stars.

When the ride ended, Diego left me and Audrey hanging out by the Tilt-A-Whirl while he hunted for a toilet. I didn't say much, and neither did Audrey. I was pretty sure we were both thinking about Jesse. Audrey picked at the peeling paint on the side of the ride and kept repeating that she was having *so much fun*. After the hundredth time, I craned my neck to look for Diego.

"How long have you guys been together?" Audrey asked.

I was standing on my tiptoes, looking over the crowd, and her question didn't register right away, so I said, "Yeah, sure." Then, "What?"

Audrey had this way of making you feel like the dumbest person in the room. She didn't do it on purpose, but when she looked at you, you knew her brain worked on a level many times greater than yours. "I'm glad you're not with Marcus anymore. If he doesn't roofie someone before graduation, I'll be shocked."

"Diego and I aren't together. He's straight."

"Really?"

"Yup."

Audrey furrowed her brow like she was staring at a math problem that had been marked wrong when she was certain it was correct. The calculations didn't make sense, and Audrey hated for things to not make sense. "The way you were looking at him on the Gravitron . . ."

"I was thinking about Jesse."

"Oh. But you like Diego, right?"

I wanted to tell Audrey how conflicted I felt. How I sometimes thought about Diego while jerking off; how, when I tried to recall memories of Jesse, Diego appeared in them instead. Jesse was dead, he'd committed suicide, but I still felt like I was betraying him for liking a guy who wasn't even capable of liking me back. Audrey was maybe the one person who could have understood, and I wanted to tell her, but I didn't. "Drop it, okay?"

"Fine. What do *you* want talk about?"

I spotted Diego walking toward us, but he stopped in front of the bumper cars, and I couldn't see why. "I don't know, Audrey."

"Come on. Don't be like that." Everything about her was pleading with me to let it all go. Her eyes and her lips and the way her shoulders slumped.

"We did fine not talking at all for the last year," I mumbled.

"Maybe you were fine, but I needed you."

Diego had clearly run into someone, but I couldn't see who it was. "I was here. I'm not the one who left." I just needed that stupid kid with his stupid balloon to get out of the way so I could see who Diego was talking to.

"I was hurting too, you know."

Standing in the middle of the fair was not where I wanted

to have this argument. I didn't want to have it at all, but Audrey was maddeningly persistent. "Yeah, you were hurting so bad you took a three-month vacation to Switzerland. That must have been horrible for you."

"Henry—"

A passing family obscured Diego, so I turned my full attention to Audrey. The festering wound split open anew, spewing a geyser of pus. "You didn't even say good-bye, Audrey. I showed up at your house, and your dad told me you'd gone to stay with family in Switzerland. I thought you'd come back after winter break, but you were gone for three months." People turned to stare at us, but I couldn't stop draining the abscess. "Jesse killed himself, and you were the only person I could talk to about it. I needed you, but you didn't answer my e-mails, my calls, nothing. My boyfriend, your best friend, committed suicide, and you abandoned me. You both abandoned me."

Tears filled Audrey's eyes, and I hated myself for causing them. I hated myself for needing her. I wanted to hate her for leaving, but I didn't, and I hated myself for that too. "You got to see Jesse at his best, but I saw him after he punched a brick wall so hard, he broke his fingers, when he cut his thighs with razor blades, when he put out lit cigarettes on his hands and told you he'd burned himself baking brownies. I was the one who cleaned up his blood and made sure he didn't drink himself to death. Me, Henry. Not you."

I didn't learn about those things until after the funeral. I spent weeks scouring old texts and pictures, looking for the clues I'd missed. Thinking about the times I suspected something was wrong but didn't push Jesse to talk about it keeps me awake most nights. I failed Jesse. We all failed him. "Why'd you leave, Audrey?"

"I needed space to breathe."

"So you went skiing?"

Audrey was shaking. I looked for Diego; he was still by the bumper cars. She clenched her fists so tightly, I thought she was going to punch me. "I wasn't in Switzerland, Henry."

"What?"

"I don't have family in Switzerland." Audrey bit her bottom lip and said, "My parents checked me in to a psychiatric hospital. I spent eight weeks there and then another month with my grandparents in Jersey."

I was tempted to believe she was lying to gain my sympathy, but going on an extended vacation after the death of her best friend had never seemed like an Audrey thing to do. I'd accepted it as the truth because she'd given me no reason to think she was lying. But this—that she'd been in a hospital—made sense. "Why didn't you tell me?"

"Jesse and I had a pact. He swore he'd call me if he were thinking about hurting himself. He called me that night, but I didn't answer. He was upset all the time and . . . I needed a night off." She paused. "I thought it was my fault he'd killed himself, and I didn't tell you because I couldn't bear for you to blame me too."

"Instead you ran away, and I blamed myself." The crowd blocking my view finally moved. Diego was talking to a short girl, perky with pink glasses and a blue stripe in her blond hair. I think she attended our school, but I didn't know her name. She covered her mouth with her hand when she laughed and kept touching Diego's arm. Diego hugged the girl and pointed toward me and Audrey. He probably wished he'd come with her and was likely plotting some way to ditch us.

"I needed to leave," Audrey said. "I was hurting so bad that I wanted to die too. It took me a long time to realize Jesse's suicide wasn't my fault. Don't you know how sorry I am? I don't know what else you want me to do."

Diego walked toward us; the crowds parted for him. He waved. I returned it robotically.

"I wish I'd killed myself instead of him." I kicked at the ground, blinking to keep from crying.

"I wish no one had died," Audrey said. "I wish Jesse were

here, singing and telling bad jokes and going on and on about some stupid book he read."

"But he's not," I said. "And it's our fault. Yours, mine. It's everyone's fault. Or no one's. Fuck. I don't know."

When Diego reached us, he stopped a foot away and said, "What's going on?"

Audrey wiped her eyes. "Sometimes I hate him, Henry. Mostly I miss him."

"Yeah."

"And I miss you."

I didn't know what to say. Audrey had been Jesse's friend first, but I missed her too. My feelings for her were buried under scar tissue built up over 103 lonely nights spent wondering what I'd done to drive away everyone I cared about. My father, Jesse, Audrey—they'd all abandoned me. Audrey had her reasons, and I could see that, but it didn't erase the pain. Not entirely. I stood there, my arms hanging limply at my sides, unsure what to do next.

Audrey glanced at her phone. "Maybe we should call it a day."

Diego furrowed his brow. "But we haven't even gone on the Ferris wheel yet." His voice was filled with a child's enthusiasm, a desire for life that Jesse's suicide had stolen from me and Audrey both.

The suggestion of a smile played on Audrey's lips. "What do you think, Space Boy?"

"Don't call me Space Boy."

Diego threw his arm around my shoulders and Audrey's, too, drawing us to him. His skin was warm and sweaty, but I didn't pull away. "No deal. You're our space boy, Space Boy."

The way Audrey looked at me—as if we could somehow fill the canyon that had grown between us with laughter and meet again in the middle—made me want to hug her and tell her how much I'd missed her, but I wasn't ready for that. Not yet.

"Fine," I said after a moment, "let's ride the goddamn Ferris wheel."

CTRL-ALT-DELETE

CURRENT DATE IS FRI, 29-01-2016

CURRENT TIME IS 11:11:51.78

THE COSMOS SIMULATION COMPUTING ENGINE MDR

VERSION 4.2 © COPYRIGHT COSMOS INTERNATIONAL

COMPUTING ENGINES

© COPYRIGHT MDR INC, 2010, 2013

C> DEL C:\SIMULATIONS\PLANETS\EARTHV3.SIML

C> ARE YOU SURE? Y/N

C> y

14 November 2015

Life isn't fair. That's what we tell kids when they're young and learn that there are no rules, or rather that there are but only suckers play by them. We don't reassure them or give them tools to help them cope with the reality of life; we simply pat them on the back and send them on their way, burdened with the knowledge that nothing they do will ever really matter. It can't if life's not fair.

If life were fair, the smartest among us would be the wealthiest and most popular. If life were fair, teachers would make millions, and scientists would be rock stars. If life were fair, we'd all gather around the TV to hear about the latest discovery coming out of CERN rather than to find out which Kardashian is pregnant. If life were fair, Jesse Franklin wouldn't have killed himself.

Life is not fair. And if life's not fair, then what's the point? Why bother with the rules? Why bother with life at all? Maybe that's the conclusion Jesse came to. Maybe he woke up one morning and decided he simply didn't want to play a game against people who refused to obey the rules.

I lay in bed all day Saturday, thinking about Jesse. Sometimes thinking about him made my body too heavy to move. The fragments of Jesse left behind were dense in my pockets and weighted me down, pulling me toward the center. I thought about Jesse and I listened to the sounds of my brother making a mess in the kitchen, and of my mother arguing with Nana, trying to get her ready to go visit my great-uncle Bob, who lives in a VA home in Miami. The sounds eventually quieted, and I knew I was alone. I still didn't move, not until the shadows grew longer across my bedroom and the bright morning light began to dim.

With great effort, I rose from bed and sat at my desk. Waited for my computer to fire up. I wanted to see Jesse, so I pulled up his SnowFlake page. The Internet is a strange place for the dead. All those digital pieces of you become frozen. You will never again post selfies with friends from the movie theater or while waiting for a concert to begin. Your friends will never tag you in another photo at a drunken party. You'll never update your page with your thoughts about how shitty South Florida drivers are or about how the lonely asshole in front of you at Target just bought twenty frozen dinners, an economy-size bag of cat food, and the box set of *Bones*; is using twenty coupons; and is paying in quarters. The Internet version of you becomes enshrined so that pathetic people like me can visit occasionally and try to pretend you're not really gone. That some small part of you lingers.

I've spent so much time on Jesse's SnowFlake page that I've practically memorized it. There's Jenny Leech's wall of text about how Jesse touched her life in ways he didn't even know, despite the extent of their relationship being the one class they shared in tenth grade. Coach VanBuren's picture of Jesse running a 440 against Dwyer High—Jesse lost that race, but from the picture you couldn't be faulted for believing that he was about to sail to victory. A hundred variations on, *I'll miss you, dude*, from people who probably stopped missing him before he was in the ground. Audrey's last post was a picture she'd taken on the sly of me and Jesse kissing by her pool. We'd spent the day turning lobster red, drinking iced tea, and laughing. I don't even remember what was so funny; I only remember thinking I'd suffocate before I stopped laughing.

That kiss wasn't our last. It was just another one of many, or so I'd thought. I think if I'd known Jesse was going to kill himself, I would have locked my arms around him and never let that kiss end. I would have pulled us into the pool together and died like that, his lips on mine, certain that I loved him and that he loved me.

The last thing I posted on Jesse's SnowFlake page was a picture of a book I wanted to buy the next time we went to Barnes & Noble. Jesse and I spent hours roaming the stacks, paging through books. It was our favorite place to go. Sometimes I wish I could post something new so the last thing I said to Jesse wasn't about buying *Naked Lunch*, which I only wrote because Audrey despises the Beat writers, but his profile is locked. I've said everything to Jesse I'll ever say.

When Jesse's SnowFlake page loaded, I knew something was wrong. Jenny's lame memorial was still there, as were all the semi-heartfelt good-byes from barely there acquaintances. But staring at me from inside of Jesse's pictures was an alien face. My alien face. Someone had Photoshopped the image of me on the floor of the locker room into every photo on Jesse's SnowFlake page. They hadn't simply vandalized his photos; they'd vandalized my memories. Whoever had done this had practically gone to Jesse's grave, dug him up, and desecrated his rotting body.

I collapsed in the chair. I couldn't take any more. January 29 wasn't soon enough; I needed the pain to end immediately.

Mom kept sleeping pills in her bathroom. One handful, and I could reunite with Jesse.

Beautiful resolve flowed through me. I imagined it was how Jesse had felt when he decided to hang himself. I wasn't scared; I wasn't conflicted. This was what I was meant to do. If nobody else was going to play by the rules, then neither was I.

I flung open my bedroom door and nearly bowled Zooey over. She was standing in the doorway with her fist raised like she was about to knock. I stumbled into her, and we fell into the wall. I babbled an apology and tried to get away, but she was talking too, and rubbing her swollen belly.

"I didn't think anyone was home."

Zooey smoothed out her long violet shirt. Her face looked fuller, and sometimes her belly resembled a beer gut rather than a baby, but she glowed as if her entire body were bragging to the world that she was growing a life inside of her. "Charlie's working at the house with my dad, and he asked me to get him his tools, but I don't know where they are and I thought you might help?"

I nodded and slid past Zooey into Charlie's room. Clothes were flung everywhere, the blinds were shut, and it smelled like sweaty feet. It was a miracle Zooey could stand to sleep there. Charlie's toolbox was in his closet. I handed it to her.

"Thanks." She turned to leave but stopped and stared at me for a moment. It felt like she knew what I'd been on my way to do. Like it was tattooed on my skin that I was a weakling, a loser, that I was planning to give up and die. "I can give you a ride somewhere if you want."

Zooey and I didn't know each other well. She was my brother's girlfriend. I'd seen her sneak from his room to the bathroom in her underthings, and she was carrying his kid, but it's not like we were friends. "Where?"

"Wherever you want. I'm not in a hurry."

If I stayed home, I was going to end up swallowing those pills, but the certainty I'd felt minutes earlier was retreating. I'd loaded Jesse's SnowFlake page because I needed to feel close to him, and they'd taken that away from me, but the need hadn't abated. I needed Jesse more than ever.

"Can you drive me to the bookstore?"

"Sure."

I carried the toolbox for her. "Okay. Yeah. Let's go."

Zooey drove a little blue Volvo that was so old, it still had a tape deck and crank windows. The inside smelled like vanilla or roses—I couldn't tell which, maybe both—and her music collection included every terrible power ballad in existence. Worse yet, she knew all the words to every song.

"Are you excited about being an uncle?" Zooey asked after a while. She looked at me until the persistent thump of the road dividers told her she was about to get us killed.

"I guess. Are you excited to become a mom?"

I expected Zooey to answer yes immediately, but she didn't. She kept her hands on the steering wheel and her eyes on the road. "Don't tell anyone, but I'm fucking scared as hell."

"Of giving birth or the stuff that comes after?"

"All of it," Zooey said. "I constantly worry about whether I'm taking enough vitamins or the right kind of vitamins. I worry about whether the pot I smoked before I knew I was pregnant hurt the baby. My older brother has schizophrenia, and I worry it might be genetic and I might pass it to my child. Every action I took in the past and that I'll take in the future could impact my baby, and that scares the shit out of me."

Maybe that should have shocked me, but I admired Zooey for admitting those things to me. "You're going to be a great mother."

"It helps knowing I won't have to do it alone. I don't think I've seen Charlie this excited about anything."

"Listen," I said. "I love my brother because he's my brother, but he's going to be a terrible father."

I waited for Zooey to yell at me or slap me or tell me I was wrong. Instead she giggled. Maybe it was the pregnancy hormones.

"I'm serious," I said. "Honestly, I don't even understand what you see in him."

The bookstore was a twenty-minute drive, and the only way I could have escaped the car would have been to throw open the door and leap into the street. Don't think I didn't consider it.

"I knew Charlie in high school. Did you know that?"

"I thought you met in college."

"We did," Zooey said, "but we were in the same grade in high school. We didn't really know each other, but I knew of him. I thought he was a jerk. He ruined homecoming by streaking across the football field with his buddies during the parade."

I leaned my head against the window. "That's my brother."

"Do you know what changed my mind?"

"No," I said, but I was sure she was going to tell me.

Zooey smiled, maybe at the memory, maybe from gas. "We had college algebra together. Our professor was new, an older woman who had decided to change careers late in life. She was a pretty terrible professor, but she tried hard.

"There were these guys who talked through every class.

When Dr. Barnett stuttered, they'd laugh and imitate her. She ignored them, but it was bad. One class, she was reviewing for an exam, and the guys were watching videos on their phones. Like, not even trying to pretend they cared about the class. Dr. Barnett asked them to shut off their phones, but they ignored her."

I glanced at Zooey. "Let me guess: Charlie told they guys to stop, and that's how you knew he was an okay guy."

Zooey laughed so hard, she nearly drove off the road. I clutched the door for dear life. "God, no," she said. "Charlie was one of the guys cutting up."

"And *that* made you decide he was worth dating?"

"It was after class. I'd left my graphing calculator behind, and I went back to get it. I saw Dr. Barnett sitting at her desk, crying. Charlie was still in there. He asked her why she was crying, and she told him she didn't think she was cut out to be a professor. Your brother told her she was the first teacher who'd ever made him understand math. I don't know if it was true—she really was a terrible teacher—but he never cut up in class again after that." Zooey was quiet for a moment, and I didn't have anything to add. Then she said, "Charlie doesn't always do what's right, and he can be insensitive, but he tries, Henry, which is more than I can say for a lot of people."

"He can try all he wants," I said. "He's still going to be a terrible father."

Zooey glanced at me again, and the entire car swerved to the right, barely remaining on the road. "I need a burger." Without another word, she detoured into the nearest McDonald's, bought herself two cheeseburgers, and forced a chocolate milk shake on me despite my protests because, in her words, "Milk shakes make the world seem less shitty."

When we reached the bookstore, Zooey pulled in front of the doors to drop me off. "I can pick you up later if you want."

"I'll find a ride."

"You're wrong about Charlie, you know."

"I wish I were." I started to open the door, stopped, and said, "When things got tough, my dad left. I needed him, and he abandoned me—walked away and never looked back— and one day Charlie's going to do that to you and that little parasite you're carrying."

Again I waited for Zooey to smack me or scream, but her expression was serene and never wavered. "Can I tell you something, Henry?"

Seeing as I'd just trashed her future kid's father, I didn't feel like I could say no. "Sure."

"When I found out I was pregnant, I wanted to abort. I wanted to finish college and start a career, and I thought a baby would derail my hard work." Zooey's voice was soft and soothing. "I made the appointment at Planned Parenthood before I even told your brother."

"Obviously, you changed your mind."

"No," Zooey said, locking her eyes onto mine. "Charlie changed it. He told me our life wouldn't be easy, that we'd struggle to pay our bills and put food on the table, that we'd argue and fight, and that there was a good chance we'd end up hating each other."

I rolled my eyes. "How could you resist a pitch like that?"

Zooey smiled. "But he also told me that no matter what happened, we would love our baby like no parents had ever loved a baby in the history of the world. He said he would sell every last thing he owned to give our child the life it deserved." She stopped speaking for a moment, but I could tell by the way she bit her lip that she wasn't done. "Even though I agreed to have the baby, I still wasn't sure until Charlie took the job with my father."

"That's not commitment; it's survival."

"Your brother gave up his dream for me, Henry."

The pregnancy was making Zooey crazy. "Charlie doesn't have any dreams that don't involve naked cheerleaders and muscle cars."

Zooey frowned. "Do you really not know?"

"Know what?"

"Charlie was enrolled in the firefighting academy."

"Bullshit."

"He gave it up to work with my father because he didn't want to risk getting hurt and not being around for the baby." Zooey seemed to be speaking both too slow and too fast. I heard what she said, but I couldn't process it.

"I guess I don't really know my brother at all." I got out of the car and wandered into the bookstore in a daze. Charlie had secretly wanted to be a firefighter—something he'd never mentioned—but he'd given it up for a fetus. The little parasite wasn't even born yet, and Charlie was already rearranging his life. That's love. That's what you do when you love someone. Maybe Jesse hadn't really loved me at all.

When Jesse and I visited the bookstore together, I'd disappear into the science section, lost in books about quantum mechanics and space travel and theories I hardly understood but that fascinated me anyway. I'd lose track of time and Jesse, and have to go up and down every aisle because he couldn't stand to remain in the same place. I loved science, but he loved everything. Sometimes I'd find him in home improvement, sometimes in philosophy, sometimes in fiction, his arms straining under the weight of all the books he was considering buying. It was always a surprise to turn a corner and see him standing there, totally immersed in whatever he was curious about that day.

As I wandered among the stacks, I kept hoping I'd stumble upon him reading about the life of Rimbaud or searching the pages of cooking books for a great lemon meringue pie recipe. The most upsetting part isn't that I never found him; it's that he was everywhere.

"Henry?"

I dropped the book I was holding. I didn't even remember taking it off the shelf. Audrey stood at the end of the aisle. She rushed toward me, grabbed the book off the floor, and looked at the cover. "Are you taking up cake decorating?"

"No."

Audrey and I hadn't talked much since the fair. "Looking for something in particular?"

I shook my head. "I just needed . . . Forget it."

"What?"

"I wanted to feel close to Jesse." I stared at my feet. "It's stupid."

"Not really."

"Whatever," I said. "I'll see you later."

Audrey stood aside to let me pass, but before I turned the corner, she said, "Wanna get a cookie?"

I stopped, turned around. "What?"

"A cookie. I can drive us across the street to the mall. If

we time it right, we can get some fresh from the oven."

"I don't know."

"You can't hate me forever, Henry."

"I can try."

"But if you come with me, you can hate me *and* eat cookies. Win-win."

I rolled my eyes. "Fine."

Audrey grinned. "It's a date."

"It's a cookie."

"It's a cookie date."

"So we were making out, and my nose was running a little, but I had it in my mind that if I stopped kissing Jesse, he'd realize I was a loser and never want to kiss me again, so I ignored it and snogged on. I'm pretty sure we made out for hours, but when we turned on the lights, I screamed because Jesse's face was covered in blood."

"Gross!" Audrey ate her cookie as we sat outside the entrance of the mall.

"Turns out I'd had a bloody nose. It was smeared over both of our faces." We'd gotten six cookies to split, and they'd been gooey and delicious at first, but all the sugar was beginning to sour my stomach.

Audrey laughed, and if I closed my eyes, I could imagine

Jesse was with us, swapping stories and cracking up at our lame jokes. "Jesse never told me about that."

"I swore him to secrecy. It's not the sort of thing I wanted getting around."

"I won't tell a soul." Silence fell, and we both turned our attention to our uneaten cookies. The conversation sputtered along in fits and starts; one second everything was good, the next uncomfortable as the past overwhelmed us. "I've missed you, Henry."

The statement stopped me because I knew she was waiting for me to say it back. To tell her that I missed her, and I had, but it used to be me and Audrey and Jesse, and we were still incomplete.

"What was it like?" I asked.

"What was what like?"

"The hospital?"

Audrey stood and walked toward the parking lot, stopping when she reached the curb. Her shoes dragged on the ground like her feet were too heavy to lift properly. I brushed the crumbs off my lap and followed. I wasn't sure whether she was going to answer, but I gave her the space to decide. "It was lonely," she said. "But it was like this whole other world where you didn't exist and my parents didn't exist and Jesse wasn't dead. Nothing seemed real there. Time was blurry, and maybe that was because of the meds they had me on, but I think it was just me. I needed a pocket of space to curl up in and wait out the pain of losing my best friend."

I leaned to the side, bumped Audrey's shoulder with my arm to let her know I was there. "I thought you left because you blamed me."

"I did," Audrey said. "I mean, I didn't leave because of that, but I did blame you for a while."

"Oh."

Audrey looked at me. The golden hour of the setting sun cast Audrey's skin in bronze. "Jesse loved you so much, Henry, but he was terrified of never being good enough for you. You told him constantly how perfect he was, but Jesse wasn't perfect, and he was worried that if you ever saw his flaws, you'd leave him."

Those words hurt more than being kicked in the testicles in the locker room. "I knew Jesse wasn't perfect. He exaggerated everything. If he were on the phone with someone for an hour, he'd say it'd been five. If he bought one shirt, he'd tell me he bought twenty. And he had terrible taste in books. He said his favorite book was *The Catcher in the Rye*, but he had a copy of *Twilight* under his bed with pages so battered, he must've read it a hundred times."

Audrey leaned her head against my arm, and I didn't

move away. "I know, and I don't blame you now. I just . . . I had to leave."

"You didn't have to leave me."

"I know."

"How come you never told me about Jesse hurting himself?"

Audrey sighed and sat on the brick wall of the decorative fountain near the bus stop. I sat beside her. The water gurgled behind us, and wishes glittered at the bottom of the pool. She looked fragile right then in a way I'd never seen her look before. I felt I had the power to break her in that moment, to destroy her utterly. A few months ago I might have done it, but it didn't seem important anymore. I think Audrey Dorn was punishing herself worse than I ever could.

"Jesse was mine." Tears rolled down Audrey's cheeks, but I doubted she was aware of them. "He was mine before he was yours, but he'd never given me all of himself. Then you came along and got everything I ever wanted."

"You didn't just love Jesse," I said. "You were in love with him, weren't you?"

Audrey sniffled. She dug a tissue out of her purse and wiped her nose. "I hated when Jesse hurt, when he cried, and when he cut himself, but he only showed those parts of himself to me. Oh, I rationalized that I didn't tell you because Jesse made me swear not to or because I didn't seriously believe he'd really hurt himself, but deep down I knew it was because I wanted something of Jesse that belonged only to me."

If Audrey had admitted that immediately after Jesse died, I never would have forgiven her. But the year between us had given me the distance I needed to understand. I even envied a little that she knew Jesse in a way I never did or would.

"Don't hate me," she said.

"I think I would have done the same thing."

"Jesse's parents hate me. They blame me."

"I don't hate you, Audrey."

Though we weren't touching, I still felt the tension she'd been holding all those months drain from her body, and I realized how difficult it was for Audrey to admit the truth to me without knowing if I'd ever forgive her. Only, there was nothing to forgive. Audrey may not have told me about Jesse's troubles, but I had willfully ignored their signs. I'd let myself believe the lies because it was easier than digging for the truth.

"I don't hate you either, Henry."

I stood and put my hands in my pockets as the last of the day's light retreated below the horizon. "Then that makes one of us."

24 November 2015

Lunch raged around us, but I was too absorbed watching Diego and Audrey argue to notice anything outside of our bubble.

"Only an idiot could prefer Matt Smith to David Tennant." Audrey was so worked up, her nostrils flared and her eyes had gone full-bore crazy.

Diego remained calm, which only seemed to infuriate Audrey more. "Then I'm an idiot." He popped a chip into his mouth, chewed, and swallowed, while holding his free hand in the air to let Audrey know he wasn't done speaking. "I'll give you that Tennant brought a gravitas to the Doctor that grounded the insanity of the ludicrous situations he got himself into, but Matt Smith didn't *play* the Doctor, he *was* the Doctor."

"You guys know I've got no clue what you're talking about, right?"

Audrey and Diego both turned to look at me like I'd climbed atop the table, dropped trou, and hosed them down.

"You've never seen *Doctor Who*?" Diego glanced at Audrey. "You have failed as a best friend."

"Hey, I only got hooked last year," Audrey said. "There was nothing to do at my grandma's house except watch a ton of TV."

"How'd you watch it, Diego?" I asked. "I thought you didn't have a television."

Diego focused on eating his sandwich, chewing each bite deliberately. His smile and laughter vanished like he'd blown a fuse, and an impenetrable wall rose between us.

"Look." Audrey pointed toward the door, where Marcus McCoy stood sweeping the cafeteria with his eyes. His forearm muscles bulged from clenching his fists, and his lips were twisted into a snarl. I'd spent enough time with Marcus to know that it took skill to make him seriously angry. He was rich and popular, which insulated him from the effects of most humiliation. He started walking and wound through the crowd until he reached a table occupied by Larry Owens, Shane Thorpe, Tania Lewis, Missi Lizneski, and Zac Newton. Everyone was watching Marcus—taking pictures and video with their phones—and I had to stand to see over their heads. He was yelling at Zac, but his words were lost in the excited murmuring of the lunch crowd. Zac's shorter than Marcus, but he's on the wrestling team and built like an inverted pyramid. He got in Marcus's face, using his weight to bully him backward.

Marcus sucker-punched Zac in the jaw and followed with a left to the nose that sent him reeling into the table. Zac's friends rushed to help him, but Marcus didn't even wait to see if Zac was going to retaliate before he stormed out of the cafeteria. Mrs. Francesco chased after him while Mr. Baker cleared a path to Zac.

"What the hell was that?" I asked. Zac's nose was gushing blood, and Mr. Baker was trying to stanch the flow with a handful of napkins. If I hadn't witnessed it, I wouldn't have believed Marcus capable of breaking Zac Newton's nose.

"You didn't hear?"

"Hear what?" A small knot of students had gathered around Zac and Mr. Baker, offering ice and towels. It took the combined strength of Larry, Shane, and Mr. Brown to keep Zac from running after Marcus.

"Someone smashed the windows of Marcus's car," Audrey said. "Obviously, he thinks it was Zac."

"Do you think it was Zac?" I asked. Audrey's only

answer was a shrug. "Why the hell would he have busted Marcus's windows?"

Audrey's voice rang with a note of satisfaction. "Because he's dating Natalie Carter—*was* dating Natalie. I'm not too clear on the current status of Zac and Natalie's rocky romance."

"That's no reason to take it out on the car."

Mr. Baker led Zac out of the cafeteria, and I sat back down. Audrey was gathering her trash and babbling about how Zac learned Natalie and Marcus had hooked up because someone posted pictures from Marcus's party on their SnowFlake page, and when Zac confronted her about it in the quad before classes, she hadn't denied it, reducing Zac to tears.

Diego hadn't spoken since the beginning of the afternoon show. I kicked him under the table, gave him a smile. He barely returned it.

"You have econ with Zac, don't you, Diego?" I asked. "Do you think he did it?"

"Don't know. Don't care. I'm just glad Marcus got what he deserved." Diego picked up his tray, dumped his trash, and returned to his seat. He didn't say another word until lunch ended.

"Everything all right?" I asked Diego as we walked to study hall. He seemed preoccupied. "Diego?"

"What?"

"I asked if you were okay."

Diego shrugged. "Sure. Why wouldn't I be?"

"You've been somewhere else since lunch."

He shifted his backpack from his left to his right shoulder. He smiled, but there was something off about it, like milk that was about to turn. "Really, I'm good."

I had no reason not to believe him, but my gut told me something was wrong. Maybe he wasn't lying, but he wasn't being entirely truthful, either. It reminded me too much of the way Jesse had deflected my questions and pretended that life was wonderful even when it wasn't. "If something's wrong, you can talk to me."

"It's nothing. Drop it, okay?"

"Sorry." We got to my class and stopped by the door. "You don't need to walk me to class every day."

"It's not a problem."

"I can't believe Zac trashed Marcus's car. Pretty ballsy move."

Diego glanced at his watch. "I guess. Listen, I can't give you a ride home today."

"It's cool."

"You sure?"

"Yeah."

"See you later then." He took off down the hall and disappeared into the crowd, leaving me to wonder what the hell I'd done.

Audrey's dog yapped at the waves and skittered backward as the water rushed toward it. The tiny terror was barely the size of a football, and answered to the name Plath.

"Aren't you afraid she's going to drown or be eaten by a shark?" I asked as we walked, the setting sun burning up the sky behind us. The daytime crowds had disappeared, leaving behind a few strays desperate to soak up what little light remained.

"I wish." Audrey glared at Plath with derision. "Come on, stupid mutt!"

Plath ignored her and barked at the water as if she thought she could annoy it into submission.

"My mom only adopted her because the Becketts have one." She rolled her eyes. "They got a Mercedes, Mom got a better Mercedes. They rented a house in Colorado for the winter, Mom bought a summer house in Martha's Vineyard. It's like she doesn't know what to do with the money, so she buys whatever the neighbors buy."

"But you got that sweet ride."

"Only because Stella Beckett got one for her sweet sixteen."

I laughed at the thought of Mrs. Dorn keeping a tally of everything her neighbors purchased, and tried not to be jealous that Audrey got a car because of a game of wealthy one-upmanship. "Is she working on anything?"

Audrey shook her head. "She's decided she's going to write a book. Only, instead of actually writing, she spends her time buying things she hopes will turn her into a writer. First it was the expensive laptop, then she needed to redecorate the study, and now she's convinced that real writers do it long-hand and with a fountain pen. And Dad's so bored, he joined the homeowner's association so he can harass people whose bushes need trimming or roofs need reshingling. I don't know who they are anymore."

Growing up, I'd admired the Dorns. While my parents were busy slamming doors, her parents ate Sunday dinners and baked cookies together. They were the picture of a perfect family. I suppose even perfect pictures fade.

"How's Nana?"

I dug my toes into the sand. "It's rough, you know? She looks like the same person, sounds like the same person, and sometimes she even acts like the same person, but she's not, and every day it gets worse." Plath rolled around in the sand in front of Audrey. "Her health is great—cancer's gone, heart's good, no other real problems—but her mind is a balloon with a slow leak. Sometimes I think . . ."

Audrey looked at me when I didn't finish. "What, Henry?"

"Nothing." But it wasn't nothing, and I think Audrey was the only person I could admit it to. "Sometimes, I think Nana would be better off dead. I mean, if I got to where I couldn't take care of myself or didn't recognize my own family . . . what's the point?"

We walked farther down the beach, the light growing dimmer. The moon had already risen, but it was still too bright for stars. "Do you think that's how Jesse felt?" I asked.

Audrey's shoulders turned inward slightly, and she became smaller. "Jesse was sick, and I think he just wanted to end the pain."

"I guess."

"Do you feel that way, Henry?"

I couldn't tell Audrey the truth, partly because I knew she'd feel obligated to tell my mom, but mostly because she didn't deserve that kind of burden. "It doesn't matter either way."

"The end of the world?" Audrey glanced at me, and I nodded. I don't think she ever believed I'd been abducted, though she had always humored me because of Jesse and had laughed when I told her about the button. It's not that she doesn't believe in the possibility of aliens or other life in the universe; she simply doesn't think it's plausible that beings from another planet would travel hundreds or thousands of light-years to abduct cows and teenage boys. I can't blame her for her skepticism; sometimes I'm not sure I believe it myself. "How do you think it's going to happen?"

"Superbug, nuclear war, man-made black hole, asteroid. I have a lot of theories."

"You've clearly put some thought into this."

"I'm surprised we haven't wiped ourselves out already." I sat down in the sand and pulled my legs up to my chest. Plath crawled into my lap and licked my chin. "If I save us, who's to say another disaster won't come along and obliterate us anyway? I sort of feel like I'm doing everyone a favor. Take Charlie and Zooey, for instance. I'm saving them the pain of raising a kid in this fucked-up world."

The dampness from the sand seeped through my shorts. I threw a stick down the beach for Plath to chase. Audrey plopped down beside me and leaned her head on my shoulder. "Did Diego convince you to go to his barbecue?"

"Mom and Zooey are planning a whole Thanksgiving meal, and either one would castrate me if I tried to bail."

"Ouch."

"Right?" I paused then said, "Do you think Diego could have broken Marcus's car windows?"

"No. Why would you think that?"

I struggled with how to explain it without coming off paranoid. "You should have seen him after I got attacked in the shower. I know I don't know him that well, but I've never seen him so angry."

"Diego's a good guy. He was worried about you, that's all."

"It was more than that. He told me this story about how he took a beating from his father to protect his sister, and I don't know, Audrey. I feel like his whole the-world-is-beautiful-and-we-should-be-happy-to-be-alive shtick is just an act."

"He's not Jesse."

"You're right," I said. "I know you're right, but I can't shake the feeling he's the one who smashed Marcus's windows. And that's scary, you know? Who does shit like that? It's psycho."

Audrey cleared her throat. "Speaking of Marcus. Have you talked to him lately?"

I shook my head. "No. Why?"

Audrey whistled when Plath wandered too close to the water, but the stupid dog ignored her. If she got pulled out to sea, I was not going in after her. "No reason," Audrey said in a singsong way that meant she absolutely had a reason.

"Spill it."

"Well, he got suspended for punching Zac, and Cheyenne

said that he's going off the rails. The rich boy trinity: booze, pills, and meaningless sex."

It shouldn't have surprised me, but it did. I'd seen him eat the occasional oxy he'd stolen from his mom, but his drug use had been strictly recreational. "Why are you telling me?"

"I thought you'd want to know."

"Well, I don't."

"Okay." Audrey paused for a moment. "I know you liked him, Henry."

"We were only fooling around."

Audrey snapped her fingers in front of my face to get my attention. It was getting too dark to see her expression, but I didn't need light to feel the intensity of her stare. "You can't lie to me."

I tried to shake my head, to tell her that none of it had meant anything, but I couldn't. I dug at the sand, unable to face her. "He took my mind off Jesse, but I didn't worry about having feelings for him because I thought I'd never have feelings for anyone again."

"Are you in love with him?"

"No!"

"You wouldn't be the first person to fall for a jerk, Henry."

I dug the hole until it was so deep that the sand at the bottom was wet and cold. "After Jesse's funeral, after everyone else disappeared or went back to their normal lives, Marcus was there for me."

"He's an asshole who doesn't deserve you." Audrey took my hand, kissed the top of it, and held it to her chest. When she let go, she pushed my mountain of sand into the hole and packed it down.

"His parents put a lot of pressure on him," I said. "And his friends—"

"Don't you dare make excuses for him, Henry Denton."

"I'm not."

"You are!"

I raked my hair with my free hand as I wrestled with how to explain what I meant. It was so clear in my mind, but when I tried to say it out loud, it fell apart. "All of this . . . all of them . . . it matters to him. What they think matters to him. Their opinions form the foundation of Marcus McCoy. Without them, he's nothing."

Audrey tut-tutted. "You know that's not true."

"He believes it." Most people hadn't seen Marcus the way I had. They'd never seen beyond the facade. Even I'd only glimpsed a little of who he truly was, but I worried that, the longer he wore it, the easier it would be to forget that the mask wasn't the truth. Marcus wasn't a lost cause yet, but convincing Audrey of that was.

"As far as I'm concerned, he's a waste of good hair."

I made gagging sounds. "I've already forgiven you. You don't have to keep insulting him on my account."

"I'm serious!" Audrey began giggling, and Plath took that to mean it was time to play. I hopped up and ran down the beach, letting the yappy beast chase me until I was out of breath. When we returned to Audrey, she was brushing sand off her jeans, hugging her knees to her chest. "I know it was Marcus who attacked you in the showers."

Plath was still barking at me and trying to bite my fingers, but I stopped cold. "You can't tell anyone, Audrey."

"Why shouldn't I?"

"Because it's not worth it."

"If he hurts you again, I'll tell everyone."

"He won't. Anyway, it's the end of the world. What does it matter?"

"It matters, Henry." She clipped the leash to Plath's collar, and we started walking back toward the road. The bright lights from the cars sped past like comets.

I wanted to believe Audrey, I really did, but I knew better.

Mom was parked in the driveway, sitting in her old Buick, smoking and listening to the oldies station on the radio. She's always had a soft spot for Motown. I stood quietly and listened to her sing along with "You Can't Hurry Love" in her raspy but beautiful voice. When the song ended, I cleared my throat so I didn't scare her.

"Henry?"

"Hey, Ma."

Mom scrambled in her seat, waving her hands around. It took a second for me to realize she wasn't smoking a cigarette. "What're you doing sneaking up on me?"

"Are you high?"

"No." Silence. "Yes." Mom climbed out of the car, shame-faced. She was still wearing her waitressing uniform, and the puffy skin under her deep-set eyes sagged heavily. I snaked the joint from her and took a hit. The weed was cheap and burned my throat. "Henry!"

"I won't tell if you won't."

Mom chewed on that for a moment and then shrugged. We sat down on the driveway behind the car and passed the joint back and forth in silence. After a while Mom said, "I'm glad you're spending time with Audrey again. She makes you smile."

"I wish you'd smile more."

"Things are hard right now."

It felt like I hadn't talked to my mom in a long time. She was always so angry or exhausted. "Why don't you try cooking again? You could easily snag a good job."

Rather than snapping at me like usual, she took a hit off the joint and held the smoke in for what felt like forever. When she exhaled, it was like she'd blown the last dusty remnants of her hope out with it. "I can't do that anymore, Henry."

"Why not? Your food is amazing, and you love cooking." The pot loosened my tongue, gave me the courage to be honest. "You haven't been the same since Dad took off."

Mom sniffed and then giggled; I couldn't tell whether she was crying or laughing. "Your father took the best parts of me when he left."

"That's not true, and you know it."

"You don't understand, Henry."

"Don't bullshit me, Mom."

"Watch your mouth." Mom scowled and flicked the joint into the grass. I'd seen Nana use the same look. It was probably passed from mother to daughter like that horrible meatloaf recipe.

It killed me to think Mom was so willing to give up because Dad had disappeared. If the world was going to end in sixty-six days, she deserved to enjoy every last one of them. "Dad might have helped you see the best parts of yourself, but they were always there, and no one can take them away."

Mom clenched her jaw, and I swore for a moment she was

going to slap me or start sobbing or shut down completely and never leave the driveway. Instead she said, "If that's true, how am I supposed to see them now that he's gone?"

"Get a mirror."

"Chain of Fools" played on the radio, and I crawled around the side of the car to crank it up. Mom didn't sing, but I leaned my head on her shoulder as we sat in the driveway and listened together.

26 November 2015

My Thanksgiving nightmare began with family pictures.

Mom forced me and Charlie to wear white button-down oxford shirts tucked into jeans, while she, Nana, and Zooey wore white sundresses. We looked like a cult on our way to the beach, where Mom was convinced we'd find the perfect backdrop somewhere among the dunes. I spent the entire walk trying to devise an excuse to escape family dinner so I could go to Diego's barbecue. He'd sent me a couple of texts, but I hadn't written back.

"Why are we doing this again?" I asked.

"Because I want a nice photo of us all together." Mom had been chain-smoking all morning, puffing and ashing with violent flicks. Bonding over illegal drugs hadn't magically solved our problems. Mom hadn't woken up the next day and decided to quit waitressing. However, she had planned a more elaborate Thanksgiving dinner than usual, so maybe that was something.

"Well, I think this is really special," Zooey said. She carried her sandals dangling from the ends of her fingers. "And when we take this picture next year, we'll have little Milo or Mia with us."

"Mia or Milo? Please don't saddle your child with either of those names. It's already starting at a disadvantage having Charlie as a father."

Charlie lunged at me, but I hopped out of the way. Zooey chuckled. "We're only trying out names to see how they fit. Nothing is certain."

Nothing was certain. Not even that we'd be alive next year. Last night I dreamed I was on the ship, but rather than aliens, I was surrounded by Mom, Nana, Charlie and Zooey, Audrey, Diego, Marcus. Even Officer Sandoval was there. They were screaming at me to press the button, but none of them could offer a convincing reason why I should. And we were all speaking Latin because, apparently, I'm fluent in Latin in my dreams.

After walking for twenty minutes, Mom finally found her perfect spot. Tufts of sea oats waved gently in the breeze, and the blue sky was smeared with white clouds to match our outfits.

"Mother, I want you in front." Mom directed us into position as she set up the tripod and camera. When Charlie attempted to help her, she snapped at him. "And Henry, don't forget to put your tongue behind your teeth when you smile; otherwise, you look goofy."

"Where's your father?" Nana squawked, and each time she did, Charlie whispered something into her ear to calm her, but it never stuck. Nana was lost in time, and I wished I could have traveled with her. Sometimes her ignorance of the present was a blessing, whether she knew it or not.

"Ready? Let's try not to screw this up." Mom pressed the timer on the camera and dashed to take her place between me and Charlie.

"Say 'cruel and unusual punishment,'" I muttered.

Charlie laughed and ruined the picture, and Mom dressed me down in front of the strangers who'd gathered to witness our group humiliation.

By the time Mom was satisfied she'd gotten the shot she wanted, my shirt was stuck to my back, and I'd been forced to wear a fake smile for so long that my lips were stiff. We were a dour group that trudged back to the house, and the first thing Mom did when we arrived was uncork a bottle of wine, fill the glasses, and pass them around.

It was a tradition in our house to binge on bad disaster

movies instead of football or parades. Watching the world end in various, ever more ludicrous ways sanded the jagged edges off the day. We made it through *Runaway Gamma-Rays* and three bottles of wine before Mom started yelling.

"What did you do? I can't believe this! Are you stupid?"

Dulled by wine and lethargy, my reflexes were sluggish, but I scrambled off the couch and stumbled into the kitchen. Black smoke belched from the oven, and Nana stood beside it, looking dazed. "You were cooking it wrong. I added salt to your stuffing too. You never add enough salt."

I grabbed Nana by the crook of her arm and led her out of the way while Mom threw open the oven door, releasing a gob of smoke that immediately set off the smoke alarm. The pulsating squeal made my brain throb.

Charlie shoved past me, frantic and confused. When he saw the blackened turkey smoldering in the oven, he grabbed two dish towels and hauled the bird into the backyard, where he unceremoniously lobbed it into the canal.

"What the hell are you doing?" Mom screamed, following after him.

"Keeping the house from burning down."

"I could have salvaged that!"

Charlie dropped the roasting pan. "A Thanksgiving miracle couldn't have saved that."

Mom was shaking with rage. "Will someone shut that goddamn alarm off!"

Zooey said, "I'll open the windows," and tugged my sleeve, motioning for me to help. I climbed onto a chair and yanked the alarm out of the ceiling, but it kept shrieking until I popped the battery out as well. The house was smoky and smelled like charred turkey. Zooey tried to laugh it off after she'd opened the windows and brought the fan from Charlie's bedroom into the kitchen to help blow the smoke out. "All we do at my house is smile politely and trade passive-aggressive compliments."

I peeked my head outside but wished I hadn't. Mom and Charlie were going at it for the whole neighborhood to hear.

"I'm not the one who cranked the oven to five hundred degrees!" The muscles on the sides of Charlie's throat bulged, and he was sweating profusely.

"You had one job, Charlie! One job! Keep Mother away from the food. You couldn't even do that, and now we have no dinner. Thank you. Thank you very much."

Charlie stormed inside and pulled Zooey toward the front door. "I'm done. We're going to your parents' house."

"But they're not expecting us until three."

"Then we'll be early."

Nana shuffled to me and held my arm. I didn't notice

she was crying until she sniffled and wiped her nose with a crumpled tissue she produced from her pocket. "I only meant to help."

"I know, Nana, but I don't think anyone can help this family."

Diego arrived to pick me up wearing a tacky Hawaiian shirt and Bermuda shorts, and didn't look embarrassed by either. "Is there a dress code?" I asked.

"Yes, but don't worry, I can loan you a shirt." Diego waited until I'd buckled my seat belt before taking off.

I didn't know if Diego was joking about the dress code, but I would have worn clown shoes and a tutu to get out of my house. After Charlie and Zooey left, Nana passed out on the couch and Mom disappeared into her bedroom with a bottle of Chardonnay. "I've never been to a Thanksgiving barbecue before."

Diego hadn't stopped grinning since I'd gotten in the car. I even thought I'd heard him grinning over the phone when I'd called him to ask if the invitation was still open. "It's Viv's anti-Thanksgiving celebration."

"Who's going to be there?"

"Mostly Viv's work friends. They're cool, though."

"Anything's better than my house."

"Yeah, so what happened?"

As we drove to Diego's house, I told him the whole miserable story. It sounded worse the second time. "The problem is, I think my mom might be right about putting Nana in a nursing home. What happens when she actually *does* burn down the house? What if she decides to cook while we're sleeping, and we die of smoke inhalation?"

"All the more reason not to press that button, yeah?"

"I guess." Except, when I was with Diego, the button was the last thing on my mind.

We pulled up to a ranch house painted the color of key lime pie. The shutters were white with pineapple cutouts in the center, and the front yard was meticulously manicured. It threw off a vibe that said: *Come in! Relax! Don't track dirt on the floors!*

Diego parked on the swale and motioned for me to follow him inside. It was even more colorful than the outside. The living room felt like a Key West bed-and-breakfast, complete with a stuffed sailfish mounted on the wall above a wicker sofa set upholstered in palm-tree-patterned fabric. Everything—the lamps, the entertainment center, the picture frames—was island themed. The only thing missing was steel drum music in the background.

"This is . . . unique."

Diego chuckled. "Viv kinda went overboard, but she wanted it to look as different from home as possible." I didn't know what a typical house in Colorado looked like, but it probably wasn't this. "Viv? You home?"

"Valentín? Is that you?"

"Valentín?"

"Don't ask." Diego led me into the kitchen. The counters were loaded with cut vegetables, and Diego's sister stood by the sink, shucking corn. She was tall and curvy, with a devious gleam in her eyes. She and Diego looked so different from each other, and yet there was no mistaking they were siblings.

"Viv, this is Henry. Henry, my sister, Viviana." Diego stole a cherry tomato from a ceramic bowl, and Viv smacked his ear.

Viviana smiled and offered me her hand, which was damp but strong. "Nice to meet you, Henry Denton. Valentín never shuts up about you."

"Why do you keep calling him Valentín?"

"That's his name."

"My *name* is Diego."

Viviana rolled her eyes as she checked a pot of something on the stove. She moved like an acrobat but spoke like a car salesperson. "Your middle name is Diego." Her face tightened, and a look passed between them. "May I have a moment alone with my brother?"

"You can hang out in my room." Diego motioned toward the living room. "It's down the hall. I'll be there in a minute."

I'd stumbled into something I didn't understand. Maybe I should have stayed home, where I could have hidden in my room and pretended it was any day other than Thanksgiving, but I was already there, so I walked back through the living room and down the hall, peeking into each room. There was a tidy bathroom decorated with peach seashells, a bedroom with a four-poster bed that I suspected belonged to Viviana, and two rooms at the end of the hall. Both doors were closed, so I chose the one on the right.

It was definitely not Diego's bedroom. The smell of paint and turpentine blanketed the air, and diffuse light streamed through the windows. The room lacked furniture, but count-less paintings hung on the walls. So many that hardly any naked wall remained. It was overwhelming and beautiful, and I stood in the center of the room, trying to absorb it all.

An oil painting of a raven clawing its way out of a young boy's chest caught my attention. The boy was sprawled on a frozen lake, his eyes white and blind, his mouth open in a last word. What clothes he wore were shredded and soaked with blood and saliva. The bird emerging from the boy's chest looked toward the sky. Its wings were spread as if preparing to fly, and its hooked talons pierced the boy's heart. But it wasn't the gore or broken ribs or the frozen heart that disturbed me. It was the last word. The raven was going to strand it on the boy's lips. It seemed beyond cruel to leave the word behind where no one would ever hear it.

"I see you've found the museum."

I turned around, too awed to feel guilty. "I didn't mean to snoop."

Diego leaned against the doorway, his hands in his pockets. "What's the point of going to a stranger's house if you're not going to poke around?"

Even though he didn't seem upset, I was still embarrassed. "This is brilliant." I pointed at the raven painting.

"Yeah, it's okay." Diego motioned toward a smaller painting on the adjacent wall. It was crowded by the work surrounding it, and I wouldn't have noticed it if he hadn't pointed it out. "This one's my favorite."

It was a portrait, but the subject had no skin. No, that's not accurate. Some frayed ribbons of skin were still stuck to the muscle, as if the subject had been flayed hastily by someone who hadn't cared enough to do it properly. A gaping hole yawned where the nose should have been, and the bulging eyes gazed heavenward and to the left at something or someone off the edge of the canvas.

"Self-portrait," Diego said after a moment of quiet.

I had to tear my eyes from it. "That's you?" Diego nodded. "That's what you see when you look in the mirror?"

Diego said, "It was when I painted that."

"Who tore your skin off?"

"I tore it off myself."

"Why?"

Diego sighed, and I wasn't sure he was going to answer,
but then he said, "Snakes get to shed their skin, why
shouldn't we?"

"But why would you want to shed your skin?" I couldn't
stop staring at the painting, looking for any detail that would
give me insight into the real Diego Vega. If his paintings were
any indication, then there was more to him than I imagined.

"Because sometimes it's easier to start over with a clean
slate than to drag the baggage of your past with you wherever
you go."

"What do you see when you look in the mirror now?"

Diego pointed at a charcoal drawing. It was larger and
more prominently displayed. The background was unfin-
ished, and it wasn't exactly a portrait. It was just a portion of
a shoulder and the back of Diego's head as if he were walking
out of the painting. "I painted that on the happiest day of
my life."

"What'd you paint on the worst day of your life?"

"The one you like."

The real Diego was hanging on these walls, but I didn't know how to reconcile the images of agony and anger with the boy who'd tried to show me the stars and loved my mother's fried chicken and who'd screamed his name from the apex of the Ferris wheel. I wanted to know what secrets Diego was hiding under his ever-changing wardrobe and disarming smile, but I didn't know how to ask. I didn't know if I even had the right to ask.

"I could paint *you* sometime."

"I'm afraid to ask what you see when you look at me." I wondered if he saw Henry Denton or Space Boy, or if there was even a difference anymore.

"You wouldn't believe me."

I could have spent days examining Diego's paintings, peeling back the layers for meaning, searching for insight into what drove him, but even though we were surrounded by bits and pieces of Diego's naked soul, I was the one who felt exposed. "Is everything cool with your sister?"

Diego nodded. "Of course."

"You didn't tell her I was coming, did you?"

"I might have forgotten to mention it."

If he was in trouble, he didn't let on. "So . . . is that your room across the hall?"

Diego seemed as eager to leave the gallery as I was to stay, and he shut the door behind us. His bedroom was the only one in the house that didn't look like it had been lifted out of a Tommy Bahama catalog. His twin bed sat unmade in the corner with the blankets and pillows piled in the center, clothes adorned every surface—pants on the floor, shirts hanging off the edge of his dresser, boxers swinging from the doorknob—and a distinctly musky smell lingered in the air, like sweat and sneakers and hair gel.

"It's a little messy."

It was so different from Marcus's bedroom, which was enormous and always spotless, and from Jesse's, which always looked on the verge of being condemned. Diego's room felt lived in and real. I spied a stack of comic books on his desk, the topmost issue was a series called *Patient F*, and next to it was a cramped bookshelf. I crouched down to scan the titles. He must have owned everything Ernest Hemingway had ever written. "I take it you're a fan?" I held up *The Old Man and the Sea*.

Diego flopped down on the bed, shoving the dirty clothes aside. "Kind of."

"Mr. Kauffman forced us to read *A Farewell to Arms* last year. I hated it. Hemingway's writing is so bland. He never *says* anything." I leaned on the edge of his desk.

"It's not about what he says but what he doesn't say."

I sniffed the air. "I smell bullshit. Do you smell bullshit?"

Diego snatched the book out of my hand. "It's not bull-shit." He returned the book to the shelf, lining up the spines so that they were all even. "Hemingway wrote in the negative spaces. His stories were shaped by what he didn't tell you."

"It still sounds like bullshit," I said with a smirk.

The doorbell rang before Diego could reply, and Viviana shouted at him to answer the door. He sighed. "Forget it. Let's go have some fun."

If the inside of Diego's house was a bed-and-breakfast, the backyard was a tropical island. Viviana had built the deck herself, and erected a fully-stocked tiki bar, complete with carved masks, coconuts, and a thatched roof. The centerpiece of the yard was a stone fire pit surrounded by the comfiest chairs my ass had ever graced. By the back fence she'd strung a hammock between two palm trees that looked over a lazy canal. It was paradise.

Diego and I mingled, inserting ourselves into various conversations with Viviana's friends. Their names slid in and right back out of my brain. The conversations were painless—mostly about how I liked school and what colleges I was applying to. Before Jesse, I assumed I'd wind up at whatever school he decided to attend. After, I stopped considering college at all. Rather than endure endless lectures about the necessity of being prepared for my future, I told anyone who asked that I wanted to go to Brown, but only because I'd heard Jesse mention it once.

When the food was ready, Diego and I loaded our plates. Viviana cooked burgers and hot dogs and steak and ribs. I grabbed a little of everything; Diego focused his attention on the meats. While his back was turned, Viviana nudged me and smiled. "I'm happy you came." She was wearing one of those joke aprons that said I LIKE PIG BUTTS AND I CANNOT LIE and had practically been chained to the grill all afternoon, but she still managed to carry on conversations with everyone within a five-foot radius and not burn the food.

"Really?"

She glanced at Diego as he served himself a preposterous helping of ribs. "Really." The way she said it sounded like I was doing Diego a favor by coming when he was the one who'd saved me, but before I could question Viviana further, Diego finished filling his plate and waved for me to follow.

We found a quiet spot by the hammock, where the music was loud enough to hear but didn't drown out our conversation—though we were both too focused on eating to talk much. Everything tasted amazing except for the potato salad, which had competing flavors of curry and celery. It *was* difficult to believe anything could taste so repulsive. Diego tore into the ribs with zeal, and his lips and chin were soon slathered with barbecue sauce. By the time he finished, which he announced with a belch loud enough to draw Viviana's attention from the other side of the yard, he looked like he'd devoured them with his hands tied behind his back.

"Did you get enough to eat?" Diego asked, motioning at my empty plate.

"I'm stuffed."

"If you say so." Diego whipped a handful of napkins from his back pocket and set to cleaning his hands methodically, scraping the sauce from under his fingernails. When I laughed, he said, "If you're not going make a mess when you eat ribs, you may as well not bother."

I looked at my clean hands. "Now I feel like a failure."

Diego dipped his finger into a puddle of leftover sauce and smeared it down my nose. "Better."

It took everything to resist reaching for my napkin to wipe it off. "If you say so."

He stared at me, and for a moment it reminded me of the way Jesse would watch me when he thought I wasn't looking, like I was the only person in the world worthy of his attention. Except Diego wasn't Jesse. No one was. "Why a Thanksgiving barbecue?" I asked.

Diego balled up his napkin and tossed it onto his empty plate. "What comes to mind when you think of Thanksgiving?"

"Turkey and stuffing. Gravy. Disaster movies. My mom drinking too much wine. Green bean casserole."

When I'd finished listing off all the regular Thanksgiving things I could recall, he said, "Oh. For me, it's cat piss and Devil Dogs."

I waited for Diego to elaborate, but he didn't. He just sat across from me, running his finger around the edge of his dirty plate, refusing to look me in the eyes. "Come on," I said, "you can't leave me hanging like that."

"It's not important."

"You know all kinds of stuff about me. Hell, you and half the world have seen me naked. You won't tell me anything about your life before you moved here, you won't tell me why you're living with your sister instead of your parents. I don't get you."

Diego clenched his fists. "Would you let it go, Henry?"

"No."

"Fine," Diego said. "If you tell me more about the aliens, I'll tell you why I was sent here."

If he was betting I'd drop it rather than discuss the sluggers, he was going to lose. "Sometimes I ask the sluggers to take me with them instead of sending me back."

"Why?"

"Because I hate it here."

"Why?"

"Because I'm a joke, that's why! I'm Space Boy, and I'll never be anything else." I hadn't realized I'd raised my voice until a couple of Viviana's friends glanced in our direction, but I didn't care. Diego wanted answers, and I gave them to him.

Then Diego said, "But I like Space Boy," and all the anger drained out of me.

"Your turn."

Diego shook his head and leaned back in the grass. "I want to hear more about the aliens."

"That's not fair."

"Fine. Ask your question." His voice was flat.

"Did you smash the windows in Marcus's car?" Up until the moment the question left my mouth, I was planning to ask why he'd been exiled to Calypso to live with his sister, but at the last second I changed my mind and immediately wished I hadn't.

Diego's mouth hung open, but he didn't answer. And the longer he remained silent, the more nauseated I felt. I'd gone too far. I'd accused him, and I had no right. Diego had been nothing but nice to me, had given me no reason to suspect him, but that hadn't stopped me. I should have kept my stupid questions to myself. I ruined everything. I should have stayed home. I needed air. "I have to go." I ran inside to Diego's bedroom and locked myself in his bathroom. The moment I was alone, I sat on the edge of the toilet and buried my face in my hands.

How could I have been so dumb? Despite knowing Diego wasn't capable of reciprocating my feelings, I needed to know if he'd busted the windows of Marcus's car, and what it meant if he had. I don't even think I would have been upset if he were responsible.

I never thought I'd have feelings for anyone after Jesse, and I wanted to carve them out of my brain. I wanted to shove an ice pick through my eyes and give myself a transorbital lobotomy, scrape Diego from the inside of my skull. The best thing for me to do was go home and forget about Diego Vega.

When I'd pulled myself together, I stood at the sink and washed my face. The barbecue sauce was still on my nose; it looked like dried blood. I wet some toilet paper and used it to scrub the stain off.

Diego's bathroom was messier and more disorganized than his bedroom. Inside the medicine cabinet were three kinds of deodorant, shaving cream, a razor, and two bottles of face wash. Globs of spent toothpaste were stuck to the side of the sink, and the shower was covered with a soapy film. My mom would have beaten me with the toilet brush if I ever let our bathroom get so filthy.

When I opened the door, I crashed into Diego. We hit the floor in a tangle of arms and legs. His elbow dug into my stomach, knocking the breath out of me.

"Sorry!" Diego said, laughter tingeing his voice.

"Just . . . It's fine." I disentangled myself from Diego, but he didn't move.

"I came to find you so I could apologize."

I already felt like an asshole for accusing Diego of smashing Marcus's car windows and then running off, and now he was apologizing when he had nothing to be sorry for. "I should go."

"You don't have to."

"Yeah, I do."

"Henry, I'm sorry." Diego grabbed my wrist when I tried to stand, and pulled me toward him. I opened my mouth to tell him to let go, but he swallowed my words. He pressed his lips to mine and wrapped his arms around my waist. Diego tasted like root beer and barbecue sauce. He smelled better than summer. Bigger than the ocean.

"Is this okay?" Diego whispered. His lips grazed my ear. All I could do was grunt.

The first time I'd kissed Jesse was the first time I'd kissed anyone, and it had felt like remembering the name of a song I'd forgotten but had been humming for days. Marcus was the second boy I kissed, and it was best described as frustrated mouth wrestling.

When Diego kissed me, I forgot about every kiss that came before. His kisses were impatient but cautious. They teetered on the edge of losing control, and I imagined him painting with the same kind of frenzy—stripped to the waist and covered in smears of more colors than the human eye was capable of detecting. My arms trembled, I could barely breathe, but I pulled him closer than a blanket on the coldest night.

I lost track of time, but eventually Diego rolled onto his back with a contented sigh. "I've been dying to do that."

I leaned on my elbow. "I thought you had a girlfriend."

"Ex-girlfriend."

"Okay," I said. "Ex-girlfriend."

"Yeah?"

"In case you haven't noticed," I said, motioning at myself. "No girl parts."

Diego winked impishly. "Oh, I noticed."

"So, when you said you liked Space Boy, you meant you *liked* Space Boy."

"Definitely."

Tangles of my hair were plastered to my forehead, and I brushed them out of my eyes. "I'm so confused."

"Don't be," Diego said. "I like people, not the parts they have." Diego frowned. "Well, I mean, I definitely like the parts; they're just not why I like the person."

"It's . . . whatever."

Diego laughed and reached for me again, but I pushed him away. "What?" he asked, like I'd physically hurt him.

When Diego was kissing me, nothing else had existed, but now that there was space between us, Jesse rushed in to fill it. My breath came in gasps. I tried to put into words what I was feeling, but every time I tried to speak, my tongue felt leaden and dry. It was a worthless chunk of meat in my mouth.

"Jesse?" he asked.

"I miss him, and I wish he were here." I couldn't look Diego in the eyes, but I felt him looking at me. Looking into me. "In a way, he is. He never leaves. Jesse never leaves. And how can I kiss you while Jesse's here?"

"You're not the one who died."

I bit back a laugh. "Maybe I should have."

"Don't be stupid."

I leaned my forehead against Diego's, and all I could think

about was kissing him again, and Jesse. Two thoughts that couldn't coexist. "What if I'm the reason Jesse killed himself?"

"You're not," Diego said.

"But what if I am?" I closed my eyes, and I expected Diego to have disappeared by the time I opened them again. But he hadn't. He was still there. "Sometimes I think it's my fault. Other times, Audrey's. Or maybe his parents'. I just need someone to blame. Might as well be me."

"Sometimes things just happen, Henry, and they're no one's fault."

I pulled back and looked into Diego's eyes. They swirled like slugger skin. I wondered what they were saying. I didn't know what to do. I wanted Diego and I missed Jesse and the world was going to end, and I didn't know what to do. "I . . . Do you think I could have a drink?"

"Done." Diego hopped up and headed for the door. He darted back and stole a kiss before disappearing into the kitchen.

There were only so many ways this could end. Jesse had said he loved me but hanged himself, Marcus had claimed to have feelings for me but then beat me up in the showers. I couldn't see Diego doing either of those things, but I didn't really know *what* Diego was capable of. There were so many ways I could screw this up, and even if I avoided them all, the world was still going to end in sixty-four days.

Yet I found myself wanting to see what could happen next. Diego managed to keep surprising me. I wasn't exactly having second thoughts about the end of the world, but I was glad I had a choice.

Diego had been gone awhile; he should have been back with the drinks. When I opened my eyes, the room was draped in shadows. I couldn't move my arms. I tried to yell for Diego, but I was voiceless.

The shadows creeped. The darkness collapsed.

I don't want to go.

But the sluggers didn't hear me or didn't care.

Mind's Eye

It's unveiled at the Commercial Electronics Show in Las Vegas, where it is hailed as the greatest technological advancement in entertainment since the television. Its inventors, Nate Duggin and Taylor Bray, call it Mind's Eye. Mind's Eye promises to deliver entertainment directly to your brain through its patented NeuroFace technology.

Smaller than a pack of gum, Mind's Eye attaches to the base of the skull and inserts microfilaments into the brain. It is painless, harmless, and worry free. That's the Mind's Eye guarantee™.

The pornography industry is the first to embrace Mind's Eye, followed by gamers. People don't play games anymore; they live them. The experience is so realistic, few people can tell the difference, and many consider Mind's Eye better than real life.

Within a year, people hardly have a reason to leave their houses. Mind's Eye devices allow them to visit their friends, work, and relax from the comfort of their couches. Crime falls to its lowest levels in recorded history, while airline corporations and automobile industries across the globe collapse. People no longer need to travel to see the world.

On 29 January 2016 the South Korean government passes a law giving incentives to citizens who use Mind's Eye for a minimum of sixteen hours daily. The program reduces pollution and conserves natural resources. South Korea becomes the model for the rest of the world. The first Mind's Eye is introduced that can be used continuously, and it is quickly adopted.

Other nations rush to pass mandatory Mind's Eye legislation, and in a matter of months every person on Earth is living in a fantasy world.

30 November 2015

I sat alone and watched the stars and dreamed of Diego. I saw the world from the stars' point of view, and it looked unbearably lonely. It took so long for starlight to reach me in the sluggers' ship orbiting Earth that some of those stars were already dead. When their light set out, we were younger, not even born. Our parent's parents weren't born. Humanity was still waiting to crawl out of the ocean and evolve. It was beautiful to think that starlight persisted even after the star itself had died, until I realized that humanity would vanish from the planet, the planet would disappear from the cosmos, and no one would remember we existed. No one would care.

Jesse was *my* star. He was gone—buried and rotting and cold—but he lingered. He sat with me in the transparent bubble of the slugger ship as I dreamed of Diego and watched the clusters of stars, other galaxies filled with other people like me and not, staring back, touching their lips and wondering if anyone would remember them. Spoiler alert: they won't.

I blinked. I was in Diego's bedroom, waiting for him to return with sodas; I blinked, and I was on the slugger ship. No sluggers greeted me; none poked at me or prodded my body with their strange alien instruments. The holographic Earth and the button were missing as well. I think I would have pressed it. I screamed for those slug-headed bastards to send me back, but they didn't. When my voice was raw, I walked into the darkness and arrived in the star room, where I remained.

I wonder what preventing the destruction of Earth means to the sluggers. In all of the universe, are we unique? Is there something humans possess that makes us worth saving? Maybe out of all the billions of planets, music is unique to Earth. Or books. The sluggers have fallen in love with Kerouac and Keats and Woolf and Shakespeare, and hope I'll press the button to preserve our literature for other alien races to explore. Then again, maybe we really are the ants. If I don't press that button, the sluggers will simply collect a couple of breeding pairs and restart the human experiment on another planet.

It seems unfair that an entire civilization could vanish from the universe and leave no trace behind, while Jesse lingers on. It isn't fair that he burned out, but his light remains to remind me of everything we had and would never have again.

But that's the difference between people and stars. A star's light still shines even if there's no one to see it, but without someone to remember Jesse, his light will disappear.

Maybe I would have pressed the button when the sluggers abducted me from Diego's house if they'd given me the chance. Maybe it was better that they'd taken me before things with Diego went too far. Maybe we were better off just being friends.

It doesn't matter. Maybes won't save the world.

The one thing I never thought to hope for was to not be awakened by a sandy kick to the ribs from a homeless man with curled, yellow toenails because aliens from outer space had dumped me in the middle of nowhere mostly naked again. I'd prayed to God for money and for my parents not to get a divorce, I'd begged Santa for a new computer, I'd even offered the devil my soul in exchange for a passing grade on my *Beowulf* exam, but I'd never thought to hope for something useful. Not until after the fact, anyway.

"Kid, you okay?" I peeked through my crusty eyes as a fungal zoo of a toe prodded my arm, and a grizzled, bearded face framed by ashy predawn light leaned over me. He reeked of piss and seaweed.

My mouth felt like I'd gargled used urinal cakes, and my cracked lips stung.

"Kid?" The man dipped nearer. His foul breath jolted me awake as surely as if I'd been electrocuted by sluggers.

"Where am I?" I asked instinctively, though the familiar sand dunes and sea oats were a dead giveaway. A cool breeze blew off the water, misting me with salt. Though it could have been any beach on any part of the planet, I knew it wasn't. It smelled like home.

The old man cackled and coughed and hacked up a glob of phlegm that he spit into the sand too near my feet for comfort. "Must've been some party."

"What time is it?" I asked. The sun was still little more than a vague promise in the eastern sky. "God, what day is it?"

"Bit young to be living so rough," the bum said, and I wanted to laugh at the irony of being told off by a man who clearly hadn't showered since Clinton was president.

"Just . . . what day is it?"

"Monday. I think." He scratched his beard and tapped at the sky, mumbling about dates, trying to recall where he'd been yesterday. "Definitely Monday. Maybe."

That meant I'd been missing since Thursday, which wasn't possible. People only went missing for that long in sitcoms, which always ended happily, or horror movies, which rarely ended happily unless you were white and chaste and not gay.

I remembered kissing Diego—Diego who liked me and wanted to kiss me and didn't care who knew—and he'd gone to get us drinks. Then the sluggers abducted me. Which meant that when Diego had returned to his bedroom, I'd disappeared without saying good-bye. He must have thought I'd freaked out and run away. I instinctively reached for my phone, but the aliens had stripped me of everything but my festive turkey boxers. Gobble, gobble.

"I have to go." When I tried to stand, I stumbled, but the old man caught me. His fingers were rough and grimy, and left streaks of filth on my arm that I fought the urge to wipe off. "Thanks," I muttered, and pointed myself toward the road, ignoring his offer of help.

Charlie's legs stuck out from under the Wrangler when I trudged home twenty minutes later, and country music filled the morning silence. It wasn't loud, but I was still surprised Mr. Nabu hadn't called the cops to complain. He complained about everything, including the fact that we still had our Christmas lights up in July. By that time, Charlie refused to take them down because it was already closer to next Christmas than it was from last.

I exaggerated my stride, letting my feet smack the driveway so I didn't startle Charlie. When I got within two feet of the Jeep, he froze and said, "Zooey?"

My throat felt like a lemon was lodged behind my Adam's apple, and I tried to work up a mouthful of saliva to swallow so I could answer. "Nah, I'm much prettier."

Charlie scrambled out from under the Jeep. His face was smeared with grease, and he was wearing his WIZARDS DO IT WITH WANDS T-shirt. In one motion, he embraced me and squeezed out my breath, wordless but shaking. He'd pinned my arms to my sides so I couldn't even hug him back, not that it seemed to matter.

"Where the fuck have you been?" He held me at arm's length, examining me.

"Nowhere."

"We called the fucking police, bro."

"When?"

"Saturday." Charlie knuckled his temple. "Some guy came by looking for you Friday. Said you were at his house on Thanksgiving."

"Diego?"

Charlie grabbed a rag from his back pocket and tried to clean his hands, but they were so filthy, all he did was smear the dirt around. "Maybe. Yeah, I think so. He was worried about you."

Diego had come to look for me. I *was* an asshole. He'd probably spent the weekend searching Calypso for me. I had to let him know I was okay. "Do you have your phone?"

Charlie swore. "I gotta let Mom know you're home." Even though Mrs. Melcher was standing in her front yard with her fluffy dog, Barron, and I was in my boxers, shivering, I waited while Charlie called her. "Yeah, Mom? He's home. I don't know. I don't know. Okay, hold on." He shoved the phone at me.

I shook my head and backed away. I couldn't deal with Mom until I'd had coffee and a shower; I needed time to figure out what to tell her. She couldn't handle the truth, but I didn't know what lie I could conjure up that would satisfy her rage. No matter what I said, I was in for it when she got ahold of me.

Charlie curled his lip like he wanted to punch me. "Yeah, Mom . . . he's going to take a shower. He's fine. Okay . . . okay . . . I'll tell him." Charlie tossed the phone into the Jeep. "Mom wants you home right after school."

"Thanks, Charlie."

"Don't thank me." Charlie frowned at me with disgust. Growing up, he'd called me a botched abortion, shit stain, fucktard, faggot, asshat, dipshit, and Henrietta. But in all our years together he'd never looked at me like he was ashamed to be my brother. "Where the fuck were you, Henry?"

"Nowhere."

Charlie shoved me with so much force that I stumbled backward and fell onto the lawn. I threw my hands behind me as I fell, and landed on my ass. Dew soaked my boxers, grass stained my palms. I scrambled to my feet. "What the hell, Charlie?"

"You've been gone for days—days, Henry—and 'nowhere' is all you can say? Mom thought you were beat up again, or worse!"

I had a pretty good idea what worse meant. When I found out that Jesse had hanged himself in his bedroom, I overheard my mom tell Nana that she couldn't imagine anything worse than finding her son's dead body, but I knew that wasn't true. Worse would be never finding me, never knowing what had happened, but I wouldn't have done that. Not to her, not to anyone.

"I'm sorry," I muttered.

Charlie shook his head. He could barely look at me. "No shit."

"What's wrong with the Jeep?" I asked, unsure what else to say.

"Nothing."

"Then why aren't you in bed?"

Charlie sneered. "If you think any of us could sleep not knowing whether you were dead or alive, then you don't know dick about this family."

I walked into Faraci's class, rubbing my head to try to ease the persistent pounding in my temples. Not even ten minutes brushing my teeth had been enough to scrub the sticky film from my mouth, and if I took any more aspirin, I'd probably start leaking blood from every orifice.

Relief flooded Audrey's face when she saw me, and she started babbling the moment I sat down. "Your mom came to my house, looking for you. Did you talk to her? Are you all right? I told her you were probably fine, but she said you hadn't come home in a couple of days and I hadn't heard from you and you weren't answering your phone. She was really worried."

My eyeballs throbbed, and it hurt to smile, but I forced one for Audrey. "I'm good. She knows I'm okay."

"Thank God."

"Thanksgiving was kind of a mess at my house, and I lost my phone." I hoped if I were vague, she'd drop it, but Audrey was tenacious.

"Diego called me, freaking out. He told me what happened,

and he was scared he'd messed things up, but I thought maybe you'd . . . Jesus, Henry, I was worried sick." She glanced around the room, but we were the only people in it other than Ms. Faraci, whose head was cocked to the side slightly. She appeared to be grading papers, but her pen hadn't moved since I'd walked into class.

My cheeks burned as I wondered how much Diego had told Audrey. "I'm not going to hurt myself, Audrey. Everything's just complicated."

"You can't disappear like that."

"It's not like the sluggers gave me a choice."

Audrey fell silent while I stewed. I was tired of apologizing for things that were beyond my control. I didn't ask to be abducted. I didn't ask for Diego to kiss me. I didn't deserve any of it. I only wanted to lie low until the end of the world.

"Diego really likes you, Henry. I knew he liked you."

"Aren't you smart?" A mob of students entered the classroom as the warning bell rang, and Marcus was among them. I tried to shush Audrey, but she wasn't listening.

"Have you talked to him yet? He went crazy when you disappeared."

"Disappeared?" Marcus stood over my desk, flanked by Adrian and Jay. "Abducted again, Space Boy?" His red-rimmed eyes held no laughter. They were hollow. He was hollow.

I tried to ignore him, but Audrey snapped. "Thank God aliens never abducted you, Marcus. I'd hate for you to represent our entire fucking species."

"Is there a problem?" Ms. Faraci asked from the front of the room.

"Did you hear what she said to me?"

Ms. Faraci glanced from me to Audrey to Marcus and offered a shrug. "I did not, Mr. McCoy. But if I hear you call anyone Space Boy again, you'll find yourself in Saturday detentions for the remainder of the year."

It would have been best if I'd faced Diego at lunch and gotten it over with, but instead I hid in an empty classroom and watched him wait by my locker, pacing back and forth, checking his phone every few seconds. After ten minutes passed he punched the locker door and left.

Regardless of what he said, I doubt he believed my stories about the sluggers. Who would? Maybe it's for the best that they abducted me before things between us got serious. There's so much I don't know about Diego. Jesse used to say I was oblivious to the world around me. I thought he was referring to things like poverty and hunger and wars in countries I didn't know the names of, but now I think he was talking about himself. I didn't know what had been going on with my own boyfriend, and we'd spent nearly every waking second together for more than a year. I've only known Diego for a few weeks.

Despite my brother hating me and my mom waiting to yell at me and the whole end-of-the-world thing, all I could think about was Diego. It was ridiculous. I hated movies and books where people ignored bullets whizzing by their heads and zombies chasing after them so that they could make out, but I finally understood. Kissing Diego dominated my every thought. I tried to think about something else, but I always returned to him, and I wasn't sure what to make of that.

Instead of going straight home, I took a detour to the beach and sat on the rickety staircase to watch the tide go out. The ocean retreated, exposing the bones of the shoreline. It was one of those days that was neither rainy nor sunny. A layer of clouds muddied the sky, bleeding the surrounding color, leaving everything monochrome and drab. If this was how dogs saw the world, it was no wonder they humped anything they could mount. It was probably the only thing that kept them from committing doggy suicide.

The steps creaked behind me, and I scooted to the side to let whoever it was pass, but they didn't.

"I figured I'd find you here," Diego said. "Also, I already tried everywhere else."

Diego Vega was the person I most and least wanted to see. He sat down beside me, leaving space between us that hadn't existed the last time we were together, and it was all I could do not to push him to the ground and kiss him until he knew I was sorry. He handed me my cell phone.

"Was it a dream?" I asked.

"Was what a dream?"

It was raining over the ocean, the wall of it so heavy that it appeared nothing existed beyond. The world consisted of only me and Diego and the beach. Maybe that's all it ever was. "Thanksgiving? Your bedroom?"

Diego shook his head. "Was it *them*?"

"Yeah."

"Why?"

"I don't know. I asked. I begged them to send me back, but the sluggers aren't keen on taking commands." I wished I knew how to make Diego believe me; I wished the aliens had abducted him, too, so we could have watched the stars together. "Maybe it was for the best, though."

"How do you figure?"

Finding the words to explain to Diego that I couldn't be with him—that no sane person should want to be with a disaster like me—was one of the most difficult things I'd ever done. But Diego remained silent until I was ready to talk.

"In case you haven't heard: the world is ending. I can't start something with you knowing it can't last."

Diego tensed like he was afraid to move. "If you're not over Jesse, if you need more time to grieve, tell me." He caught my gaze for the first time since joining me on the staircase, and utterly disarmed me with the intensity behind his hazel eyes, like the endless fire of the Crab Nebula burning in space.

"I hate Jesse," I said. "And I love him. I'll never be done grieving for him."

"You miss him—I get that—but the world doesn't stop because he's gone."

He was wrong. The world had stopped. The world had stopped and it was going to end, but I didn't tell Diego that; Jesse was just a name to him. "Tell me why you moved to Calypso. You hardly talk about your family, and when you do, it's all horrible."

"That's because it's not important, Henry." Diego rocked back and forth on the step. "This is confusing for me, too. You're not the only one with a past, but unlike you, I don't live in mine."

"I like you, Diego—so much, it scares me. But what does it say about me that I can like you as much as I do and still not want to press the button?"

"We can forget it happened," Diego said.

"I don't want to."

"Then where does that leave us?"

Diego ignored the past, and I believed we had no future. It was impossible to look at him and not want to kiss him. It was impossible to look at him and not know the world was going to end and drag us to hell with it. It was impossible to look at Diego and be anything but honest. "I don't know."

It wasn't the answer Diego wanted—I could see it in his bent back and slumped shoulders—but it was all the truth that was in me. The world wasn't worth saving without Jesse in it.

"My mom's going to kill me."

Diego kept his hands in his pockets as we walked up the stairs, like he didn't trust himself not to touch me. "Do you want me to drive you home? Your mom might not freak out with me there."

The offer was tempting, but Diego's presence would only delay my mother's wrath, and time had a way of concentrating her anger. "I'll walk."

"Try not to get abducted."

"Funny."

We lingered at Please Start. Diego sat on the rusted hood and traced lines in the dirt, while I kicked at the gravel on the side of the road. Maybe we were both thinking about that kiss on his bedroom floor. I certainly was. Making out with Marcus had always felt like a race to the finish line, but with Diego I felt like I'd already won.

The house felt lonely inside. Mom's car was parked in front of the duplex, but it didn't feel like anyone was home. Nana wasn't on the couch, and it looked abandoned without her sitting on it, reading while she watched the twenty-four-hour *Bunker* live feed.

"Hello?"

Smoke drifted into the living room from the kitchen, a spectral finger beckoning me onward. Mom sat at the kitchen table, still in her uniform, the black apron stained with salad dressing and other unidentifiable food particles. She looked a little like a slug herself, flabby and limp, leaning on the table with her face buried in her hands. The only sign of life was the lit cigarette smoldering between her fingers.

"Mom?"

"Sit." She took a hard drag from her cigarette, the cherry flaring, and lit the end of a new one off the old before stubbing it out. I chose the seat across from her, hoping to stay out of arm's reach. "I can't do this with you, Henry. I need you to be okay."

I'd expected anger, rage. I'd come to the table, garbed in heavy plate armor capable of deflecting my mother's barbed and poisonous words. I was not prepared for this. The emptiness of her voice. "Mom—"

"I put Mother in a home."

"What?"

Mom sucked on the cigarette like it was the only thing anchoring her to the world. "My mother is sick and I put her in a home, my oldest son dropped out of college to have a baby out of wedlock, and I can barely gather the strength to get out of bed in the morning. I need *you* to be okay." Mom looked me in the eyes, but I didn't see my mom anymore. I saw a woman struggling and failing to hold the tattered shreds of her life together. "Are you okay, Henry?"

After the first abduction, my mom sent me to one doctor after another. She never believed the various diagnoses—she hadn't believed I was being abducted by aliens either. When they said I was depressed, she refused to let them medicate me. When they said I had avoidant personality disorder, she told them I just hadn't learned to be comfortable in my own skin. She didn't believe the psychiatrists, she didn't believe in aliens, but she always believed in me. Through everything, she held fast to the notion that I didn't need help, that all I needed was time to figure out who I was. I'm not sure if she was right, or if I would have been better off on pills or locked up in a mental hospital, but her belief in me was absolute. If I told her I was still being abducted, that I'd been fooling around with the same boy who attacked me in the showers, that the world was ending and I could prevent it, but that I wasn't sure I wanted to, it would have destroyed that belief, and it was the only thing holding her together.

I reached across the table and rested my hand on hers. I'd never labored under the false notion that my mom was infallible. I knew that my mom was a human being, frail and confused, but I'd always thought she was just a little less confused than everyone else. She wasn't, though, and that's the moment I knew it.

But in the end, it wasn't her belief that kept me from telling her the truth. It wasn't her frailty. It was the certainty that we'd all be dead in sixty days. It was the knowledge that none of our choices mattered, that all our pain and all our suffering would end with the world, and we'd be free of those burdens. No faulty memory, no baby, no shitty job, or dead boyfriend. Just the perfect peace of nothingness. That's what *I* believed.

"I'm okay, Mom."

5 December 2015

Audrey's bedroom hadn't changed much in the year since I'd seen it last. More pictures of Jesse were framed and hung on the walls or arranged on her desk and nightstand and dresser, but it was still the pink, obsessively organized room where I'd spent dozens of afternoons and evenings hanging out with her and Jesse.

"Are you even studying?" she asked without looking up from her chemistry book. "If you're not going to do the extra credit for Faraci, you need to ace every test between now and the end of the term."

My book lay open in front of me, still on the same page I'd opened it to an hour ago. The science was easy; it was concentration that eluded me. "When the world ends, grades won't matter."

"What if the world doesn't end on January twenty-ninth?"

I leaned against Audrey's bed and looked at the ceiling. She had glow-in-the-dark star stickers plastered up there, clustered together in constellations she and Jesse had named. They'd been stuck up there so long, they hardly glowed anymore. "Then it'll end some other day, and my chemistry grade still won't matter." I stretched and grabbed her laptop off the edge of the bed.

Audrey peeked up at me. "What're you doing now?"

I checked my SnowFlake page, but no one had posted anything not related to Space Boy. Audrey had fixed Jesse's profile, but I didn't have the nerve to look for myself. "I think I want to find my dad."

"What? Since when?"

"Since now."

"Do you know where he is?"

I shook my head. "He split while Charlie and I were at school, and we haven't seen him since. I don't think he's ever paid child support."

Audrey tapped her pencil on the inside of her book. "Is this some end-of-the-world thing? You want to find your father and reconcile before your alien friends nuke the planet?"

"I don't think so." It had seemed like a good idea a few

minutes ago, but I wasn't sure how to explain it to Audrey. "Jesse killed himself without leaving a note."

"What's that got to do with your father?"

"He left me too, but he's still alive to tell me why. I think he's still alive." Charlie was right: my father hadn't abandoned us; he abandoned me. I needed to know why. I needed to know what was wrong with me that made everyone want to leave.

Audrey shut her book and crawled over beside me. She slid the computer into her lap and started searching. It didn't take her long to figure out there was nothing to find. My father's trail ended with the divorce. "Well," she said after an hour, "we know he's probably not dead and hasn't been arrested in the last three years."

"But?"

"He hasn't filed his taxes or gotten a job, either."

"How do you know that?"

"The IRS would have taken his tax return for child support if he'd filed and, if he had a job, the state would have garnished his wages."

"He could be working off the books."

Audrey sighed and passed the laptop back to me. "That won't make him any easier to find."

"Forget it. It was a stupid idea."

Before Audrey could respond, Mrs. Dorn popped into

the doorway, carrying a tray of assorted cheeses and two bottled waters. She was a more polished version of her daughter, but lacked Audrey's intensity, which she claimed to have inherited from her father. Mrs. Dorn had practiced ballet for most of her life and still moved as if dancing.

"Henry, dear." Mrs. Dorn set the tray on top of Audrey's television stand when I got up to hug her. "Boy, have I missed you. Your hair's getting so long!" She held me at arm's length, eyeing me critically the way only a mother could. "I don't like it."

"I missed you too, Mrs. Dorn."

Audrey gave her mom a sour look. "We're studying, Mom."

Mrs. Dorn threw the look back at Audrey. "I just wanted to see Henry, sweetheart."

"You've seen him. Now go."

"I heard you're working on a book."

"Gave up," Mrs. Dorn said. "As it turns out, writing is hard. But I do have an idea for an automatic doggie bath." She launched into a detailed description of her doggie bath concept, which sounded more like doggie torture, while Audrey and I snacked on cheese. She probably would have talked forever if Mr. Dorn hadn't come home. Audrey and her mom went downstairs to greet him, leaving me alone.

I opened Audrey's laptop to hunt for my father again, but I typed Diego's name into the search box instead. Less information existed about him than about my father. Then I remembered that his sister had called him Valentín. That search returned few results, but I found an article dated three years earlier about the trial of a Brighton, Colorado, boy arrested for assault. The details were vague, and the majority of the article was hidden behind a paywall.

"Sorry." Audrey shut the door behind her and flopped onto the floor. "Dad's been harassing the neighbors again."

I showed Audrey the article. "What do you think it means?"

Audrey took a minute to read it. "I don't know. It might not even be about him."

"How many Valentín Vegas do you think live in Colorado?"

"Good point."

"Maybe this is why he moved to Calypso."

"Have you asked him?"

I nodded. "He won't talk about it."

Audrey took the laptop from me and shut it. "I'm sure he has his reasons. You're making this into something it's not."

"That's what I used to tell myself about Jesse."

"Diego's not Jesse."

"Nobody is."

An object must travel at approximately 11.2 kilometers per second to break free of Earth's gravity. This is known as escape velocity. Escaping the pull of a town like Calypso requires much higher velocity but is easier with money and a car.

The days between Thanksgiving and Christmas break passed in a blur of exams, aliens, Diego, and Audrey. I haven't been abducted since the barbecue, but I've been thinking about the sluggers more than I care to admit. I want to believe the sluggers told me about the end of the world and gave me the choice to prevent it for some purpose other than because they simply want to see what I'll do. That they chose me for a reason and not at random. But if that's true, then it would mean they'd considered what would happen if I *do* decide to press the button. It would mean the sluggers had thought about my future beyond January 29, 2016, which is something I've been afraid to do.

If the world is irreparably fucked, it doesn't make sense for the sluggers to give us a second chance. If my life is meaningless, it makes no sense for the sluggers to spare it.

Unless that's part of the experiment. They want to see if I'm willing to endure a lifetime of misery simply to keep breathing.

I've been driving myself mad thinking about it, but I haven't come any closer to an answer.

Diego hasn't kissed me since Thanksgiving, but we still spend much of our free time together. He even tagged along with me to visit Nana in the nursing home. I tried to find a way to ask him about the article I'd dug up but never found the right time.

The last day of school before winter break, Ms. Faraci played a movie about the life of Nikola Tesla. I tried to pay attention, but the monotonous voice of the narrator kept lulling me to sleep. I was grateful for the distraction when Marcus sent me a text.

ALL-STAR PLUMBERS: behind the auditorium at lunch?
ME: why?
ALL-STAR PLUMBERS: want 2 talk

I glanced at Marcus, but his head was on his desk with the hood of his sweatshirt pulled up. I didn't answer because I didn't know how to. It should have been an easy decision—don't acknowledge the guy who attacked and humiliated me—but Marcus had been there when no one else had, and I couldn't ignore him when he needed me.

I was still debating whether to meet him, when the bell rang. I lingered behind, waiting for Marcus and his friends to leave before gathering my things to walk out with Audrey.

"Have a nice break," Ms. Faraci called after us. I wondered whether she had family or if she was going to spend her vacation preparing lessons and grading tests. I wondered if teachers were people who, for whatever reason, couldn't reach the escape velocity of high school. Ms. Faraci deserved better than to be marooned on such a lonely planet.

"Tell Diego I'll catch up with you guys in the cafeteria in a few minutes."

Audrey eyed me suspiciously. "What're you up to, Henry?"

"Who says I'm up to anything? There's just something I've got to do." I tried not to sound evasive, but I'm pretty sure I failed miserably.

"Please tell me you're not going to see you-know-who."

"He just wants to talk."

"Are you stupid or what, Henry?"

I pulled Audrey to the side of the hallway to avoid being trampled. "Jesse called you before he killed himself, right?"

"Yes."

"And you regret not answering, right?"

Audrey glared at me like she was considering kicking in my teeth. "This is different. Marcus attacked you!"

The bruises were gone, but the memories persisted, especially when I closed my eyes. "If he needs help and I ignore him, I'll never be able to live with myself."

"If you have to," Audrey said, "you can learn to live with anything." She shook her head. "Be at lunch in ten minutes, or I'm coming to find you."

Marcus was waiting behind the auditorium, pacing in front of the back door. It was an open space with few hiding places, and I scoured the area for signs of a trap, but as far as I could tell, Marcus was alone. The weather had turned cooler, but I was still sweating, anxious to get this over with, paranoid that Adrian and Jay were going to jump me and do worse than pour paint over my head.

Marcus looked up when I approached, and broke into a splintered grin. "I didn't think you were gonna come."

"I wasn't."

"You look good."

"You . . . don't."

Marcus stopped pacing and stuffed his hands into the front pocket of his hoodie. "I miss you."

"Is that why you wanted to see me?"

"Isn't that enough?"

"Whatever we had ended when you jumped me in the showers."

"You used to like it when I jumped you in the shower."

"Good-bye, Marcus." I turned to leave, but he called for me to wait. His voice cracked, as did my resolve. "What do you want?"

"You're with that Diego guy, aren't you?"

"No . . . it's complicated."

"Does he make you happy?"

"Marcus . . ."

"We were happy, weren't we?"

"You were horny, and I missed Jesse."

"It was more than that," Marcus said. "For me, anyway."

"Then how come you never told your friends you were fucking Space Boy?"

Marcus looked at the sidewalk, the grass, rarely at me. "Why didn't *you*?"

The question caught me off guard. "Obviously because you didn't want me to."

"Did you ask? Did you ever think maybe I was hoping you'd tell people because I was too scared to do it myself?" His voice was colder than the Boomerang Nebula.

I tried to recall the many opportunities I'd had to out Marcus. There was the time his parents came home early from Greece, and I hid under his bed while his mother recounted the horror of nearly having to fly coach because the bastards at the airline had overbooked first class. Or the time Adrian nearly caught us making out behind the English building. Marcus shoved me to the ground to cover, and I skinned my palm. We had quite a few close calls, but I thought Marcus liked the thrill. I never once wondered if he was hoping we'd be caught. "Did you really want that?"

"Remember when you asked me if I'd save the world?"

"I didn't think you'd heard me."

Marcus snorted like I was stupid to think otherwise. "Well, I would."

"Why?"

Instead of answering, he pulled a folded envelope from his back pocket and handed it to me. "Merry Christmas, Henry."

Marcus tromped off, leaving me standing behind the auditorium still trying to think up a reply. A sane person would have reveled in seeing Marcus brought so low, but I hated him that way.

I tore open the envelope. The Christmas card sported a picture of a hunky frat boy who resembled Marcus in a revealing Santa suit. Across the top it said *I'll jingle your bells.* He'd taped a prepaid calling card to the inside and written *Space Boy, use this to phone home. And if no one answers, I will. Love, All-Star Plumbers.*

19 December 2015

If I weighed 146 pounds and Diego weighed 162 pounds, and the distance separating us was fractionally nothing, then the gravitational force between our noncelestial bodies was approximately equal to three times the force a seat belt applies to a restrained passenger in a vehicle traveling at sixty-three miles per hour when it collides with a stationary object.

You can't fight gravity. Gravity is love. Love requires us to fall. Anyway, I couldn't have reached the escape velocity required to break free of Diego even if I'd wanted to.

"Why do you keep laughing?" Diego asked. His skin was damp with sweat, but I didn't mind.

"Your hair tickles my nose."

"Then stop kissing my neck." Diego paused. "On second thought, definitely don't stop." He pulled me on top of him, running his hands up the back of my shirt, holding me like the last note of a song.

When Diego kissed me, I could hardly believe it was real. Believing Diego liked me and wanted to be with me seemed more implausible than being abducted by aliens who wanted me to decide whether to save the world. If I thought about it too long, doubt burrowed into my brain, multiplying and feeding on my fears. Mom was working, and I'd only invited Diego over to play the new Zombie Splatter, but we started kissing and I knew we should stop, but I didn't want to.

Diego sat up, breathing heavily. "I think my lips may fall off."

"That would be unfortunate. And gross." I grabbed one of the glasses of water sitting on my desk, and drank. My tongue felt heavy and my lips raw.

Diego started rifling under my bed before I could stop him. He ignored the dirty socks and went straight for the spiral notebooks. "What are these?"

"Nothing important." I tried to sound casual, but my voice cracked.

"Are they stories? Read me one."

"They're my journals." I grabbed the notebook and shoved it back under the bed.

Diego raised himself onto his elbows. "What do you write about?"

"Personal stuff."

"You've seen my paintings."

"Those weren't hidden under your bed."

"Only behind a closed door."

"Why don't you tell me why you were arrested for assault? Then maybe I'll read you something." I hadn't meant for it to come out like that, but I couldn't stand how easy it was for him to demand to know my secrets without giving away any of his.

Diego's eyes narrowed. "I don't know what you're talking about."

"I read about it online."

"You Googled me? What the hell, Henry?"

"Forget it. This was a mistake." I pulled my knees to my chest and tried to wipe the feel of Diego's lips off my mouth.

I waited for him to leave, but he didn't. "Why does the past have to matter? Can't now be enough? Can't *this* be enough?"

"I want it to be." If Jesse had asked me to read to him from my journals when he was alive, I would have. Maybe if I'd shared my secrets with him, he would have told me how much pain he was in. I'll never know. I lost my chance with Jesse, but Diego was sitting right in front of me. One of us had to blink, and I had nothing to lose. "Sometimes I write about how the world might end. Sometimes I write about the abductions. . . . You know, for science. I forget the details otherwise."

"What're they like?" Diego spoke softly, like he was afraid he'd spook me if he spoke too loud.

"It'll be easier if I read you something." I reached past Diego and retrieved the notebook. The pages were filled with my cramped hieroglyphics, a byproduct of being born a lefty. I cleared my throat and began to read before I lost my nerve.

"Last night I was created from light. Stoplights and patio lights and campfire lights and Christmas lights still up in summer. Sunlight and moonlight and starlight and light that's taken a million, million years to arrive. I was made of them all.

"It happened like always: the shadows, the urge to pee, the helpless paralysis. The dark room. I love and loathe that room. It's there that they deconstruct me, study me, and rebuild me. It's there that they probe me, searching for answers to the mystery of Henry Jerome Denton. I try to tell them there is no mystery. I am not special, not unique, not even a little important. They never listen. As they perform their experiments, which make little sense to my primitive intellect, my mind wanders. It wonders. Why me?

"Do mice ask the same questions when scientists study them? Do they believe in their uniqueness as they are injected with syringes of experimental drugs? When a hand reaches into a cage, grabs one by the tail, and vivisects it, do they marvel at their specialness? Will the sluggers kill and cut me open one day?

"Tonight something unusual occurred. The tallest slugger touched my forehead, and I ignited like a sparkler on the Fourth of July. Shards of dazzling light rippled under my skin. I was the constellation Grus. The Trifid Nebula. I was the Big Bang, expanding endlessly through time and space forever.

"I thought I was dying. That I was going to expire on a cold slab, trapped inside a UFO, my body filled with every light that had ever existed. I couldn't imagine a better way to die.

"But I didn't die. The lights rose to the surface of my skin, through it and into the air where they hovered over me, maintaining the form of my body. I was no longer filled with light; I *was* light. My photonic heart beat, pushing my glittering blood through my glowing veins.

"This was probably a routine procedure for the aliens— no more wondrous than a CT scan or an X-ray is to us—but seeing that twin of myself created from heavenly particles made me believe that I *was* special to them in some way.

"One by one, the lights began to fade and slowly die. Not

with the big bang that birthed them, but with a whimper and a gasp.

"They returned me to Calypso shortly after, I think. I woke up in Mr. Haverty's backyard. I really wish they'd stop taking my pants."

My throat was scratchy, so I drank the rest of my water while I waited for Diego's reaction. His mouth hung open, and his eyes seemed unfocused. I couldn't read his expression, but I felt exposed under it.

"That was a dumb one, I can find you one where they cut—"

Diego grabbed the back of my head and pulled me to him, kissing me like I was the only water in the desert. He sucked the air out of me, but it was okay because he breathed for both of us—his heart pumped blood for us too. We were a closed system, complete.

"Read me more."

"It's bullshit."

"It's beautiful, Henry. You're beautiful."

Diego never did answer my question, and after a while, I wondered if it even mattered.

Midnight Sun

When scientists at NASA first observe the sun dimming, a small division is funded to study the phenomenon, but the consensus is that the anomaly will self-correct.

A year later a secret conference of scientists is convened to debate the dimming of the sun, which many now believe presents an imminent threat to life on Earth. Already the effects are noticeable. Colder, longer winters and more glacial ice than has been seen in decades. Conservatives in Washington, DC, claim these phenomena are proof that global warming is and always was a sham. While most scientists at the conference agree that the global cooldown is being caused by the dimming of the sun, none can offer a viable solution to halt or reverse it.

Over the next two years, the pace of climate change

rapidly increases. Glaciers form over Canada, snows fall regularly in Florida and Central America. People flee the northernmost states to more temperate climates.

The sun is dying. That's what people say.

Unable to hide the truth any longer, the world's leaders announce that the sun is experiencing a cycle of dimming, and that its light and heat will continue to diminish. Eventually the dimming will reverse itself, but scientists predict all multicellular life on Earth will perish long before that occurs.

People move as close to the equator as possible. Lakes turn to ice and food becomes scarce. Those who do not freeze to death, starve. There are no wars over the world's meager resources; soldiers are too cold and hungry to fight.

On 29 January 2016, at 11:23 p.m. EST, a boat off the coast of Maryland becomes trapped in ice. It is the first reported instance of the Atlantic Ocean freezing. It is not the last.

By the time the sun grows bright again, no one is left alive on Earth to feel its warmth.

21 December 2015

The first time I visited Nana at the nursing home I expected to find her alone in a dreary room, sitting in her own feces while the orderlies ignored or berated her. Shady Lane was nothing like that. It was bright and cheerful, with sky blue walls and so many windows, they hardly needed to use the overhead lights during the day. The staff was friendly and seemed to genuinely enjoy their jobs.

A few days before Christmas, Audrey joined me to visit Nana. TJ was the nurse on duty, and we swapped small talk while he signed us in at the front desk before telling us we could find Nana in the community room. During my other visits, I'd only seen Nana's room and the garden, but TJ assured us the community room was easy to find. We had only to follow the music.

Nana was playing show tunes on a weathered piano while a pair of older men—one a gravelly baritone and the other a tuneless tenor—sang along.

"Well, this is just appalling," Audrey said, stifling a giggle.

I waited until they finished "I Could Have Danced All Night" from *My Fair Lady*, and added my applause to the smattering from the handful of patients and nurses seated about the airy room. "That was great, Nana!"

Nana's eyes lit up when she saw me, and she played the opening notes to "Son of a Preacher Man." "Henry, sweetheart." She spun around on the bench to face us. "Have you come to take me home?"

Her question was a knife that slid neatly between my ribs and left me bleeding. The two men who'd been singing with her continued smiling with their big, glossy fake teeth. "Nana, this is my friend Audrey. You remember Audrey."

Nana offered Audrey her hand. "Audrey, dear, a pleasure. My name is . . . is . . . I seem to have misplaced my name." She looked distressed.

"You told me the first time I met you to call you Georgie." Audrey's grace under pressure was astounding. "But I don't have a grandmother of my own, so it'd be an honor if I could call you Nana too."

"Georgie," Nana said. "That's me, right?"

298 · SHAUN DAVID HUTCHINSON

I hugged Nana as hard as I could, taking care not to break her. "That's you."

The men's names were Miles and Cecil, and they knew all the words to "Bohemian Rhapsody," "Dancing Queen," and every song from *West Side Story*. Audrey and I sang with them until we were hoarse, and after, Nana showed us her room as if I'd never seen it.

Audrey gravitated toward the picture on the dresser. It was the only photograph in the room. "When was this taken?"

"Thanksgiving," I said. Charlie looked like he was chewing a lemon, Mom's smile looked painful, and I'm pretty sure the only reason I was smiling was because I was imagining pushing both of them out of an airplane without parachutes. The tension radiated from the surface of the photograph like heat off a summer sidewalk. Only Nana and Zooey looked genuinely happy.

Nana shuffled to stand beside Audrey. "That's my family. Aren't they lovely? My daughter could stand to eat less, but she always did have a sweet tooth."

"Mom?" I asked. She liked her wine and cigarettes, but I couldn't remember her eating many sweets.

Nana took the picture and sat on the edge of her bed. "Oh, yes. Eleanor was quite a little piggy growing up. She especially loved to watch me bake because I would let her lick the spoons and beaters. Once, she became very ill. Vomiting all night. I nearly called Dr. Wadlow to come out to the house, but your mother confessed that she'd eaten an entire stick of butter."

I clapped my hand over my mouth, laughing. "Gross!" Audrey was also laughing.

"Why in the world would she eat butter?"

The lines and wrinkles seemed to smooth out on Nana's face as she recalled the memory. Nana couldn't remember that I'd visited her two days earlier, but she remembered every detail of something that had happened more than forty years ago. The farther we are from someone, the further we live in their past.

"Eleanor saw me put butter in everything I baked, so she must have thought it would be delicious on its own."

"I bet that's why Mom hates baking cookies," I said. "She always made me take store-bought treats for the bake sales in middle school."

Audrey shuddered. "I love cookies, but I'd never eat butter."

Nana sighed and touched the picture. "And yet, cookies would taste terrible without it."

Audrey and I hung out for another hour, listening to Nana's stories. She told us about the detective who lived on the third floor and the nice woman down the hall named Bella who was a stage magician, while Audrey brushed Nana's hair. I wasn't sure how much was real and how much was fantasy, but it didn't matter because it made her smile.

When we signed out, I flipped through the pages to see if anyone else had visited Nana. Charlie's careless scrawl popped up once, but Mom's was there every day.

I wasn't in the mood to talk on the drive back, and Audrey gave me some space. We stopped for coffee, and after we left, she said, "Nana seems okay."

"I guess."

"I mean, I've heard of worse places."

"Me too." I burned my tongue and swore. "Truth is, I'm not worried about her being mistreated. You just don't know her. She was barely forty when my grandfather died, and she's been on her own ever since. She's so stubborn that Mom had to practically force her to come live with us."

Audrey only ever drank iced coffee, and she sipped hers through a ridiculously long straw. "I don't think she remembered me."

"She called me Henry, but I think she thought I was my grandfather."

"They'll take care of her." Audrey patted my leg. "How are things with Diego?"

I leaned my head against the window. "Confusing."

"He doesn't seem confused."

"Maybe that's the problem." I'd been so sure that staying away from him was best for us both, but then we'd kissed and I'd read to him from my journals and he still hadn't told me why he moved to Calypso, but I think maybe he wanted to. I couldn't think when we were together. Diego took the clarity granted to me by the sluggers and twisted it around until I didn't know what I wanted anymore.

Audrey drove slower the closer we got to my house. "Henry, Jesse would want you to be happy."

"If either of us had known what Jesse really wanted, he might not be dead." It was a terrible thing to say, but I had so many terrible things bubbling inside of me that it was inevitable some would occasionally spill out. "Whatever. It's not just Jesse. It's complicated."

"I know, I know. End of the world." Audrey pulled up in front of my house. She came to a stop but didn't put the car in park.

"Maybe the end of the world isn't the problem, Audrey. Maybe it's the solution. And right now Diego's a complication."

Dust clouded the air in the living room when I got into the house, and settled on every surface. Boxes of Nana's belongings were stacked against the walls. Clothes mostly, but also picture albums and scrapbooks I remember Nana displaying on bookshelves in her old house. The walls rattled, and I followed the twang of a cheerful country song toward Charlie's room. The doorway was covered with plastic sheeting that I ducked through, and Charlie was dressed in board shorts, flip-flops, his old workout shirt, and a breathing mask, swinging a hammer at the wall that used to divide his room from Nana's. She'd only been gone a few weeks, and it was already like she'd never lived there.

"What the fuck do you think you're doing?" I pulled my shirt over my mouth and nose to keep from breathing in the drywall dust.

Charlie slipped the hammer into his waistband. "Making room for Zooey and the baby."

I surveyed the mess. "You're going to bring the house down on our heads!"

"I know how to Google shit, asshole. I'm not a total moron." He tore a down a chunk of drywall and tossed it onto the heap with the rest.

"You failed woodshop in high school."

"I was stoned through most of high school." Charlie lifted the mask and rested it on top of his head. White dust coated his face, and he looked like the surface of the moon. He reached into a cooler under the window, grabbed two beers, and tossed me one.

"I'm pretty sure this is the cheapest beer you can buy."
I'm not a beer connoisseur, but I know shit when I drink it.

"Babies are expensive." Charlie shook his head. "I'd give
up drinking completely if I didn't live with you assholes."

"Mom could drive the pope to drink."

Charlie chugged his beer. "If I could afford to get my own
place, trust me, I would."

"Do you really think this is worth it? The job, living here?"

Charlie sat down on the cooler and wiped the sweat from
forehead. He was gaining back some of the muscle he'd lost
after high school, but he'd lost the war with his hairline. "I'm
doing what I have to do."

"Wouldn't you rather do something you love?" I thought
back to my conversation with Zooey, about Charlie giving up
his dream of being a firefighter.

Charlie finished his beer and grabbed another. I'd barely
taken two sips of mine. "I'm gonna love being a dad. I'll get
to teach my kid how to throw a punch and a football. It's
going to be fun."

"Raising a kid isn't supposed to be fun."

"Says you."

"What makes you think you'll be any better than our dad?"

"Because I want to be."

"Is it really that simple?"

Charlie stared at me for a second, his brow furrowed. "Yes! It's that fucking simple. I'll be a better father than our father because I want to be. I'm sure I'll screw up loads of other things, but I won't make the same mistakes as him, and I won't ever leave."

"Was it my fault? Did Dad leave because of me?"

"Damn it, Henry." Charlie rubbed his head and looked at me like he hoped I was joking, but I wasn't. "You know what your problem is? You overthink everything."

"Yes or no, Charlie?"

"Dad left because he was a dick. It doesn't matter if it was because of you or me or Mom. He left because he was a selfish prick, and that's all you need to know."

It was as close to an honest answer as I was going to get without being able to ask my father directly, but it didn't make me feel any better. "Why would you want to bring a kid into such a fucked-up world?"

"Are you kidding, bro? About the only good thing I *can* do is bring this kid into the world, give her the best life I can, and believe that she can make it a better place."

Charlie's transformation blew my mind. This was the same guy who delighted in sticking freshmen's heads in toilet bowls in high school, and thought flicking boogers on me was hilarious. He was still an ass, but he was an ass with a purpose. I was so stunned that I almost missed what he'd let slip. "Wait. Did you say 'her'?" He couldn't contain his grin, and I hugged him, clapping his back. "Congratulations, Charlie."

Charlie socked me in the shoulder. "Don't tell Mom. Zooey wants to do it. Some kind of chick-bonding thing."

"I won't." I couldn't believe Charlie was going to have a daughter. She wasn't a little parasite anymore; she was my niece. She wasn't going to grow up and go to high school and become a porn-addicted, chronic-masturbating alcoholic. She was going to have a mother and father who loved her and didn't slam doors. She was going to have an uncle who was sometimes abducted by aliens. She was going to grow up and grow old and fill her head with memories that time would never be able to steal from her.

Except she wouldn't because the world was going to end. "I saw Nana today."

"How is she?"

"We're her family; she should be with us."

"This way's better," Charlie said. "A month ago she tried to crawl into bed with me and Zooey at two in the morning." He shuddered.

"It's not right." I couldn't shake the image of Nana sitting alone in her bedroom staring at that one lonely picture. Even though she'd made friends, they weren't her family. We were her family, and we'd abandoned her. But it was more than Nana. It was how bitter and cynical Mom had become, and Marcus's downward spiral, and my not being able to get over Jesse and give Diego a fair chance. "Everything's so fucked up."

Charlie tossed the hammer at my feet. It hit the floor with a thud. "Help me tear down this wall."

"Why?"

Charlie pointed at the hammer with his chin. "Break the drywall, or I break your face."

"Yeah, you're going to be a great dad." Charlie feinted toward me, and I snatched the hammer. I'd seen Charlie do it, but I felt silly. What was he hoping to accomplish? Anything? Or was I just free labor? Still, I knew he wouldn't let me escape without trying to tear down the wall. I swung the hammer. It barely made a dent. "Sweet. That was fun. Thanks."

"Weak." Charlie pushed me toward the wall. "Hit that motherfucking wall, Henry!"

I cocked my arm back and let it fly. The drywall cracked. Again, and it made a hole.

"Yeah!" hollered Charlie. He cranked up his shitty music until I couldn't hear myself think.

Adrenaline surged through me. Testosterone and electricity.

I began to understand the power of aggression, of fists and fighting and pain. With this hammer, I wasn't Space Boy or Henry Denton, I was a mighty warrior and I could do anything. I attacked the wall, punching hole after hole into it, and when I'd made enough holes, I tore it down with my bare hands and bloody knuckles. The wall was my bad grades in school. The wall was the sluggers and their fucking button. The wall was Marcus. The wall was Jesse. The wall was Mom's job and Charlie's daughter. The wall was Diego. The wall was everything I hated, everything I loved.

I probably would have dug through to the other side if Charlie hadn't grabbed my arms and pulled them behind my back. "Whoa, little bro."

My breath heaved. I still heard music even though the radio was silent. Charlie let me go, and I looked at my bloody, dusty knuckles. Red smears painted parts of the discarded drywall.

"You want to do the rest?" Charlie asked. "You'd have it done in half the time it'd take me." He laughed. I didn't.

My arms were weak and my shoulders sore, but they weren't what hurt worst. Diego had made me happy these last few weeks, but it wasn't enough. I thought about Jesse looking down on me, seeing me with Diego. Teenage boys who are dead probably can't masturbate, and it made me sad to think about Jesse stuck in the afterlife, lonely, frustrated, and unable to get off. I loved him, and I just don't know if a world without Jesse Franklin is worth saving. Either way, I only have thirty-nine days to decide. "Thanks," I said to Charlie, and stumbled toward the door.

"Hey, bro," Charlie called after me. "You're not just gonna be an uncle. You're gonna be a godfather, too."

22 December 2015

From Earth, Venus is a beacon in the night sky, beautiful and bright. However, the surface of the planet is a scorching 467 degrees Celsius, the ground is barren and rocky, and clouds of sulfuric acid roam the atmosphere. Much like my face.

Looking in the mirror, I could identity every disgusting, clogged pore, every hair out of place, every imperfection on my imperfect body. I hated how my nipples were sort of oval, and my belly button was deeper than Krubera Cave. I'd spent an hour brushing my teeth and scrubbing away blackheads and digging Q-tips into all my face holes. I even paid special attention to the slum areas, not that I expected Diego to visit them. So far, he'd kept his hands in the touristy regions, showing a restraint Marcus never had. He respected that I still had no idea what we were doing.

After pulling every piece of clothing I owned out of my closet and drawers, I settled on my best jeans and a button-down shirt my mom had bought me that still had the tags on it. I felt like a little boy in his father's suit, a fraud everyone could see through.

Mom whistled when I walked into the living room. She was smoking and drinking and watching *Bunker* with the volume muted so she could read. It must have been her day off from the restaurant because she was still wearing her pajamas. "Don't you look nice?"

"Whatever."

"I'm serious, Henry. You've grown into a handsome young man."

"You're my mom; you're contractually obligated to say that." There's probably be a genetic reason every mother believes her son to be the apex of male beauty. I suppose if they didn't, they'd smother the ugly ones, and the human race would have died out or been much more attractive as a result.

Mom flicked her ash into the ashtray. "Well, yes, but for a while, your father and I were worried you were never going to grow out of your ugly phase."

"Mom!"

"What? You had those knobby knees, and your front teeth were so big, you could barely shut your mouth." I liked seeing her laugh, even if it was at my expense. "Who are you dressed up for?"

"I'm hanging out with Diego. You met him." I didn't want to remind her that she'd met him over Thanksgiving break because I'd disappeared.

Mom raised her eyebrow. "You two have been spending an awful lot of time together. Do we need to have *the talk*?"

"Jesus, no. We're not even dating." I held up my hands and backed toward the door.

"Sex is nothing to be ashamed of, Henry, and I want you to be informed. We should have had this discussion sooner."

My face was burning, and I wanted to escape, but Diego wasn't going to pick me up for another ten minutes. "I'm not sleeping with Diego," I said. "And anyway, I already know about that stuff."

Mom looked skeptical. "I know you've seen it on those Web sites you visit—"

"Oh my God! Mom! Have you been going through my computer?"

"Only to make sure you weren't experimenting with drugs or planning to shoot up your school."

"That's an invasion of privacy!"

Mom took a drag from her cigarette and blew the smoke at me dismissively. "Don't be so uptight, Henry. Compared to

Charlie, you're pretty vanilla." She shuddered.

The thought of my mother knowing what kind of porn Charlie and I browsed was mortifying, and I couldn't get out of the house quickly enough. Waiting outside was preferable. Having needles driven into my eyeballs would have been preferable. "Please stop."

"I want you to be happy. You know that right, Henry?"

To be honest, it never occurred to me that my mother was concerned about my happiness. My safety, yes, but not my happiness. It seems obvious now, but before she said it, I wouldn't have put it at the top of a list of things my mother wanted for me. "I'm trying."

"That's what worries me."

"Why?"

Mom stubbed out her cigarette. "Because a smart, handsome boy like you shouldn't have to try so hard to be happy."

"I'll be back by eleven," I said, and dashed out the door.

Diego's hand lingered on mine when he passed me the popcorn. His fingers were butter-slick and warm. He smiled, looking far less nervous than I felt. The movie theater was mostly empty, which only amped up my anxiety. Diego had convinced me to let him take me on an actual date, arguing that it wouldn't have to mean anything and that it would be a good way to see what I was missing out on. He wore me down and I finally agreed, but only to prove to him that it was a disastrous idea.

"What's the name of this movie again?"

"*Dino and July*," Diego said. "It's about a guy whose family owns a funeral home, and this girl he has a crush on dies but then comes back to life and helps him become cool. Sort of like *Cyrano de Bergerac* meets *Pygmalion*. With a zombie."

"Sounds . . . interesting."

"It got good reviews."

I grabbed a handful of popcorn, immediately regretting it. What if my breath smelled like butter and salt? I dropped the popcorn and sipped my soda instead.

"Any word from your slug friends?"

After reading to Diego from my journal, I felt less like a freak discussing the aliens with him, though they still weren't my favorite conversation topic. "Not since the barbecue."

"Is that strange?"

"I've gone a whole year without being abducted before, but January twenty-ninth is barely a month from now, so you'd think they'd want to give me plenty of opportunities to push the button."

"Would you? Press it?"

It should have been an easy answer. It was true that I

didn't want to live in a world without Jesse—I'm not sure any of us deserved to live in a world where Jesse Franklin felt like killing himself was the only solution—and if I didn't press the button, I'd never have to worry about Diego leaving me like Jesse and my father had, Charlie and Zooey wouldn't have to watch their daughter grow up in an increasingly hostile world, Nana wouldn't have to lose her memories, and Mom wouldn't be so sad anymore. If I didn't press the button, the future would never disappoint any of us. But, despite how hard I fought him, Diego made me curious about my future. About *our* future together.

"I don't know," I said. Before I could explain, laughter echoed through the theater as a group of people rounded the corner at the front. I recognized Marcus immediately. "Shit." I slid down in my seat.

"What?" Diego craned his neck. Marcus was with Adrian, and they each had their arm around a different girl. I think one of the girls was Maya Anderson, but I couldn't place the other.

I kept still and quiet, hoping to remain invisible, but Marcus zeroed in on me like I was tagged with a tracker and yelled, "Look, it's Space Boy! And he brought his girl-friend. That's one ugly bitch, Space Boy." Adrian and the girls cracked up and took seats a few rows ahead of us, but Marcus lingered in the aisle. His clothes were winkled and his cheeks were flushed. I could practically smell the booze on him.

Diego elbowed me in the ribs. "Problem?"

"No."

The lights dimmed, the projector lit up the screen, and I ate popcorn, but I don't remember anything about the movie. I spent two hours watching Marcus and Adrian out of the corner of my eye. When the show ended, I waited in my seat until only Diego and I remained in the theater.

"You want to talk about it?"

"Nope."

"Want me to slash their tires?"

I tried to laugh it off, but there was a scary intensity to Diego's voice that made me think he wasn't joking. "No. It's nothing. Really."

Diego nodded, but I doubted he believed me.

We walked next door to Barnaby's, an old-style arcade, where we played Skee-Ball and avoided talking about what had happened in the theater. Finally Diego said, "Listen, if you're going to let that guy ruin our night, I'd rather go home."

His bluntness caught me off guard, and I felt like an asshole. I rolled the last ball and walked away without bothering to see where it landed. Diego followed me to a table that reeked of fries and grease and baby wipes, and sat across from me.

"It's always been like that," I said. "People calling me names, making me feel like I don't belong. Before Space Boy, it was fag or knob gobbler or the Ass Pirate Roberts. My personal fave was Henry Diarrhea."

Diego raised an eyebrow. "Henry Diarrhea?"

"I had a nervous stomach in middle school."

"Oh." He tried to catch my eye. "Those names, they're not who you are."

"I'm Space Boy. I'll never be anyone else."

"You're whoever you want to be."

"Come on," I said. "That's bullshit and you know it." A mother with young kids scowled at me from two tables over.

Diego leaned his head back and sighed. I figured I'd finally done it. I'd convinced him I was damaged goods, not worth the time or effort he'd invested in me. In a way, I was relieved. I could stop pretending the possibility existed that we might have a future. My future died with Jesse, and I was killing time while the rest of the world caught up.

"Before I moved to Calypso," Diego said, "I spent one year, ten months, and ninety-three days in prison."

That was definitely not what I'd expected Diego to say, and I was sure I'd misheard him. "What?"

"Juvenile detention, actually." Diego's eyes, so like the

slugger's skin, grew distant and hard. "I should have told you sooner. I wanted to tell you."

I had so many questions, but the first one to come out was, "Why?"

"It's complicated." Diego traced lines on the table with a dab of partially dried ketchup. "I was thirteen and angry and everything was so fucked up. I'll be on probation until I'm twenty-one. No drinking, no drugs—I can't even get a speeding ticket, or they'll lock me up again."

I'd sensed darkness in Diego, a stifled rage hidden behind broad smiles and laughter, but I'd have believed Audrey was a criminal before Diego Vega. His confession clobbered me like a sucker punch. I felt as blindsided as I had in the days after Jesse's suicide, when I began to learn how truly broken the boy I thought I knew everything about had been. "Why didn't you tell me?"

"Because the past isn't important. History is just a way of keeping score, but it doesn't have to be who we are."

"Great," I said, laughing at the absurdity. "I'm Space Boy, and you're a criminal."

Diego squeezed my hand. "We're not words, Henry, we're people. Words are how others define us, but we can define ourselves any way we choose."

I pulled my hand away. "Is that why you dress so oddly?"

"Part of it," Diego said. "Compared to other kids, I wasn't in juvie for that long, but it felt like forever. Being inside, it strips you of your identity. I was who the lawyers and the judge and the guards told me to be. Now I can be whoever I want, and I'm still struggling to figure out who that is, but the point is that the choice belongs to me."

Maybe he believed that, but it sounded to me like a lie he fed himself so that he could wake up in the morning believing he could change. That people would let him. "Can you take me home?"

We didn't talk on the drive, and I hated Marcus for fucking up the night. If I'd never seen him, I would have enjoyed the movie with Diego and we would have kissed and he wouldn't have told me about being in juvie and I wouldn't have been sitting in his car wondering what he'd done to deserve being there and what other secrets he was keeping from me. I understood he had his reasons, and it shouldn't have mattered what he'd done in the past, but it did. The past overshadowed everything I thought I knew about Diego. It made me think maybe he *had* smashed Marcus's car windows. And if he was capable of that, what else was he capable of?

Diego parked Please Start in front of the duplex. "I'm sorry, Henry. I should have told you the truth."

"Yeah."

"I've really fucked this up, haven't I?"

I brushed my hair out of my eyes and tried to look at him, but when I did, I was too tempted to forget the past. It didn't matter that history was our way of keeping score, since the points didn't matter, but I couldn't just ignore it. "Diego, I like you but . . ."

Diego ran his thumb down the side of my face. His touch was soft, and I wanted him to kiss me so badly. "I spent nearly two years locked up in juvie, dreaming about the outside world. I thought about my choices, about the things I'd done and the things I hadn't. I've never been to Paris or water-skied or fallen in love. When they let me out, I swore not to waste one second of my life. My counselor used to tell me that we remember the past, live in the present, and write the future. Even if the world ends next month or in a million years, we can still write our future, Henry."

"I want that to be true." I leaned my forehead against Diego's, felt his breath on my nose.

"Do you hate me now?"

"Kind of the opposite."

23 December 2015

Audrey and I braved the mall two days before Christmas. It was a demonic landscape of strollers and shoppers and bad holiday music that made me want to cut off my ears so that I would never again be forced to endure Wham! singing "Last Christmas." We killed time at the Apple store, waiting for someone in a blue shirt to acknowledge our presence while hordes of tiny, teething infidels ran screaming around us.

"Why do people who so obviously hate children have so many of them?" Audrey asked. I stuck out my tongue when she took my picture with one of the display phones.

"Because they hate everyone else more. Their bratty kids are their revenge on a society that has denied them the riches they so rightly deserve." As if to emphasize my point, an exhausted father watched his little angel pull a laptop off the table and throw it onto the ground with dead-eyed glee.

"You complete me, Henry Denton."

The mobs of people were making me claustrophobic, and I wanted them to die slowly of plague almost as much as I wanted to get the hell out of there. I felt as if each person within visual range were slowly draining the life from me. We were all connected, and the more of them there were, the more I wanted to crawl under a table and cry. "Can't you buy the computer online?"

Audrey shook her head. "It won't arrive in time, and I promised Mom I'd pick it up for her. Remember when she called the UPS guy a heartless, baby-killing Nazi because they lost the knives she ordered from Amazon?"

"Oh, I remember."

"Christmas makes her insane."

"I still need to find a gift for Diego."

A blue-shirted employee passed within arm's reach, and Audrey pounced on her, ignoring her protests. I wandered toward the front of the store while I waited for Audrey to finish.

I don't know how long he was standing there, but I noticed Adrian Morse on the other side of the store. He was wearing a blue shirt and grinning. I'd always assumed he was rich like Marcus, and it surprised me to find him working in the Apple store. A moment later every demo computer screen, monitor, phone, and tablet blinked, and their displays lit up with the picture of me covered in paint wearing the alien mask. Most of the shoppers were confused, but a few began to laugh. My face was hidden by the mask in the photo, but Adrian wasn't the only CHS student in the store, and they recognized me immediately.

I drew breaths in ragged jags, my heart raced, and my skin burned. The world went *waa-waa-waa* at the edges, and the floor seemed to tilt to the side. I tried to find Audrey, to focus on her and regain my equilibrium, but the crowd had swallowed her up.

"Oh my God. Is that him?"

"Space Boy?"

"What a freak."

"Really thinks aliens took him?"

"The mask's an improvement."

I fled the store, not caring where I went. I rounded a corner and blew through a side door into a dark labyrinth that led into the bowels of the mall. It reeked of trash and cigarette smoke. The taunts couldn't follow me there. I steadied myself against the wall. A kid in a hairnet, carrying a bag of garbage, trudged past, nodding in my direction before disappearing down the maze of walkways.

This part of the mall was quieter. Some doors were labeled with store names, others with numbers. Being in that store with all those shoppers laughing at me dragged me back into the gym showers. I felt my knobby wrists rubbing together painfully, felt my groin ache and the hair on my legs yanked off when Coach Raskin removed the tape. Marcus and his friends hadn't victimized me once; they did it every time they called me Space Boy or left a mask on my desk or paraded that fucking picture around for the world to see. I was tired of being the victim, but I didn't know how to be anything else.

I'm not sure how long Audrey had been calling, but I felt my phone vibrate in my pocket and answered it. She was frantic, so I rejoined her at the food court. The moment she saw me, she threw herself at me, crying. Her heavy shopping bag whacked me in the back, probably leaving a bruise.

"Sorry for running off."

Audrey's tears quickly became rage. "Don't you dare blame yourself."

"It was Adrian."

"I saw him." An evil grin lifted her lips. "But he won't cause problems anymore."

I waited for Audrey to spill, but she was savoring her victory. "Are you going to fill me in or what?"

Audrey pulled me out of the way. The mingling smells of

fried rice and pizza and burgers made me hungry. I hadn't eaten all day. "I may have e-mailed an anonymous tip to Principal DeShields from one of the phones in the Apple store."

"Wait, what?"

Audrey couldn't stop smiling the whole time she recounted her story. "I cornered Adrian's manager and explained what Adrian had done, but he didn't take me seriously. He's one of those dicks who calls everyone 'bro,' even girls, and he was never going to take my word over Adrian's." Audrey glowered, still fired up. "So I confronted Adrian myself."

A supernova occurs when the gravitational force of a star's core becomes greater than the star's energy output. The core collapses in on itself, ejecting the outer layers in a display of light and energy greater than that which the sun will produce over its entire lifetime. Adrian never stood a chance.

"You shouldn't have done that."

"You're right," she said. "You should have." Audrey gave me her Hell-yes-I-did-just-go-there stare, so I kept my mouth shut. "It was easy. I set a display phone to record video and confronted him about the picture. I'd only planned to use it to get him fired, but then the fool blabbed about actually snapping the picture. He went on and on about how much you struggled. I pretty much lost my shit."

My knees felt weak, like I'd stood up too fast. The blood

rushed to my head, and the world turned to static. I leaned against the wall until it passed. "Did you really record him saying that?"

"Yep!" Audrey had never looked more proud of herself. "Then I saved the video and e-mailed a copy to Principal DeShields. I'm sure she'll know what to do with it." She stood on her toes and kissed my cheek. "Merry Christmas, Henry."

I knew there would be repercussions, but I didn't care. Adrian was going to get what he deserved. I wish that made me feel some sense of relief or closure, but the victory was hollow. No matter what Principal DeShields did to Adrian, I'd still be Space Boy. Nothing could change that.

Despite the crowds, neither of us was ready to go home, so Audrey and I grabbed slices of greasy pizza, had our picture taken together with Santa, and each bought toys for the donation tree in the center of the mall. It was nearing closing time, and I still hadn't found a present for Diego.

"I'm terrible at gifts, Audrey."

Audrey tried to reassure me. "Pshaw. What are you talking about? I love my talking Gollum doll. Nothing says best-friendship like an emaciated demon who hides under your pillow snarling, 'My precious!' even after you remove his batteries and drown him in a bucket of water."

I laughed so loud, it sounded like a seal barking. I don't

know why I'd bought that doll except that Audrey once said she loved *The Lord of the Rings*. It was so creepy, I hid it in Charlie's closet until I was ready to wrap it. "Did Jesse ever show you the smittens I got him for his birthday?"

"What the hell is a smitten?"

"It's a mitten that two people can wear while holding hands." Audrey turned red; I thought she was choking on her tongue. "Come on! I thought it was cute!"

"We live in Florida!" Audrey linked her arm through mine and pulled me toward the coffee shop. "Tell me what you know about Diego."

"He's a good kisser."

"Yuck. Other than that?"

The more time Diego and I spent together, the less I felt I knew about him. Every layer I peeled back revealed a hundred more. "He likes to read. He's an artist. He doesn't drink."

"That's a list of stuff," she said. "What do you *know* about him?" Audrey ordered us coffees while I tried to come up with an answer. I knew loads about Jesse—he loved baths but hated hot tubs, he listened to self-important indie music, cologne made his eyes puffy, he never washed his jeans—but Diego was an enigma. Even though he'd finally fessed up about being in juvie, that had only raised more questions.

I wracked my brain for something. "He's sweet," I said.

"He'd give you his last dollar. Nothing scares him. He cuts a path through this world like he's got a plan, but I'm pretty sure he's making it up as he goes along." I sat down on the ledge surrounding one of the fountains with my head bowed. "I don't know, Audrey."

"Stop stressing. You'll figure something out."

"I shouldn't even be doing this."

Audrey sat beside me and rested her head on my arm. "Doing what?"

"Looking for a gift for Diego, thinking about Diego, imagining that we might have a future together. Even if the world doesn't end, he'd still end up abandoning me."

"You don't know that."

"Jesse did. It's my fault he's dead."

Audrey slapped my shoulder. "Are you soft in the head?"

"Jesse always said I didn't love him the way he loved me. He must've been right; otherwise, he wouldn't have killed himself."

She took my hand and kissed my fingers. My knuckles were still scabbed from punching the drywall with Charlie. "Jesse didn't die of a broken heart, Henry; he died of a broken brain." I tried to interrupt, but she cut me off. "It took a lot of therapy for me to understand that Jesse committed suicide because he was sick. It wasn't my fault, it wasn't his fault, and it sure as hell wasn't your fault."

"I should have been a better boyfriend."

"Depression isn't a war you win. It's a battle you fight every day. You never get to stop, never get to rest. It's one bloody fray after another. Jesse got worn down and didn't think he could fight anymore."

"Why? Why did he do it, Audrey?" My voice caught in my throat, and tears weren't far behind, but I didn't care. Fuck it, and fuck them.

"I don't know." Audrey shook her head.

To Jesse's parents, I was just some boy their son was dating. I'd eaten dinner with them a couple of times, but the conversations were awkward and unmemorable. "Sometimes I think about going to their house and asking to see Jesse's room one last time. He had to have left something behind explaining why he killed himself."

"What if he did? What then?"

"I don't know."

"Would it make you feel better?"

"No, but at least I'd know the truth."

Audrey said Jesse's suicide wasn't anyone's fault, but I think we all shared the blame. Me, Audrey, Jesse's parents, the kids at school. Sometimes when a star collapses, it becomes a fiery supernova, but other times the core density is so great that it quietly consumes itself, forming a black hole, its gravitational pull so terrible that nothing can escape, not even light. You can't see a black hole, but if you look closely, you can witness its effect on those objects nearest to it—the way it changes the orbits of solar systems or draws off a star's light a little at a time, sucking it down to its dense center.

Maybe we couldn't have stopped Jesse's collapse, but we should have seen it happening. If I can figure out why, I can stop it from ever happening again.

Audrey tossed her empty coffee in the trash. "You want to get out of here?"

"I still don't know what to get Diego for Christmas."

"You'll figure it out, Henry."

"And if I don't?"

Audrey took my arm and led me toward the parking lot. "Then give him the gift every horny teenage boy wants for Christmas."

"An Xbox?"

"I love you, Henry."

"I think he already has an Xbox, Audrey."

24 December 2015

As Mom studied Diego across the table, her fingers twitched, itching for a cigarette. She regarded him the way a battle-hardened general regards the enemy on the other side of a blood-soaked battlefield, which was weird since she was the one who'd invited him to dinner.

The whole thing had happened suddenly. Charlie and Zooey were arguing over paint colors for the baby's room while Diego and I played video games on the couch. Then Mom burst into the house and herded us all into the car for a surprise family dinner at Neptune's.

"So, Diego, where in Colorado are you from?"

Diego's mouth was full of a tomato wedge from his salad. His eyes grew wide, and he chewed quickly while everyone watched him, before spitting out, "Brighton."

"How's the renovation coming, Charlie?" I was trying to rescue Diego—I'd never seen him so adorably flustered—but my mother was not easily deterred.

"What brought you to Calypso?"

Diego set down his fork. Unlike at the barbecue, he had impeccable manners. He kept his elbows off the table, didn't talk with his mouth full, and used his napkin frequently. "I got into some trouble, so I came to live with my sister, Viviana."

"What kind of trouble?" My mother, the Grand Inquisitor.

"This isn't an interrogation," I said. As mortified as I was at her merciless prying, I was as anxious to hear the answers as she was. Only, I didn't want Diego to know that.

"Sounds like one to me," Charlie said. Zooey elbowed him in the ribs. She couldn't scoot all the way up to the table because of her bulging belly, but she didn't let that stop her from eating everything within reach—her salad, all the bread, Charlie's salad. Zooey's pregnancy was turning into a great diet for my brother.

"I'm only trying to get to know your boyfriend, sweet-heart."

"He's not my boyfriend."

Diego blushed. "We're just friends—"

"That make out," Charlie added. Diego blushed redder

332 · SHAUN DAVID HUTCHINSON

than ketchup, and I flashed my brother a death stare. "What? Don't leave your door open if you don't want me to record video of it and post it to SnowFlake."

"Henry, if you're going to have a friend you sometimes make out with, I have to get to know him." I couldn't believe we were discussing my nonrelationship with Diego in a restaurant on Christmas Eve. How could I explain my feelings for Diego to them when I didn't understand them myself? Not that Mom gave me the chance. "You were saying, Diego?"

Diego managed to remain calm, though I have no idea how. When he spoke, his voice was even, flat almost, and barely rose above the background noises of the restaurant. "I spent two years in a juvenile detention center for breaking my father's arm. Both arms, actually. And his nose. He also had a fractured skull, but that probably wasn't entirely my fault."

And the table descended into silence. Even my brother, who had a smartass remark for everything, was struck dumb. After Diego told me he spent time in juvenile detention, I'd tried to imagine what he'd been put away for. Nearly killing his father never made the list.

"My father believed in Jesus," Diego said quietly, "but he believed in meth more. He'd go on binges, spend weeks high and crazy, beating up my mom and sister. When he sobered up, he'd find the Lord and beg forgiveness, and we were supposed to accept that. My sister kept me out of trouble when she was home, but the day she turned eighteen, she packed a bag, boarded the first bus out of Brighton, and left. I was ten.

"For my thirteenth birthday, my mom fried up fresh fish for dinner and baked me a cake. Carrot, because it was my favorite. My dad came home, tweaking, and laid into my mom. Sometimes he used his fists, but that night he grabbed the dirty skillet off the stove. It was one of those heavy, cast-iron skillets that my mom had gotten from her mom who'd gotten it from *her* mom." Diego clenched his jaw, shook his head. "I don't actually remember what happened after that. My court-appointed shrink said that I'd been suppressing my anger for years and that I might have experienced a psychotic break.

"I pled to a lesser charge on my lawyer's advice, but my one condition was that I be allowed to live with Viviana after my release. So here I am."

No one ate a single bite during Diego's explanation. Charlie was still holding a loaded fork, but had forgotten it entirely. Based on what Diego had told me, I knew his father was abusive, but I wasn't prepared for the truth. Here I'd been whining about my life, and Diego had lost a chunk of his for protecting his mother from his bastard dad. If anyone should have wanted to not press the button, it was Diego.

"Jesus Christ, Henry, you sure know how to pick 'em." Charlie chuckled like this was a joke.

As soon as Diego stopped speaking, Mom began to eat again. Small bites that she chewed about a hundred times before swallowing. When the waiter passed nearby, she waved him down and ordered a vodka tonic.

Diego squeezed my hand under the table. I didn't squeeze it back.

Zooey rubbed her belly and offered Diego the table's only smile. "That must've been a horrible way to grow up. My psych professor says we never truly know what we're capable of until we're put into a hopeless situation."

"It's true," Diego said.

Mom wiped her mouth with the cloth napkin and set it on the table. The waiter returned with her drink and she drained it before saying, "I hope you learned how to deal with your anger while you were in juvenile detention."

"Not living with my father helps. And I paint."

Charlie slapped the table. "Shit, I've got two rooms that need painting. When my little bro pisses you off, come on over and grab a brush."

Zooey's eyes lit up. "Could you do a mural for the baby's room? I'll pay you."

I tried to intercede, but Charlie and Zooey sank their

claws into Diego, and he'd soon agreed to paint the baby's room, though he refused to accept money for his work. Charlie and Zooey got caught up wrangling over the color palette and only stopped when Diego suggested a combination of colors. He got along with my family better than I did.

Mom signaled the waiter for another drink. After he dropped it off, she cleared her throat to get our attention. "How do you like the restaurant?"

I hadn't given the place much thought. I'd been so nervous about Diego joining us for dinner that I'd barely noticed the surroundings. "It's cool, I guess." Neptune's was a quaint seafood restaurant with views of the intracoastal. Small and chummy, the decor was thrift-store chic, and the food was outstanding. It wasn't a normal dinner joint with bland selections you could find anywhere. The menu was inventive and playful and definitely not cheap.

Zooey was more enthusiastic. "My dad adores this place. He brings all his clients here."

"Five stars," Diego said, looking down at his completely clean plate. "I'd definitely eat here again."

"Good." Mom leveled her gaze at me and Charlie. "Look, I'm going to need you boys to pitch in around the house. Things are going to be tight for a while."

336 • SHAUN DAVID HUTCHINSON

Charlie cast me a questioning glance, but I was clueless. "Yeah," he said. "Okay, Mom."

"What's going on?" I asked.

"I quit Tutto Fresco."

My stomach dropped. I'd spent my savings on Christmas gifts. I began mentally calculating how much money I could give Mom to help with the bills if I returned them. And maybe I could get a job.

Charlie said, "You quit? Right before Christmas?"

"Yes." Mom sipped her vodka tonic. She sounded unconcerned, but her jaw muscles twitched, and she clutched her drink glass so tightly, I worried she might break it. "But don't you boys worry. I've got a new job."

"Where?" As soon as I asked, a smile blossomed on Mom's face, the tension fled. "Here? You're working here?"

Mom nodded. "I start after the new year."

"You think the tips will be better?" Charlie asked.

"I'm not waiting tables," Mom said. "I'm the new sous chef."

"Congratulations, Mrs. Denton," Diego said, unaware of how big a deal it was. Actually, I was glad he said it because I was too blown away to speak.

Mom glowed as she described how nervous and tongue-tied she'd been during the interview. She thought she'd blown it because of the way the owner's attention had wandered, but rather than give up, she marched into the kitchen and prepared a spicy tuna tartare. All it took was one bite, and the job belonged to her. It was a gutsy move, and I smiled thinking about how scared she must have been to ignore the head chef yelling at her for being in his kitchen while she chopped and sliced her way into a new job.

"I'm really proud of you, Mom." In fact, I'd never been more proud.

Zooey said, "What made you decide to go for it?"

Mom smiled at me. "Someone gave me a mirror."

After dinner, Diego and I meandered down the street in front of my house. Neither of us said much. The silence grew between us like a weed pushing through the cracks in a sidewalk. Finding out that my mom had quit her job waiting tables to follow her dream was huge, but Diego occupied my thoughts. I wondered who he'd been before he was locked away, and who his time in juvenile detention had turned him into. My Diego—with his carefree grin and slugger-green eyes—hardly seemed capable of hurting anyone, but he'd admitted to beating his father so badly that he'd broken his bones. Dinner had left me with more questions than answers. Was Diego a nice boy who sometimes lost his temper or a monster who'd mastered pretending to be nice?

"Your mom's cool," Diego said.

"Sorry about the interrogation."

"At least she didn't pull out my fingernails or electrocute my genitals."

"She's probably saving that for next time."

The weather had finally turned cooler, though it still didn't feel like Christmas. I grew up in Florida, where it's a miracle if it gets cold enough to need a hoodie, but Christmas just doesn't feel right without snow and hot chocolate and a roaring fire. I suppose television and movies have brainwashed me. Or maybe we're just born with some beliefs in our bones. "How come you never told me about your dad?"

Diego stopped in the middle of the road. I stood beside him, unsure what to do next. The houses on my street were decorated with bright holiday lights, displaying their glowing Santas and candy canes, but it still felt like Diego and I were alone in the world.

He started walking back toward my house, and when the silence was almost too much to bear, Diego said, "You know that painting you like?" I nodded, remembering the bird clawing at the boy's heart, and the last word frozen on his dead lips. "I painted that the night before I reported to juvie. The judge had accepted my plea agreement, and I was living with my uncle because I couldn't go back to my parents' house. It was going to be my last night of freedom for a long time—I should have gone out with my friends or spent time with Viviana—but I spent the whole night painting. That was the worst day of my life, and that painting was me on the worst day of my life." Diego knuckled tears from the corner of his eyes.

"Maybe that's not how I see myself now—some days, I don't know—but it's how everyone else sees me—my family, my friends, my sister. Everyone who knows the truth." Diego stopped walking and turned to me. "I never wanted you to see me that way."

"It wasn't your fault."

"I almost killed my dad!" Diego shouted. He clenched his fists and bit his lip. He trembled and shook, and I didn't know how to help him. "When it comes to the people I care about, everything gets messed up in my head. I don't know who I am, but I know who I don't want to be."

We stood in front of my duplex. Light peeked through the curtains of my living room window, and I thought I saw my mom's shadow. I couldn't look at Diego without imagining his dead-eyed stare as he attacked his father, without wondering if he'd enjoyed the sound of cracking bones or smiled when he saw the blood on his hands. "Did you smash the windows of Marcus's car?"

"If you have to ask, then my answer won't matter." Diego's voice was flat, and he wouldn't look me in the eyes. He sat on the hood of his car, fidgeting with his keys.

"Tell me you didn't do it, and I'll believe you."

"No, you won't." Diego stood up, kissed my cheek, and got in his car. "Merry Christmas, Henry."

I called Audrey as soon as Diego's car disappeared down the street. She was waiting outside of my house fifteen minutes later. We drove to IHOP and got a corner booth and some pancakes, which didn't make me feel any better. Audrey talked about inconsequential things while I tried to sort out what had happened with Diego. It felt like a breakup even though we were never a couple. His leaving hurt like the punch of finality that only comes from a broken heart. I recognized the pain because I'd felt it the day I found out Jesse was dead.

"I miss him," I said. I hadn't meant to say it out loud; I'd only been thinking it.

"You'll work it out with Diego."

"Not Diego. Jesse."

"Oh." Audrey chewed a bite of soggy pancake, but I imagined it tasted like gravel to her, the way everything had tasted like gravel to me since Jesse's death. "I miss him too."

"He should be sitting beside me, holding my hand under the table, kicking my foot with his foot, turning everything into a dirty joke." I dragged my fork through the syrup on my plate, creating trenches that quickly filled in again. "If Jesse were here, everything would be different."

"Yeah," Audrey said, "it would be. But Jesse's not here. I am and you are. Jesse's dead, Henry."

"Why? Why did Jesse kill himself?"

Audrey shook her head, raised her napkin to her face like she was going to cry. I waited for her to give me the answer I'd been waiting months and months for. "I don't know. I wish I knew, but I don't. I wish I could point to one specific reason that caused Jesse to give up, but I can't. Sometimes, people just quit wanting to live, and there's no good reason for it. It's so fucking selfish and cruel to the people left behind, but we can't change that. We can only live with it."

The rational voice in my head knew Audrey was right, but the other voice—the one that loved Jesse and hated him and felt terrible for not trusting Diego—refused to accept what she was saying. "I know Jesse, Audrey. He would have left something behind."

"He didn't."

"I tried to ask his parents at the funeral, but they wouldn't speak to me."

"I'm sure the police searched Jesse's belongings for a suicide note."

"They didn't know Jesse; they wouldn't have known what to look for."

Our server approached with a cheery smile that disappeared the moment he saw Audrey's grim expression. He dropped the check and scurried away. "I can't make this better for you, Henry. Jesse's gone, and we've got to move forward with our lives. You've got your family, a niece on the way, and a guy who really likes you."

All those things were true, but I'd stopped paying attention as an idea struck me. It began as a spark and exploded, spreading like a universe within my mind. Audrey was still talking when I said, "Let's break into Jesse's house."

"What?"

My thoughts whizzed around my skull so near the speed of light that I could never catch them. "It's Christmas Eve. Jesse's parents dragged him to Providence every year for Christmas. They won't be home. I know where they keep a spare key, and I know the alarm code."

It was a perfect idea, and I couldn't understand why Audrey was staring at me slack-jawed and bewildered. "Why on Earth would we break into Jesse's house?"

"To figure out why he killed himself."

"But why, Henry? Why does it matter?"

I slammed my fist onto the table, causing the plates of soggy pancakes and mugs of bitter coffee to jump. The other diners turned to stare, but I couldn't be bothered. "Because if Jesse didn't have a reason for killing himself, then his death was meaningless. And if Jesse's death is meaningless, then so are our lives. So is everything, Audrey. I thought you out of everyone would get that." I threw some cash onto the table and walked to the parking lot. The night sky was clear, but I could hardly see the stars for all the streetlights. They were up there, though. I'd seen them from the slugger's ship. I'd seen them all.

The door opened and closed behind me, but I didn't turn around. "You know," I said, "if we were on one of the planets in the Alpha Centauri system, looking toward Earth, we'd see Jesse still alive."

"But he wouldn't be, would he?"

I shook my head.

"What would be the point of watching Jesse die all over again if we couldn't do anything to prevent it?"

"At least we'd know."

Audrey walked to her car, unlocked the doors, and got in. She started the engine and rolled down the windows. I stood watching the stars. "Come on. If we're going to commit a felony, we've got to do it before my curfew."

• • •

I spent a lot of time at Jesse's house when he was alive, but I never really looked at it until Audrey and I parked on the street and sat quietly in her car with the lights off. It was a typical Florida house, which is to say there was nothing architecturally interesting about it. It had no history, no quirky lines or idiosyncratic ornamentations. It was solid and functional, though larger than most of the other houses on the street. The hedges under the windows were trimmed so perfectly, I doubt I could have found a single leaf out of place. The grass was green and neat, the mulch surrounding the various trees bright and woody. The driveway was marred by nothing, not even a single drop of oil. The Franklins' house was pristine, perfect, and sterile, right down to the tasteful white holiday lights that lined the edge of the roof, and the festive wreath hanging from the front door.

"Are we doing this?" Audrey asked. "If we're doing this, we should go now." She'd been rambling like that for fifteen minutes, reciting everything she'd ever seen on TV about how to not get caught breaking into someone's house, and the penalties if we were. I wanted to tell her this wasn't an exam to be failed, but I got the feeling she'd melt down if I tried to silence her.

Audrey's car didn't stand out, which was a boon to us,

as were the Christmas Eve parties happening at a few of the Franklins' neighbor's houses. One set of teenagers would hardly be remembered by someone who might have glimpsed us as they stood on their front porch, guzzling spiked eggnog and trying to avoid one more pinch on the cheek from Aunt So-and-So.

"In and out," I said. "Mr. and Mrs. Franklin probably haven't even gone into Jesse's room since . . . Everything will look the same as it did the last time I was there." I tried not to think about that last time or about what we'd done. I had to remain focused.

"What if Jesse didn't leave a note, Henry?"

"Then he left a journal entry or an e-mail he never sent or a video he recorded on his phone that no one thought to check. There has to be something."

Audrey grabbed my hand and held it to her chest. She was sweating through her thin Muppets shirt. "Finding out why Jesse killed himself won't change anything."

"You're right. It'll change everything."

I got out of the car before I lost my nerve. I was halfway across the lawn when Audrey caught up. I hoped to find out that Jesse had killed himself because someone had molested him when he was little or because his parents beat him or because he'd had a crisis of faith and couldn't reconcile being gay with his belief in God. I didn't actually believe any of those things were true, and I didn't want to think that Jesse had been tormented by them, but if there had been some horror in Jesse's life that had driven him to suicide, at least I'd know it wasn't my fault.

Audrey stumbled, and I caught her by the elbow. Anyone watching would have thought we were just a couple of tipsy kids. I led her around the side of the house to the back patio. The waterfall splashed into the pool, reminding me that I needed to pee. I pushed my bladder aside and went straight for the Christmas cactus on a metal shelf with a dozen other plants. Red-and-white blossoms burst out of the padlike stems. The key was under the pot. Jesse's parents hadn't even known he'd kept a spare for those nights he needed to sneak in. I put it to its intended use one last time.

As we entered the house, Audrey hooked her finger through the belt loop of my jeans and crept so closely behind me that her breath warmed my neck. The alarm beeped its insistent warning, and I silenced it with Jesse's birthday. The outside lights poured through the windows, but even without them, I could have navigated my way through the kitchen, to the living room, and up the grand staircase to Jesse's room—third door on the right.

"We don't need to do this, Henry." Audrey whispered

even though the house was empty, and there was no one to hear us. The house felt more than empty. It felt gutted.

"There are answers behind this door." There was also truth, memories of times that sparkled in my mind like exposed bits of broken glass in a heaping pile of shit. Some of my best days happened behind that door, and they would never happen again.

I turned the knob, pushed open the door, and turned on the light. Jesse's bed stood in the center of the room, unmade; his long chest of drawers lined the far wall, the surface crowded with dirty clothes and half-empty water bottles and whatever scraps of the day he'd pulled out of his pockets and tossed there; across from his bed was a TV stand with a TV and four game systems, the controllers on the floor; and a small desk hunched in the corner, bearing the weight of a hundred books on its back.

Only, none of those things were there.

They should have been; they'd always been before. The books changed, the dirty laundry rotated items, but the fundamentals remained constant.

Audrey poked her head in, pulled it back out, and looked around. "Is this the right room?" She already knew the answer. She'd spent more time in Jesse's house than I had.

The bed was gone, the dresser gone, the desk and books and

game consoles. Gone. Even Jesse's posters of the Broadway shows he'd seen—*Miss Saigon* and *Little Shop of Horrors* and *Wicked*— were gone. Jesse's parents had transformed his bedroom into a sewing room. The walls were painted a tasteful yellow, antique shelves filled with bolts of cloth in every color lined the walls. Drawings of gowns were tacked to a corkboard, and racks held examples of work in various stages of completion.

Jesse wasn't there. It was as if he'd never existed at all.

"Henry . . ."

Audrey put her hand on my shoulder, but the weight was too much, and I sank to my knees. There were no truths to find in Jesse's bedroom. No absolution.

I didn't cry. There was no point. There was no point to anything. "It's all fucked up, Audrey. Jesse's dead, and it's probably my fault because I didn't love him enough or I wasn't good enough for him and he kept so many secrets from me that I thought maybe if I'd known I could have stopped him from killing himself, so I pushed Diego because he's the first person who's made me think maybe I was wrong, maybe it wasn't my fault, and maybe I could press the button and have a future that wasn't meaningless, but I pushed him too far and now he's gone too."

Audrey knelt beside me. She held my hand to her chest. "Henry, Diego's not gone."

"He told me about being in juvie and about how he got sent there for beating up his dad to protect his mom, and I accused him of smashing the windows in Marcus's car."

"Oh, Henry, you didn't."

"I fucked up so bad, Audrey."

As she was about to say something, the floor beneath us vibrated. I leapt to my feet. "Shit!"

"What?" Audrey asked, but I was shutting off the light and grabbing her hand to run.

"Someone's home." Jesse's bedroom had been over the garage, and it had always given us plenty of warning when his parents came home so that we could dress and compose ourselves and pretend we'd been playing video games while alone in his house rather than what his parents knew we'd actually been doing.

"I thought you said they were out of town!"

"They should be." We flew down the stairs, but I stopped at the landing.

"What?" Audrey whispered.

"I need to check one more place." Audrey pulled my arm. "You go. I'll meet you at the car." I dashed back up the stairs before she could stop me.

Jesse's parents had practiced a fairly distant approach to parenting. They did the things parents were supposed to do, but they'd generally let him do whatever he wanted. He hadn't needed to password protect his computer to keep them from prying or hide anything he didn't want them to see. They respected his privacy. It was the cleaning people that made him nervous. Mr. Franklin couldn't keep a housecleaner for more than a month, so the ever-changing array of people parading through his bedroom while he was at school had caused Jesse to develop a healthy sense of paranoia. Jesse owned few valuables he considered worth hiding, but those he did he kept in a hollow space under his bathroom sink.

I didn't have much time, so I gave up attempting to be quiet, and ran through Jesse's bedroom to the connecting bathroom. His parents had redecorated it as well, though not as radically. I dropped to my knees, opened the cabinet doors, shoved the stacked toilet paper out of the way, and reached into the hole. I felt around for the cigar box he kept his treasures in, but it wasn't there. I reached as deeply into the hole as I could, twisting my arm around to feel with my fingers, but I felt nothing. The box was gone. Everything was gone.

I'd never know why Jesse killed himself. My sole consolation was that I only had to live with that for thirty-six more days.

I crept out of the room that no longer belonged to Jesse, and stood at the top of the stairs. Mr. and Mrs. Franklin were arguing in the kitchen.

"Don't use that tone with me, Russell. I set the alarm before we left." Mrs. Franklin's voice was an iron rod.

"You're right. It must have disarmed on its own."

They fought while I stood quietly trying to figure out how to escape. The stairs were the only way down. When I heard footsteps coming my way, I ducked into the linen closet and shut the door behind me. I held my breath, praying that neither of Jesse's parents needed clean sheets or towels. Five minutes must have passed before I heard water running from the direction of the Franklins' bedroom, though it felt like days. I cracked open the door and peeked down the hallway. It was empty.

I ran down the stairs, through the dining room, and to the back door. I opened it, and as I prepared to dash to freedom, a voice called my name, and I froze.

"Henry Denton?"

I could have kept running. I should have kept running. Mrs. Franklin hadn't seen my face. She wouldn't have been able to prove that it had been me in her house. But I turned around anyway.

"Hi, Mrs. Franklin."

The last time I'd seen her was at Jesse's funeral. She'd worn a dignified black dress and hadn't cried. The last year hadn't changed her. She still wore black. Her blond hair was wavy and loose, curling around her neck. So much of Jesse's looks had come from her—the slightly upturned nose, the eyes that saw through all bullshit, the long, thin fingers—and it hurt to see pieces of him standing right in front of me.

"I wanted to . . . I needed to see . . . I can't believe you turned Jesse's bedroom into a sewing room."

Mrs. Franklin's mouth moved, but no sound came out. Her face was emotionless, a blank lump of clay. There was nothing left for me to say, nothing left for me in that house. All traces of Jesse had been eradicated.

"Henry, I—"

I didn't wait around to hear the rest. I bolted out the door and didn't stop until I reached Audrey's car. The lights were off, but the engine was running, and she peeled out as soon as I was inside.

We were both quiet until we reached Audrey's house. She parked and shut off the engine. I climbed out and walked to the end of her driveway. Audrey sat beside me.

"There's something I need to tell you, Henry."

I wasn't in the mood to talk. Mrs. Franklin's face haunted me. The way she'd hardly seemed surprised to see me. How she'd disposed of Jesse like he'd never mattered. I hoped when the world ended, she would die terrified and alone. Even that was better than she deserved.

"Can I sleep here tonight?"

Audrey nodded. "Sure, but, Henry—"

"Whatever it is, it doesn't matter."

"Diego didn't smash up Marcus's car. I did." She spit out the words fast, sending them hurtling toward me like photons from the sun, and I didn't see them coming until they blinded me.

"You?"

"Me."

"But . . . why?"

Audrey shrugged like committing a felony was no big deal. "Marcus McCoy is a dick, and you're my best friend."

I was still trying to wrap my head around the idea that Audrey had busted the windows of Marcus's car. For me. "You could have gotten arrested."

Maybe it was only the shadows, but she loomed over me in her driveway that night. She carried herself like a warrior, and spoke as fiercely. "I did it, and I'd do it again."

I leaned my head on Audrey's shoulder. "Thank you."

Bees?

The phenomenon is first observed in France. The year is 1994. Bees exposed to a new type of pesticide known as neonicotinoids exhibit confusion and odd behavior. Bees often abandon the hive, leading to the collapse of the entire colony.

In 2006, United States beekeeper David Hackenberg reports to Congress on an unexplained phenomenon known as Colony Collapse Disorder (CCD) that had spread to over 70 percent of the bee populations in the country. The cause is yet unknown, but there is speculation linking it to pesticides, fungicides, mites, and parasites.

In 2013, CCD contributes to the deaths of 60 percent of all hives. Scientists speak out against the use of certain neonicotinoids, and some countries limit or ban their use on crops, but the rate of collapse remains unchanged.

On 29 January 2016, the last hive of honeybees, located on an almond farm in California, succumbs to CCD.

The price of orange juice skyrockets overnight. Blueberries and almonds disappear from shelves. Onions become impossible to purchase. Within the first year, many common fruits simply vanish. Their juices, stored in tanks, become more precious than caviar. Pumpkins become too expensive to carve on Halloween.

The effect of the loss of honeybees ripples to other crops. Coffee becomes a luxury few can afford. Worldwide food shortages lead to riots. The economies of states and countries that depend on honeybee-pollinated crops collapse shortly after the hives.

The United States is the first. Unable to feed its people, unemployment soars to more than 50 percent. Disease runs rampant because few can afford health care, but starvation remains the number-one killer. Other nations soon follow.

War, famine, and death become the rule of the planet. The poison that caused the collapse of the honeybees spreads to the human population, and, just as the bees did, humanity goes slowly mad.

25 December 2015

Grief is an ocean, and guilt the undertow that pulls me beneath the waves and drowns me.

I woke up in Audrey's bed, clutching my throat, gasping for breath. In my dreams I was drowning. I was in Jesse's bedroom. It still looked the way it had when he was alive, except the ocean was rushing in to fill it. I tried to keep my head above water, but Jesse was at the bottom, pulling me down.

Light streamed through the windows. Audrey was deep asleep, hugging her pillow, a shirt covering her face. It didn't feel like Christmas morning. I wanted to close my eyes and sleep until the end of the world, but I needed to go home before my mom realized I wasn't there.

Rather than wake up Audrey, I left her a note and borrowed her bicycle. Her house was only a couple of miles from mine, and the ride gave me time to think. A little about Jesse, but mostly about Diego. I'd screwed everything up. He was right that I shouldn't have had to ask him if he was responsible for smashing Marcus's windows. I should have trusted him. I wasn't sure if he'd accept my apology, but I needed to try.

When I reached home, I was sweaty and out of breath. I dropped the bike in front of the duplex. Mr. Nabu was watching me from across the street. I waved; he waved back. I wondered how many times he'd seen me sneak home in the morning wearing nothing but my underwear or a trash can lid.

I figured I'd peek through the window to make sure the rest of the house was still asleep before I snuck inside. When we were kids, Mom had discouraged me and Charlie from waking up at dawn on Christmas morning by instituting a rule that the first person out of bed had to make breakfast for everyone else. By the time we hit our teens, it was a competition to see who could stay in bed the longest. Usually, we didn't get around to opening presents until after noon.

I eased into the bushes and spied through the window. To my surprise, everyone was awake and gathered in the living room. Mom must have picked Nana up from the home early, and they sat on the couch together. Zooey was relaxing in the recliner next to the sofa, and Charlie had his back to me, digging around for something under the Christmas tree.

Mom clapped her hands and held up a chef's knife. The knife I bought for her. They were opening gifts without me. Had they gone into my room to see if I was awake? Did they even know I wasn't home? I was about to storm inside when Charlie stood in the center of the room. I couldn't hear what he was saying, but Zooey's hand flew to her mouth as Charlie took a knee. He slipped a ring on Zooey's finger, and she threw her arms around him and kissed him. I imagined her shouting, "Yes! Yes, I'll marry you," acting like it was a surprise even though she had to have been expecting it.

I couldn't believe he'd proposed to Zooey, and I'd missed it. He hadn't even waited until I was awake. They were opening presents and proposing without me.

"Everything all right, young man?" called Mr. Nabu. He was tough and stringy, like old celery, but his bright eyes missed nothing.

I walked toward Mr. Nabu's house. "If you knew the world was ending and could prevent it, would you?"

Mr. Nabu set his newspaper in his lap. His bald head was speckled with liver spots, and his spectacles sat low on his nose. "It's Christmas, young man, and I'm reading my newspaper alone on my front porch."

"Merry Christmas, sir." I nodded and trudged around to the side of the house to crawl in through the bathroom window.

Physicists theorize that up to 27 percent of the mass-energy content of the universe is composed of what they refer to as dark matter. Dark matter is nonreactive to light and has so far eluded all efforts to prove its existence. However, the existence of dark matter is widely accepted because it explains the discrepancies found between the mass of large astronomical objects and their gravitational effect. The argument for the existence of dark matter can be observed in the motions of galaxies. Most do not contain enough observable mass to support the gravitational forces necessary to hold them together. Much like my family. Sometimes I watch them and wonder how we all don't fly apart.

The engagement was all anyone could talk about for the rest of the day. No one heard me when I accidentally tore down the shower curtain sneaking into the house. They didn't even apologize for not waiting until I was awake to open presents. Every ten minutes, Nana gave me a sticky kiss on the cheek and told me how glad she was to see me. Charlie and Zooey couldn't stop touching each other, and Mom spent nearly every minute in the kitchen, making trays of hors d'oeuvres a troupe of traveling acrobats couldn't have finished.

I couldn't wait to leave.

Mrs. Franklin must not have called the police to report me, though I jumped at every sound and spent hours peeking out the windows, waiting for a patrol car to arrive. Honestly, spending a few days in jail might not have been the worst thing to happen to me. When my mom and brother were tipsy enough that I knew they wouldn't notice I was gone, I rode Audrey's bicycle to Diego's house. I stood at his front door, sweaty and stinky, clutching a bag of gifts.

Diego opened the door, wearing pajama bottoms decorated with cartoon elves, and a gray tank top. His hair was rumpled like he'd just woken up, even though it was mid-afternoon.

"I'm sorry." Before Diego could tell me to leave, I rambled on. "Audrey smashed the windows and I should have believed you but I trusted Jesse and he kept secrets from me and killed himself and I don't think I could ever go through something like that again."

"I'm not Jesse."

"I know."

"I'm not going to kill myself."

"I know."

Diego stood in the doorway, blocking it with his whole body. I hoped he could forgive me, but I doubted my chances. "I wish I *had* smashed Marcus's car windows. I wanted to smash his face for what he did to you. I will if he ever hurts you again . . ." He shook his head. "I think you were right about us just being friends. You're still messed up over Jesse, and I've clearly got my own issues to work through."

I couldn't argue. Starting a relationship under the best of circumstances is difficult. For us, it would have been a disaster. That didn't stop me from wanting to push Diego into the house and kiss him until the world ended. From imagining what a future might look like with him in it. But I couldn't afford to think like that. I held up the bag. "Christmas gifts."

"I got you something too." Diego hesitated before standing aside to let me in.

"Where's Viviana?"

"Her boyfriend's house."

"She left you alone on Christmas?"

"Nah," Diego said. "We had breakfast and opened our presents earlier. She had to go do the Christmas thing with her boyfriend's family."

"Oh."

"Wait here." Diego left me in the living room, and I sat on the couch. He returned a moment later with a couple of wrapped packages that he set on top of the coffee table.

"You first." I pulled the presents out of the bag and handed them to him.

"What's this?" Diego tore the paper like a pro. None of that prissy trying-to-spare-the-paper-to-reuse-next-year stuff. He was a ripper, and I adored that. "I love Frida Kahlo." Diego fingered the book's cover before flipping through it, stopping at some of his favorite works.

"Your paintings remind me of hers."

"It's . . . perfect!" Diego sat with the book in his lap, just staring at it for a moment before opening the rest of his gifts. Along with the book, I got him a pair of real flip-flops, *Doctor Who* pajama pants, and a one-pound bag of cereal marshmallows. "What am I going to do with all these marshmallows?"

"I don't know, but everyone should have a bag of emergency cereal marshmallows." I pulled a last gift from the bottom of the bag.

"Henry!" Diego frowned but accepted the gift.

"The others were . . . you know . . . This one is special."

Diego tore into it with the same zeal as the others but froze when he saw the front. It was a simple black journal with leather front and back covers, and pages with a deckle edge. But it wasn't the journal that had caught his attention; it was what was etched into the front.

REMEMBER THE PAST,

LIVE THE PRESENT,

WRITE THE FUTURE.

Diego traced the words. I couldn't tell if he liked it or not. He'd practically gone catatonic.

"I thought you could use it to record all the stuff you want to do," I said. "I don't know. It's stupid. If you hate it, I can take it back." Of course, I couldn't take it back because of the etching, but whatever.

"Thank you, Henry." It was only three words, but it felt like more to me. It felt like a wish that we could go back and forget I'd accused him of breaking Marcus's windows, that we could forget about his past and my Jesse and meet at a time before tragedy had consumed either of us. But that wasn't possible, and this was all we had. For these last thirty-five days we could be friends, and that would have to be enough.

Diego handed me my gifts.

I looked at the wrap job, and grinned. "That was so sweet of you to let those poor orphans with no fingers do your wrapping for you."

"Whatever," Diego said. "It's abstract wrapping. You just don't understand my art." There were four badly wrapped gifts in all. A book about rockets and space travel written in

1948, a retractable fountain pen, a bottle of dark red ink that looked like blood, and a star chart.

"You shouldn't have done all this."

Diego grinned like crazy. "There's one more." He handed me an envelope. "Open it."

I expected it to be a card, and I felt like a jerk for not getting Diego one. Only, it wasn't a card. Inside were two tickets to see Janelle Monáe in concert. I'd only mentioned liking her once. "I can't believe you remembered." I turned the tickets over, scanning them for the when and where. The show was at a club in Fort Lauderdale. On February 2, 2016. "Diego—"

"If the world doesn't end, we can go. Or you can take Audrey if you want. Either way, I thought having something to look forward to might help you make your decision."

"You still want me to press the button, even after what I did?"

Diego smiled. His hand twitched like he wanted to touch my cheek but was fighting the impulse. "I still want *you* to want to press it."

I wish I could say that it was my idea, but that honor belonged to Jesse Franklin. Jesse believed stories were the collective memories of the world, recorded in books so that each of us could know who we were before we became who we are. He said that's why people love *The Catcher in the Rye* when they're teenagers, but fall out of love with it as adults. We're all Holden Caulfield at fifteen, but when we grow up we want to be Atticus Finch. I didn't exactly buy Jesse's theory, but I stumbled upon the copy of *To Kill a Mockingbird* he'd loaned me, and it came back to me. That's when I knew what I needed to do.

Audrey and Diego were both in on the plan—it'd been easy to convince them. Convincing TJ to let us into Nana's room without her permission required a more devious approach.

"And that, gentlemen, is what boobs are good for," Audrey said as she shut Nana's door behind us and dropped the box she was carrying onto the empty bed. We hadn't spoken about breaking into Jesse's house, and I was happy to forget it had ever happened.

I rolled my eyes, but I doubt we would have gotten in without her. "You can finish patting yourself on the back later. Mom said she'd have Nana here by three thirty, which leaves us less than an hour."

Diego scanned the bare room. "Where should we start?" It was difficult to resist holding his hand or leaning over to kiss him. I caught myself a couple of times, forgetting we'd agreed to just be friends, and I wondered if it were easier for Diego.

"Let's start at the beginning."

It took the entire hour, all three of us working quickly to finish before Nana returned. That didn't include our preparation from the last two days. This was my belated Christmas gift to Nana, and one that she wouldn't need to remember to appreciate.

Mom wasn't in on the plan. Not the real plan. I'd only told her that I wanted to hang something in Nana's room at the nursing home as a surprise, and convinced her to delay bringing Nana back after spending Christmas with us. My phone buzzed, letting me know they were close. We finished in a mad rush, and were waiting outside the door for Nana when she arrived.

"What's this, Charlie? What are all of you doing here?" A few of the residents shuffled from their rooms, drawn by Nana's annoyed tone.

"Come on, Nana. There's something I want to show you." I held out my hand and led her into the room.

I already knew what was on the other side of the door, so I watched Nana's face when she saw it for the first time. Her tight frown eased, fell, and disappeared completely, replaced by confused awe as she tried to take in everything at once. The walls were almost completely covered in pictures of Nana's life. There had been hundreds of photographs in the boxes Charlie had taken from her room, and the ones we'd chosen barely represented a tenth of them.

"This is the story of you."

Nana touched the nearest picture. She was dancing with a handsome young man. Her left arm was raised, and her flowered dress twirled around her, open like an umbrella. If you listened closely, you could hear the Coasters singing "Poison Ivy" in the background. Nana couldn't have been older than I am when that photo was taken. That girl's face was unlined, untroubled, and unconcerned about the future.

Framed next to the picture was a photocopy of a hand-written journal entry. The boy's name had been Kenny Highcastle, and Nana had only allowed him to escort her to the dance because her mother insisted, but she'd had the time of her life that night. Each picture we'd hung had a corresponding journal entry, and Nana's life filled the spaces of all four walls.

"Even if they steal all your memories, they can't steal the amazing life you led. Whenever you forget, just come in here until you remember again," I said.

Nana shuffled around the room, moving from photograph to photograph, stopping at some longer than others. "Oh! I remember this. Your father and I bought our very first car. A Pontiac Tempest, Teal Turquoise. I never did learn how to drive it."

"Yes, but you were the only mother on the PTA who could drive a tractor." Mom stood behind me and rested her hands on my shoulders.

A few of the other residents trickled in. "Look, Hannah. Charlie found my missing memories. They're all here." Watching Nana show off her life, all the things she'd done, was the most amazing feeling in the world. I didn't even care that she called me Charlie.

Maybe our lives did have meaning. Nana's did. It meant

something to her and to the people in her photographs. Each and every one of those memories was a moment that had mattered, even the ones that hadn't seemed important at the time.

Mom kissed my cheek before she left. Audrey, Diego, and I stuck around a while longer, listening to Nana recount stories from the pictures. I figured, even if she didn't always know she was the woman who'd lived this life, she'd know how important it was.

On the way out, Audrey said, "For a guy who thinks the world is going to end in a few weeks, that was a pretty amazing thing to do."

"Nana deserves to be happy, for however long we have left."

Diego shrugged and said, "She's not the only one."

31 December 2015

Mom decided to celebrate New Year's Eve with her girl-friends at the Hard Rock Casino, leaving the house to me and Charlie with explicit instructions not to throw a party, which we obviously planned to ignore.

We weren't going to host a rager—just Zooey, a few of Charlie's friends who were home from college, Audrey, and Diego. I told Audrey she could go to Marcus's party if she didn't want to hang out with us, but she said she'd rather eat a flaming cockroach, which seemed a little dramatic. And gross. Marcus had been bragging about his New Year's Eve bash on SnowFlake all week. He even texted me an invitation, but I never responded.

After I finished moving Mom's breakables into her bed-room and locking the door, I checked on the snack and alcohol situation. Between Diego's Christmas gifts and the picture frames for Nana, I'd blown most of my meager savings. Mom had given Charlie her engagement ring, which was a family heirloom, but remodeling the baby's room meant he was also broke. Hopefully, no one would notice we'd bought the off-brand sodas and chips, no dip, and liquor so bottom shelf it was practically on the floor. Charlie filtered the vodka through our water purifier—a trick he'd learned from his college-going buddies—and paired it with the off-brand sodas that had names like Pop! and Lemony-Lime Fresh. I checked on the cocktail wieners baking in the oven. Those, of course, were nothing more than a family pack of hot dogs cut up and wrapped in croissant dough. The only thing worse would have been if we'd served ramen, and don't think we didn't consider it.

"Charlie! Charlie, where are the cups?" I searched cupboards for the stack of red plastic cups I knew we'd bought.

"In here!" Charlie yelled.

Why in the world did Charlie have them? People were going to start showing up in a few minutes, and I still needed to shower. I stomped back to his bedroom. The plastic sheeting was gone, and Charlie stood in the doorway, grinning. "I wanted to finish before everyone arrived."

"Finish what?"

"The baby's room."

"Oh." Even though I still had a ton to do, I knew he wanted me to ask. "Can I see?"

Charlie nodded, manic and proud. He stood aside and motioned for me to enter. What had once been his bedroom was transformed from a smelly, dreary man cave into a simple, neatly organized room. He'd replaced his lumpy twin bed with a new full-size mattress, added curtains to the windows, and bought a new dresser. They'd settled on painting the walls a soft blue. On the baby's side of the room, they didn't have much in the way of furniture, but they'd found a crib, a changing table, and rocking chair.

"Isn't that Nana's old rocking chair?"

"Mom got it out of storage." He was beaming. I wondered how many generations of our family had been rocked in that chair. Around the time my mom was rocking Charlie in it for the first time, light from the star Delta Pavonis was beginning its journey toward Earth. From its point of view, Charlie was still a colicky baby who barely slept for his first few months of life. In the triple-star system 26 Draconis, Mom was the baby and Nana the beautiful woman nursing her.

I walked deeper into the room. A mural of a tree decorated the far wall. Its branches reached high and stretched wide, and under it sat a little girl who resembled both

Charlie and Zooey, staring at the stars overhead, a secret smile on her face.

"Your boyfriend did that," Charlie said.

"He's not my boyfriend."

Charlie rolled his eyes. "Whatever." He smacked my arm playfully. "He says it's not finished, that he's got to paint stars on this wall, and the sun on the other side. Zooey knows all the details. It's supposed to be, like, the turning of a whole day or some shit."

"Jesus, Charlie, I can't believe you did all of this."

"It's not permanent, you know, but it's a start." I stood there admiring the work my brother and Zooey had put into creating a perfect little corner of the universe for their family. My brother wasn't a kid anymore. I don't know that anyone is ever ready to have a baby of their own, but Charlie was as prepared as anyone could be.

"Hey, so what do you think of the name Evie?"

"Evie . . ." I said, trying it out. "I like it."

"Good."

"Evie Denton." The more I said it aloud, the more real it felt. She wasn't the little parasite anymore. She had a room and a mural and a crib to sleep in. She had a name. My niece and goddaughter, Evie Denton.

· · ·

It was still an hour until midnight, but I was drunk. No, *drunk* isn't the right word for it. I was blitzed. Blitzed and surrounded by the best people in the world.

"I love you, Audrey." I hung off of her while Diego and Charlie tried to light the cheap firecrackers Charlie had bought from Target as a surprise. Charlie kept trying to light the whole box, and Diego was doing his best to make sure no one blew off their fingers, while Zooey watched from a lawn chair, her belly big and her ankles swollen. "I do. Love you. I was an ass."

Audrey looked stunning. She'd worn a simple black shift dress that highlighted how beautiful she was. Sometimes I forgot. "I love you too." I didn't know if Audrey was drunk, but perspiration beaded her upper lip, and she sipped her vodka and Pop! through a Krazy straw.

A bottle rocket zipped through the air, over Diego's shoulder, narrowly missing his ear, and exploded with a frantic crack. Charlie's buddies hooted and crowed. He seemed to have reverted to his teenage self in their presence, but he deserved this time to be dumb—parenthood offers no vacations or sick days. Diego silently begged me for help before telling off my brother for shooting fireworks at his face. I suppose I should have been glad his aim wasn't as good with a bottle rocket as it was with toast.

"I think I love that guy too."

"Yeah?" Audrey said. "Does he know?"

"No. Maybe." Diego wrestled the lighter from my brother and then lit three Roman candles, which sent streamers of blue and red and green sparks into the air. Charlie pumped his fist and hollered. "It doesn't matter, though. We're just friends."

"You're obviously more than that, Henry. Any idiot can see it."

I couldn't look at Diego and not see Jesse. I couldn't think of the future and not imagine all the ways it could fall apart. Maybe Diego wouldn't kill himself, but he could end up back in jail or find someone better or move home to Colorado. Only, those weren't the reasons holding me back. "I don't think I deserve him."

Audrey shrugged. "Probably not. But he doesn't deserve you, either. Maybe that's why you're perfect for each other."

"Do you think it could last?"

"Who cares?"

"I care."

Audrey sucked up her drink and tossed the empty cup onto the ground. There was no way we were going to be able to hide the fact that we'd had a party from Mom. Fuck it.

"You like bacon, right?" Audrey asked.

"Duh."

"So, when you're offered bacon for breakfast, do you refuse because you're worried about what's going to happen when it's gone?"

"No."

"No!" Audrey smacked me in the chest. "You eat that bacon and you love it because it's delicious. You don't fret over whether you'll ever have bacon again. You just eat the bacon." Audrey stood in front of me and held my face between her hands. Her expression was so solemn that it was difficult not to laugh. "Eat the bacon, Henry."

A roar erupted from Charlie and his friends. Audrey and I turned in time to watch a plume of fire and sparks shoot into the air and explode like a supernova. Diego winked at me from across the lawn.

"I'm assuming Diego is the bacon in that analogy."

"I need another drink."

Diego and I stood in my bedroom, the lights off, our arms wrapped around each other. The TV blared in the living room. It was still ten minutes to midnight, but it could have been ten seconds, and I wouldn't have cared.

The bright moon shone through my window, and I froze Diego's face in my mind, committing to memory the curves of his cheeks and the scar on his temple and the way he shivered when I touched him.

Diego's skin pressed against mine as he kissed my lips and my neck, lingering only long enough in one spot to make me want more. This was prolonged euphoria, better than the carrot the sluggers used to turn me into their trained monkey.

"It was my mom."

I stopped kissing Diego. "Is this really the best time to talk about your mom?"

"She's the reason I came to live with Viv instead of going home when I got out of juvie." He spoke so softly that I felt his words vibrate against my skin. I stroked Diego's hair but didn't move otherwise. "It was self-defense—even my lawyer said so—but my mom refused to testify against my dad. It was my word against his, and my father had a silver tongue when he wasn't tweaking. I needed my mom to back me up, but she refused. He's going to kill her one day, and she chose him over her own son." His voice broke.

"You don't have to talk about it." I tried to imagine being betrayed by my own mother, but I couldn't. Despite her flaws, my mom was always there for me.

Diego rested his forehead against mine. "I wanted you to know." He pulled me to him and kissed me as if that might erase his memories of the past. He slid his hands under my shirt and pulled it over my head. I couldn't unbutton his shirt fast enough. I lost track of time. We were arms and legs and lips, fearless and frenzied.

"Is this all right?" he asked as if I wasn't the one who'd wrestled him out of his black dress pants. "You've had a lot to drink."

"It's good," I murmured, tipsy but not drunk. "Is it okay for you?" I looked into Diego's eyes, feeling self-conscious now. I'd been poked and prodded by aliens, wandered Calypso without a stitch, but standing in front of Diego was the most naked I'd ever felt.

"Better than okay."

"Have you ever done it with a guy?" I asked. Diego shook his head. "Not even in juvie?"

"It's not like that," he said with a chuckle.

"I have . . . with Jesse. And Marcus."

Diego laughed. "So much for just being friends."

"We can stop."

"I don't want to. Unless you do."

"I don't."

I led Diego to the bed, and we eased under my sheets, letting instinct and hormones take control. I thought it must've been midnight because I heard shouting, but I ignored it. Only Diego and I existed.

My bedroom door burst open. "Henry! Henry, you gotta come quick!"

I scrambled to cover Diego and myself with the sheets. "Jesus Christ, Charlie, we're fucking busy in here!"

Charlie was crying. I didn't notice that at first because I was freaking out about my brother walking in while Diego and I were naked and about to have sex. But when I did, I knew something was wrong. "Henry, please. It's Zooey."

1 January 2016

I watched my brother chew his fingernails down to the quick, and then keep biting. He gnawed on the ends until they bled, and I finally had to pull his hands away from his mouth. He looked at his fingers and shook his head.

"How long are they going to be in there?" he asked.

"I'm sure someone will be out soon." The hospital waiting room was far from comforting, and our coffee cups sat forgotten on the small plastic side tables. We'd been waiting for more than an hour, starving for even the smallest scrap of news. Diego had been the only one of us sober enough to drive, and we'd rushed Zooey—moaning in pain and clutching her belly—to the nearest hospital in Audrey's car. I wanted to call an ambulance, but Charlie refused to wait.

"Do you think I should call her parents again?"

"You left them a message, right?"

Charlie nodded. "I don't think they get reception on their boat."

Diego held my hand and smiled when I glanced his way. It was difficult to think of anything other than what we'd been about to do when I looked at him, but Charlie needed me, so I tried to pretend Diego wasn't there.

"Do you think she's going to be all right?" Charlie asked.

Audrey's eyes were half closed—she never could hold her liquor—but she said, "It was probably false labor. Sometimes it happens."

Diego and I agreed, but I'd seen the blood on Zooey's hands and between her legs. I didn't know what it meant, but I doubted it was good.

"Well, she'd be the first Denton in history to be early to anything." I tried to loan Charlie my smile, but he wasn't in the mood.

"Zooey's always early," he said. "If she's not at least fifteen minutes early to wherever she's going, she starts to get physically sick."

Audrey said, "I thought I was bad."

"You are," I said.

Charlie wasn't listening to us so much as talking to fill the void where Zooey should have been. "She has this saying:

'Early is on time, on time is late, and if you're late, don't bother showing up.'"

"I'd hate to work for her." Diego couldn't figure out which cup of coffee was his and so just took one at random. He grimaced. "This is worse than what they served in juvie."

Audrey blinked to clear the sleep from her eyes, and tried to sit up straight. "What was it like?"

Diego's back stiffened, and he bit the corner of his lip. He hadn't talked about it, and I hadn't asked. I was about to change the subject, when he said, "At first it's scary. When you go inside, they strip you and search you in the most humiliating way imaginable. Guys'll hide drugs and weapons anywhere they think they can get away with it, but I think the strip search is more about the guards showing you that your ass is theirs. No matter how tough you think you are, you're their bitch."

I wondered if that's why the sluggers always sent me back without my clothes. They had the technology to travel the universe and draw out my memories; surely, they could have returned me to Earth fully dressed.

"I tried to keep to myself, and read every book I could get my hands on, but it's tough. Most every kid in juvie is inside because they screwed up pretty bad, but they're all just boys hiding under layers of false bravado. They act like thugs, but most of them miss their mothers. Most still believe they can do anything."

"Do you believe that?" Audrey asked.

Diego nodded. "If a kid looks like he doesn't give a shit, it's not because he doesn't believe in himself anymore; it's because no one else believes in him."

I thought about Jesse. I wondered if that's why he killed himself. If he thought no one believed in him and that his only escape was at the end of a noose. I wondered about Marcus, too. People believed in him, but the person they believed in was a lie. I don't know when Marcus stopped being himself and started pretending to be the person others expected him to be.

Charlie was chewing on his fingers again, biting the skin around the nail, and Audrey looked like she was going to fall asleep. "Did it work?" I asked. "Juvie, I mean. Did it change you?"

Diego cocked his head and looked at me as if that wasn't the question he'd expected me to ask. "People don't really change; they just find something else to give their life meaning."

"Do you regret what you did?" Audrey asked.

"Sometimes . . ."

I sensed Diego was going to say more, but Charlie stood up, drawing our attention. I followed his line of sight to the doctor walking through the double doors. She was short and stocky, and carried herself with confidence. Charlie rushed to meet her, and Diego held my hand while we watched. I knew it was bad news the moment I saw her pinched lips and tired eyes. Charlie went rigid, offering the doctor robotic nods as she explained what happened. We were too far away to hear.

"They're going to take me to see Zooey," Charlie said when the doctor left. "You should go home."

"What about you?"

"Just . . ."

Audrey stood, her keys jingling in her hand. "We'll drive your car here and leave it in the parking lot."

Charlie nodded, but I doubted he'd heard the words.

"Mr. Denton?" A nurse stood waiting by the doors.

"I'm gonna . . ."

I slugged Charlie lightly in the arm. "She's okay. You're both going to be okay."

"Yeah, Henry. Sure." Charlie followed the nurse into the bowels of the hospital, and I watched him go. I jumped when Diego touched my shoulder.

"We should get out of here," he said. "Clean the house before your mom gets home."

"What do you think happened?" Audrey asked.

"I think I'm not going to be an uncle anymore."

· · ·

Audrey tried to make me sit in the front seat on the way home, but I refused. It was her car, after all. I stared at the streak of blood on the leather and wondered if the baby were already dead or if it had offered the world one mewling cry—a first and last protest—before succumbing to gravity.

We sat parked in my driveway for a while. I didn't even realize we'd arrived until Audrey looked at me in the rearview mirror and said, "We missed midnight."

I didn't know if the stain would come out or if some shadow of it would always remain. "We didn't miss it," I said. "It just happened without us."

It seems silly to worry about the arbitrary moment some person long dead declared to be the end of one year and the beginning of another, as if our attempts to divide time into meaningful chunks actually mean anything. People wait for the countdown to tell them that it's okay to believe in themselves again. They end each year with failure, but hope that when the clock strikes twelve, they can begin the new year with a clean slate. They tell themselves that *this* is the year things will happen, never realizing that things are *always* happening; they're just happening without them.

"I should get home," Audrey said.

"Are you okay to drive?" Diego asked.

"Yeah."

When Audrey's BMW disappeared into the night, Diego hugged me close. I wanted him to kiss me, to kiss away everything that had happened. To kiss me until time reversed and we were back in my bedroom. But you can't live in the past; you can only visit. I wasn't sure what was happening between us, but I didn't want it to happen without me.

"Happy New Year, Henry."

"Happy New Year, Diego."

Hardly giving us time to breathe, Ms. Faraci launched into her lecture on acids and bases and the importance of a neutral pH. I already knew most of what she was teaching, and glanced over my shoulder at Marcus out of boredom. He'd snuck into class at the last minute, looking ragged. I searched for the boy who'd given me the calling card behind the auditorium before winter break, but couldn't find him. Marcus's eyes were bloodshot and his cheeks hollow. His New Year's Eve party was all anyone had talked about in the halls and before classes. Rumor was that Marcus had leapt from his roof into his pool wearing nothing but his grin; that he'd passed out pills like candy; that the party had devolved into an orgy of Dionysian proportions. But the more Marcus tries to prove that he's the life of the party, the less I believe him.

Adrian's seat was noticeably empty, though most specu-
lated he'd been expelled and questioned by the police. I wondered if he'd ratted out his friends or if he was the kind of guy
who'd take the fall rather than snitching. I suppose I already
knew the answer, since Adrian was gone but Marcus wasn't.

After class, I hung back to talk to Ms. Faraci. "Did you
have a nice break?" she asked.

I didn't want to tell Ms. Faraci about Charlie and Zooey,
so I said, "Yeah. It was all right. You? Tell me you didn't spend
the whole break buried in books."

Ms. Faraci flashed me a wry smile. "Despite your insinu-
ations, I do have a life outside of this classroom." If she'd said
it with even a hint of conviction, I might have believed her.
"So, what can I do for you, Henry?"

"Is your offer to do some extra credit still on the table?"

"Of course!" She looked relieved and surprised simulta-
neously. "Do you know what you want to write about?"

I hung my head. "Well . . . it's just . . . I've been keeping
journals since I was a kid, and I thought I could put them
together, maybe write about how the world ends." I glanced
up at Ms. Faraci to judge her reaction, but her expression
didn't change. "It's stupid, I know."

"As long as it's got something to do with science, no matter how tenuous the relation, I'll take it." Her lip twitched, and

I wondered if she was going to ask me about the sluggers—I suspected even my teachers had heard the rumors of my abductions—but instead she said, "What changed your mind?"

"I don't know. I guess I just like having choices."

I'm not sure my answer made sense to Ms. Faraci, but she smiled anyway, her round cheeks so high, they brushed the bottom of her glasses. I was about to leave, when she snapped her fingers and said, "I almost forgot." She dug around in her bag and plopped an ancient yearbook on her desk from a school called Jupiter High. "I brought this to show you something."

"You graduated in 1996?" I would have guessed she was older than that, but didn't say so.

"Indeed. It was quite a year. They cloned Dolly the sheep in 1996."

"Good for Dolly." Diego was waiting for me in the cafeteria, so I said, "What'd you want to show me?"

Ms. Faraci flipped through the pages. She stopped on the only section of color photos. The boys were all wearing tuxes, and the girls, black dresses. "In high school one of my nicknames was Spacey Faraci because I always had my head in the clouds."

I wanted to ask her what her other nicknames were, but I had a feeling she wouldn't tell me. "No offense, but I already knew you were a nerd."

"None taken." Ms. Faraci pointed at a picture of a boy

with a flattop and a bold smile. "Andrew Darby once told everyone I had a penis. These days he sells insurance and has been divorced three times." She pointed at a girl. "Molly Roswell stole my clothes during gym all through tenth grade. She has four children with two different fathers, and a DUI.

"Tyler Coombs, Gregory Nguyn, and Chris Brentano tormented me during lunch. Tyler runs a successful Internet business, Greg now goes by Caryn, and Chris works with special needs children at a school in Miami."

I tried to stop her, but Ms. Faraci cut me off. "I'm almost done." She pointed at a picture of a beautiful girl with a prom queen smile. "Nasya Boulos. Everyone loved her. She tortured me for four years. No matter what I did, she made certain I knew I would never be as beautiful or as popular as she was." Ms. Faraci took a breath and smiled. "She's a heart surgeon in New York, married to a handsome man in publishing. She's got a beautiful child and the life she always dreamed of."

I waited to make sure Ms. Faraci was finished before I said, "Is this supposed to make me feel better? That the people who bullied you didn't get what they deserved?"

"It's meant to show you that these people don't matter, Henry. Their successes and failures mean nothing to me. I am exactly who I want to be, doing exactly what I want to do. After graduation, the people who torment you will disappear, and they'll never have the power to hurt you again. When I tell you it gets better, this is what I mean."

"I guess it's just hard to believe that right now," I said.

Ms. Faraci closed the yearbook and smiled. "And one day you'll wake up, look around, and wonder how you could ever have believed otherwise. If the world doesn't end, of course."

"Thanks, Ms. Faraci."

I was in a hurry to get to lunch. Diego had texted me to find out where I was, and I was busy typing a reply instead of paying attention to what was in front of me. I turned the corner out of the science building and pain exploded in my face. The suddenness of it paralyzed me. It felt like I'd been hit by a brick instead of a fist. The force of the blow knocked me into the wall, and I banged my head, the pain of the collision spreading through my skull like ripples on a pond.

"Rot in hell, Space Boy." A large figure in my blurry vision darted past me, leaden footsteps pounding down the hall. I didn't need to see his face; I'd heard Adrian's voice in my nightmares often enough to recognize it.

Mr. Curtis poked his head out of his classroom. "What's going on out here? Mr. Denton?"

I leaned against the wall and held my hand over my throbbing, watery eye. "Nothing, sir."

· · ·

Diego punched the steering wheel so hard, the dashboard shook. "I'll fucking kill him." I'd skipped lunch to avoid Diego seeing my eye, but he found me after last period. We'd been sitting in the school parking lot for ten minutes while he raged, blaming himself for not being there to protect me. "I'll rip his fucking hands off."

"Calm down, Diego. It's not a big deal." It was difficult to sell it with a swollen eye and a plum-colored bruise running across the bridge of my nose.

"It's a big fucking deal," Diego yelled. "Which one of them was it? Was it Marcus?"

"No."

"Don't protect him!"

I flinched. The air around Diego vibrated the way it does before a thunderstorm, warning me that worse was coming. "Stop, Diego, just stop. It doesn't matter who did it."

Diego clenched his fist. He punched the steering wheel until his knuckles bled. "Don't you get it, Henry? I love you. I love you so much, and I know this is all a big joke to you because the world is ending and you don't think any of this matters, but when it comes to you, it always matters."

I unbuckled my seat belt and twisted around. I held Diego's face in my hands and kissed him despite the agony that exploded around my nose and eye. Pain has a way of reinforcing memories. It binds them to the moment so you never forget, and I didn't want to forget.

"I think . . . I think I love you too, Diego." They words hurt. Saying them to someone other than Jesse, but I knew they were true. And that made them hurt even worse. "But that's why we shouldn't see each other." I don't remember when I started crying, but I couldn't stop. "I wish the sluggers had chosen you to save the world. I just . . . I can't be the reason you end up back in juvie."

Diego was shaking, but I couldn't tell if he was crying or going to punch me. "I don't need you to look after me. You can't even look after yourself."

"What's that supposed to mean?"

"You won't press the button to save the world because you don't think you deserve to live in it."

"I was going to do it, Diego. Because of you."

Diego shook his head. "Maybe you're right. We shouldn't see each other." He laughed bitterly, but I didn't get the joke. "I wanted you to press the button because *you* wanted to, not for me or anyone else. If you can't see how amazing you are, then . . . forget it."

I tried to think of something more to say, but I'd run out of words. I got out of the car and walked back toward school to call Audrey for a ride. I half expected Diego to chase after me, but he didn't.

Superbugs

The first case of untreatable gonorrhea is observed in Maxx Costanza of Warwick, Rhode Island. It is estimated that he infected thirteen sexual partners before being diagnosed.

Within months, outbreaks of antibiotic-resistant *Pseudomonas aeruginosa*, *Clostridium difficile*, and E. coli are observed in patients around the world. Not even last-resort antibiotics are effective in controlling the diseases.

Governments around the globe direct their resources to the development of new antibiotics. As deaths from simple infections rise dramatically, a new sense of teamwork spreads throughout the world. Knowledge is shared freely, old barriers are eliminated as humanity races to find cures for diseases once considered beaten. Economic and military rivalries are set aside to save the world.

An unparalleled level of global collaboration leads to the

first breakthrough nearly two years after Maxx Costanza's initial diagnosis. The potential new antibiotic is found in the chemical secretions of cockroaches. While attempting to isolate enough of the compounds in the cockroaches, an international consortium of scientists develops revolutionary technologies to increase the size of the cockroaches through genetic manipulation. These novel insects, named *Blatella asmithicus* after the geneticist responsible for creating them, Dr. Andrew Smith, measure nearly a meter in length, and have an astounding resiliency and immunity to all known toxins. Capable, even, of withstanding significant exposure to radiation. They are more commonly referred to as CroMS: cockroaches of mighty size.

The first new successful antibiotic in a decade is tested on 8 January 2016. Within days, the mortality rate from bacterial infections decreases to levels never before achieved.

United by their cause, a new age of peace and prosperity envelops the world. It is the golden age of humanity.

On 29 January 2016 a pair of CroMS escape from a laboratory in Austin, Texas. They begin to breed. As a result of their increased size, CroMS possess a ravenous appetite and devour everything in their path.

Austin is overrun in three days. Texas in two weeks. The United States in less than a year.

When CroMS are the only living creatures remaining on the planet, they consume each other.

7 January 2016

After Adrian punched me in the hallway at school, which I read on Marcus's SnowFlake page was retribution for his expulsion, despite not even being the one who'd e-mailed his video confession to Principal DeShields, I spent most of my free time in my room, contemplating my existence.

I've been wondering why the sluggers haven't abducted me since Thanksgiving. They've had plenty of opportunities, and there were definitely a few times I might have pressed the button. Maybe they don't want Earth saved after all. Maybe they're messing with my head. They want to see if I'll break under the pressure. Maybe the world isn't going to end, and I'll spend January 29 waiting for an apocalypse that won't come.

Diego sent me a couple of texts, left some messages, but I deleted them unanswered and unread. I'm not sure I did the right thing, breaking up with him. I'm not sure we were ever actually a couple. I'd seen him naked and he'd seen me, so we were more than friends; I just don't know what *more* actually means. I wasn't kidding when I told him I loved him. Somewhere between his bursting into my chemistry class and punching his knuckles bloody on his steering wheel, I fell in love with Diego Vega.

As human beings, we seek meaning in everything. We're so good at discovering patterns that we see them where they don't exist. One summer my parents sent me and Charlie to stay with our uncle Joe in Seattle. I had to share a room with Charlie, and his snoring kept me from sleeping. Uncle Joe gave me a white-noise machine. When it was time for bed, I fired it up and listened to the static. It was nice at first—like crumpling paper or a fly's endlessly buzzing wings—but after a while, I began to hear things in the noise. Random words or bits of music repeating. I woke up Charlie and made him listen, convinced I'd discovered a secret message left by spies, but he punched me and went back to sleep. Once I heard the pattern, I couldn't stop hearing it, and I spent the rest of the summer looking and listening for patterns in other random sources—the wind, clothes tumbling in the dryer. I even pulled out one of Uncle Joe's old television sets to watch the snow.

We look for the same patterns in our lives to give them meaning. When someone says, "Everything happens for a reason," they're trying to convince you there's a pattern to your life, and that if you pay close attention, it's possible to decipher it. If my mom hadn't packed my lunch on 18 September 2013, I wouldn't have gotten to the cafeteria early and sat at a table that belonged to a group of seniors, which included my brother. Charlie wouldn't have stolen my lunch, and I wouldn't have been forced to buy something to eat and sit at another table on the other side of the cafeteria. Jesse never would have seen me, and we wouldn't have met. We wouldn't have dated, fallen in love, and Jesse's suicide wouldn't have destroyed me. I wouldn't have gone to the boys' room to cry and run into Marcus on his way out. Marcus and I wouldn't have started fooling around, and I wouldn't have gone to his party to prove that I could. I wouldn't have bumped into Diego and gotten to know him, and we wouldn't have fallen for each other. A person who believed in patterns might be tempted to believe Diego and I were fated to meet.

Only, it wasn't fate. It wasn't destiny. And it certainly wasn't God. It was chance. A random series of events given meaning by someone desperate to prove there's a design to our lives. That the minutes and hours between our birth and death are more than frantic moments of chaos. Because if that's all they are—if there are no rules governing our lives—then our entire existence is a meaningless farce.

If Jesse didn't have a reason for hanging himself, then his death was pointless. And if Jesse died for nothing, how can I live for anything?

The doorbell rang, but I didn't move. Mom was somewhere in the house; she could answer the door. I was inert, still in my school clothes, lying on top of my sheets, dozing in a transitory space between asleep and awake. My skin was moist, but I was too lazy to crank up the fan. I must have drifted off, because I didn't hear my mom calling my name until she was standing over my bed, shaking me.

"Henry, wake up."

"What?"

"There's someone here to see you." She hesitated in a way that made me think it was Diego. I hadn't told her we'd broken up or whatever, but she wasn't stupid, either.

"I'll be out in a minute." Mom left. I got a whiff of my pits, slapped on some deodorant, and changed into something less pungent. I wasn't sure what was left to say to Diego. Nothing had changed. If he stayed with me, he'd end up hurting someone, and I didn't want him to spend the last days of Earth behind bars. But I missed him. I missed his goofy smile and his stupid jokes and how he blushed when his stomach gurgled. I wasn't sure if I could see him and hang on to my resolve.

As it turned out, I didn't have to worry.

Mrs. Franklin sat at the dining room table with my mom. She looked out of place in our house, like finding a van Gogh displayed amongst an army of Thomas Kinkades. Even dressed in a simple outfit of shorts and a blouse, she radiated refinement. A crispness that my mother, in her shabby clothes, could never match.

I thought she must have come to confront me about breaking into her house, and that cops would surely be busting down my door any moment, but I resisted the urge to panic. If police were on their way, freaking out wouldn't help. "Hi, Mrs. Franklin."

She turned toward me, the bare hint of a smile on her lips. "Henry. I can't believe that for as long as you and Jesse dated, I've never met your mother."

"Lucky you."

Mom scowled at me. "You know, I have a box of baby pictures around here somewhere. Keep it up, mister." She pushed back her chair. "It was really nice to meet you, Helen. We should have lunch sometime."

"Absolutely." She waited for Mom to disappear outside

before motioning for me to sit. When I did, she stared at me for so long that I began to feel the same way I did when the sluggers examined me. "I never liked you, Henry."

Mrs. Franklin's pronouncement should have shocked me, but it didn't. "Thanks?"

The hard edges of her face softened momentarily. "It wasn't you—I'm sure you're a fine young man." I noticed the way she lingered on my black eye, and wasn't sure I believed her. "It was Jesse. I wanted him to focus on his studies. You were a distraction."

"Jesse would have been valedictorian if—"

"I'm glad he found you, though. You made him happy." Mrs. Franklin's voice was wooden, like she was reciting lines, but I didn't know whether it was because she was insincere or because if she allowed any emotion to creep into her voice, she'd fall apart.

"About the other night—"

Mrs. Franklin held up her hand. "I think I understand."

"You do?"

"No, I suppose not. But I'm sure you had your reasons."

"You turned Jesse's bedroom into a sewing room."

"I'd burn down that house if I had the nerve." Mrs. Franklin's composure cracked. A mad giggle escaped from her mouth, and she seemed as surprised by it as I was. "Jesse is

402 · **SHAUN DAVID HUTCHINSON**

imprinted all over that house. Down every hallway, in every wall. He's gone, but he'll never be *gone*."

I considered taking her hand, offering her comfort, but if that was what she wanted, there had been plenty of opportunities after Jesse's death. His funeral, the wake, the lonely days after when even eating had become an unbearable chore. "Why are you here?"

Mrs. Franklin cleared her throat. "We didn't speak at Jesse's funeral—I was too bound up in my own grief to be concerned with yours. I hope you can forgive me."

"There's nothing to forgive."

"I wanted to ask you . . . I wanted to know . . . Did Jesse tell you he was sad?"

The question blindsided me the same way Jesse's suicide had. "No more so than anyone else."

"Did he ever talk about wanting to hurt himself?"

"Not with me," I said. "Audrey knew a little, but he kept that part of himself from me."

For some reason, that made Mrs. Franklin smile. "So like Jesse. He hated to be a bother, and only wanted to make people smile. Especially you."

"He did. I don't think I was ever happier than with Jesse."

"Neither was I." Mrs. Franklin folded her hands in front of her, and I think we both got a little lost remembering how amazing Jesse was. The way the sun shone brighter, and no trouble seemed to matter when he was near. "Do you think it was my fault?"

"I don't know." It probably wasn't the answer Mrs. Franklin hoped for, but it was honest, and she deserved the truth. "Maybe. Maybe it was my fault. Maybe nobody is to blame."

"My son was very lucky to have had you in his life." Mrs. Franklin pushed back her chair and stood. She was even more imposing towering over me. "Please don't break into my house again."

"Yes, ma'am." As she turned to leave, I stopped her. "Did you find anything when you were cleaning out Jesse's room?"

Mrs. Franklin furrowed her brow. "Like what, Henry?"

"I don't know. Anything that might have explained why he killed himself?" The whole time we were talking, I kept hoping she'd reveal that she'd discovered a letter addressed to me, something Jesse had left behind that would make sense of everything.

She shook her head, eyes downcast. "What would it have changed if I had?"

"At least we would have known."

"But knowing wouldn't return Jesse to us."

She began to head toward the door again. I'd broken into

her house looking for closure, and I think she came to mine looking for the same. I'm not sure either of us found what we were looking for, but maybe continuing to search was the best we could do.

"Mrs. Franklin?"

She sighed. "Yes, Henry?"

"If you knew the world was going to end, but you had the power to stop it, would you?"

"Yes."

"Why?"

Mrs. Franklin's back was to me, but I imagined I could see the determined set of her jaw, the same resolute expression I'd seen on Jesse's face a hundred times. "Because Jesse believed that life wasn't worth living, and I refuse to prove him right."

I was having a dream. The sluggers abducted me and cut off my limbs. Then they reattached them wrong. My left arm became my right leg, my right leg became my left leg, and so on. Then they tossed me onto the floor and forced me to try to crawl to the button. I wanted to reach the button more than anything, but it was impossible to walk with an arm where my leg should have been.

Jesse was in the dream too. He was lecturing me on the impermanence of memory. Most of the words jumbled together because I was busy having my body parts rearranged, but I remembered him telling me that memories are often amalgams of truth and fiction, sewn together in our heads by our subconscious to support our personal beliefs about the world. He droned on and on about dendrites and voltage

406 · SHAUN DAVID HUTCHINSON

gradients, but in my dream I couldn't stop wondering how much of what I remembered about Jesse was truth and how much was fiction.

As the aliens prepared to switch my hands, feet, and genitals, I heard a banging from the shadows. The sluggers turned as a unit to look toward the source of the noise, but Jesse hadn't noticed and was still talking about memory, this time in rhyming couplets. He might have also been speaking Italian. Apparently, I am also an Italian poet in my dreams.

The banging grew louder and I tried to sit up, but, lacking limbs, I fell off the table instead. My last thought before I hit the ground and woke up was, *Not the nose.*

The pounding sound traveled with me out of my dream, but I was groggy and confused, so it took me a moment to realize someone was knocking on my window.

It was 1:37 a.m. Who the fuck was knocking on my bedroom window at 1:37? I lifted the window a crack. "What?"

"Bro. I lost my keys. Let me in." Charlie slurred his words, barely able to form a coherent sentence. Luckily, I'd been speaking Charlie Denton my entire life.

"Do you know what time it is?"

Charlie was too busy puking to answer. I threw on some clothes and snuck through the house to avoid waking Mom. Charlie wasn't waiting by the door, and I was shocked by a blast of arctic air when I walked outside in nothing but shorts and a tank top.

"Shit." Charlie's car was parked on the front lawn. The headlights illuminated the front of the house, and the hazards were blinking. "You've got to be kidding me." The keys were in the ignition, so I quickly backed the Jeep into the street and parked behind Mom. I couldn't do anything about the tire tracks marring the grass. Mom was going to strangle Charlie when she saw them.

Charlie stumbled toward me. The front of his work shirt was crusty with vomit, and he was sweating profusely, even in the cold. "Jesus, Charlie, we have to get you inside."

"When did I eat broccoli?" He lurched and opened his mouth; I thought he was going to throw up again, but he fired off a wet burp that made my skin crawl. "Better."

"Where's Zooey?"

"Parents' house."

It's been nearly two weeks since Zooey's loss, and I haven't seen much of her or Charlie. Their obstetrician suspects the baby suffered from chromosomal damage. Mom told me those types of pregnancies frequently miscarry early on, but not always. Only, Mom didn't use the word *miscarry*. She referred to it as *nature's fail-safe*, as if that could draw the poison from the sting. I didn't have the heart to tell her that with

Zooey so far along, the correct term was actually *stillbirth*. Anyway, it doesn't matter what word we use; their baby is dead.

"You reek," I said. "Let's get you washed up."

Charlie didn't put up a fight when I led him inside and got him out of his work clothes, which probably needed to be burned. He stood compliantly under the shower, letting the water run over his head. I turned it up as hot as he could bear to warm his bones so he didn't get sick. I had no idea how long he'd been outside my window, but his skin was icy. When we ran out of hot water, Charlie dressed and followed me to his room. His eyes were bloodshot, and he was sweating cheap booze.

"Don't go anywhere." I left Charlie sitting on his bed while I ran to the kitchen for water and aspirin to mitigate his inevitable hangover.

I heard the first crash as I was filling the glass, and ran back to Charlie's room. He'd knocked over the crib, spilling out the mound of stuffed animals within, and I couldn't get to him before he punched a hole in Diego's mural.

"Charlie, what the fuck are you doing?" I tried to tackle him before he hurt himself, but he lunged at me. His fist glanced off my shoulder. I wrestled for his arms, but Charlie was bigger and stronger than I was, and the alcohol flooding his body amplified his rage. He punched me in the stomach, knocking the breath from me, and followed it with a knee to my groin that dropped me to the floor. Before I knew it, Charlie was straddling me, punching my ribs and my arms. All I could do was protect my face and plead for him to stop.

The blows slacked off, and Charlie staggered to the rocking chair. He collapsed into it, sobbing.

"Evie Nicole Denton." Charlie repeated the name over and over.

My entire body hurt. Every breath felt like I had rusty fishhooks for lungs, but I crawled toward my brother.

"When was the last time you slept, Charlie?"

He looked at me like it was the first time he'd really seen me all night. "She had a name! We gave her a fucking name!"

"It's a beautiful name."

"She was tiny, Henry. Littler than my hand." Charlie's body shook. He pulled his knees to his chest and buried his face in them.

When Jesse died, people said a lot of things to try to make me feel better:

He's in a better place.

At least he's not in pain anymore.

God has a plan.

Bullshit platitudes that made me want to rip their faces

off. Even Mom tried to tell me that everything happened for a reason. The only person who didn't was Charlie. After the funeral, he told me that Jesse Franklin was an asshole, and I was better off with him dead. I decked Charlie on our front lawn. Split his goddamn lip. My second punch left him with a black eye that lingered for two weeks. It was the only fight with my brother I ever won.

"You need to hit me some more?" I asked. "I think I've still got some unbruised ribs on my left side."

Charlie sneered. "Such a fucking pansy."

"We'll see who's a pansy when Mom rips you a new asshole for driving home drunk and tearing up the lawn."

"Whatever."

"You could've killed yourself, idiot."

"That was the point."

I hugged my ribs, breathing shallowly. At least he hadn't hit my face. My eye was only just healed from Adrian's surprise punch in the hallway at school. "Don't bother," I said. "Unless the aliens abduct me again, we're all going to die in a couple of weeks."

Charlie glanced at me. "Do you honestly believe that shit?"

"Did you think I was making it up?"

"I always figured you belonged in a mental hospital."

"Maybe I do."

Charlie's eyelids began to droop, and his breathing slowed. I should have left him to sleep in the chair. It would have served him right to wake up at least half as sore as I was going to. But I grabbed his wrist and helped him to his bed. He crashed into the pillows, asleep before he hit them.

"I really wanted to be a dad," he mumbled.

I pulled the blankets over Charlie and set his phone beside him before turning off the lights. I stood in the doorway, listening to my brother snore.

"For the record, I think you would have been a good dad."

I stood at the edge of the ocean, letting the water wash over my feet. My eyes were closed, but I was looking up, and I swore I could still see the stars through my eyelids. On my left was mighty Hercules, and on my right Mars and the constellation Libra. Somewhere out there the sluggers were orbiting Earth in their spaceship.

"I don't know if you can hear me, but I'm ready to press the button now." The air was still. There was no moon and no shadows. "I want to press the button."

I shivered uncontrollably, but figured it was my due to suffer for this. If I'd pushed that button when I'd had the chance, I wouldn't have needed to stand outside in the cold night, begging the aliens to save me.

Only it wasn't myself I wanted to save. It was my brother, who wanted to be a father, and Zooey who deserved to finish college. It was Mom and Nana and Audrey and Diego. Even Marcus. They deserve to live, even if I don't.

"Please."

The Big Bang released so much energy that the universe has been expanding outward from it for more than thirteen billion years. Eventually, that expansion will cease, and gravity will cause the universe to contract. All those galactic clusters and far-flung stars ringed by planets—some dead, some teeming with alien life—are going to come zipping back toward one another, faster and faster as the pull of gravity draws them toward the center. No one is sure what will happen in the Big Crunch. The universe and everything in it could collapse into a massive singularity, or it could initiate another Big Bang, a new beginning to the universe. Maybe that wouldn't be such a bad thing. Maybe the only way to really start over is to tear everything apart.

At least, that's what I told myself.

Mom was cooking when I walked into the kitchen.

Buzzing about, happier than I'd seen her in ages. Audrey was picking me up to go to Calypso High's winter carnival in fifteen minutes. I had no real desire to waste my time throwing balls at bottles to win cheap prizes, but Audrey refused to let me spend another Friday night wallowing alone in my room. I tried to ignore the possibility that Diego might be there, but when I realized I'd spent an hour obsessing over what to wear, I knew I was hoping to see him.

"Smells good in here," I said. There were so many aromas, it was difficult to separate them, but I was pretty certain one was fish.

"Pancetta-wrapped salmon with asparagus and lime crème fraîche." She glanced at me over her shoulder as she stood at the sink washing asparagus. "You look nice."

I peeked at the bowls on the counter, looking for something to nibble on, but none of it looked edible. "Audrey and I are going to the winter carnival."

"That'll be fun." She sounded doubtful, and I was right there with her.

"Sadly, I have nothing better to do." I settled on a banana. It was still too green, but I had to quiet my chatty stomach. "You seen Charlie?"

Mom shook her head. "I think he's staying with Zooey at her parents' house."

Charlie and I hadn't spoken since the other night. My ribs looked like a weather map predicting a winter storm, but I'll count it a worthy sacrifice if Charlie never drives drunk again.

"You think they'll get through this?"

Mom transferred the asparagus to the cutting board. She smiled as she chopped. I hadn't seen her smoke since New Year's either, but I didn't mention it. She'd tried to quit before but had never lasted longer than a week. I hoped she succeeded, but I didn't want her to feel like a failure if she didn't.

"It's hard to tell."

"I like Zooey," I said. "I like Charlie with Zooey." It didn't matter that Charlie didn't deserve his beautiful, brilliant fiancée. For some unknown reason she loved him, and he was a better person for it.

"Me too." Even Mom seemed surprised that she meant it. "Though, I do hope your brother changes his mind about college."

I chuckled. "Fat chance."

"Can't blame a mom for dreaming." She set to work descaling the salmon. I've never been able to get past the meaty pink of it, so similar to human flesh, the white stripes of fat running through it.

"Are you having someone for dinner?"

She shook her head. "Just experimenting for the restaurant."

"How's it going?"

"Good . . . I think." Mom leaned forward and made a face. "Henry, will you scratch my forehead?" She held up her fishy hands.

Mom arched her back like a cat when I finally hit the itch. "Better?"

"Much."

"You seem happier."

"I guess I am," Mom said after thinking about it for a moment. "It's tough work, and Chef Norbert can be a real asshole—"

"Nice way to talk about your new boss."

She rolled her eyes. "What? His only mode of speaking is yelling, and sometimes he barks orders in French and I have no idea what he's saying." Mom laughed, and I couldn't help thinking there hadn't been enough of that in our house this last year. "Maybe I'll open my own restaurant one day."

I cringed at the idea of Mom running her own place, stress smoking and screaming at the help, but there were worse dreams to have. "Well, someone ought to put Charlie's college fund to use."

"Good thinking."

I watched Mom while I waited for Audrey. She chopped and mixed and moved so quickly that I couldn't always follow what she was doing, but every action was confident. Cooking is practically magic to me, and my mom is a wizard.

"Mom? Did Dad leave because of me?"

She froze. The knife hovered over the cutting board, and her eyebrows dipped to form a V. "Why on Earth would you think that?"

"Lots of reasons."

"Henry, sweetie, your father loved you."

"I know."

"You aren't the reason he left."

"Why then?"

Mom sighed and set down her knife. She moved more slowly, like she'd been waiting years for me to ask and, now that I had, she realized she wasn't prepared to answer. "Your father and I fell out of love. Joel was never the marrying type, and I was naive. In love with the idea of love. His devotion to you and Charlie is the reason he stayed as long as he did."

"If he loved us so much, why'd he abandon us?"

"Because he hated the person he was becoming, and he wanted to leave before you and your brother hated him too."

My memories of my father are all jumbled together. They say when we recall a memory, we're actually calling up the last time we remembered it, and I'm not sure I can trust that my anger at him for leaving hasn't tainted those memories. I tried to think back to the last few months he lived with us. Had he been stressed? More distant? If he'd stayed, would my life have turned out differently? Would I hate him more than I hated him for leaving us?

"Do you think Dad made the right choice?"

Mom resumed chopping at a leisurely pace. "I don't know, sweetie, but I think we're doing pretty well without him. Everything happens for a reason."

The Calypso High winter carnival was held in the school's senior parking lot. Gone were the cars and neatly lined spaces, replaced by game booths and food booths and a Ferris wheel that looked like it had barely passed its last safety inspection. The cold weather had stuck around, but the heat from the bonfire and the press of bodies made me wish I'd worn shorts rather than jeans and a button-down shirt.

Audrey spent the drive describing her mother's next invention: an office chair that grew more uncomfortable the longer you sat in it. It was supposed to remind cubicle workers to stand and stretch every hour, but it sounded like an ergonomic torture device. I did my best to camouflage my anxiety by singing along to the stupid songs on the radio.

I wasn't thrilled with the idea of spending the evening surrounded by my peers, most of whom I imagined whispering
"Space Boy" as they passed. There were too many dark cor-
ners to hide in, too many shadows to launch punches from.
Still, I tried to enjoy myself.

We ran from booth to booth, looking for trouble. I made
a valiant effort to win a stuffed whale by pitching a ball at a
pyramid of bottles, but never managed to knock down more
than two. Audrey, however, had perfect aim, and dunked Jay
Oh into a tank of freezing water. Seeing him shiver and sput-
ter wasn't exactly revenge, but it didn't suck, either.

Somewhere along the way, my fake smile became real. I
was with my best friend, and no one could hurt me. I didn't
even mind when she had to leave to work the debate team's
booth—for two dollars, they'd try to help you win any argument. I wandered through the maze of booths and tents,
thinking how much Jesse would have adored the spectacle
of it all. He loved anything loud and manic. The laughter
and smiles of crowds had given him strength, whereas they
drained me even when I enjoyed them.

The Calypso Crooners were hosting a karaoke booth, and
I couldn't listen to one more off-key rendition of "Summer
Nights," so I ended up on the far side of the carnival, where it
was quieter. I noticed a blue-striped tent with a meticulously

painted sign that read: CALYPSO HIGH ART GALLERY. Diego had mentioned an art show, and I wondered if any of his paintings were on display. I had thirty minutes to kill before Audrey rejoined me, so I decided to take a peek inside.

The outside of the tent may have been dingy, but the inside was wondrous. Framed art hung from the walls and was displayed on freestanding easels. A sculpture of Medusa that bore an eerie resemblance to Principal DeShields haunted a space by the entrance, glowering at all who passed; a cityscape constructed of cigarette butts had attracted a crowd of admirers; and a painting of an ocean sunrise caught my attention. It was so realistic, I could hear the waves and smell the salt water. Each piece of art had a little placard indicating the artist and name of the work. I didn't want to admit I was looking for one bearing Diego's name, but I was. I finally found it in the back of the tent, beside an eight-by-ten painting in a simple black frame.

Diego had painted a boy sitting cross-legged in a dark room. He was naked, with shadows for underwear and cracked cement for skin. Sections of his arms, legs, and shoulders had crumbled, revealing a core of rebar rather than bone. As if hinged, the boy's skull hung open, and the hollow space inside was crowded with familiar faces. I recognized my mom, Nana, Charlie and Zooey cradling a tiny bundle between them, Ms. Faraci, and Audrey. Jesse's translucent face peered back at me too. It took me a moment to notice, but hidden in the back stood an algae-skinned alien with marble-black eyes mounted on wobbly stalks. The boy's hand hovered over a button, and his lips bore a cheeky Mona Lisa smile, as if he were hoarding all the secrets of the universe and would never share.

It was me. I tried to digest the details, but there were so many. Rather than beating in my chest, Diego had painted my heart as cut from the night sky—full of stars—and pinned to the concrete skin of my upper left arm, and a crow hovered overhead, so dark it nearly blended into the background. I could have peeled back the layers of meaning for hours and not discovered them all. This was how Diego saw me. I was Henry Denton and I was Space Boy. I was broken and I was beautiful. I was nothing and I was everything. I didn't matter to the universe, but I mattered to him.

The person in that painting would have pressed the button. The person in that painting with the steel bones and legions in his skull would have saved Jesse. The person in that painting would have fought back in the showers, he would have told the police who had attacked him. The person in that painting wasn't real.

An average-size human being jumping out of an airplane

will reach 99 percent of terminal velocity—approximately 122 miles per hour—within about fifteen seconds. If the body remains horizontal, the air resistance gives the illusion of floating. That's how I've felt since meeting Diego. Like I was floating. But I'd been falling the entire time.

A hand on my shoulder. "Henry?"

Diego.

"Henry, are you—"

"That's not me."

Diego's hand slid away. The ground was rushing to meet me. I was falling and falling. I was running.

But I could never run far or fast enough to escape the impact because gravity is inevitable.

Vega is the brightest star in the constellation Lyra, and the third brightest star in the northern hemisphere. Lyra is traditionally associated with the Greek musician Orpheus, though it is also sometimes referred to as King Arthur's Harp. Upon the death of Orpheus's wife, Eurydice, he marched into the Underworld and played his lyre for Hades until the lord of Death, so moved, agreed to return his wife. The hitch was that Orpheus was forbidden from looking backward until he was clear of the dread god's domain. Failure to abide by this one rule would nullify his victory, and Eurydice would be lost forever. Orpheus looked back. Orpheus was an asshole.

I, however, did not look back. Not even once I reached the football field.

I sat on the bleachers and buried my face in my hands, crying until I couldn't cry anymore, wondering how I'd fucked everything up. I wasn't the person Diego thought I was. I could never be that person. I hadn't even pressed the goddamn button. I screamed as loud as I could, letting the noise explode from my throat and ripple across the world. I didn't care who heard me.

"You don't answer my texts anymore, Space Boy." Marcus startled me when he sauntered up behind me. I hopped to my feet and scanned the surrounding area for Adrian or Jay, but either they were well hidden or Marcus was alone.

"Go away."

Marcus climbed the bleachers and sat next to where I was standing, leaving space between us. His face was drawn and pale, but he still looked good in jeans and a V-neck sweater. "Listen, about that thing in the hallway . . . That wasn't me. I didn't know about that."

I touched my eye involuntarily. "Whatever, Marcus. I'm not in the mood." I marched down off the bleachers toward the football field, hoping he wouldn't follow me. But he did. I turned around and shouted, "Leave me alone!"

"I miss spending time with you, Henry."

"Publicly humiliating and attacking me was a bizarre way to show it. A box of chocolates might have been more appropriate."

"I'm sorry." The funny thing is that I believed him. Jesse had faked being happy, Diego had hidden his past from me, but Marcus had always told me the truth. Even when he beat me up, it was honest. He pulled a flask from his pocket and offered it to me. When I didn't take it, he drank from it first and offered it to me again. Drinking was the last thing I needed, but I didn't want to feel anything anymore, so I accepted the flask. I don't know what it was, but it burned my throat.

I sat down on the grass and buried my face in my hands. "Why are you being nice to me, Marcus? Why now?"

"Do you want to know the truth?" He passed me the flask again, and I swallowed a couple of gulps, feeling the alcohol loosen my limbs and my brain.

"Sure." I was only half listening. I could still hear the distant sounds of the carnival, but it occurred to me how isolated we were.

Marcus sat across from me and pulled his feet in so he was sitting cross-legged. "I'm not strong like you, Henry. My parents expect me to be their perfect son; my friends expect me to be Mr. Popular. It's so hard to be everything to everyone. I feel stretched thin sometimes. You're the only person who doesn't expect anything from me."

I sat up and tried to clear my head, but my thoughts were stuck in a pool of tar, and I couldn't pull them out. "You're drunk. You don't know what you're saying."

Marcus sat forward, his eyes were unfocused and red. "I knew in the beginning I was just not-Jesse to you. You needed someone to take your mind off of Jesse, and I was not-Jesse. But I fell for you, Henry, and I thought you'd fall for me too."

"You. Attacked. Me."

Marcus crawled across the grass until his face was so close to mine that I could smell his rancid breath. "I fucked up." Marcus brushed my lips with his, and I didn't turn away. "Is this all right?" Here was Marcus offering to be not-Jesse for me again. All I had to do was accept, and I could blunt the pain of living for a little while longer.

I looked at the stars, wishing the sluggers would abduct me so that I didn't have to make a choice. That's what this was all about, after all. Making choices. Diego had made a choice. My mom had made a choice. Charlie had made a choice. Even Jesse had made a choice. It had been a selfish, stupid, heartbreaking choice, but one he'd made for himself.

Marcus pushed himself onto me, the weight of his body

against mine made it difficult to breathe. A rock dug into my back while Marcus kissed my neck, his hands pulling at the button on my jeans. I didn't have to choose. I could close my eyes and let it happen the same way I was going to sit back and let the world end. Marcus rubbed his hips against mine and struggled with my zipper.

I didn't have to choose. It was easier not to choose.

"I can't . . ."

"What's wrong?" Marcus cupped my head with his hand and stroked the side of my face with his thumb, kissing me hard, desperately.

"Stop." I wedged my hands between our chests and tried to shove Marcus away. "I don't want to do this, Marcus."

Marcus stopped kissing me. "You're a fucking tease, Henry."

"Get off me!"

Marcus grabbed a handful of my hair and slammed my head into the ground. The world melted and blurred. There were so many stars. Too many. There shouldn't have been that many stars in the sky. I tried to name them, but there were constellations I'd never seen.

Torpid from the booze and dizzy from hitting the rock, I tried to fend off Marcus, but he was yanking my jeans down around my knees. This was another slugger hallucination.

Only an hour ago I was laughing with Audrey, I was seeing myself the way Diego saw me. Somewhere along the way I'd stumbled into this nightmare world where Marcus was on top of me, panting in my ear and telling me what a fucking loser I was. How he was going to fuck Space Boy, and no one would believe me because no one believed loser space boys.

I pressed my head against the rock, digging it deeper into the cut on my scalp, clutching the pain, using it to drag me out of the fog. I elbowed Marcus in the face and scrambled to my feet, pulling up my pants and sprinting toward the flashing lights and laughter and nauseating smell of popcorn.

Marcus screamed my name. He tackled me by the bleachers, and I fell on my wrist. It bent back in a way wrists weren't supposed to bend, but I ate the pain, swallowed it down with blood, and became stronger. I kicked like an animal until I connected with something that made him howl. And then I ran again. I didn't look back this time either.

I spotted Ms. Faraci standing by the candy apple booth.

"Henry?" Ms. Faraci dropped her apple and brushed my hair from my eyes. It was sticky with blood. The color drained from her face. "Henry, what happened?"

Now that I was safe, I finally looked back. Marcus wasn't there, but Diego was. He trotted toward us, panic in his algae eyes. "Henry, I've been looking for you everywhere." He saw me cradling my wrist, touched the blood on my ear. He saw my pants undone, hanging off my hips. "What happened?"

"Were you attacked again?" Ms. Faraci asked. She guided me to a quieter spot behind the roasted nuts tent. The smell made me want to vomit.

Diego followed us, his eyes an expressionless wasteland.

"Henry? Tell me what happened." Ms. Faraci grabbed her cell phone out of her purse. "That's it. I'm calling an ambulance."

"It was Marcus McCoy."

Ms. Faraci dialed 911.

"What was Marcus?" Diego's voice was flat; he hardly sounded like the boy I knew.

"I need an ambulance and police at Calypso High School. One of our students has been attacked." Ms. Faraci regarded me like she was afraid I was going to shatter to pieces in front of her.

"What did Marcus do?"

I couldn't look Diego in the eyes. "It's not your problem."

"Did Marcus hurt you?" I nodded. "Did he . . . ?" Diego glanced at my jeans, and I fumbled with them but couldn't button them because my wrist was swollen and useless.

"He tried."

Diego's mouth twisted.

Ms. Faraci touched my shoulder, and I jumped. "It's okay, Henry. You're okay. The police are coming. Let's get you somewhere safe." She put her arm around my shoulders to lead me toward the school.

"Come on, Diego," I said, but Diego was gone.

I sat on the back of an ambulance while the cops questioned me and paramedics pressed gauze to my head. My wrist was definitely broken, and I probably had a concussion. I told the police officers everything, including who had attacked me in the showers. The paramedics wanted to take me to the hospital, but I refused to go until someone found Diego. Audrey stayed with me, holding my good hand. She hardly said a word.

A crowd of onlookers had gathered around the emergency vehicles, and my mom shoved them aside to get to me, not caring who she elbowed. "Henry! Henry, what the hell happened?" She was wearing pink pajamas, and her hair was pulled back with an elastic band.

I smiled weakly and tried to assure her I was okay, but what she really needed was a Xanax. "Someone attacked me," I said. "He tried to . . . He tried to rape me." None of this would have happened if I hadn't run from Diego. "I needed to be alone, so I went to the football field."

"Young man," said the red-haired paramedic with blood-shot eyes. "We need to take you to the hospital."

"Not until they find Diego." I turned to Audrey. "You have to find him."

"I'm not leaving you." Her voice was so fierce that I didn't even try to argue.

The paramedic was about to explain for the fifth time why I needed to go to the emergency room, when two cops led Diego through the crowd, his hands zip-tied behind his back. Dried blood stained his face and was streaked across his shirt. I jumped off the edge of the ambulance and ran to him.

"Diego! Are you okay?" I looked for the source of the blood but couldn't find any injuries.

"Don't worry," Diego said. "It's not mine."

16 January 2016

We stayed at the emergency room until nearly two a.m. A chatty doctor put four stitches in my scalp and a cast on my wrist. When we got home, I passed out on the couch with my phone beside my head so I wouldn't miss it when Diego returned one of the hundred texts or voice mails I'd left for him. I just needed to know he was okay. Audrey messaged me that Marcus had been released to his parents, who immediately checked him into a drug-and-alcohol treatment facility.

Mom peeked in on me repeatedly throughout the night. At around eight in the morning, I sat up and said, "I'm not sleeping."

With a cup of coffee in one hand and an unlit cigarette in the other, Mom sat beside me on the couch. She fidgeted with the cigarette like she was dying to put it to her lips and light it, and didn't seem to know what she was supposed to be doing. Finally she set the mug on the coffee table and hugged me so tightly that I thought she was trying to break my spine.

"Why didn't you tell me it had gotten so bad?"

"You needed me to be okay."

"I didn't know. . . ." Mom hugged me again, and this time I hugged her back. I tried to be strong, I tried to hold myself together, but I couldn't do it anymore. I told her everything. About the sluggers and the end of the world and the button and Marcus and my guilt over Jesse's suicide.

"It's my fault Diego's in trouble," I said. "All of this is my fault."

I expected my mom to tell me that it wasn't my fault and that nothing was broken we couldn't mend, but there were lines on her face I'd never seen before, like she'd aged a decade overnight. "Tell me why you didn't press the button."

"Who cares about the button, Mom? Diego's in jail because of me!"

"This is important, Henry."

"Mom!"

"Henry." Mom's bottom lip trembled. "Do you wish you were dead?"

We slammed doors in my family. We beat each other up and we asked questions we didn't want answers to and we wielded silence like a dagger. I wasn't sure how to respond to her blunt honesty except with honesty of my own. "I don't want to die, but I don't want to live, either. I don't know why anyone would. This world is so fucked up, Mom, I think we'd all be better off if I didn't press that button. Everything, everything just hurts too much. And I miss Jesse, and I tried to be okay. I thought Marcus could help me forget, and Diego could replace Jesse, but I miss him so much."

Mom was quiet for a long time. Her silence stretched across the morning and led me back through the past hundred days, and I knew what she was going to say before she finally said it. "I think you need help, Henry."

"I don't need help."

"Then answer me truthfully: Are you okay?"

I was confused and woozy from the pain medication. I didn't have time for doctors or therapists; I needed to know what was happening with Diego. He was still on probation, and I didn't know what being arrested for beating up Marcus would mean for him. All I had to do was tell my mom I was okay, and she'd believe me. I could go to the police station and explain everything. All I had to do was say three little words, and I could fix all that I'd broken. But I was broken too, and I didn't know how to fix myself.

"I'm not okay."

19 January 2016

Miranda, one of the moons belonging to Uranus, features a patchwork of ridges and cliffs, grooved structures called coronae, and massive canyons up to twelve times deeper than the Grand Canyon. Some scientists have theorized that Miranda's piecemeal structure is the result of a massive impact that broke the moon into several pieces that—held together by her gravity—were reformed into something entirely unique. I feel as broken as Miranda, but I can't begin to guess at what's holding me together.

Audrey and I walked through what passed for a garden at the Quiet Oaks Inpatient Treatment Facility. Most of the plants were stunted or dead, and cigarette butts poked out of the dirt like signposts. There wasn't much for the patients to do between therapy sessions other than smoke or write or fuck with the nurses.

"You should see what happens when I try to take a pudding cup out of the kitchen. One step off the linoleum, and Katy starts screaming about breaking the rules. That sets Matthew off. All he ever does is drone on and on about how cruel we are to eat in front of him. And I have to wear socks around Brandy, or she tries to molest my feet."

"Sounds . . . fun?" Audrey laughed. I wondered if the hospital she'd been at was like mine, and if she'd been afraid they'd never let her leave.

"It's really not."

Nurse Curtis watched us from the door to make sure Audrey wasn't sneaking me contraband. They took my shaving razors and my shoelaces. The only thing I was allowed to keep was a pencil so I could keep writing in my journal. "Are you doing . . . better?"

Better was such a relative word. I wasn't even sure what the baseline to measure better against was. "Dr. Janeway put me on antidepressants. They take time to work, I guess. I think she wants me to let Jesse go, but I haven't figured out how I'm supposed to do that yet."

Audrey sat on one of the faded plastic patio chairs, and I sat across from her. "Is that progress?"

"I don't know. I mean, how am I supposed to say good-bye to Jesse?"

"You don't," Audrey said. "Not really."

I shook my head. "Dr. Janeway and I talk about the aliens a lot. Jesse too. Sometimes we talk about Marcus, but I don't really like to, and she's cool about not pushing me."

"Speaking of Marcus. Principal DeShields expelled him."

"Seriously?" Without any concrete evidence, the police were reluctant to charge him with attempted rape. It didn't matter how many times I repeated my story to the cops; they couldn't hide their skepticism. Marcus was right: no one believed loser space boys. But it didn't matter. I'd made a choice.

Audrey's tentative smile morphed into a grin. "The police searched him and found a handful of OxyContin in his pocket. Since he was on school grounds, that was all the excuse DeShields needed to give him the boot."

"I hope he gets help."

"I hope he gets what's coming to him."

He probably wouldn't. He'd probably still get into a good college, end up rich like his parents, and have everything he thought he ever wanted. But it was like Ms. Faraci had said: Marcus didn't matter to me.

"Have you heard from Diego?"

Audrey hesitated, and I knew she had. Mom had driven me to his house on our way to Quiet Oaks the morning after the winter carnival, but he hadn't been home. I'd left a note on his front door, begging him to call Audrey or Charlie or my mom, but it had been three days and he hadn't called. I'd even used the calling card Marcus had given me, and called Viviana from the hospital, but she hadn't answered.

"He's in Colorado."

My heart was beating so hard, I thought it would explode. "Is he . . . ?"

"His sister is with him. He's got to go before a judge for violating his probation, but since Marcus's family isn't pressing charges, he's hopeful the judge will be lenient."

I raised my eyebrow. "Marcus isn't pressing charges? Diego broke his nose."

"Don't forget about the tooth." Audrey chuckled. "Their darling boy tried to rape another boy at a high school carnival. It's not the sort of thing his parents want to draw attention to."

"Did Diego give you a number?" The hospital had a pay phone for patients to use, and I wanted to call him so badly. I didn't expect things to go back to the way they were, but I was hoping he'd still be my friend.

Audrey shook her head.

I'd figured as much. Even though Diego had risked being locked up in juvie for me, I wasn't sure I could fix the damage I'd done.

"Just focus on getting better, Henry. That's what's important."

21 January 2016

On my fifth day in Quiet Oaks, Dr. Janeway took me on a field trip. It was my idea, but she agreed without hesitation. It was one of those nice Florida days that makes you forget about the months of steamy air teeming with blood-hungry mosquitos. A salty breeze blew in from the ocean, and it was cool even in the sunlight.

Dr. Janeway remained in her car, giving me enough distance to feel like I was on my own.

Jesse Franklin's headstone was simple and uncomplicated. I think maybe people thought that's how Jesse was, but there was so much under the surface that no one, not even I, knew about. I wish I had.

"Now that I'm here, I don't know what to say." I stood over Jesse's grave, my hands folded in front of me. "Apparently, letting the world end is sort of the same as wanting to kill myself, so I guess I'm just as screwed up as you."

It hurt to imagine Jesse all alone under the ground. I wasn't sure whether I believed in heaven or hell or reincarnation. All I knew was that Jesse was gone and that I'd loved him.

"Dr. Janeway says I'll never really know why you took your own life. I hope you knew that I loved you so fucking much. Maybe we don't matter to the universe, Jesse Franklin, but you mattered to me."

Mom and Charlie visited me yesterday, but I think it was difficult for Mom to see me in the hospital. I think blaming ourselves for situations we have no control over must be genetic. Maybe the sluggers should pay her a visit.

Zooey was waiting for me when I returned from the cemetery with Dr. Janeway. It hurt to see her without her round belly. Part of her was missing, but only those of us who knew her could see it.

"Hey, Henry."

"Checking in?" Zooey didn't laugh at the joke. "You look good."

I didn't know what else to say. The truth was that she looked tired, worn-down, and worn-out. Maybe she knew I wasn't being entirely honest, but she said thanks, anyway.

"Where's Charlie? Did he find the fridge? The nurses count those Jell-O cups." I looked around for my brother but didn't see him.

Zooey shook her head. "Just me."

I led her to a threadbare couch, ignoring and ignored by the other patients.

She said, "I had class yesterday and couldn't come with your mom and Charlie. I just wanted to see how you're doing."

"I'm good, I guess."

Zooey seemed as at a loss for words as I did. She'd hidden herself away after New Year's, and I felt guilty I hadn't visited her. "That's good."

"What about you? How are you holding up?"

As soon as I asked, Zooey's bottom lip began to tremble. I didn't want her to cry in the crazy hospital, for fear they'd never let her leave. "I shouldn't have come."

She tried to stand, but I took her hand and pulled her back onto the couch. "I'm glad you came," I said. "This place gets super boring."

Zooey smiled a little. "Can I ask you something, Henry?"

"Sure."

"Do you still want the world to end?"

I wasn't kidding about the hospital being boring. No TV,

no books, just a lot of time to write and think. And I'd spent a fairly huge chunk of that time thinking about the sluggers. "No. I don't think so."

"What changed your mind?"

"Honestly?" I said. "It wasn't any one thing." I looked at Zooey—into her eyes, into the deep pools of amber. I recognized what I saw there. The emptiness, the grief. I could have been looking into a mirror. I could have told her something inspirational, something to hang her hope on that would help her through the long, lonely nights where she wouldn't be able to think about anything but the little life that might have been. Instead I told her the truth. "Jesse's still dead, Diego might end up back in juvie. The world pretty much sucks. But the bad shit that happens doesn't cancel out the good. I mean, a world with people like you in it can't be totally crap, right?"

I wasn't sure if anything I'd said had helped. Zooey's eyes were wet around the edges, but she wasn't crying. Not really.

After a moment she said, "I'm considering changing my major."

"Oh yeah? What to?"

"Premed," Zooey said. "I think I want to be an obstetrician."

"That's pretty cool. But you'll definitely have to trade up from Charlie."

That made Zooey laugh. A real laugh. Beautiful and alive.

"Hey, Zooey?"

"Yeah."

"Will you tell me about her? About Evie?"

It took her a moment to get started, but once Zooey began talking, she didn't stop until visiting hours ended.

23 January 2016

On the seventh day, Dr. Janeway released me from Quiet Oaks under strict orders to continue taking my antidepressants. I also had to meet with her twice a week at her office for therapy.

I expected Mom to pick me up, but Charlie and Zooey were waiting for me instead. Zooey hugged me fiercely, and Charlie slugged me in the arm. They weren't there to take me home, though. They had a different destination in mind.

Mom and Nana were waiting for us at the county courthouse for Charlie and Zooey's wedding. I stood beside Charlie as his best man, and Mom fussed over a radiant Zooey. Nana filled the courtroom with stories about the time she caught a shark off the coast of Key West, and the time she single-handedly uncovered a plot to murder the pope. When the judge finished, she took a group photo of us, and Nana played Mr. and Mrs. Charlie Denton out on a little keyboard that was stashed in the corner. She didn't miss a note.

The ceremony was brief but wonderful. We had dinner afterward at Neptune's because Mom couldn't take the day off, not even for her son's wedding. That's how life is; it just goes on.

Diego's painting from the winter carnival was leaning against my bed when I finally got home. Charlie said he'd found it outside the door the day I was admitted to the hospital. A note was taped to the frame that read *This isn't a painting; it's a mirror.*

28 January 2016

The smell of popcorn filled the living room, and Charlie and Zooey wouldn't stop kissing on the couch. It was pretty disgusting. Mom and I had a bet on how long it would take before they were pregnant again, though I thought it was gross for Mom to be wagering on her eldest son's sex life.

I was emptying popcorn into a plastic bowl while Audrey prepared our drinks, when the doorbell rang.

"Get that will you, Henry?" Charlie yelled from the living room.

"You're closer."

"*Bunker*'s already started."

I sighed and set the popcorn bag aside. "Ten to one, it's Charlie's friends."

Audrey poured the root beer too quickly and it overflowed. "Shit!"

"Smooth." I laughed as I walked to the door. When I opened it, Diego was standing on the step, dressed in gray shorts and a black sweater. I hadn't seen him since the winter carnival, and I didn't know he'd returned from Colorado. I was too stunned to speak, so I stood there like a moron.

"I really hope you're the one who ordered the nude model, because the last house I went to let me strip down to my underwear before telling me they weren't."

I threw my arms around Diego, accidentally knocking the back of his head with my cast, but I didn't care because he was here and not in jail and I'd missed him so much.

"Why didn't you call me?"

"I can't help it; I love to make an entrance." He grinned so big, it hurt to look at him.

"Everything cool, Henry?" called Charlie.

"Yeah," I said. I pulled Diego outside. "What happened to you?"

Diego filled me in on the hearing and how he almost ended up in juvie again. "It was pretty close. The judge was ready to toss me back in, but my lawyer argued that since Marcus wasn't pressing charges, there was no one to refute my story that I'd been acting in self-defense."

"I don't know what I would have done without you."

"You would have been just fine, I think."

Once the shock of seeing him wore off, I remembered all the things I'd said to him, the things we'd said to each other, and I wasn't sure where we stood. That he was at my house was a good sign, but I was uncertain how to act. I tried to cover my awkwardness by telling him about Quiet Oaks and how I finally made my peace with Jesse.

"I've still got a lot to figure out, but I like having choices."

Diego rocked back and forth on his heels, his hands in his pockets. "I'm seeing a therapist about my anger issues. Apparently, it's not okay to beat the shit out of anyone who hurts someone you love. Go figure."

"I still think Marcus deserved it."

"Maybe."

"And I love you too, you know?"

"I know." I kissed Diego. We floated free and unfettered. Maybe love doesn't require falling after all. Maybe it only requires that you choose to be in it. I wasn't sure what was going to happen with us or how much time we had left, but I wasn't going to waste a second of it.

Audrey joined us outside, and we walked to the beach together. It was a clear sky full of stars with a bright moon overhead, and we passed the time naming the constellations.

"Did you ever press the button?" Diego asked.

We sat in the sand at the water's edge. Audrey on my left, Diego on my right. The rest of the world didn't exist. "The sluggers haven't abducted me in a while. I would if they'd give me the chance."

Audrey checked her watch. "There's still a few hours left until the twenty-ninth."

Diego leaned his head on my shoulder. "What do you think's going to happen?"

I'd imagined dozens of ways the world could end, but I still wasn't any closer to an answer. I watched the sky and wondered where the sluggers were. Why they hadn't given me another opportunity to press the button and whether they were ever real at all. I didn't know if the world was going to end tomorrow, nor did I care.

"Honestly? It doesn't matter."

Ms. Faraci

I know this isn't what you had in mind when you assigned me this extra credit project. You probably expected a thousand words on gravity or the four laws of thermodynamics, not a journal recounting the last 144 days of my life—possibly of all life—interspersed with crazy doomsday scenarios. It's entirely possible we won't even be alive to discuss it. The world will probably end in a flood that cleanses the stink of humanity from the face of the planet. No, strike that. It's the acidification of the oceans that'll do us in. Climate change causes the glaciers to melt, which causes the acidification of the world's oceans, resulting in the death of most sea life. This triggers a worldwide food shortage, which leads to wars and the end of mankind.

Or maybe robots rise up and murder us all. Gamma rays

from deep space blanket the earth and annihilate all living creatures. A supervolcano erupts or aliens invade or a genetically modified virus is released by a terrorist organization that kills 99.99 percent of all humans, leaving the remaining .01 percent to die slowly of starvation and loneliness.

It doesn't matter.

Rising temperatures could trigger the release of massive amounts of methane trapped beneath the ocean; a scientist could create a strangelet, which would immediately begin converting all matter it comes into contact with into strange matter, including our planet and everything on it. It doesn't matter.

Famine, war, nuclear winter, black holes, or coronal mass ejections. It doesn't matter.

It doesn't matter, because one way or another we're all going to die. A blood clot could lodge in my brain and kill me ten minutes from now; a car could hit you while you're walking your dog. It doesn't matter. We could all die, the world could end, and the universe would simply carry on. A hundred billion years from now, no one will exist who remembers we were space boys or chronic-masturbating alcoholics or science teachers or ex-cons or valedictorians. When we're gone, time will forget whether we swapped spit with strangers. It will forget we ever existed.

And it doesn't matter.

We remember the past, live in the present, and write the future.

The universe may forget us, but our light will brighten the darkness for eons after we've departed this world. The universe may forget us, but it can't forget us until we're gone, and we're still here, our futures still unwritten. We can choose to sit on our asses and wait for the end, or we can live right now. We can march to the edge of the void and scream in defiance. Yell out for all to hear that we *do* matter. That we are still here, living our absurd, bullshit lives, and nothing can take that away from us. Not rogue comets, not black holes, not the heat death of the universe. We may not get to choose how we die, but we *can* choose how we live.

The universe may forget us, but it doesn't matter. Because we are the ants, and we'll keep marching on.

Acknowledgments

Every book is a challenge, but this one more than most. It began life as a haunted-house story, then became a murder mystery, then somehow morphed into a sci-fi story set on a space station before finally revealing its true self to me. And, as always, I had a crazy amount of help along the way.

First and foremost, I'd like to thank my wonderful agent, Amy Boggs, who talks me down off ledges and keeps my compass pointing north. Every book from me is a surprise to her because what I say I'm going to write is rarely what I turn in. But she's always game, and I am eternally grateful. I'm also grateful to everyone at Donald Maass for taking care of me. You all rock.

I received some wonderful advice from Bruce Coville through a friend of mine who attended a writing retreat with him. He said that when you're lucky enough to find an editor who believes in you, understands you, and pushes you to be better than you thought you could be, that you should follow that editor anywhere. That editor for me is Michael Strother. My books wouldn't be the same without his intelligence, insight, and *How to Get Away With Murder* tweets. Thank you, Michael.

I owe a debt of gratitude to the entire Simon Pulse team.

Liesa Abrams for introducing me to Franks. Regina Flath for always designing the perfect covers. My thorough and semicolon-loving copyeditor, Kaitlin Severini, who saved my butt multiple times. Candace Greene McManus, Faye Bi, Anthony Parisi, and everyone in the marketing, publicity, and educational departments I haven't yet met. I write the words, but you all make the magic happen.

Margie Gelbwasser was my tireless cheerleader throughout this journey, Skyping with me when I needed to gripe, and holding my hand when I wanted to quit. Matthew Rush gave me more encouragement than I deserved, and prodded me with a pointy stick when he knew I could do better.

The Spinners (Jenn and Chelsea and Caragh and Stephanie and Denise, and everyone else who pops up from time to time), who have been around since Deathday, continue to be a source of inspiration and support. I'd probably go crazy without our weekly check-ins.

As always, Rachel Melcher is my first reader, offering the support, wisdom, and tough love that only she can. Even when she had to hide from her kids in the bathroom to get the quiet time to read what I sent her. I will never be able to repay you, Pookie!

I can't thank my family enough for their unwavering belief and support. They may not always understand what

I'm writing, but they never make me feel too guilty for disappearing to write it.

Matt Ramsay (aka Captain Schmoopy Von Cuddlebum) remains the most supportive partner any guy could ask for. Writing is stressful, and he's always game to bring me iced teas and frosty treats, and to listen to me complain when I've had a bad day, even if he can't make sense of half of what I'm talking about. Love you!

Finally, I'd like to thank *you*. All the enthusiastic readers and librarians who talk up my books and send me e-mails and remind me why I have the greatest job in the world. We may be the ants, but we're some pretty damn awesome ants, and if the world were to end, I'd count myself lucky to have taken this journey with each and every one of you.